GUNNER ASCH GOES TO WAR

HANS HELLMUT KIRST is one of the most successful post-war novelists, not only in his native Germany but also throughout the English-speaking world where he outsells all other living German authors.

He was born in 1914 in East Prussia, and has been successively a farmer, playwright, gardener, factory worker, book reviewer, soldier and inmate of German prisons and Allied internment camps. After the War he began writing: his most famous books include the four 'Gunner Asch' novels, satires on Nazi army life, and *The Night of the Generals*.

H. H. Kirst now lives in Switzerland.

Available in Fontana by the same author

The Revolt of Gunner Asch
The Night of the Generals
Nights of the Long Knives
The Return of Gunner Asch
What Became of Gunner Asch
Party Games

HANS HELLMUT KIRST

Gunner Asch
Goes to War

Translated from the German by
Robert Kee

FONTANA/Collins

First published in Great Britain by
Weidenfeld and Nicolson 1956
First issued in Fontana Paperbacks 1965
Tenth impression January 1983

Made and printed in Great Britain by
William Collins Sons & Co. Ltd, Glasgow

A strange motor-car was standing in the middle of the village street. A forlorn conglomeration of metal, rubber and canvas. Its wheels were covered in the thick mush of snow and mud churned up by the endless convoys.

Sergeant Asch was approaching the obstruction in a heavy caterpillar truck. He looked quickly across at his driver and half raised his hand. But the driver had already begun to brake. The gun they were pulling swung about behind them a little and then came to a standstill.

"What idiot's gone and left that there?" asked the driver.

"We'll soon see," said Asch, jumping down.

The soldiers seated on the back of the truck paid little attention to all this. They lay huddled up in their greatcoats like so many sacks. One of them lifted his feet up on to the seat, making a terrible scraping noise with his boots. Another pulled the collar of his greatcoat right up over his head and the smoke from his cigarette came out of the top like smoke from a chimney. They waited patiently for whatever would happen next. They hardly even bothered to exchange glances. There was certainly no sense in saying anything. They just waited. Waiting was something they had grown used to.

Asch made his way over to the car. On closer inspection it turned out to be a small Mercedes coupé. The radiator was still warm. The doors were shut but there were rents in the canvas hood through which Asch could see a couple of suit-cases and a very full kit-bag.

The driver of the caterpillar left his engine running at first but switched it off after a while. He leant over the steering wheel and said:

"Shall I push the little bastard into the ditch?"

"I suppose you're longing to?"

"If you give me the order, I'll carry it out with pleasure."

Asch looked up and down the road. The stubble on his chin was the first thing that caught one's attention. There was a cool, cynical, rather tired look in his eyes.

The village lay only a few kilometres behind the front. It seemed deserted. But there were several military vehicles parked in front of the houses; and smoke was pouring from some of the chimneys.

The war was in a state of hibernation on this particular

sector. And no one seemed to want to wake it up. But it was already nearly spring. And spring affected war like everything else. The war would soon be stirring again. This long sleep of the first winter in Russia couldn't last much longer.

Not far from the abandoned Mercedes stood a wretched little hut which looked as if it were trying to crawl away into a hole in the ground. A strip of canvas hung across the door with the letters F T crudely painted on it.

"I suppose the man's trying to put a call through," said the driver. Even he knew that the yellow letters on the canvas stood for Field Telephone. "Making a date for to-night perhaps." He grinned to show that he had made a joke.

Asch grinned back. He went over to the hut, were F T was also scribbled on the walls in chalk. He put his shoulder to the door. It stuck badly at first. Then it flew open, banging against the inside wall. Flakes of whitewash fell to the ground.

There was a strong smell of socks and tobacco inside. He seemed to meet a great wall of fug. The whole place was in semi-darkness. It took him a few seconds to get his bearings.

"Shut the door, man, for God's sake!" someone shouted at him, amiably enough. "You're not at home now!"

Asch slammed the door behind him. More whitewash fell. He looked critically round him as if he were thinking of buying the place.

The room was packed with men. They lay about, smoking, dozing, feeling bored, playing cards and from time to time shouting an odd remark across to one another. Asch felt as if he had forced his way into a tin of sardines.

Close to the door and just under the window stood a telephone switchboard. A soldier in a shabby old fur coat was lounging against a beam nearby. Another man, in a brand new greatcoat stood in front of the switchboard trying to telephone. He was shouting so furiously in his effort to make himself heard that his cap had slipped on to the back of his head. It was an officer's cap.

Asch took no notice of the man.

"Who does that old crock outside belong to?" he asked at random.

No one answered him. No one seemed to take any notice of him at all. Once inside the tin he was just another sardine like the rest of them.

Asch raised his voice.

"I said: who does that old crock outside belong to?"

"I'm the driver of that car," said the man in the shabby fur coat at last. He didn't alter his position. He seemed to be collecting a mouthful of spit.

"Then kindly step outside and move the bloody thing out of the way. It's blocking the road."

"There's quite enough room to pass," said the man sullenly. He spat expertly between two men on to the stove.

"Not for a caterpillar there isn't," said Asch raising his voice still louder. "Come on, man! Out of here! Clear it out of the way. I'm not going into the ditch just because you're too lazy to move that bloody little thing."

"That's a Mercedes coupé, I'd have you know," said the man. He made no effort to move.

"Come on out—at once!" yelled Asch. "Or I'll plough it up for scrap."

The officer at the telephone was having difficulty in putting his call through. He seemed to resent the disturbance.

"Will you hold your tongue, man!" he said sharply, although not without a trace of patronising heartiness. "Can't you hear I'm trying to telephone?"

"Yes," said Asch, "I can hear."

"Then kindly stop interrupting me!"

Asch nodded briefly. Then he went up so close to the driver of the Mercedes that the man could feel his breath on his face. He tried to take a step back.

"Now then, my friend," said Asch, "are you coming outside or not? Or would you like me to give you a little helping hand?"

"You're not to order my driver about," said the officer sharply. "I'm the one who gives him his orders, see?"

"Then will you please order him to come outside?"

The officer at the telephone who was still without his call, put down the receiver and stared at Asch in utter astonishment.

"Who do you think you're talking to?" he asked. "Can't you see I'm an officer?"

"Yes," said Asch, "I can."

"My rank is Captain."

"Yes, Captain."

The other men in the room who had been killing time as best they could, slowly began to take an interest in the conversation. Some of them even went so far as to sit up. Certainly, as field telephone personnel, they were not exactly strangers to conversations of this sort, especially on days when things were going badly, but there were usually several kilometres of telephone cable between the two antagonists. An out-and-out

7

row face to face was far rarer and always bound to attract a certain amount of attention.

"Captain," said Asch, restraining himself so that the advice he was about to give should seem as tactful as possible, "our gun position is about four kilometres farther on towards the front."

"Are you in the artillery then?" asked the Captain with sudden interest.

"Yes."

"Not in Luschke's regiment by any chance?"

"Yes."

"Remember that I'm a Captain please."

"Yes, Captain."

"Which troop are you in?"

"No. 3 Troop, Captain."

"Well, well, well!" cried the Captain. There was a look of triumph on his smooth slightly angular face. "Really, now! No. 3 Troop, eh? Francy that! That's really excellent."

"Yes, Captain," said Asch, quite unperturbed. "And just at the moment only three of our guns are in position. The fourth has been away for repair the last two days. It's my job to bring it back again, only unfortunately that car of yours is blocking the way."

"If the troop's been without the gun for two whole days already it won't do it any harm to have to wait another ten minutes until my call comes through."

"But, Captain, couldn't your driver . . ."

"I'll look into the matter myself as soon as I've finished." said the officer furiously. "You've made your demand in a thoroughly undisciplined manner. I shall see for myself whether there's any justification for it or whether you're merely being lazy and incompetent. I suspect you're just trying to put something over on me."

"But all your driver needs to do . . ."

"And that's an order, Sergeant."

"But what if, in the meantime . . ."

"Naturally I take full responsibility for my orders, Sergeant. Kindly take note of that fact. You may find it convenient to remember later on."

Asch decided to say no more. He looked slowly round the grinning faces in the room. The whole incident had been quite a treat for the men. It had brought a little colour into the drabness of their everyday lives. Asch couldn't grudge them their fun.

8

The driver, however, continued to lounge quite impenitently against the wooden beam. He had a broad grin on his face. He spat again, more ferociously than before, and hit the top of the stove right in the centre. The Captain started bellowing down the telephone again in a last desperate effort to get through.

Sergeant Asch turned round, flung open the door and shouted out to the men on the caterpillar:

" Get down and come inside. It looks as if this is going to take some time."

" What's the matter?" called out Asch's driver. " Someone trying to make trouble?"

" No," said Asch calmly. " Just insisting on a little discipline."

" Where the hell's he come from? The moon?"

" Home I should say, at a glance."

Asch's men left the caterpillar and gun where they were and pushed their way, grumbling, into the hut. The crush was almost unbearable. The air was so thick you could have cut it with a knife. In the farthest corner of the room someone let out a groan of despair and looked around in vain for something to throw. The men on the switchboard cursed and swore; it was quite impossible to hear anything.

The Captain still hadn't got through. He wiped the sweat from his forehead.

" Can't your men wait outside?" he shouted angrily.

" No," said Sergeant Asch. " It's extremely cold outside."

The Captain was unable to take him up on this at once for at that very moment his call came through at last.

" Can I speak to Major Baer, please?"

Major Baer was obviously some sort of officer on the Divisional Staff. He answered at once. He appeared to be a bosom friend of the Captain, who was now on top of the world.

" How are you, Richard? Witterer here. Captain Witterer— Paul Witterer. A surprise for you, eh? Well, I've made it at last!"

The two dozen or so men who were jammed up against one another in the Captain's immediate vicinity listened to his conversation without any particular interest. The Captain gushed on heartily:

" A terrible mess!" he shouted. " Just what I expected. But we'll soon put things right. I must say, I hope I've seen the worst of it though. It's all quite bad enough. New blood is what's wanted. But enough of that. How's little Lisa, my dear fellow?"

The men pricked up their ears. The mere mention of a woman's name was enough to arouse their interest. They prayed that Lisa wouldn't turn out to be just another code name, for ammunition or something, but the Christian name of a real live woman—a woman of flesh and blood.

Even Sergeant Asch showed a certain amount of interest. This Lisa whose name was being bandied about a few kilometres behind the front in the middle of Russia reminded him of his own Elizabeth. To most people it was only another girl's name. To him it stood for a whole world. And the only world that counted if anyone were to ask him. But nobody did ask ordinary soldiers. Some of them were even glad of the fact. They preferred to risk their lives rather than have to think for themselves.

The sound of the Captain roaring away down the telephone brought Asch's mind back to the immediate situation. This was just as well. There were so few people who shared his view of things that it wasn't worth wasting time on such thoughts. The only thing to do was to take life as it came and make the best of it.

"Splendid!" trumpeted Captain Witterer gaily. "And in our sector too, and so soon! My dear fellow, you can be quite sure I'll be only too delighted to have the little girl entertain me! Well, good-bye then, old man. You'll be hearing from me."

Captain Witterer handed the receiver to the man at the switchboard. He was still beaming with pleasure. His conversation seemed to have put him in an excellent mood.

"Does it always take as long as that to get through here?" he asked the man at the switchboard.

"Usually."

"One just has to go on trying until one's blue in the face, eh?"

"No one's actually died on us yet," muttered the man at the switchboard. And rather less audibly, he added: "Worse luck."

But Captain Witterer was no longer paying any attention to him. He pulled his cap forward, straightened it and looked challengingly at Asch. After a carefully calculated pause he said:

"And now, Sergeant, I'll deal with you."

Asch turned round and walked out of the hut without a word. The Captain followed him. His driver joined the procession. The gun crew tacked themselves on behind.

Outside in the road Asch waved a hand in the general direction of the Mercedes, the caterpillar and the gun. Captain Witterer went up and examined the situation at close quarters. After considerable deliberations he said "Hum."

The gun crew grinned to themselves.

The Captain could see at once that Asch was in the right. The road was far too narrow for the caterpillar to be able to pass. Thousands of vehicles had churned their way over it in the course of the winter and left it in an appalling state.

"Pull in to the side," said the Captain curtly to his driver.

"Ah!" said Asch, "and why couldn't that have been done in the first place?"

Fingering his belt Captain Witterer went over to Asch and drew himself up in front of him. The Sergeant was amazed by the brand new state of his equipment. His fur-lined greatcoat was almost spotless. A remarkable sight altogether.

"Your attitude," said the Captain severely, "is thoroughly insolent."

The Sergeant said nothing. He stared out into the empty landscape. For a minute or two he watched a chimney from which smoke was rising slowly. He continued to say nothing.

"What's your name?"

"Asch."

"And you're a member of No. 3 Troop, No. 1 Battery in Luschke's regiment?"

"Yes, Captain."

"And do you know who your troop commander is?"

"Yes, Captain: Lieutenant Wedelmann."

"That," said Witterer with a nasty smile on his face, "is just where you're wrong. As from to-day, your troop commander is myself!"

"One look at your honest patriotic German face," said Colonel Luschke, brusquely, but at the same time with unmistakable friendliness, "and I always know at once that it's going to be a long war. Sit down all the same."

Lieutenant Wedelmann muttered a few conventional words of greeting.

"Really, we're not in the mess now, you know," said Luschke sarcastically. But he meant it well. "We're in Russia, my dear fellow. My entire quarters here are about the size of the clothes cupboard I had in barracks."

Wedelmann smiled but there was no question of him trying to ingratiate himself with the Colonel. This wasn't just one of those " subaltern's smirks ", to which Luschke was known to take such violent objection. Wedelmann respected Luschke; he had no need to ingratiate himself with him. He wasn't one of those smooth young men who spent their time toadying to senior officers.

" There's something I want to discuss with you," said the Colonel. " Make yourself at home."

Wedelmann drew up a plain wooden chair. The Colonel was sitting in a rocking-chair which creaked as he moved slowly backwards and forwards.

One of the many reasons why the two of them got on so well was that they were both equally sceptical about all forms of heroics. Neither of them held that there was any glory attached to death. Their only difference of opinion—and that a strong one—was on the subject of what was to be understood by the term " Germany ".

The room in which Luschke had been living for some months now was a small one with a low ceiling. It contained only the bare minimum of furniture: a camp-bed, a few chairs, and a relatively large table with maps on it. There were also maps on the walls, which had been newly whitewashed, but these were there for hygienic rather than strategic purposes, being used to cover up the hundreds of little blood-stains which marked the last resting-places of an army of squashed lice.

" What are your men up to?" asked the Colonel, apparently on the spur of the moment. He leant back in his chair.

Wedelmann was immediately on his guard.

" Everything's in order, sir, as far as I know. Or . . .?"

" Your conscience is never really entirely clear, eh, Wedelmann?"

" As far as I know . . ."

" It's a long time since I've had a clear conscience too," said the Colonel in a calm matter-of-fact way as if he were discussing the weather. " I'd always imagined myself to be the ideal type of defender of the Fatherland. But you know, Wedelmann, all is not well with the Fatherland. Sometimes I feel that it's like a firm about to go bankrupt."

Wedelmann began to protest, but Luschke merely waved a bored hand in his direction.

" We're all really just a lot of sheep nowadays," he said. " We let them do what they like with us. We're only brave when it's a question of saving our own skins. And even then sometimes only when it's possible to do so without risk. No one's really his own master any more. And anyone who doesn't behave like a sheep is either a man of enormous courage or unbelievable stupidity. It's this partnership of the idealists and the half-wits that worries me."

The Lieutenant didn't reply but looked up into the foxy little eyes of his regimental commander. "Lumpface" sat motionless in his chair. His tunic was as usual buttoned right up to his neck in the regulation manner and lay in folds across his narrow frame. His feet were stuck into a pair of fur-lined boots.

"Not a very promising outlook, eh?" asked Luschke softly.

Wedelmann felt confused. This wasn't the first time the Colonel had succeeded in upsetting him. Even the strongest of men were like wax in Luschke's hands.

"Never try to hide what you're thinking, Wedelmann," said "Lumpface" quietly. "You never know: the day may come when you'll wish you hadn't."

"Yes, Colonel," said Wedelmann obediently, and it was obvious that he wasn't quite sure how his C.O.'s remark was meant to be taken.

"And by the way," said Luschke, suddenly changing the subject, "one of your N.C.O.s seems to have been up to his old tricks again."

"Soeft?"

"Who else? It seems he's been drawing rations for a unit that simply doesn't exist in our sector at all!"

"I'll look into the matter at once. . . ."

"You'll do nothing of the sort, my dear Wedelmann. In the first place because it's still impossible to prove that it *was* Soeft who has made such fools of them up at Army H.Q. And secondly because I don't see why it should always be the man at the front who has to pay for the blunders of the men back at base. If on the other hand they do succeed in pinning it on Soeft . . ."

"I don't think there's much danger of that, sir."

"Neither do I. But you never know: one day even the people back at base may start doing a little thinking. And if the unexpected should happen and they succeed in catching Soeft, then don't expect me to turn a blind eye to it all, Wedelmann."

"I'll have a word with Corporal Soeft, sir. I'll see if I can't appeal to his conscience."

Luschke laughed quietly. The idea of Soeft having a conscience and of Wedelmann solemnly trying to make an appeal to it struck him as amusing. He picked up his field telephone, turned the handle a few times and then said quietly:

" Bring some more wood for the fire and my tea. And then see that I'm not disturbed for the next half-hour."

The Colonel's batman came in and threw a few logs on to the stove. He put two tumblers, a jug of hot water and a bottle of rum on to the table and disappeared again as silently as he had come.

" Help yourself, Wedelmann," said the Colonel, pointing towards the bottle, " Give yourself a drop of Dutch courage. You may be needing it sooner than you think. And don't stint yourself. You can drink a whole quarter of a litre without upsetting my economy. If you want more than that you'll have to get your friend Soeft to replenish my stocks."

Wedelman poured himself out a large tumbler. The Colonel filled his own glass with hot water and only added a drop or two of rum. He raised it to the Lieutenant and began to drink in a series of little sips. Then he said:

" We've been hibernating here for some months now. It could all come to an end any day. You can feel the spring over the whole front. In a few weeks' time the war will be back on its feet again."

" High time too, sir."

" Eager for fresh exploits, eh?"

" It's just that I don't much want to spend the rest of my life here, sir."

Luschke nodded understandingly.

" You won't be doing that, Wedelmann. Don't worry."

" We've made good use of the winter, sir. We've had a thorough overhaul of all weapons, equipment, vehicles, etc. We're well stocked up with ammunition."

" Bravo, Lieutenant!" cheered Luschke ironically. " And while you've been doing all that the Russians have been fast asleep I suppose. For of course Hitler is a genius and Stalin an idiot. Nothing but heroes on our side and morons on theirs, eh! *Deutschland über alles*! and nobody else worth a damn! My dear Wedelmann, kindly use a little intelligence. Even when you're being carried away by patriotism. Then most of all, in fact."

Wedelmann said nothing. He felt rather at a loss. He took hold of his tumbler with both hands. Luschke was always the same—far less confident about the final outcome of the war than he ought to have been. But Wedelmann respected the little man with the foxy eyes far too much ever to think seriously of reproaching him for this.

"The supplies we've received," said Luschke in disgust, "have been utterly worthless. Oh yes, they've sent us plenty of stuff, I grant you that. But in my sector at least, I haven't detected the slightest effort to improve our fighting efficiency or learn from experience in any way."

"I expect other types of weapons have been getting priority, sir."

"It's usually only those in charge of supplies who get priority."

Luschke looked sideways at the astonished Lieutenant.

"You're wondering what's come over your C.O., eh, Wedelmann? You're not used to this sort of talk, I suppose. You can hardly believe your ears, eh? Not only is the Colonel fed up—he actually dares to say so!"

"I'm sure the Colonel has his reasons."

"I certainly have, Wedelmann. Dozens of them. For instance, I've been trying to get hold of radio transmitters for months now. You know where our weakness has been every time we've been in action: intercommunication—it's been simply appalling. Sometimes I've been unable to make contact with one of my batteries for twenty-four hours at a time. They've been wandering about in the blue somewhere. You can't keep in touch by field telephone in the middle of a tank battle."

"Perhaps the transmitters are on their way."

"Oh, they're on their way all right. But we're not going to wait for them. We're going to fetch them ourselves!"

"Fetch them ourselves? But where from, sir?"

"From home, of course; where else do you think? They've got everything we want back there in the reserve battery, Wedelmann: transmitters and the personnel to operate them. All we have to do is to go and fetch them. And once we've got them we'll distribute them to No. 1 Battery, which is where by rights they belong."

Wedelmann found himself completely under Luschke's spell as usual. Luschke smiled at him. Slowly he began to rock his chair backwards and forwards. It creaked horribly. His Iron Cross First Class gleamed on his puny little chest.

"It's all quite simple," he announced. "A friend of mine is in charge of the corps airfield. Some of his JU 52s are at this moment bringing stuff up to the front from the factories in our home town. And there, there's another friend of mine. Well, my friend at this end is prepared to let a reliable man of ours fly back home on one of these JU 52s. And it'll be up to such a man to get the equipment and personnel for us out of the reserve battery. When he's done that he can fly back here with them."

"Perfect," said Wedelmann. He was full of admiration for the plan.

"Who do you pick for the job? Choose one of your own men."

Wedelmann thought for a moment. Then he said:

"A job like that is worth getting."

Luschke nodded. "And carries with it quite a bit of responsibility. It won't be all plain sailing, you know. Well, who do you think? Is it as difficult as all that to decide? Now, surely you're not going to say you'll have to consult your Sergeant-Major. Spare me that at least, Wedelmann."

"I propose the best man I've got," said Wedelmann, "Corporal Vierbein."

Luschke didn't say anything, but he stopped rocking his chair backwards and forwards. His lumpy face was quite inscrutable. He folded his little hands and waited for Wedelmann to continue.

"Corporal Vierbein," said Lieutenant Wedelmann, "is the best gun-crew leader in the whole troop. He and his crew have knocked out seven tanks altogether between them. He's been awarded the Iron Cross First Class, you know."

"Yes, I know that," said the Colonel and then fell silent again.

"If anyone deserves this job," went on Wedelmann enthusiastically, "it's Corporal Vierbein. Besides, he hasn't had any leave for over a year."

"Yes," said Luschke thoughtfully, "I dare say that's all true, but don't forget that the qualities needed to deal with red tape back home aren't quite the same as those needed at the front."

"I'd stake my life on Vierbein."

"It does you credit," said "Lumpface". He smiled to himself, but it wasn't yet clear whether he agreed to the proposal or not. "If I had to do my time in the ranks all over again, Wedelmann, yours would be the troop I'd choose to do it in. You're only a youngster still, but you've got quite a fatherly touch."

Wedelmann acted as if he hadn't heard the C.O.'s remark.

"If the Colonel doesn't agree with my proposal," he said politely, "then in place of Corporal Vierbein, I'd like to suggest Sergeant Asch."

"Asch? For God's sake, Wedelmann! This is a very delicate mission. I can't afford to have anything go wrong. If it does there'll be hell to pay. I'll have half a dozen Generals down on me at once. And that'll mean this regiment will be looking for a new C.O. Anyone but Asch! Even Vierbein!"

"Very good, sir: Corporal Vierbein then," noted the Lieutenant with satisfaction.

"Oh, all right," said Luschke. He laughed aloud and said: "But don't try that trick on me too often, Wedelmann. I don't much like being beaten at my own game."

Wedelmann laughed too. The Colonel raised his glass. The two of them understood each other very well.

"This damn' war has brought you and me much closer together," said Luschke genially. "But then war's like that. Either you treat the next fellow like a long-lost brother or else you can't stand the sight of him."

The telephone rang quietly. Luschke picked up the receiver and said "Hallo!". His face took on a serious expression. "Right," he said, "in five minutes' time."

He put the receiver back thoughtfully. He looked at Wedelmann quizzically as if he were a new gun he was examining. Then he said:

"There's a Captain Witterer waiting outside."

"Oh yes, sir."

"This Captain Witterer has arrived about eight days too soon. He seems to have been in a hurry. Still, there he is and there's nothing we can do about it. Sorry, Wedelmann."

"Yes, sir," said Wedelmann. He couldn't quite understand what Luschke was driving at.

"Just to make matters clearer: Captain Witterer is the new Commanding Officer of No. 3 Troop."

"My troop?"

"Exactly. Of the troop which was yours until to-day."

"But what about me?"

"I'll let you know what I've decided for you later on, Wedelmann. In the meantime you're to hand over command of the troop to Captain Witterer, but to stay on here until he's found his feet."

Wedelmann found himself quite unable to speak. The heat from the stove had dried up the air in the room and he felt drowsy and stupified. Outside a truck could be heard churning its way towards them through the mud.

Luschke, still deep in his chair, rocked himself backwards and forwards. He gave Wedelmann an encouraging smile.

" Now then, Wedelmann, off you go! "

It was obvious that Wedelmann not only felt utterly bewildered, but also deeply hurt. His strong sense of discipline, however, prevented him from commenting on the situation, even to Luschke.

The Colonel leant right back in his chair.

" My dear Lieutenant Wedelmann," he said affably, " I know perfectly well what you're thinking. Nothing would give you greater pleasure at this moment than to be able to let yourself go and kick your old C.O. round the room. Or am I wrong? I don't hear you deny it, Wedelmann."

" Sir, you know I've always . . ."

" Quite so, Wedelmann; quite so. I keep my eyes open, you know. I know you're far and away the best troop commander I've got. I also know that you've always been a loyal supporter of the Führer. The first does you credit; the second I forgive you for. In any case what is undoubtedly true is that but for you Luschke's regiment would never be better than average; as it is, it's one of the *élite*. I know all that. It's really largely your troop I've got to thank for this Iron Cross I'm wearing. I haven't been blind to all this."

" Then if I may say so, sir, I don't quite see why . . ."

Luschke brushed the remark aside.

" My dear Wedelmann," he said, " how do you know I may not have some other plans in store for you? Well? You just trust your old C.O., my boy; this damn' war is only just beginning."

" But sir, the Führer . . ."

" Now, none of your fancy speeches here, my boy. Just because I find something to swear at there's no need to go and drag in National Socialism. But enough of all this. Tell me now: how are the girls? "

" Who, sir? "

" Now then, come off it," chaffed Luschke good-naturedly. " When I was driving through your village the other day I saw Soeft talking to a magnificent-looking creature. There was only one thing I didn't like about it and that was that they were such an ill-matched pair. The girl looked really intelligent. How long has Soeft been going about with her? "

" I don't take much interest in that sort of thing, sir."

"But you should, Wedelmann! While you've got the chance. Things may start warming up here again much sooner than any of us expect."

No. 3 Troop's orderly-room Corporal shot out of the hut which housed the Sergeant-Major and his records like a bullet from a gun. He hurried across the open space around which the forward base had been constructed, went past the field kitchen and stopped at a wooden building which had C S chalked up in large letter on the door. C S stood for Commissariat Soeft.

The orderly-room Corporal opened the door and found himself in a little hall-way. This in turn led into a small ante-room, the walls of which had recently been whitwashed. Two men in dark overalls were busy cutting up enormous lumps of sausage which they weighed generously on a pair of scales and then parcelled up into rations.

"Soeft about?" asked the orderly-room Corporal, staring hungrily at the lumps of sausage.

Soeft's assistants shook their heads.

"Anyone know where he is?"

The sausage slicers shrugged their shoulders one after the other.

The orderly-room Corporal found himself profoundly disturbed by the sight of so much sausage. He couldn't help thinking of his very inadequate breakfast. He withdrew. He stood outside on the square for a moment, an unhealthy-looking little man, tortured by anxiety. He rubbed his hands together to try and keep warm.

He looked about him with the air of a disgruntled sparrow. Finally he set off down the village street at a smart trot. He was making for a little house which was shaped like a mushroom and set back a little from the side of the road. There, as he had expected, he found Soeft, who was just saying good-bye to a Russian girl. The orderly-room Corporal stood and waited. After a time he seemed to have become frozen to the spot; only the mechanical rubbing of his hands continued.

The girl seemed to be dressed entirely in sacking. This gave a loose bulky effect to her figure which was certainly sturdy but not altogether unattractive. The orderly-room Corporal stared at it as if it were an important paper that had just come on to his desk.

"Nothing doing, then, Natasha?" said Soeft.

The girl shook her head vigorously in a series of short jerks like a stubborn pony.

"I am afraid not," she said in her good schoolroom German. She spoke very slowly, emphasising each syllable carefully. "Not for you at any rate, Herr Soeft."

"You're not trying to raise the price, I suppose, Natasha?"

"Send me your officer. Perhaps I would make a deal with him."

Soeft stood there eyeing her. He seemed annoyed. He turned on the orderly-room Corporal.

"What do you want? You're interrupting some business."

"Very important, Soeft."

"Not before breakfast," said Soeft. "Not for at least another quarter of an hour."

And with that he turned on his heel without even another glance at Natasha. He wanted to put her in her place. But before he turned the corner he looked back and saw her smiling at him scornfully. This made him furious. He stamped on through the slush. A truck which was ploughing its way along the street had to pull up to avoid running him over. The driver swore. Soeft took not the slightest notice. He was too busy with his calculations.

He went over to his own quarters, pausing for a moment as he always did in front of the C S chalked up on the door. The orderly-room Corporal who had come up alongside, tried to push his way in through the door with him. But Soeft slammed it in his face.

The orderly-room Corporal waited patiently outside for a few minutes. He paced up and down trying to keep warm. And as he did so the smell of soup was wafted across to him from the field kitchen. He strolled across to it and smiled in friendly fashion at the cook. The cook gave him a friendly smile back. And that was all he got from the cook.

He found this very irritating, and his irritation put new spirit into him. He strode briskly over to Corporal Soeft's establishment.

The two sausage slicers were still at work and looked up at him as he came in.

One of them nodded at the Corporal and jerked a free thumb over in the direction of a door on which hung a notice saying: "Private. Knock Before Entering."

The Corporal hesitated for a moment and then went in without knocking.

20

Corporal Soeft who felt more secure now that he was once more on his home ground, was busy demolishing the breakfast he had referred to. It was obviously his second breakfast that day, for it consisted of little more than a light snack of tunny fish, toast and red wine. These delicacies, together with a large lump of butter, were spread out on a large dazzling white cloth. Behind them sat Soeft chewing methodically.

"The Sergeant-Major wants you," said the orderly-room Corporal, staring hard at the table. "You're to come over at once. I've been looking all over the place for you."

"Help yourself," said Soeft, chewing calmly on.

The orderly-room Corporal didn't wait to be asked a second time. He stretched out both arms, took a large slice of toast, spread it thickly with butter and then piled it high with tunny fish. Then he opened his mouth wide, shut his eyes and crammed the whole lot in at once. He began to chew, almost choked, and swallowed. A warm flush spread slowly over his face.

Soeft didn't even smile. He was still busy with his calculations. He was never happier than when engaged on a problem of this sort and refused to let anything interrupt him. He opened a fat-looking packet of foreign cigarettes, took one out, lit it and threw the match away on the floor.

The way he saw it, the situation was something like this: every girl has her price—this one was worth an officer. She should have him then if there was nothing else for it. He had to admit that interpreters were worth their weight in gold in this God-forsaken country. That the interpreter in this case should also be a woman merely added to the value! Almost as good as being in France again!

"What does the Chief want me for actually?" he asked. He took a long pull on his cigarette, for he was feeling very pleased with himself. He considered he had every reason to be. "I haven't got much time to-day, old man; there's some business I want to attend to over at the regimental bakery."

The orderly-room Corporal nodded eagerly. But his mouth was so full he was unable to get a word out. He swallowed desperately.

"I want to make quite sure," Soeft went on, taking no notice of him, "that we get fresh rolls on Sunday."

"Man . . ." was all the orderly-room Corporal was able to get out and then immediately set about licking his greasy fingers.

"So you see I haven't a moment to spare, really. Tell the Chief that, will you?"

"Come on, Soeft. You tell him. Besides I think you may find it worth your while to come over."

"What do you mean?"

"I'm not giving anything away," said the orderly-room Corporal making a mysterious sign with two fingers. "But I will say this: it's women!"

"What sort of women?" asked Soeft, showing a sudden interest.

"You'll find out if you come over to the Sergeant-Major's," said the orderly-room Corporal, and immediately turned and left the room, managing to slip an opened tin of tunny fish into his pocket as he went. For, as it said on the label, there was nothing like tunny fish.

Soeft took his time; but his curiosity had been aroused. He drank up his coffee—made of course from the genuine coffee beans—a good deal more quickly than usual. Then he put on the lighter of his two greatcoats, the one with the detachable fur collar, looked quickly over the work of the two sausage slicers, found nothing about it to take exception to and made his way across to the orderly-room.

Sergeant-Major Bock received him with an air of brisk impatience. He tried to convey the impression that he was simply overloaded with work.

"About time too, Soeft," he said, and he made it clear that it had been in his mind to deliver a severe reprimand; "just about time too, I must say."

"Must you?" said Corporal Soeft, and he slowly sat down on top of a packing-case, not without dusting it first with an enormous handkerchief made of parachute silk which he took out of his pocket.

The two of them stared at each other, although this was quite unnecessary for they knew each other inside out. Each had the other perfectly sized up. Each thought of himself as having No. 3 Troop under his thumb.

The Sergeant-Major, deprived of the splendour which was his on the barrack square, was here little better than a buffer between the gun positions and the forward base. But though he had lost his influence he retained all his old self-confidence. The Corporal in charge of the Commissariat, on the other hand, a man whose contacts were legendary, was able to do exactly as he liked; for the present high standard of living enjoyed by No. 3 Troop was due solely to him.

"What's going on actually?" asked Soeft, moistening his lips with an enormous tongue.

"As you already know," said the Sergeant-Major, "we're getting a new C.O. here."

"Well, what about it? That's not going to change anything. My liver sausage will taste much the same as before. The old firm under a different name, that's all. These creatures are all the same. Mass produced. The ones with defects are the most interesting. And if this new fellow doesn't come up to Wedelmann standards right away—which would perhaps be expecting too much—well, it won't be long before we have him just where we want him. Or don't you agree?"

Sergeant-Major Bock acted as if he hadn't heard a word Soeft had said. He was a good tactician. He knew that it was sometimes advisable to appear not to have heard Soeft's suggestions. There was no sense in arguing with him; the fellow knew the strength of his position and exploited it shamelessly.

"I haven't been able to have more than a few words with Captain Witterer, the new C.O., so far. I spoke to him on the telephone for a moment. He'll probably be arriving to-morrow. He's got some business up at Regimental H.Q. to-day."

Soeft nodded knowingly.

"Luschke will be wanting to look him over," he said.

"In any case," said the Sergeant-Major, once again prudently ignoring Soeft's remarks, "Captain Witterer wanted to know if there was any N.C.O. in the troop who was particularly reliable."

"He's in a hurry, isn't he?" said Soeft, grinning broadly.

"Naturally I gave him your name, Soeft."

"Naturally. And in what particular sphere am I to be of service to him?"

"It's something of a rather confidential nature."

"Just my speciality," said Soeft, obligingly.

"Some time this afternoon," said the Sergeant-Major, "there'll be an aircraft landing at the base airfield with a Wehrmacht concert party on board."

"How many women?"

"Three ladies and a gentleman." There was no hint of reproach in the Sergeant-Major's voice. "One of the ladies is called Lisa Ebner."

"And she's the little lady we're interested in?"

"Captain Witterer's request," went on the Sergeant-Major, not without a certain dignity—he took a cigar from the case which Soeft offered him—"is that Fräulein Ebner should be well looked after and that everything in our power should be done to make her stay as comfortable as possible."

"Well, and why not?" said Soeft. He pointed at the Sergeant-Major's cigar. "Do you want a light?"

"I have already told Captain Witterer that he can leave everything to you, Soeft."

"Anything else?" asked the Corporal. He had a vast nose and little foxy eyes. He blew out the match with which the Sergeant-Major had lit his cigar.

"Not as far as I'm concerned."

"And now what about that Henschel eight-tonner?"

"My dear Soeft," said Bock very emphatically, "I've told you a hundred times: we've got to let the ammunition section have the eight-tonner."

"Ah, I see," said Soeft with sinister composure. "So ammunition is now to have priority over food. I'll make a note of the fact."

"Be reasonable, Soeft! Lieutenant Wedelmann isn't petty about these things, you know, but . . ."

"And he isn't C.O. here any longer either! And the new C.O. hasn't arrived yet. So it's a perfect opportunity. I tell you what: you let me have the eight-tonner for the supplies and you can have my Ford!"

"What? That old hearse?"

"The M.T. section is quite agreeable."

"But Sergeant Asch will not be so agreeable, Soeft. And so long as Asch is still acting as adjutant to the C.O. . . ."

The Corporal's eyes became smaller than ever. He blew a whole smoke-ring up to the ceiling. "Asch isn't going to be adjutant here for ever, you know. When the Lieutenant goes his Adjutant will presumably go with him. Or do you imagine Asch is a permanent fixture? If the new C.O. is a different sort of fellow from Wedelmann—and this job he's given me to do makes me think he must be—he's not going to put up with Asch for long."

The Sergeant-Major seemed to come to a difficult decision. Of course Soeft was right. It was an ideal moment for little adjustments of this sort.

"If you really think," he said, "that you can't get on without the Henschel and the M.T. people don't mind . . ."

"Fine," said Soeft. "I'll get on to that right away." And turning the situation to his advantage with his usual brazenness, he added: "And what about Lance-Corporal Kowalski? I could use him too, you know."

24

"Out of the question," said Sergeant-Major Bock, without a moment's hesitation. "He remains the C.O.'s driver whatever happens. I'm prepared to do a lot of things for you, Soeft, but not that!"

Soeft nodded. The rebuff didn't surprise him. Nor did the relatively sharp tone in which it was delivered. The Chief wasn't caught napping as easily as all that. He knew that Soeft was a formidable enough force in the life of No. 3 Troop as it was; in combination with Kowalski there would have been nothing to stop him. Like almost everyone else at the front, Sergeant-Major Bock had his own little private war to wage.

Soeft seemed not to mind much at first. But it was a favourite saying of his that everything comes to him who waits. At least he had made sure of the Henschel eight-tonner for himself. It would mean a big increase in his loading capacity. He had needed it badly too; during the months of inactivity on the front his stores had grown to astonishing proportions.

"It's most important," said the Sergeant-Major, "that you and I should continue to get on well together." He puffed out his chest beneath his tunic. The action didn't escape Soeft. "It will then be quite clear to the new C.O. that the unit he's come to is one on which he can rely implicitly."

"Provided he's reasonably human," said Soeft, "it shouldn't be long before we have him round to our way of thinking."

Before leaving for the rear to organise the reception for the ladies, Soeft decided that it would be wise to make sure of the Henschel eight-tonner he had been promised. He knew enough about this sort of thing to realise that the transfer could hardly be expected to take place without a certain amount of friction.

He decided to go about it systematically. First he went to his quarters where he filled his cigarette-case and stuffed several more packets, including a number of foreign brands, into his pockets. Then he went across to the M.T. section.

Everything went smoothly enough at first. He told the N.C.O. in charge that the Sergeant-Major had allotted the Henschel eight-tonner to him, Soeft. The N.C.O. nodded. He didn't care who drove his trucks. All he minded about was whether they were serviceable.

Soeft had known that he would have a bit of trouble with the drivers. One of them, the driver of the Henschel, would of course be only too delighted to have the chance of carrying rations. But the other, the driver of the Ford, would be bound to be furious—who indeed would not dislike the prospect of driving live ammunition about at the best of times, above all in war-time? So long as he was merely furious, everything would be all right. But if he were to lodge a complaint—and such a thing was by no means beyond the bounds of possibility —then there might well be trouble.

"Very good, Corporal," said the driver of the Henschel enthusiastically. "By all means. And what shall I do with the ammunition?"

"Just unload it," said Soeft. "Anywhere. Put a tarpaulin over the lot and leave it."

"Just as you say, Corporal," said the driver, and at once shouted for some men to come and help him.

Soeft didn't say anything to the driver of the Ford for the time being. The important thing was that he now had the new truck. He could always give the old one up at any time. And perhaps—who could tell?—the front might move suddenly. And then there were the two C.O.s! Neither knowing anything about the other's orders! And before either could have time to look into the matter Soeft would be in possession not only of the new truck but of the old one as well. Only a half-wit would give anything up before he was asked for it. The prospect of all this delighted Soeft so much that he began to feel like a drink. He hurried back to his own quarters and pulled out a box which was one of his most treasured possessions. He fished around for the key in his pocket for a moment, and finally pulled it out and opened the box. It was filled with various bottles of spirits of extra special quality, all packed away in wooden shavings. He selected a bottle of Benedictine, uncorked it and put his nose to it.

"Ah, France!" he said, and an expression of ecstasy came over his face.

He sat down and poured himself out a glass. A gentle feeling of well-being spread through him as he drank. I only need to close my eyes and I might be back in France again, he thought. But his foxy little eyes remained wide open. He was far too careful to risk being taken by surprise.

And thus it was that he heard the sound of approaching footsteps in time. Certainly it would have been difficult not to have heard the commotion which the new-comer made as he came into the ante-room. Soeft didn't find it hard to guess who his visitor was.

"You'll have a drink, I suppose?" he said as the door opened.

Sergeant Asch took in the scene before him but made no comment,

"What's this about the Henschel?" he asked. "The N.C.O. in charge of the ammunition section is furious. You can't just go and commandeer the best truck in the whole troop for yourself like that!"

"Can't I?" said Soeft winking. "Can't I just?"

Soeft looked blandly up at his visitor like some benevolent uncle regarding a Christmas tree.

"Asch," he said. "You know, I always thought you were a perfectly normal sort of human being. But sometimes it seems to me that you're almost as mad as the worst of them. So you consider ammunition more important than food, eh? You'd rather spend your time killing your fellow human beings than filling your own belly?"

"Now just listen to me, Soeft. This war's none of my doing but here I am in the middle of it and I'm going to look after myself. And I can't do that if I haven't got any ammunition."

"You're just one of Wedelmann's toadies—fighting for Germany and Western Civilisation and all the rest of it!"

"Soeft! If I'm offered the choice between an empty belly and a hole in the head I'll choose an empty belly, thank you very much!"

"Why the hell doesn't Wedelmann give some of his attention to the girls and leave the war to look after itself for a bit? The man's not normal. Now I've got just the thing for him. Natasha, she's called. Typical Russian, you know—the soulful type." His hands described a few curves in the air. "Full of soul!"

"Come off it," said Asch impatiently. "Don't start trying to play the pimp with me. Give the Henschel back and you can go on boozing away to your heart's content."

"Asch," said Soeft, "this is my final offer: a girl for Wedelmann and a case of goodies for yourself. And in return: the Henschel eight-tonner for me!"

"Stand up," said Asch, "so that I can kick you properly."

"That's your last word on the matter?"

"If you don't hurry up and return that truck," said Asch, "you'll find you've spoken your last word on any matter."

Soeft nodded. He tried to look calm.

"All right, Asch. That's all I wanted to know. Just so long as I know where I am."

"It's about time you did!"

"As far as the Henschel's concerned, Asch, it's an order from the C.O."

"Don't be an ass, Soeft. I know what Wedelmann's orders are and what they aren't."

"Who said anything about Wedelmann? The C.O.'s name is Witterer."

"But he hasn't arrived yet!"

Soeft poured himself out another glass of Benedictine. He needed it. What he was about to say required all the courage he could muster. He moistened his lips and said:

"In case you'd forgotten, Asch, there happens to be such a thing as the telephone. And Witterer has already given me a number of orders—down the telephone!"

"We'll see about that," said Sergeant Asch, "and if it turns out that you're lying, God help you!"

Soeft's eyes narrowed as he watched Asch turn on his heel and leave the room. He rubbed his left hand thoughtfully up and down his face. Then he drank up the rest of the Benedictine. But it didn't taste nearly so good as before.

"Hm," he said, "things are beginning to get a little complicated."

But he didn't lose his self-assurance for a moment. He was still firmly in the saddle. It was Asch who was riding for a fall. On the other hand, it would of course be a great mistake to underestimate Asch.

And he decided that he would show Captain Witterer that if there was one man in the troop who was indispensable to him it was Corporal Soeft.

The Corporal got out his private car, a captured Russian limousine, the back of which he had converted into a capacious boot. This car of course also bore the inscription C S.

The main base lay some eighteen kilometres to the rear. It was humming with activity. The din of the repair shops could be heard echoing through what had once been churches. The more important staffs had taken over the Communist Party buildings. The smaller ones preferred private billets, if possible with families still living in them.

Vehicles of every sort and description were parked alongside the houses. One or two officers with brief-cases were searching for their cars. Two other ranks appeared merely to be taking a little stroll along the pavement. Smoke was pouring from every chimney in the village.

Soeft decided to put his ability to the test at once. He approached the whole thing systematically. He knew how to cut his way through the jungle of red-tape which invariably

28

surrounded a situation of this sort. He went straight to the heart of the matter. It was mainly a question of practice. For the rest what was needed was a bit of luck, the right opportunity, and a great deal of nerve.

Soeft drove straight to Divisional Headquarters. He sought out the intelligence officer, who was also the officer in charge of entertainments for the troops. He told him quite coolly and entirely convincingly that he had come from the Kommandantur. He said he'd come to discuss the question of the concert party which was arriving that afternoon. As a member of the Kommandantur he found himself immediately showered with curses which he bore docilely enough, thereby picking up most of the information he wanted.

Next he drove to the Kommandantur where he said he'd come from Divisional H.Q. to discuss the question of the concert party which was arriving that afternoon. As a member of Divisional H.Q. he found himself immediately showered with curses which he bore equally docilely and thus picked up the rest of the information he wanted.

"It's always the same," said the officer with a bad grace. "Divisional H.Q. gives the movement orders and we have to find somewhere to put the people."

"Can I see the quarters you've allotted, please?" asked Soeft coldly.

With some reluctance the officer agreed. He detailed a Sergeant to show them to Soeft. The Sergeant took him off to what had once been a school. On the top floor a relatively clean little room had been set apart with three camp-beds it it.

"This is for the women," said the Sergeant; "we've rigged up a special toilet as well. It wasn't so easy doing that. You've got to know how to improvise in this game. You should thank your lucky stars you don't have to work in a Kommandantur. The man, by the way, will be sleeping downstairs with the officers."

"I'm not interested in where the man sleeps," said Soeft in typical Divisional H.Q. fashion. "But it's obviously impossible to expect all three ladies to sleep together in the same room. One of them will have to have a room to herself."

"What do you mean: 'will have to'?" said the Sergeant. "We're not in France now, you know!"

"Unfortunately," said Soeft, sighing as he always did when his thoughts went back to his beloved France. Ah! what a time they had had during the campaign there. God, he loved that country. An El Dorado for the black marketeer! He had never felt so happy in his life as he had done then. And he sighed again wistfully.

Then he said again:

"One of the ladies will have to have a room to herself. Those are the General's personal orders." And with a wink he added: "I expect she's a relation—or something!"

"God, you people make a lot of trouble for us," said the Sergeant bad-temperedly. "Always wanting these little extras. As if this were some sort of holiday resort—St. Moritz or something! But we'll do what we can, and let's just hope the General approves. If he doesn't, it's just . . ."

"The lady's name is Lisa Ebner," said Soeft. "See that some flowers are put in her room, will you?"

"Perhaps she'd like a four-poster, too?" said the Sergeant with bitter sarcasm.

"Yes, if you can manage one," said Soeft.

Now that that was settled, Soeft drove off to the airfield where he went straight to see the Commanding Officer. This man was a friend of Luschke's and some time ago Luschke had dropped a fairly broad hint about him to Soeft, who from time to time saw that a few little extras came his way.

The C.O. received Soeft in a most friendly manner and let him have all the information he wanted.

The transport aircraft which was due at three arrived shortly after five. It floated exhausted on to the runway with engines roaring and eventually came to a halt in front of the control tower. The propellers shuddered to a standstill. Several men in uniform climbed out of the fuselage, most of them officers. Then came four civilians—three women and one man.

Soeft looked them over carefully before going across to them. The man might have been a soldier on leave and had no interest for him. The women were a very different proposition. Their long hair alone was enough to cause a stir. And then there were legs to be seen, a fact which could only be described as sensational. It was true that the ladies had a slightly crumpled look about them after their long flight. Their faces were pale and were lined with sweat and dirt, but there could be no doubt about it: all of them had distinct class.

One of them, obviously the eldest of the three, carried a portfolio with her as well as her suit-case. There was a matter-of-fact down-to-earth look about her reminiscent of a school-mistress. The second, a genuine blonde whose lips were painted bright red, jumped up and down excitedly on the tarmac. She looked, or so Soeft thought, as if she were ready to entertain half the Wehrmacht. The third was small, dark and charming. She had large round eyes and walked with a tripping little gait. She clasped a guitar-case to her slender little bosom.

Soeft went up to the ladies, introduced himself and said: " So you've arrived at last."

And he nodded amiably.

The officer from the Kommandantur, the same one with whom Soeft had had dealings earlier on, stalked stiffly up to them. He stammered out a rather tedious speech in which the words " heartily welcome " occurred three times over. The civilian stared grimly about him. The ladies stamped their feet to try and keep warm. Only the blonde stood there unconcernedly waggling her hips. She brought all work on the airfield to a standstill for several minutes.

" Cold here, isn't it?" said Soeft with a grin.

" It is what one expects in Russia," said the civilian with a certain stiffness. The blonde giggled sillily, but not without charm.

The officer from the Kommandantur now asked his distinguished guests to take their seats in the waiting car. At the same time he suddenly transformed himself into a most conscientious and efficient porter. But when even the civilian tried to get him to carry his bags, he rebuffed him coldly.

Soeft said: " Which of the ladies is Fräulein Ebner?"

The attractive little brunette with the guitar-case raised her large round eyes and said eagerly: " Oh, I am."

" You'll be coming with me. I have orders to look after you myself," said Soeft. " Follow me, will you?"

The officer from the Kommandantur at once put down the two cases he was carrying. His mouth opened and he seemed to be trying to say something. To judge from the expression on his face it would not have been very flattering.

But Soeft merely said: " General's orders," and went ahead. The girl followed him obediently.

He stowed Fräulein Ebner's luggage away in the back of his car. She watched every one of his movements wide-eyed like a child. Soeft thought that she was admiring him.

" I suppose you find all this rather astonishing?" he said.

" No, why should I?" answered Lisa Ebner gently.

" You'll soon see," said Soeft. " You'll soon find plenty to take your breath away. I can guarantee that all right. Absolutely guarantee it."

There was a look of keenness in Corporal Vierbein's honest boyish eyes as he sat beside Lieutenant Wedelmann at the table. He sat stiff as a ramrod. His bulging rucksack stood ready packed over by the door. Steel helmet, rifle and gas-mask were stacked nearby. All these objects were in perfect order and laid out as if about to be photographed for the weekly magazine, the *Illustrierte Beobachter*.

Wedelmann smiled down at the staunch but modest little Corporal beside him: " I'm relying on you, Vierbein. It's something I've always felt able to do with perfect confidence."

The Corporal nodded curtly. It was as if he were permanently on the alert for fear of missing some order which might apply to him. And on his tunic, which was well-worn but absolutely spotless, could be seen the dull gleam of the Iron Cross First Class.

Wedelmann listened for a moment to the silence of the early evening. The front was quiet, as it almost always was these days at this time. It was an ugly, sinister, unsettling sort of quiet.

On both sides men who had not yet received orders to attack one another were doing their best to make life, or rather what there was left of it, as tolerable for each other as possible. And yet everyone knew how pointless it all was in the end. The silence of the front weighed on people oppressively. It was as if a pack of ravening wolves were quietly surrounding the two armies. Even in the hut which Wedelmann shared with Asch the noiseless burning of the fire in the grate made one uneasy.

There was not even the sound of a truck on the move to break the silence. No aircraft had appeared in the sky for over a fortnight. The front lay only about three kilometres away but over the whole length of it had fallen the silence of the grave.

Wedelmann once more gave Vierbein an encouraging smile. He slapped his thigh and looked across to where Asch was staring into the fire, waiting for the kettle to boil.

" Isn't it ready yet, Asch?" asked the Lieutenant loudly. The sound of his own voice seemed to reassure him.

" There's no hurry," said Asch, " we've got all the time in the world."

Wedelmann pushed his chair back noisily. It was made out of packing-cases. He turned to Vierbein.

"Don't forget," he said, "there's something almost sacred about this mission you're being sent on."

Asch slowly got up and made his way over to the table with the kettle.

"Don't worry," he said, looking across at Vierbein, "our Vierbein will pull it off all right."

"Of course," said the Lieutenant enthusiastically. "Of course he will."

Wedelmann was now in the best of moods. He beamed across at the Corporal. This pale boyish creature always looked a little as if he were just on his way to a confirmation class. But in fact he was one of the finest soldiers in the regiment. This was that very Vierbein who had seemed such an utterly hopeless case only a few years before. To-day he was a tower of strength to his gun crew, barking out his orders with the most perfect assurance. On one occasion he had knocked out no less than three enemy tanks in a quarter of an hour. Two weeks later he had done the same thing again. And an hour later he had knocked out yet another.

"You would have had the Ritterkreuz by now, Vierbein, if I'd had any say in the matter," remarked Wedelmann. "Certainly you've earned this trip home if anyone has."

"Thank you, Lieutenant," said Vierbein modestly.

Sergeant Asch mumbled something that was difficult to hear but on the whole it didn't sound too friendly.

"To hell with it," he added, apparently referring to a cork which he was having some difficulty in getting out of a bottle of rum. There followed some further expletives after which he succeeded in opening two bottles and setting them on the table with a number of tumblers.

"Why so many, Asch?" asked Wedelmann. "There are only three of us."

"We have some visitors coming, Lieutenant," announced Asch. "I've taken the liberty of inviting Sergeant-Major Bock and Corporal Soeft round. The one will be giving Vierbein his travel papers and the other issuing him with his rations. Oh, yes, and then I've asked another guest: Lance-Corporal Kowalski who'll be driving our friend Vierbein to the airfield to-morrow morning."

Wedelmann listened to this information with the same equanimity with which he had come to listen to the identical day-to-day reports of unexpended ammunition. He had long ago ceased to be surprised by any arrangements which his adjutant made for him. Asch nearly always worked on his own and since Wedelmann found that their two minds were pretty much in sympathy he seldom had any fault to find with his decisions.

"Take care of yourself, then, my boy," said Asch to his old friend Vierbein.

"Don't worry, Asch," said Vierbein, "I know what I have to do. I'll get the job done just as quickly as I possibly can."

"But why?" asked Asch affably. "What's the hurry? Take your time about things. Have a bit of a rest at home. Make the most of your opportunity."

Vierbein began to feel rather uncomfortable. He looked up at Wedelmann. But the latter didn't seem to have heard. He started mixing himself a stiff grog: half rum, half water. This seemed to occupy his whole attention.

"Just relax for a few days," continued Asch. "Try to remember if you can that the war really can get on without you for once. Get my parents to let you have my room. My sister will look after you, though don't go making a fool of yourself with her. Take my wife out some evening. And tell them all what a lovely time we're having here."

"All right," said Vierbein, "I'll do that."

Asch took a look round the room. The dull light of the oil lamp cast shadows on the dirty floor and on the pile of straw with the blankets heaped up on it at the other end.

"You must tell the people back home we're living like kings here," he said. "Nothing we want. Only one thought in our heads: to force Russia to her knees so that the Fatherland can sleep in peace."

"I'll do all that," said Vierbein.

Wedelmann had by now tasted his grog, and finding it satisfactory, once again took part in the conversation.

"Yes, take your time, Vierbein. Don't try and rush the job. Do it thoroughly."

"In other words, Vierbein," said Asch, "in plain language: don't be a fool. You only get a chance like this once in a lifetime."

Wedelmann laughed, but he kept his thoughts to himself. He was delighted that Vierbein was getting this trip home; he knew that he had earned it more than anyone else in the troop; but at the same time he knew that he wouldn't make the most of it.

Snow was beginning to fall outside. A grey gloom was gathering round the windows. Asch put up the black-out. The lamp flickered wanly.

The sound of an engine could be heard making its way towards them in the distance. Asch looked up and said:

" Here come the guests."

Lance-Corporal Kowalski swung the car miraculously round three enormous potholes, braked hard and brought it to a stand-still in front of the C.O.'s hut.

" The surface isn't all it might be," he said with a grin, looking up and down the road.

The Sergeant-Major jumped out of the car. He held a brief-case under one arm and trudged over at once to the door of the hut. Soeft took his time. Slowly he unwound the blanket which he had wrapped round his legs and the lower part of his body. Then with calm deliberation he removed his special pair of elegant fur gloves.

" Bring the case inside," he said to Kowalski.

" I'm not your batman," said Kowalski, turning his back on him pointedly and getting out of the car.

Corporal Soeft then muttered something which could only have been an insult, although Kowalski seemed to mistake it for a joke for he laughed long and loud. Soeft's case remained where it was for the time being.

Wedelmann waved affably at his guests.

" Make yourselves at home," he said.

The Sergeant-Major did his best to draw himself up to his full height and deliver a regulation salute. But he wasn't entirely successful for the roof of the hut was too low. Soeft behind him merely sketched out the roughest possible sort of salute. Kowalski didn't even do that.

" I've brought a case of extras with me," announced Soeft.

" Excellent," said Wedelmann. " We can do with them."

" It's outside in the car," said Soeft and as this didn't seem to produce the desired effect, he added. " It'll have to be brought in."

" The sooner the better," said Wedelmann.

Soeft turned to the Lance-Corporal:

" Kowalski!" he said, " the case!"

Kowalski seemed to be having some trouble with his hearing. He put a finger into one ear to try to clear it. He gazed respect-fully down at the opened bottles of rum.

" What are you waiting for then?" asked Wedelmann.

Kowalski slowly took his finger out of his ear and with remarkable lack of enthusiasm slouched out of the room. He was back again in no time.

" I don't see any case," he said cheerfully.

35

Then Soeft's usual composure left him. This was a very rare occurrence. He went storming out of the room and, after a short interval, came back again, panting, scarlet in the face and dragging the case after him.

"Well, now," said Kowalski, "why on earth couldn't you have done that in the first place?"

Asch roared with laughter. Soeft's eyes narrowed to even smaller pin-points than usual. He glared furiously at Asch. But Asch wasn't worried in the least.

Wedelmann shook hands with his guests and asked them to sit down. Kowalski did so at once. Before the others had even time to get their greatcoats off he was sipping contentedly at his grog which consisted of almost neat rum.

The Sergeant-Major looked disapprovingly at the Lance-Corporal but no one paid any attention to him, least of all Kowalski. Then Bock brought out Vierbein's marching orders, arranged them neatly into a pile and handed them across to the Lieutenant for his signature. Asch leant interestedly over Wedelmann's shoulder and read them through.

"But these papers merely second him for duty," said Asch in astonishment. "Why doesn't he get a leave pass?"

"Because," said the Sergeant-Major, "all leave has just been suspended in this sector." And there was no mistaking the hostile tone in which he said it.

"But the people at home don't know that!"

"_We_ do, though, Asch," said the Sergeant-Major, "and I have to act accordingly." He was in a bad temper and didn't try to conceal the fact.

Wedelmann gave every appearance of reading the papers through thoroughly. But in fact he was leaning forward listening to what was being said.

Asch, who was still standing behind Wedelmann, stared at the Sergeant-Major and slowly shook his head.

"I'm not sure you're not making a big mistake," he said doubtfully.

"At least I'm obeying orders. You won't dispute that, Asch?"

Kowalski raised his glass in Vierbein's direction and winked at him. Soeft took a long pull at the enormous cigar to which he had just helped himself out of his leather cigar-case. Wedelmann was still apparently absorbed in the papers in front of him. Bock and Asch glared at each other and continued to argue.

"If you merely second our friend it means he has to go and

36

report to the reserve battery as soon as he gets home. And that means that they can do what they like with him."

"But he's got to go to the reserve battery in any case, Asch. How else is he to carry out his mission?"

"And there," put in Soeft, very much enjoying his cigar, "he'll find our old friend 'Chiefie' Schulz. Only nowadays of course he's a Lieutenant. He's in charge of the staff troop there, as a matter of fact."

"That's a point," said Wedelmann, looking up thoughtfully. "But I don't see why it should necessarily mean trouble. The war's changed a lot of things, you know. It's left its mark on everyone. And four years is a long time. Any views about this, Vierbein?"

"I'm not worried, sir," said Vierbein staunchly.

Asch slowly shook his head.

"The best thing," he said, "would be to fix Vierbein up so that he's covered either way. Give him both sets of papers so that he's in line with the regulations on the one hand but can also get a little bit of time to himself as well."

"Both at once you mean?"

"Why not? Or do you think it's putting too much strain on the orderly-room Corporal?"

"A double set of papers!" said the Sergeant-Major. He was quite beside himself. "You can't do that!"

"One can do anything, if only one has the will—the Führer said so himself."

Wedelmann drummed thoughtfully on the table with his pencil. He found it difficult to decide what to do, mainly because there were too many other people in the room. It never paid for too many people to be in the know when you were thinking of tampering with orders.

"What do you think about this, Vierbein?"

Vierbein sensed the embarrassing situation in which the C.O. found himself. As always he was prepared to play the part of a dutiful subordinate.

"I think it'll be all right if I just have papers seconding me, sir," he said.

"Just as you like," said the Lieutenant with a sigh of relief. He signed at once.

Asch drank up the contents of his glass and filled it up to the brim again immediately. Kowalski was drinking almost continuously, but seemed to be none the worse for it. Soeft, overcome by a sudden wave of generosity opened his cigar-case and offered cigars all round. Even Vierbein took one and managed not to choke as he smoked it.

"You'll be home this time to-morrow, my lad," said Soeft. "And I can guess what'll be the first thing you do when you get there!"

They all laughed. A deep blush spread slowly over Vierbein's face and they laughed louder than ever.

Asch had to assure them that the drink had run out before they would agree to go. Wedelmann decided not to open the extra case which Soeft had brought or they would have been there all night.

The guests took Vierbein with them when they left. He had said good-bye to his crew during the afternoon, before coming to see Wedelmann. He was to spend the night at the forward base and then be taken out to the airfield by Kowalski early the next morning.

"Well, have a good time," said Sergeant Asch, clapping his old friend Vierbein on the back. "Go and see my wife: tell her I'm well, in great form, and all the rest of it."

He took a step back. The murky light from the oil lamp left his face in shadow. He made way for Lieutenant Wedelmann. "I'll go with you to the car," said Wedelmann.

They walked out of the hut together. The moonlight filtered through black clouds on to the snow giving it a wan appearance. The night was cold and damp. But the warmth of the coming spring lay embedded somewhere in the clouds above.

"Now, Vierbein," said the Lieutenant, "I want this mission of yours to go absolutely smoothly. Don't let anything distract you. Come back safe and sound and see that you bring the transmitters and the trained operators with you."

"Yes, Lieutenant."

"Oh, and one more thing, Vierbein. A private matter."

Wedelmann took the Corporal to one side. He hesitated. He was obviously embarrassed.

He spoke up unusually quickly:

"By the way, I've had a couple of bottles of best brandy put in your kit. One of them is for you. And I wish you all the best, my dear fellow; may you drink it in good company. The other bottle—yes, well, that one perhaps you would give to Frau Schulz for me. Frau Lore Schulz, that is. You know her, I think. Tell her that . . . No, don't tell her anything. Just

38

give her my . . . my compliments. And say that I wish her all the best. That's all then. Good luck, Vierbein."

And before Vierbein could say anything in reply, the Lieutenant had retreated into the darkness: obviously greatly relieved. The night swallowed him up. But he didn't go back into his hut. He seemed to want to go for a little walk by himself.

"You know what the trouble with him is, don't you?" said Soeft. "He needs a woman. Now then, Asch, what about it? Shall I lay Natasha on for him?"

"Haven't you gone yet?" said Asch, who had just come out of the hut. "If you're not off by the time I count three there'll be trouble. One . . ."

"Good-bye again," said Vierbein.

He got into the car beside Kowalski. Soeft and the Sergeant-Major were already sitting in the back. Kowalski revved up the engine and darted suddenly forward, swerving violently to avoid the potholes. They hurtled away into the night.

"That man drives like the devil himself," said Wedelmann, reappearing behind Asch.

"Don't worry," said Asch guessing his thoughts, "Vierbein'll be all right. He's the sort that comes through everything."

Wedelmann put a hand on Asch's shoulder. Together they listened to the sound of the engine receding. Suddenly it died on them. The night had swallowed it up along with everything else. Once again they found themselves caught for a moment in the ominous treacherous silence which was the war.

"It's cold," said Asch. He wanted to break the silence. "Cold and damp."

A pale moon forced its way through the clouds, wreathed in mysterious vapours. The snow covered the earth like a blanket over a corpse. It seemed to absorb the moonlight and radiate it back again. The darkness slowly dispersed.

A sentry could be seen in the little valley where the guns were in position. He stamped his way noiselessly through the snow. His movements were painfully slow. He seemed to be making no progress at all. Then he came to a sudden halt. It was as if the whole world stood still for a moment. There seemed to be no more front lines with frozen corpses lying stiffly in between them; no soldiers snoring beneath filthy blankets; no base camps where they knew neither war, nor this peculiar brand of peace; no women left for a man to go for comfort to. It was as if the whole world had become simply one vast graveyard.

Captain Witterer, the new C.O. of No. 3 Troop, stepped energetically into the little car which had been waiting for him in front of Regimental H.Q. The springs creaked as he let himself down heavily on to the seat but his military bearing was maintained almost intact.

The driver continued to sit at his ease behind the steering wheel. A fair amount of luggage lay piled up in the back. The sun which seemed to hang exhausted in the sky had apparently been strong enough to send the driver off to sleep, for he sat there quite motionless.

"Right," said Captain Witterer briskly, "to my troop then! But hurry, please, if you don't mind!"

"Gun positions, forward base or rear base?" asked the driver like a waiter rattling off dishes from a menu.

"To the orderly-room first," said Witterer, and his tone was far from friendly. He didn't like this driver's attitude. He didn't like quite a lot of things he'd seen so far. He had noticed at once that almost all the men out here, but particularly those from his own battery, seemed completely lacking in discipline. He'd soon put a stop to that.

"What's your name?" he asked his driver.

"Kowalski."

"General Kowalski?"

"No, just Kowalski," replied the other. He pressed down the accelerator and swerved violently to avoid a pothole. The car lurched, righted itself and bounced into the air. Witterer clung desperately to the side of the door. His cap slipped forward over his face, "My rank," continued Kowalski, "if that's what you mean, is Lance-Corporal."

Witterer didn't answer. He stared through the windscreen at the road ahead. He was sorry to have to say it, but No. 3 Troop seemed to be in the most deplorable state. Like a lot of other things round here. But he wasn't going to let himself be got down by it. Half the pleasure in life lay in overcoming obstacles, he told himself, desperately trying to keep his balance as the car proceeded on its hair-raising journey. Yes, he'd soon have everything in No. 3 Troop looking very different. It was just the job for a man in the prime of life like himself.

Captain Witterer had been posted straight to the front from the German High Command, where he had been one of the right-hand men of a General in charge of communications.

It was only a matter of time before he became *the* right-hand man. The one thing lacking in his career to date was a little "front-line experience". But this presented no real problem to a man like Witterer. He was now in the process of adjusting the matter. A stay of two or three months out here would do the trick, and in the meantime the Wehrmacht would acquire another first-class front-line unit.

They had left the base behind them now and were rushing down the deserted main road at a terrific pace. Dirty snow, dead trees, wretched little tumbledown shacks, seemed to be flying past them. They were aware of nothing but the strong smell of petrol, the roaring of the engine and the cold damp air on their faces. The driver held on to the wheel with two fingers of his left hand. His right hand was stuck deep into his trouser pocket.

Witterer looked at the man more closely. His greatcoat could not be described as clean by any stretch of the imagination. It was positively filthy. It was covered in oil and there were even splashes of mud on it which must have been there since the autumn. In addition to which the fellow hadn't shaved. And whenever one caught a whiff of him there was that unpleasant smell of stale alcohol which hangs about bar-rooms in the early mornings. His hands, which were more like paws than hands, were so dirty that it looked as if he had been digging in the earth with them. The fellow simply wasn't a soldier at all, or at least not the sort of soldier he was going to have in his troop. He was little better than a tramp. But at least he could drive. That was something. He could drive like the very devil.

"How much farther?" asked Witterer.

"Not much farther," said the Lance-Corporal.

Kowalski headed for the village where the troop's rear base had been set up. He only slightly slackened pace, although men and vehicles now appeared on every side to block his way. He drove straight for everyone he saw at breakneck speed. They simply had to get out of his way as fast as they could. Witterer was amazed.

The Captain looked about his new domain with increasing misgiving. Tanks were standing about all over the place. A repair shop had been set up in a wretched little smithy; broken-down vehicles stood parked round it. The school had been taken over as a forward hospital. An infantry regiment had set up its headquarters in the largest house in the village. No. 3 Troop's rear base was installed in the second largest.

Kowalski drove straight for the orderly-room. Just before he got to it he jammed on the brakes so hard that Witterer almost went through the windscreen. Before the Captain could give vent to his feelings, the door of the hut was flung open and Sergeant-Major Bock himself came bursting out.

Lance-Corporal Kowalski watched the scene which now took place with considerable pleasure. The Chief was arrayed in his best uniform. He might have been just about to take a parade on the barrack square. Even his note-book was held in exactly the regulation manner. He had pinned on his little row of medals and among them his War Service Medal—First Class—was plainly visible, gleaming with metal polish. His belt, too, had been polished till it shone. And the snow and slush at his feet were beautifully mirrored in his boots. Kowalski was beside himself with delight. He hadn't known such things were possible.

Sergeant-Major Bock drew himself up, brought his hand up to his cap with a magnificent flourish and snapped it smartly down again. A perfect regulation salute.

" No. 3 Troop," he announced; " 2 officers, 23 N.C.O.s, 138 men; 2 N.C.O.s and 9 men sick, 1 N.C.O. and 4 men temporarily seconded for other duties, 1 man under arrest, 1 man in detention!"

Witterer was absolutely delighted. At last, at last someone in this troop who had made a good impression on him. An old soldier—you could tell it at a glance! Fellows like him were the backbone of the Wehrmacht—the sort of man you could always rely on, the sort of man who was badly needed here.

Witterer jumped eagerly out of the car. He walked briskly over to the Sergeant-Major and shook hands with him. The Sergeant-Major looked very proud of himself. They were like two people congratulating each other about something. Kowalski found it all highly amusing.

The Sergeant-Major now hurried back to the hut and flung wide the door. Witterer bent his head slightly, although this wasn't strictly necessary, and went inside. He found Wedelmann waiting for him, looking through the secret files.

The two officers saluted each other and introduced themselves, trying to hide the curiosity they felt for each other beneath the heartiness of their greeting. After making one or two polite remarks they began looking each other up and down like a couple of horse-dealers.

" I've been around since yesterday actually," said Witterer, "but Colonel Luschke thought it best for me to get some idea of the general set-up in the sector first."

"Yes, that's part of Luschke's technique," said Wedelmann. He glanced quickly at Sergeant-Major Bock who had taken up a good strategic position just behind Witterer and therefore had no need to hide the broad grin which appeared on his face. The same thought had crossed both their minds: it was part of Luschke's technique to give every new officer twenty-four hours up at Regimental H.Q. before he got down to regular duties. After that, if he had any sense at all, he had an idea of which way the wind blew, and, unless he was actually looking for trouble, adjusted his ideas accordingly.

"The regimental commander seems a remarkable man," said Witterer, rather cautiously.

Wedelmann nodded.

"Yes, it's difficult to put anything over on him."

"No 3 Troop has had a considerable amount of success to date, I believe?"

"You might say so."

"Not at the expense of discipline, I hope?"

Wedelmann rested his hands on his knees and leant forward. He looked like a boxer in a corner of the ring waiting for the first round to begin.

"It's fighting qualities that count here," he said. "Not discipline."

"You can't have one without the other," said Witterer assuming a rather schoolmasterly tone. He was a Captain after all. There were times when it did no harm to remind even brother officers of the fact.

"That sort of thing's all very well in theory, Captain. But it works out rather differently in practice. Or do you mean you think that one day there'll even be a regulation way of dying?"

Witterer smiled in a superior sort of way. Colonel Luschke had spoken very highly of Wedelmann, but he didn't really seem to be much of an officer. He didn't even carry himself like one. He had obviously just allowed himself to stagnate out here at the front. That sort of life wears a man down in the end; it saps his energy and undermines his intelligence. New blood was badly needed. That of course was one of the reasons why he had come.

"Have you got everything ready for handing over the troop, Lieutenant?"

"What do you mean: have I got everything ready?" replied

43

Wedelmann. "I hand over the troop, that's all there is to it. And a thoroughly experienced troop it is too, which has proved itself in battle more than once. What you make of it is your own look-out."

"But surely," said the Captain distinctly coolly, "there will at least be some sort of written statement to this effect."

"We don't keep log-books here," said Wedelmann, with mounting dislike for his successor. "The daily returns will of course give you all the information as to strength, serviceable vehicles, fuel and ammunition, if that's what you mean."

At this point the Sergeant-Major intervened in an effort to be tactful.

"The receipt for the various documents has been prepared, of course," he said.

"Ah, good," said Witterer, getting to his feet. "Well, let's take a look round then."

"Right," said Wedelmann also getting up. "We'll start with the gun positions."

Witterer was already half-way to the door, but he stopped as if something had just crossed his mind.

"There's just one thing before we go out to the guns," he said. "Where will I be living, by the way?"

Living! thought Wedelmann, and aloud he said:

"You can share my billet, Captain. We can always make room for you there. It's up in the forward base."

"I think, to start with, I'll be taking up my quarters in the rear base," said Witterer, "so that I can get to know everything from the bottom up."

"Very good, sir," said the Sergeant-Major trying to hide the displeasure he felt at this news. He looked upon the rear base as his own private domain. He didn't like the idea of anyone else setting up house there, least of all someone with the authority to interfere with his arrangements and perhaps even the intention of doing so.

Witterer looked at the Sergeant-Major and laughed curtly. This was a warning to the Chief that there were more surprises to come. Indeed, before he had fully been able to grasp the situation, the Captain said:

"I imagine that the best billet in the rear base is the one you're in, Bock."

Wedelmann grinned broadly. The Sergeant-Major stood there speechless. Both knew very well that it wasn't the Sergeant-Major who had the best billet, but Soeft. But Witterer could hardly be expected to be aware of such finer points yet.

"Ah yes!" said Witterer heartily. He felt immensely pleased with himself. "I know the way these things are. The Sergeant-Major's always the man with the cushiest billet! Everyone knows that! But you'd be only too glad to surrender yours to your new C.O., I feel quite sure, Bock."

"Of course, sir," said Bock, although he only just managed to get the words out.

"Right then," said Witterer. He obviously prided himself on his sense of humour, which was dry and to the point, the sort of thing the men understood. "Right, start clearing your things out straight away. When I come back from the gun positions, we'll see what you've seen fit to leave me."

"Very good, sir." Bock sounded extremely bitter.

"What I suggest," said Wedelmann, who was beginning to enjoy himself, "is that the Sergeant-Major goes and joins Soeft. That is, always provided you have no objection."

"Yes, all right," said Witterer, as if he were taking a very important decision. "You go and transfer your things to Soeft's place, Sergeant-Major."

The Sergeant-Major saw the most appalling trouble ahead. Not only was he going to lose his own very reasonable billet, but he was going to have Soeft on top of him as well. What on earth did this new man think he was up to? He couldn't just suddenly take on a man like Soeft like that. Soeft of all people! If things weren't ironed out in time this could lead to starvation rations all round. The fellow simply had no idea of the way things worked.

"Who's my regular driver, by the way?" asked Witterer.

"Lance-Corporal Kowalski, sir," replied Bock. He felt better for a moment for being able to say so. This at least was some sort of retaliation. Kowalski was the ideal person to deflate a man like this.

"Does it have to be Kowalski?" asked Witterer.

"He's the best driver in the troop," said Wedelmann. "He's up to every situation." He too was delighted at the idea of Witterer taking Kowalski. The Lance-Corporal missed nothing. He had a particular gift for knowing what someone else was thinking and if he sensed trouble coming he was always able to deflect it in time.

"Right," said Witterer. "Let's get moving then."

Kowalski drove both his old and his new C.O. at breakneck speed up towards the forward base. From there both proceeded on foot to the guns which were in position on the edge of the village.

Witterer did everything that the regulations prescribed. He put on his steel helmet, took advantage of every scrap of natural cover and made an intensive study of the surrounding countryside through his field-glasses. There was almost nothing to be seen of the enemy lines.

"Only two of our guns can be brought to bear on their lines at close range," explained Wedelmann, standing beside him in the snow. "The other two are covering that hill in front of us which is on this side of our own infantry. They're for use against tanks."

"And at long range?"

Wedelmann pulled a tattered map from his cuff and spread it out in front of them. It was covered with pencil marks.

"At long range all four guns can be brought to bear on the entire sector of the front."

"And how often do you send something over to keep them awake?"

"There's been absolute quiet here for the last few weeks."

"What? Nothing to start the day with? No signing off in the evening?"

Wedelmann folded up his map again.

"Captain," he said politely, "we never expend more ammunition that we have to. This troop doesn't need to practise any more now, they've had enough experience of the real thing."

Witterer made no reply. He was still taking care to keep under cover. He hadn't thought much of Wedelmann right from the start. Now his opinion of him was confirmed. Wedelmann had gone stale. And his men had caught his staleness from him. The necessary spark was missing.

Captain Witterer first made sure that the sector was as quiet as Wedelmann had said it was and then ventured across to the guns. There in a few well-chosen words he harangued first the sentries, then the men on the guns and finally the remainder of the crews in their dug-outs.

Wedelmann made no comment. He wasn't in the least surprised. The men, on the other hand, were extremely surprised, but they made no comment either. Witterer put this down to instinctive respect.

The two officers then retired to Wedelmann's quarters where they found Sergeant Asch waiting for them. The Captain jumped when he saw him. Then he smiled unpleasantly, like a schoolmaster who is just about to start correcting some exercise books.

"I didn't recognise you for a moment," he said.

"Ah, I knew you wouldn't forget me, Captain."

"Sergeant Asch is the C.O.'s adjutant in this troop," explained Wedelmann. "I didn't realise you knew him."

"Yes, I know him all right," said Witterer. "Know him quite well, you might almost say."

Witterer and Wedelmann sat down at the table. Asch didn't wait to be asked but sat down with them, as a matter of course. Witterer decided not to say anything. Later, when he'd had time to get things into shape a bit he'd put an end to all that. Yes, he certainly would.

"Anything to report from the gun positions, Sergeant?" asked the Lieutenant.

"The sights on No. 3 gun need a little adjusting. If we put it in for repair to-day we'll get it back the day after to-morrow."

Wedelmann turned to Witterer.

"Do you agree to that, Captain?"

"Can't the armourers come out and do the job on the spot?" asked Witterer. "Or are they too scared?"

"There isn't anything for them to be scared of just at the moment, Captain," said Asch. "They would, of course, come out and do the job on the spot if we insisted. But it'll be done more quickly and more efficiently if we take the gun into the repair shop."

"It's all very well for you to say that, Sergeant, but what happens if anything starts up at the front in the meantime?"

"If anything's going to start up we'll get twenty-four hours' notice of it at least, Captain. Just at the moment the enemy hasn't got a single tank in the whole sector, in addition to which he's got almost no artillery. Our spotters haven't reported any reinforcements either in the way of men or supplies. . . ."

"I think you'd better let me be the best judge of that sort of thing in future, Sergeant," said Witterer. He said it very calmly as if he were merely giving a piece of helpful advice. But, at the same time, he made it clear that he had no intention of discussing the matter further.

Asch looked across at Wedelmann who refused to catch his eye.

"Very good, Captain, I'll do that," said Asch.

The door was suddenly flung open and Kowalski slouched into the room. His dirty forage cap was pushed right on to the back of his head. Beneath his greatcoat it could be seen that his tunic was unbuttoned.

"What do you want?" said Witterer.

"A spot of warmth," said Kowalski, going straight over to the stove. He stretched his hands out towards it and grinned. He stamped his feet to get the snow off his boots.

"Was there anything else?" said Wedelmann to Asch. He was quite used to this sort of intrusion.

"Yes," said Asch. "I don't think we should let Corporal Krause take over Vierbein's gun."

Witterer asked who Vierbein was. Wedelmann told him.

Then Witterer wanted to know why Vierbein wasn't with his gun. And again Wedelmann told him. And who was Krause? Anyway why shouldn't he take over Vierbein's post?

"Well," said Asch, "you see, Captain, Corporal Vierbein has built up a particularly happy relationship with his gun crew. But Corporal Krause is . . . well, a very different sort of man, a complete contrast with Vierbein, one might say. The men would find it difficult to get on with him. It could be that he'd completely mess things up before Vierbein got back."

"I'd like to see this man Corporal Krause," said Witterer. And he added to himself: If Asch is so much against Krause, then Krause must be a very different sort of man from Asch. Which is interesting, because Asch . . .

"By the way," he said, suddenly very affable, "when did you last have an entertainment show here?"

"Here?" repeated Wedelmann in amazement. "When did *we* last have one? You must be joking."

"So that's been neglected too," said Witterer. "It seems to me that there's been a bit of initiative lacking here somewhere. You can't expect an entertainment show to materialise of its own accord, you know—you've got to be prepared to help it along a bit. And, furthermore, that's just what I'm going to do. Is my car ready, Lance-Corporal?"

"Always ready for anything like that, sir," said Kowalski, with a keenness which Asch and Wedelmann found quite astonishing.

The Junkers 52 was a huge camouflaged metal bird known familiarly as "Auntie". The pilot brought it down as calmly as if he were handling it in his sleep. As it floated to earth it seemed to hang in the air for a moment before settling gently on to the ground and then rolling forward to a standstill.

"Terminus!" shouted a soldier excitedly. "All change!"

Corporal Vierbein buttoned up his greatcoat in the regulation manner. He took his time about this as if he were considering whether or not to go through with what he was doing. Thoughtfully he slung his rifle over his shoulder and reached for his rucksack.

He stood there waiting for something to happen, but not quite certain what it was. He let everyone else off the aircraft first. They pushed and shoved their way out on to the tarmac. Only when they were all out did Vierbein make his way slowly towards the door and walk solemnly down the steps.

He looked about him like a man who has just got to the top of a hill which he has never climbed before. Dusk was already beginning to fall. A pale blue light lay over the airfield. The setting sun made a last feeble attempt to paint the horizon a vivid red, but the world seemed to be running out of colour.

A truck loomed up out of the dusk. It came rattling and swaying towards the Junkers, with its engine spluttering and back-firing. A number of cases were piled on to it and it swayed away again like some easily satisfied drunk.

The metallic breath of a loud-speaker suddenly became audible and a voice boomed out across the airfield:

"New arrivals report to the Kommandantur. Air crew report to the duty officer. Attention, please—stand clear of the runways, everyone!"

Corporal Vierbein took a firm grip on his rucksack. Well, he said to himself, I'm home at last, home after a whole year.

From what he had read in books he knew that this was a great moment. But the extraordinary thing was: it didn't now seem like one. Quite the contrary in fact. Instead of elation he was aware only of a growing feeling of anxiety. This started somewhere in the region of his heart and spread slowly out towards his stomach. Well, here he was. But what next?

He trotted after the others to the Kommandantur where a Sergeant inspected his papers, found them in order and duly stamped and signed them. Then in an unusually smart manner which immediately attracted favourable attention, Vierbein asked if he could speak to the Commanding Officer. He had a letter for him, he said.

The Sergeant was an accommodating sort of fellow. He was always ready to grant any reasonable request provided that it didn't inconvenience him in any way. He handed Vierbein over to the orderly-room who handed him over to the adjutant who in turn took him in to see the C.O.

The C.O. of the airfield was an elderly man with a bald patch on the top of his head which reflected the light even more dazzlingly than the lenses of his glasses. His one anxiety seemed to be to radiate the maximum amount of paternal goodwill. He took the letter which Vierbein handed to him, turned it over for a moment to see who had sent it and then asked the Corporal to sit down.

He began to read. What he read seemed to amuse him. He chuckled to himself and kept on putting his hand up to the shiny surface of his bald head.

Then he said: "I want you to report to me again before you fly back, Corporal. I'll have a couple of parcels for you to take. One for the C.O. of the airfield there and the other for Colonel Luschke."

"Very good, Major," said Vierbein respectfully. He realised now that he owed this trip primarily to the friendship of these three officers. He was being handed down through one of those private channels which were always so much quicker and more effective than the orthodox ones.

"If you find yourself in any difficulty, I want you to contact me right away, Corporal. Even if I can't help you myself, I can at least manage to get in touch with Colonel Luschke within a matter of twelve hours or so. My adjutant will tell you how to reach me by telephone."

"Yes, Major. Thank you very much, Major."

"A pleasure," said the C.O. He looked at his watch. "I expect you'd like to get home to-day if possible. We'll see what we can do for you. You're about thirty kilometres from the town here. If there isn't another train to-day there's probably a truck going in which can give you a lift. If not, we'll lay on special transport for you."

Vierbein had to wait about an hour or so in the canteen. The paper streamers which decorated it had once been brightly coloured, but were now grey with dust. He sat alone in a corner, peering into the haze of smoke. There was a good deal of noise. Men were talking and laughing. But somehow the atmosphere wasn't very gay. The radio droned on incessantly.

A driver in a mackintosh came into the room. He looked about him for a moment and then went over to Vierbein and told him he had orders to collect him. He was a keen, fresh-faced young man, with a rather touching look of immaturity about him. He carried Vierbein's rucksack out to a motorcycle and side-car which were waiting outside the canteen.

"Straight from Russia, Corporal?" he asked.

"Straight from Russia," answered Vierbein.

" Been in action yet?"

" Now and again."

" Pretty good hell, I suppose?"

" One makes the best of it."

Vierbein first felt his rucksack to see that Wedelmann's bottles were still intact and then stowed it away in the side-car. Then he climbed in himself, wedged his rifle in between his knees, and pulled the canvas covering over him.

" When you're ready," he said.

The driver let in the clutch and they drove away. The young man was anxious to show what a good driver he was and went as fast as he could. Probably a Staff Corporal of some sort, he thought to himself, hence the special transport. Obviously he hadn't really been in action. He accelerated harder.

" You don't need to go quite so fast," said Vierbein.

" Call that fast?" said the young man in a superior tone of voice. Typical base type, he thought contemptuously: careful, windy, no guts.

But he throttled back a bit. It was never good policy to annoy one of the C.O.'s favourites. You could land yourself in trouble that way. Why, only a fortnight ago, a fellow had been transferred straight to the Eastern Front for refusing to give a man some petrol for his lighter!

Vierbein had no idea of the thoughts which were passing through his driver's head. He leant right back in the side-car and stretched his legs. The rush of air against his face made his skin dry. He suddenly felt hot all over as if he had a fever. Now that he was approaching his destination the tension in his blood was beginning to mount.

" Only another twelve kilometres," said the driver. " Not more than twenty minutes at the most."

Vierbein nodded mechanically. He didn't feel in the mood for conversation. But he was far too good-natured to say so to the driver.

He knew every inch of the road along which they were travelling. He knew the ditches on both sides of them; he knew every tree and every footpath. One of the paths led off to a little lake in the middle of the woods. He had been for so many route marches along this road, so many walks on Sunday afternoons, so many evening strolls. The last time he had been along it had been with Herbert Asch and his wife Elizabeth and sister Ingrid. Ingrid Asch. His Ingrid.

It had been a glorious day, a day of sunshine and happiness. A day between the end of the campaign in France and the start of the campaign in Russia. The war seemed to be on another planet altogether.

Vierbein quickly tried to forget about that day.

The outskirts of the town began to loom up out of the darkness. The houses were becoming larger and taller. But there were no lights in them. A vast building suddenly blocked out the evening sky.

"That's not the barracks, surely?" said Vierbein.

"That's the new hydro-electric works," said the driver. And not without a touch of pride, he added: "We put that up practically overnight, you know. Those huts all round it are where the workers live."

He had slowed down considerably now. A cluster of wooden huts with corrugated iron roofs stretched out on either side of the road.

"A surprise for you, eh? Overnight it went up. Just like a mushroom."

Then, as if a curtain had suddenly been drawn aside in front of them, there stood the barracks in total darkness, they might have been brightly floodlit so well did Vierbein know every corner of them, every building, every shed, every inch of tarmac, every door, every window, every stone in the place.

"Do you want me to drop you at the barracks, Corporal?"

"No," said Vierbein hurriedly. "No." He could feel the sweat breaking out on his face. He gripped the canvas covering which lay across his knees.

"Where do you want to go then?"

"Take me to the centre of the town, to the market-place. Do you know the Café Asch? Right then, take me there."

The driver accelerated again. The bouncing light of the headlamps picked up one or two pedestrians and then lost them again. A few others loomed up out of the shadows and then disappeared. The town seemed utterly dead. The sound of the engine throbbed for a moment against the walls of the houses and was swallowed up by them. There was no echo at all. There was hardly any sign of life in the little town.

The machine drew up in front of the Café Asch. Corporal Vierbein climbed out and lifted out his rucksack, rifle, steel helmet and gas-mask. Then he said good-bye to the driver, who shook hands with him, revved up the engine and roared away again.

Vierbein found himself standing in the middle of the darkened market-place. Everything in the town seemed to have become smaller, gloomier, more insignificant. He stood there almost motionless, with rucksack, rifle and the rest of his equipment dangling from him. He looked helplessly about him. It was a long time since he had felt so lonely.

And Vierbein said to himself: what on earth am I doing here? I should have gone straight to the barracks to report. Then he thought: but this is where old Asch, the café proprietor, the father of my one and only friend, lives. And this is where Ingrid Asch lives, the girl whom I love and am going to marry.

With the slow ponderous steps of a man carrying a heavy burden, Corporal Vierbein went up to the Café Asch. He put his shoulder to the door. Then he pushed aside the heavy blanket which hung inside it. He found himself on the edge of a great sea of noise and light. He stood there, blinded and dumbfounded.

It was all so very different from what he had imagined. Even the Café Asch had changed. His memory seemed to have deceived him. The little café with its quiet corners and gentle murmur of conversation had changed completely. It was much fuller than it used to be. Smoke rose slowly in thick clouds above the tables. There was a smell of stale beer. A blaring loud-speaker drowned all conversation.

No one seemed to pay any attention to Vierbein. The waiters moved busily up and down the length of the room. A couple of women he didn't know performed their duties mechanically at the bar. Old Asch was nowhere to be seen. Neither was Ingrid. There was no one there he knew at all.

A group of new arrivals forced their way in at the door, pushing Vierbein to one side. He made no attempt to stand his ground. He bumped into an empty chair by the entrance and sat down in it without a word.

After he had been there a few minutes he got up again. He put his rucksack away in a corner, hung his equipment up on a hook and took off his greatcoat. Then he sat down again, a silent, patient, rather helpless figure.

But now the people at whose table he was sitting began to pay some attention to him, for they could see he was wearing several decorations, including the Iron Cross First Class. Heroes were still at a premium in those days.

"Well, and how are things at the front?" someone asked. His voice had a rough beery edge to it.

"Oh, splendid—splendid, you know," said Vierbein quickly. But he got to his feet at once. He had no wish to play the hero. He walked hurriedly over to the bar. He could see the two girls who were serving there more clearly now, but he still couldn't recognise them. There had been changes here as everywhere else in the last few years. At the same time people's faces were all beginning to look the same.

"Can I speak to Herr Asch, please?" he asked.

"He's not in," replied one of the girls, without looking up. She went on drawing the beer in a completely business-like way.

"And Fräulein Ingrid?"

"She's not either," said the girl. And then, with a quick glance at Vierbein's Iron Cross, but at nothing else about him, she said:

"Would you like a schnaps? I'll give you one. I'm allowed to give them to men back from the front."

"No, thank you," said Vierbein, turning away again. He looked helplessly round the hall. It was absolutely packed. All he could see in the smoky atmosphere were heads and hands and glasses. His ear-drums vibrated with the din.

Then he noticed Anton, the head waiter, sitting in a little compartment behind the cash register. Vierbein went over to him, delighted to have found someone he knew at last. But Anton didn't recognise him to begin with. Vierbein immediately grew shy again. He reminded Anton who he was.

"But, of course, Herr Vierbein," cried the head waiter with delight. "You're thinner, though, and paler. You look more of a man somehow. Ah, yes, war does that to people. I know all about it. I've seen my share, you know. But when did you get back? What'll you have to drink?"

"Where's Herr Asch?"

"Oh, he's somewhere around. He hardly bothers to turn up here these days. He doesn't need to. The place runs itself, as you can see."

"And Fräulein Ingrid?"

"Oh, she's somewhere around too. Probably at some committee meeting or other. Or knitting comforts for the troops. Or at the hospital. She's always doing something for the troops these days, workng for victory and so on. You know what I mean?"

"Of course," said Vierbein. "It's very understandable. I'll wait then."

"Yes, do," said Anton, "and have a drink while you're about it. On the house, of course. Herr Asch makes a point of that for men back from the front."

"Thanks," said Vierbein. He went back to his table.

But after a while he couldn't bear waiting any longer. He went over to Anton again and said:

" You've no idea where Herr Asch could be, have you then, Anton?"

" Let's see now. It's difficult to say. He might be in at any moment, of course, for it's gone ten already. On the other hand, the betting is he's still with his old friend Foreman Freiag, in which case he won't be back till late."

Vierbein thanked Anton. He asked him to look after his rifle and equipment for him. Anton was only too ready to do that. " We can't do enough for our boys," he said. " Oh, we've seen our share of it too, you know."

As soon as Vierbein got outside, he took a deep breath of fresh air. And then another. It's wonderful air, he tried to tell himself—the air of home.

He wandered off down the darkened streets. This was the town in which he had done his training. The sound of his steps echoed back from the houses. He liked that: it made him feel he wasn't alone any more.

He didn't meet many people in the streets and those he did meet were mainly soldiers, most of them ordinary rank and file. Some had girls with them. Others seemed to be quite happy on drink alone. There were artillery and infantry just as in peace-time. The batteries and battalions of former days had merely turned into reserve batteries and reserve battalions. And in addition to these there were the regiments of foreign workers, the staffs of engineers and officials. The barracks had been enlarged, they were now like one vast army encampment. But here on the home front the war still slumbered. There was a peaceful air about the town. It had always seemed a bit sleepy at the best of times, but now with the black-out as well, its sleep seemed deeper than ever. And from the façades of the houses the windows stared down at him like eyeless sockets.

Vierbein shuddered and quickened his pace. He walked past Bismarckshöh. Here too the noise was muffled by the heavy black-out curtain on the windows. A few steps more and the barracks loomed up ahead of him, vast and menacing. The building was like some great animal waiting to pounce on him. He turned quickly off to the left heading for the little colony of villas where Foreman Freitag lived.

After a moment's hesitation he pushed open the garden gate and knocked on the door rather timidly.

A few moments later, the door opened and Foreman Freitag

stood there in his shirt and trousers. The light of the hall falling on him from behind made the squat little man seem much bigger than he really was.

"Good evening, Herr Freitag," said Vierbein. "Is Herr Asch with you?"

The foreman peered out into the darkness. He leant forward a little as if he were straining his ears to hear something. "He's not here," he said. "But do my ears deceive me? That voice seems familiar. It's not Herr Vierbein by any chance, is it?"

"Yes, it is," said Vierbein. "But I didn't want to disturb you . . ."

"But man alive, come in! Come in!" cried the foreman enthusiastically, flinging the door open wide. Then he turned round and called back into the house. "Come here everyone! We've got a visitor! Herr Vierbein is here!"

"But I don't want to . . ." The unusual warmth of the welcome made Vierbein feel shy.

But Foreman Freitag seized Vierbein by both hands and wouldn't let go of him until he had brought him into the living-room. The foreman rather hurriedly made certain that the black-out curtains were drawn and then switched on all the lights.

He looked at Vierbein affectionately and said: "Well, when did you get back?"

"Just arrived," said Vierbein. "By air. This time last night I was still with my troop."

"And how is he?"

"Your son-in-law? Herbert Asch? He's fine."

"Thank God for that," said old Freitag, with a sigh of relief. "Thank God for Elizabeth's sake."

Frau Freitag came up at that moment and beamed a motherly smile at him. And then came Elizabeth herself, half excited, half drowsy. The foreman told her at once that all was well with Herbert Asch. "And Herr Vierbein was with him only this time last night—think of that—just twenty-four hours ago!"

"Oh, thank you," said Elizabeth softly, shaking hands with Vierbein.

Then he had to tell them all about it. Then he had to eat. And then drink. And then he had to see Elizabeth's child— his friend Herbert Asch's child. And he went to Elizabeth's room and saw a tiny pink infant fast asleep in its cot. And he looked at it for a long time for he wanted to be able to tell Asch all about it.

When it was close on midnight he said good-bye. Of course he had to promise to come again and to come again often. He promised. And then he went back to the Café Asch, and Foreman Freitag went with him as far as the edge of the town.

Anton, the head waiter, had just finished with the last of the guests. He was collecting all the bills together and checking the cash register. "I'm awfully sorry," he said to Vierbein, " but Herr Asch hasn't come in yet. Nor has Fräulein Ingrid."

" It doesn't matter," said Vierbein, trying to hide his disappointment. " I'll come back to-morrow."

" I'm terribly sorry," said Anton. " But that's just how it is. War messes everything up. I know it only too well, I've seen my share you know. What will you do now?"

" Oh, that's quite simple," said Vierbein. He put on his greatcoat, fastened his belt, fixed on his gas-mask, picked up his rifle and threw his rucksack over his shoulder. " That's really quite simple," he said. " I shall spend the night in the barracks of course."

One of the first decisions taken by Captain Witterer, the new troop commander, was this: " I will not have that fellow anywhere near me."

" That fellow " was none other than Corporal Kowalski, who gave up the C.O.'s car without a murmur and changed over to a Henschel eight-tonner. The Sergeant-Major did his best to prevent this happening by tactfully pointing out the disastrous consequences it was bound to have on the delicate balance of the troop as a whole. But Witterer remained adamant.

Two hours later Witterer's new driver got into a bad skid on an icy stretch of road and sailed straight into the only tree in the neighbourhood. There was a shattering crash. And then another shattering crash as Captain Witterer's head struck the windscreen. He roared like a bull.

The newly-appointed driver surveyed the ruins of the car and was himself reduced to a nervous wreck by Witterer's threat of a court martial. He was also told that from now on he was to consider himself quite unfit to drive personnel, particularly superior officers. " Nothing but ammunition!" yelled Witterer.

When the Captain got back to rear base he sought out the Sergeant-Major at once. " The drivers in this troop are all worse than useless," he declared.

Naturally the Sergeant-Major did not contradict his C.O. on

this point but at least he had sufficient character not to agree with him.

"This is the first accident we've had for four months," he said.

"The troop's been stuck here doing nothing for four months—that's why!"

"Yes, Captain."

"In any case, Bock, it's an old army rule that the best driver in the troop is automatically the C.O.'s driver. Kindly see to it that the best man is allotted to me at once!"

"But far and away the best driver we have is Lance-Corporal Kowalski, Captain."

"I've told you I'm not going to have him hanging round me any more."

The Sergeant-Major thought: and that goes for me, too. I don't want to have Kowalski hanging round me either. He was quite unable to make any use of him at rear base—particularly with Soeft about. Quite apart from which, Kowalski really was far and away the best driver.

"This fellow Kowalski has a sort of sixth sense at the wheel, you know, Captain. He's quite invaluable. He never loses his way; he can deal with every sort of breakdown; he never gets into trouble however bad the country. He never gets tired. When advancing, or in action, you can depend on him absolutely."

"Really now," said Witterer, showing a certain interest. "Really? But unfortunately the fellow hasn't got any manners."

"He'll learn them again all right, Captain. He's rather gone to seed lately, I'm afraid."

"Yes, maybe that's so," said Witterer, thoughtfully. And after further consideration, he added: "The same might be said of the entire troop, I think!"

The Sergeant-Major allowed himself to come under the suspicion of reacting slowly. It seemed to him that this was an unmistakable dig at Lieutenant Wedelmann. Now there was no doubt that as C.O.s went, Wedelmann had been a decent enough sort of fellow. On the other hand, there was also no doubt that the C.O. he had to reckon with in future was Captain Witterer.

"The Lieutenant," said Bock adroitly, "had his own way of doing things."

"And I have mine, let me tell you," snapped Witterer. "And it's my way that counts from now on. Woe betide anyone who doesn't adapt himself to it!"

"Of course, Captain," said Bock. He was really astonished

by the pace at which this new man was setting about things. He wondered how long he would keep it up. And then with all the caution that he had so painstakingly acquired in the course of two years of war, he allowed himself to wonder who would probably be the best person to see that he didn't keep it up too long.

Witterer sat down on a chair which had a folded blanket for a cushion. This was the one usually reserved for the Sergeant-Major. Papers giving details of the troop at the time of the change of command, had been drawn up in accordance with the Captain's instructions. He reached across for them. He nodded:

"Yes, that seems all right, Sergeant-Major," he said. "One top copy and three carbons. By to-day, if possible."

"Very good, Captain. But what about Lance-Corporal Kowalski?"

"All right, I'll take him back as driver. But give him a warning. Any more trouble and I'll have him posted."

"Colonel Luschke has several times inquired if he could have Kowalski for Regimental H.Q."

"Colonel Luschke takes a good deal of interest in this troop I gather?"

"Yes, I think you might say that, Captain."

"Colonel Luschke and Lieutenant Wedelmann get on pretty well, eh?"

"Apparently, Captain. There is no doubt our success in this troop has been a great credit to the regiment."

"And will, I hope, continue to be so, Sergeant-Major."

"I hope so, Captain."

"It undoubtedly will," said Witterer firmly. "What's more, we'll take good care to see that it does. Do you understand me?"

"Yes, sir," said Bock, very smartly and correctly, thinking to himself: and now on top of everything else he wants to be a hero as well! And who's going to have to pay for that, I'd like to know?

"When did you have your last practice alarm here?"

"Practice alarm, sir?"

"Yes."

"I don't know, sir—really that sort of thing . . . in the front line you know, sir . . ."

"Just as I thought, Sergeant-Major. The troop's been hibernating far too long. It can prove dangerous you know. It undermines morale!"

"Yes, sir," said the Sergeant-Major rather slowly.

"For instance, what happens if there's a dive-bombing attack?"

"There aren't any dive-bombers here, Captain. And if there were—well, everyone would take cover!"

Witterer shook his head in disapproval. But there was a look of triumph in his eye. He had really caught the fellow out.

"Oh, so they would, would they?" he said. "Have you ever heard of anti-aircraft fire by any chance? With rifles and machine-guns? And what about a paratroop attack? Or a sudden push by partisans? And what if the Russians start a surprise offensive and we have to take up new positions all of a sudden? What then?"

"Oh, of course, we're always ready for any surprises, Captain. It's just that we haven't got any special plans worked out."

"And, before I forget," went on Captain Witterer, setting his jaw grimly, "let me have a look at Sergeant Asch's personal file, will you?"

The Sergeant-Major made a note of this—Asch, personal file, C.O.—and thought to himself: now, my dear man, surely you're not going to . . . But he let no suggestion of what was in his mind appear on his face.

"What sort of a fellow is Asch actually?"

"He's the C.O.'s adjutant here."

"I know that. That's to say, I know that he was Lieutenant Wedelmann's adjutant. But, presumably, that is so no longer, since the Lieutenant no longer requires an adjutant. The question is what other post have we got to give him?"

"Asch would make a good operations officer," said Bock cautiously.

"Later—perhaps—much later. In the meantime Lieutenant Wedelmann can take over the job, that is for as long as he stays with the troop."

The Sergeant-Major now found it difficult to hide his astonishment. He lowered his note-book and stared at his new C.O. By God, that was a cool thing to do—he was actually demoting the Lieutenant. The man who had commanded the troop for over a year now—and had commanded it very creditably—was to spend his last few days as—— Pretty cool.

"What would you say to putting Sergeant Asch in charge of the ammunition?"

"Sergeant Asch has been an excellent adjutant," said the Sergeant-Major. He had decided to go carefully. He felt more than a little put out at the idea of having Asch hanging about with nothing to do in future. "He's capable of dealing with almost any situation and he's particularly useful up in the gun positions. You could give him any job, he'd do it well."

"Even make him Sergeant-Major?" asked Witterer quietly.

Bock bit his lip. That had gone home all right. But he spoke out bravely: "If I were to become a casualty then, yes, by all means."

"Well," said Witterer stubbornly, "if this man is so exceptionally gifted, then he'll certainly be able to cope with the job of looking after the ammunition."

"And who will you have as adjutant, sir?"

"Tell Corporal Krause that I wish to see him, will you, Sergeant-Major? As soon as possible. And let me have a look at his personal file too."

"Do you mean that Corporal Krause is to be——"

"I'll take that decision myself, thank you, Sergeant-Major."

Sergeant-Major Bock, suffering slightly from shock, but otherwise more or less intact, went to find solace with Soeft and his canteen supplies. Krause put in an appearance at once. He had a pretty shrewd idea what was coming though there was nothing very remarkable about that for Krause always had a pretty shrewd idea of what was coming. He was a wiry man of medium build with shady little terrier's eyes and he had a great deal of energy and a great deal of ambition.

On reporting to his new C.O. he gave him a first-class regulation salute. This immediately put him in Witterer's good books. In addition to that, he had taken the trouble to brush his uniform thoroughly and to shave himself in a manner which, in the circumstances, was really most creditable. His hair was neatly parted and shone with a high polish, for it was still wet.

After some general remarks and a few routine questions, Witterer came straight to the point.

"What do you think of Sergeant Asch?" he asked.

"An excellent soldier," answered Krause promptly. And he didn't show the slightest surprise at being asked his opinion of a superior N.C.O. in this way. "Just a little difficult, perhaps."

"Difficult? How do you mean?"

"Well—difficult to get on with. In any given situation. You might say he's not very adaptable."

Krause had no scruples or inhibitions about delivering himself of this judgement. He had been secretly prepared for the question. It wasn't difficult to guess what lay behind it. The fairly brusque encounter which had taken place between

Sergeant Asch and Captain Witterer in the telephone hut had quickly gone the rounds. The troop had spent a whole evening laughing over it.

"I suppose you know, Krause, that Sergeant Asch isn't exactly a friend of yours?"

"I did know that, yes, sir. I'm sorry about it because, as I say, Sergeant Asch really is an excellent soldier. On the other hand, I must say, I'm not surprised because our natures are really poles apart. And then, of course, sir, there is the fact that I've applied for a commission."

Witterer nodded, trying to pretend that he already knew all about that. He wanted to make it seem that he had everything at his finger-tips. And Krause went out of his way to try and show that he was taken in. They were really getting on splendidly.

Witterer now put one or two questions to Krause, about his background, his education, his civilian occupation and so on. They were answered to his entire satisfaction.

"Would you care to be my adjutant, Corporal?"

"Very much so, sir," said Krause, very correctly but at the same time in a tone of suppressed excitement. It was as if he were trying as hard as he could to keep his personal feelings out of his answer but simply hadn't got the strength of will to do so.

Shortly after this interview Captain Witterer had himself driven over by Kowalski to see Lieutenant Wedelmann. Kowalski grinned with delight as he let in the clutch and drove off at such speed that the chassis seemed to take leave of the springs altogether. The mudguards rattled and the engine roared until it seemed as if it would explode. But Witterer had to admit that Kowalski was an uncannily good driver, all the same.

Wedelmann was up with the guns as usual and had to be fetched by Sergeant Asch. In the meantime Captain Witterer spread out the documents which were to ratify the hand-over on the rickety table in the hut, one top copy and three carbons all on the regulation thick white paper. When Wedelmann came in Witterer returned his salute in a curt but friendly manner, merely maintaining that certain reserve which is the mark of the superior officer. He dismissed Asch at once.

"Your signature, please," he said to Wedelmann.

Wedelmann signed without reading the papers through. Then he collected them all up neatly into piles.

"Have you no comments to make?" asked Witterer in surprise.

"It's all only so much waste paper," said Wedelmann, without much interest.

"That may be what you think, Lieutenant."

Captain Witterer carefully folded up all the forms except one and put them away in his wallet. The extra one he handed over to Wedelmann.

"One of these is yours," he said.

"I dare say I'll find a use for it," said Wedelmann, putting it away in a hip pocket of his trousers.

"And now," said Captain Witterer, with a touch of solemnity, for he was a true soldier and liked a bit of ceremonial now and again, "I hereby formally take over command of No. 3 Troop, No. 1 Battery in the artillery regiment commanded by Colonel Luschke."

Then he made a point of shaking hands with Wedelmann very deliberately. This was a big moment for him.

"Well, what next?" asked Wedelmann.

"Yes," said Witterer, and he tried to make out that what he was now turning over in his mind was something that had only just occurred to him. He wanted to imply that he was a fast thinker. In fact, he had spent several hours considering what he should do with Wedelmann.

"Colonel Luschke wishes you to stay on with the troop for a few days longer, Lieutenant. He hasn't made up his mind what to do with you yet. It is, of course, very generous of him to let you stay here and assist me, even though it is in fact completely unnecessary. I think the best thing would be if you were to take over the job of operations officer."

"But we've got an operations officer already."

"He will be working under you until further notice."

"Is that an order?"

"Yes, it's an order. And while we're on the subject you won't, of course, be needing an adjutant any more. And I shan't be using the adjutant you had. So that Sergeant Asch will be relieved of his post and can take over the ammunition section."

And with that Captain Witterer strode athletically out of the hut. Wedelmann stood there speechless for a moment. Sergeant Asch came in and said:

"Well, is the bull still in the china shop?"

"Bang in the middle of it," answered Wedelmann, trying to laugh.

"There isn't much more china left," said Asch. He winked at Wedelmann, but Wedelmann had gone over to the window and was staring through the dirty panes like a farmer who can't help watching the shower of hail which ruins his harvest.

Lance-Corporal Kowalski pushed open the door of the hut, much as if he were making his way into a bar. Wedelmann turned round. Kowalski had brought a little parcel with him. He put it down on the table and grinned significantly.

"What's that for, Kowalski?"

"It's with best wishes from Corporal Soeft."

"Food?"

"Possibly, Lieutenant. But it's not actually for you. It's for a lady."

"What, Kowalski?"

"A pretty girl who lives in this village, apparently. At No. 17. She's got a wonderful figure, Lieutenant. Natasha's her name. Soeft thinks it would be worth your while to visit her."

"What sort of man do you think I am, Kowalski?"

"Someone who's got a certain amount of time on his hands, Lieutenant. And you ought to make use of it."

"Kowalski," said Asch. "Your new C.O. will be after you if you don't hurry up out of here."

"Oh, him!" said Kowalski. He dismissed his C.O. with a wave of the hand. "He'll learn."

Outside, Witterer was already shouting for Kowalski. Kowalski seemed delighted by the sound. "Quite a powerful organ that," he said, appreciatively. "All very well for the barrack square but unfortunately we're not in barracks just at the moment. We'll have to put him wise to one or two things like that." And with that Kowalski turned to go. But just before he left, he said to Wedelmann: "Really, Lieutenant—a wonderful figure!"

Wedelmann and Asch considered the parcel.

"I wonder what Soeft gets out of this," said the Lieutenant slowly. And he added: "But it's true I have got time on my hands now." And he smiled rather shyly for it seemed to him slightly disgraceful that he should now suddenly have time—for this sort of thing.

"Here's your greatcoat."

"Just a minute," said Wedelmann, and he seemed suddenly quite excited. "All in good time. First of all I think I'll just have a word with Colonel Luschke on the telephone."

Sergeant Asch was not the sort of man to try and meet trouble half-way. At first he simply ignored the new C.O.'s order to take charge of the ammunition section. He made no alteration in his daily routine. He just waited to see what would happen.

Lying full length on the floor of the hut, he stared at the low smoky beam above him and thought of his wife, Elizabeth, and of the child he hadn't yet seen. He smiled to himself for he could hardly believe that he was a father. The oil lamp threw a soft dull light which he found tiring on his eyes. But he couldn't get to sleep.

Some time later, Lieutenant Wedelmann came stumbling into the hut. Seeing Asch lying motionless on the straw, apparently asleep, he tried to be as quiet as possible. He turned the lamp down lower and began to undress.

That is to say he took off his greatcoat and laid it down beside Asch in the straw. Then he clamped each of his boots in turn between the bench and the table-leg and pulled them off, swearing under his breath. He folded his tunic up into a pillow and arranged it carefully on the straw. And that was as far as his undressing went.

He switched on a torch and blew out the oil lamp. Then he lay down beside Asch. He wrapped himself up in his two blankets and pulled his greatcoat over the top of him. There was a rustling of straw. Then even the light of the torch went out. The Lieutenant's breathing came deep and regular.

But he couldn't sleep. He was listening to the darkness. Asch moved an arm. He couldn't sleep either.

"It's funny," said Asch, "there are more and more nights when I find myself trying to see into the future."

"It'll be spring soon," said the Lieutenant. "I can feel it in my bones. And I can feel a lot of nights coming when neither of us'll get a wink of sleep."

Asch said nothing. His and Wedelmann's attitudes to the war were fundamentally different. Wedelmann took part in it with conviction. Asch regarded it as an unmitigated evil. Wedelmann identified Germany with National Socialism and thought of Hitler as a man of honour. Asch saw things as they were and wondered how it would all end. The one saw himself as fighting for a better world, the other merely tried to see that he came out of it all with a whole skin.

Wedelmann began searching for a cigarette. He found one

in the pocket of his tunic. It was rather squashed but he smoothed it out with his fingers in the darkness until the tobacco was evenly distributed. Asch gave him a light.

The Lieutenant took a few puffs and then handed the cigarette over to the Sergeant. Asch smoked it for a while and then handed it back again. The sweet smell of the smoke seemed to clear the fetid air in the little room.

"A remarkable girl that," said Wedelmann after a long pause.

"Another of Soeft's adopted children?"

"Not just any other—something rather special. The parcel I took did contain food. It was in return for some washing she'd done for him. It all seems straightforward enough."

"Soeft's a born business man. He doesn't do anything for nothing."

"Perhaps you're right," said Wedelmann thoughtfully. The end of his cigarette glowed strongly for a moment, then he threw it over to the stove in a high arc. There was a little shower of sparks. They were in darkness again.

"From Soeft's point of view," said Asch, "the whole war is just one big business deal. He'll do anything that shows a good return. Sometimes I think that in his eyes there are no fronts, and no enemies, only good opportunities and different people to do business with."

"She's a very unusual girl, this one, Asch. A student who got cut off here by our advance. She speaks German excellently."

"You certainly had quite a long conversation with her."

"I enjoyed it. She's a real woman, Asch. The first I've been able to talk to properly for months."

"A very accommodating sort of lady, too, I imagine."

"No, no, nothing like that."

"Wouldn't she play?"

"I tell you, Asch, it was nothing like that. We just understood each other, that was all."

"And when do you hope to be able to develop this little understanding of yours?"

"You're still sceptical, Asch, I see. I assure you I merely had a conversation with her—a nice long conversation. I'm not interested in anything else. And besides, she's not that sort of girl."

"What sort?"

"I think it's time you and I tried to get some sleep, Asch."

"Well, let's rest on our laurels then."

" Good night, N.C.O. i/c ammunition."

" Good night, operations officer."

They laughed softly, then they tried to get to sleep. But it was quite a time before they both dropped off.

They slept late the next morning, for neither had anything to get them up. By the time they did get up they found that there had been a restoration of the status quo. Asch was adjutant again and Wedelmann was no longer operations officer.

Captain Witterer had had his first reprimand over the telephone from Colonel Luschke. Luschke's technique was something quite new to Witterer. The soft, sinister, pentrating hiss of the Colonel's voice made even someone as sure of himself as Witterer, feel uneasy.

" I have great respect for initiative," Luschke had said, " but even more for common sense. An energetic approach is admirable in its way, but things must be done methodically and systematically."

" Exactly my way of thinking, Colonel," said Witterer, very full of himself again.

" Your way of thinking I have no doubt, Captain," went on Luschke. " But kindly don't forget that you have a C.O. above you and that he, too, has his way of thinking, that is if you have no objection. What's more, and this may surprise you, he knows No. 3 Troop fairly well."

" Of course, Colonel."

" I even know it rather better than you do just now, Captain. I'm not saying that that will always be so—it's a question of experience. And experience, as far as No. 3 Troop goes, my good Witterer, seems to be what you're lacking in. That is of course unless you're a genius, which at first sight doesn't seem likely. You will therefore have to acquire this experience. And for that you will need a certain amount of time. And it is precisely for that reason that I have left Lieutenant Wedelmann with you. Wedelmann is not there to work *under* you but to work *with* you."

" Yes, Colonel."

" For the time being, that is for as long as Wedelmann is there, I don't want to see any alterations made in the personnel of No. 3 Troop. I don't even wish the adjutant to be changed. Do you understand?"

" Yes, Colonel," Captain Witterer replied in consternation. He waited for the C.O. to ring off and then slammed down the receiver. He looked about him contemptuously. It was clear enough what he was thinking—what a prize mess things were in!

He sent for Sergeant-Major Bock, to whom the duty tele-phone operator had already conveyed the contents of this conversation. Bock rubbed his hands, not altogether because of the cold, and strode cheerfully over to the troop commander's quarters.

" Sergeant-Major," said Witterer, once again pretending that he was displaying his genius for improvisation. " We'll approach this thing systematically. I've been thinking things over. Of course all the various dispositions I've made will stand. But I want to make sure that the transition period goes through smoothly."

" Yes, Captain," said Bock, expectantly.

" Sergeant Asch will remain in his post as adjutant for the time being."

" But in that case we'll have two adjutants, Captain."

" We will have only one adjutant, Sergeant-Major. One adjutant is all that regulations permit. As soon as the one is ready to take over the job, the other will be dismissed."

" I see, Captain," said Bock. He was delighted by this development in the situation. " Yes, I see."

" As it happens I have a special job for Sergeant Asch to do." Sergeant-Major Bock listened attentively.

" Sergeant Asch will take over the organisation of an enter-tainment show for us here."

" Sergeant Asch?" said the Sergeant-Major. He couldn't believe his ears.

" And why not? That's a typical adjutant's job, isn't it? Or don't you think he's capable of doing it?"

" Yes, of course, sir. It's just that . . . well, that sort of thing can't exactly be done overnight. It will take quite a long time. And in the meantime we'd be without an adjutant."

" But how is that, Sergeant-Major? You don't seem to have understood me properly. While Asch is busy with the entertain-ment show—and he's to do the job properly—Corporal Krause will take over his work here."

" I see," said Bock, not without a certain respect for the Captain's technique. He had got the point at last.

Asch accepted his new job as he accepted every other. Nothing could surprise him any more. He specialised in extraordinary jobs of this sort. He'd done almost everything there was to do in this war so far. He'd led patrols, cleaned out latrines, looked after the wounded, dug graves, serviced captured vehicles, destroyed enemy tanks, and organised a tailoring factory for the process of turning old newspapers into synthetic fur. And now he was to organise an entertainment show for the first time. Well, why not?

He got hold of a motor-bicycle and rode off on it to the main base. Witterer's instructions had been clear enough. The members of the concert party which he had to organise were quartered in a school there. One of them was a singer called Lisa Ebner.

As soon as he got there, Asch inquired for Lisa Ebner and found her room without much difficulty. He knocked on the door and walked in.

The girl with the large round child's eyes was very indignant. She was not yet properly dressed.

" Kindly wait outside till I'm dressed."

" I'm in rather a hurry," said Asch. He didn't want to be any longer than necessary about this.

" It seems to me you might take a little time off to learn some manners."

" Manners are a luxury I can't afford."

" But can't you see that I'm still undressed?"

" I simply don't notice that sort of thing," he said. " Anyway, I'm married, in case you're interested."

" I'm not in the least bit interested," cried Lisa angrily. " At least you might turn your back while I get dressed."

" Yes, I'll do that for you," said Asch, turning round.

There was the rustle of a dress behind him. The little brunette with the big round eyes was furious. Her movements alone made that clear. First one slipper fell to the floor and then the other.

" Have you come from Captain Witterer?" asked the girl.

" That's right."

" He's a fine man, isn't he?"

" I couldn't say. I imagine my relationship with Captain Witterer is on a rather different level from yours."

" We'll do without the word ' relationship ', thank you," said Lisa, stamping her foot, presumably to get her shoe on properly. " There's no question of anything like that."

Asch stared at the wooden door ahead of him. The wall beside it had once been painted green but the colour had faded. The paint was beginning to flake off.

" What are you doing here, anyway?" he asked.

" And what are you doing?"

" Simply obeying orders."

" I volunteered for this, you know."

" And you're proud of yourself, eh?"

Lisa Ebner snorted indignantly through her pretty little nose.

" Captain Witterer might at least have spared me someone like you."

" Not so easy for him. There are a lot of my sort round here, as you'll soon find out. Ready?"

" Don't turn round yet!"

" Then, would you mind giving me a chair?"

She hesitated for a moment then pushed a stool across the floor. Asch sat down on it and waited. There was more rustling behind him. Then came the sound of some hard object—a bottle it sounded like—being dragged across a wooden surface. The next moment the smell of a heavy scent was wafted in Asch's direction.

" The full treament, eh?" said Asch.

" I don't want to have to smell you, that's all."

" I'd go away at once if you'd only be so good as to answer one or two of my questions."

" Such as?"

" When, on what day and at what time can you and your lot come out to us? How many of you will come? Do you want to be fetched or have you got your own transport? How long will the performance last? Have you any special requests to make?"

" None of that's anything to do with me, my dear man. You must talk to our manager. He's the conjurer and you'll find him on the floor below in one of the officers' rooms."

Asch got to his feet.

" You might have told me that in the first place without keeping me with my face to the wall all this time. Good-bye."

" Wait a moment! You can turn round now."

Asch slowly turned round. He started. He pulled himself together.

The girl with the big eyes was very pretty, but it wasn't just the prettiness that had made him start. The dress she was wearing was a plain, dark blue one, drawn in slightly at the waist. In it she reminded him very much of Elizabeth. Elizabeth liked wearing dresses like that, too. And wasn't this girl's name Lisa as well?

" Well?"

"It's extraordinary," said Asch, simply. "You remind me very much of someone I know."

"Who?"

"Someone I love."

Lisa Ebner stared at him with her big round eyes. "Oh, we've heard that one before," she said. "You all say that. It's just an optical illusion. It's because you've all forgotten what a woman looks like."

Asch nodded. He was only half convinced.

"Possibly," he said. "But then also possibly not."

Once again the barracks held Vierbein in their power. He was woken by muffled sounds of activity. He lay awake a long time before he had to get up himself.

When he had reported to the reserve battery the night before, the orderly officer had sent him to one of the N.C.O.'s rooms.

"Sleep yourself out first—we'll go into everything else in the morning," the orderly officer had said.

The two other Corporals with whom he shared the room made it clear at once that the room belonged to them, and that he was merely tolerated as their guest. "Or have you been posted to this battery?"

"No, I've only come to fetch some reserves. I'll be getting out of here as quickly as possible."

"Admirable," said one of the Corporals.

But the other added: "Just to put you in the picture: we ourselves are not reserves. We're simply responsible for supplying them."

These two creatures in whose room Vierbein had found himself a bed were called Bartsch and Ruhnau. They had a variety of other names for themselves, all drawn from current military phraseology and describing admirably, as they thought, different aspects of their present activities. Thus sometimes they saw themselves as "thousand-pounders" blasting their way through all obstacles to whatever they happened to be in need of at the moment. At other times, "mine-sweepers" or "night-fighters". They always went out together in the evenings and were even said to share their girls. In the town they were merely known as the Siamese twins. Certainly the alliance was an extremely effective one for whereas one or the other, alone, might easily have gone under in the general turmoil of war, together they managed to keep themselves pretty comfortably afloat.

" How long will you be staying, Vierbein?"

"A few days."

" There's not a great deal doing here, you know. If you've got a bottle of schnaps to spare you can join up with us. For two bottles we'll even find you a little number all to yourself."

Vierbein went out to the wash-room. Bartsch and Ruhnau had water brought to them where they were. When Vierbein came back again the two Corporals were both lying on their beds again.

" Phew! What a night," said one.

" What skirmishing, man! Why, that girl didn't seem to know there was a war on!"

Vierbein began to get himself ready for the inevitable round of reporting. He tried to put a bit of a polish on his boots but didn't have much success. He was sweating slightly by the time he had finished.

" Don't bother, man," said Bartsch. " Your Iron Cross shows up all right—that's all that matters."

And Ruhnau said: " We've got rather a weakness for heroes, you know."

" Besides, the Sergeant-Major's an absolute idiot. He doesn't care what you do so long as you give him a smart salute."

" And you don't need to worry because Lieutenant Schulz is up to his eyes in work at the moment. He's practically running the place."

" Who?"

" Lieutenant Schulz. Don't you know him? He used to be Sergeant-Major here."

" He still is a Sergeant-Major, too, at heart—acting for the whole battery now!"

Vierbein nodded. Yes, he knew Schulz all right. In days gone by Schulz had put him through it in merciless fashion. He had reduced him to a complete wreck. But Vierbein didn't hold it against him. Of course not. Schulz had merely done his duty. Even more than his duty, one might say.

Vierbein wondered whether he shouldn't first go to the canteen and ring up Asch's father. But he decided to leave that till later. He wanted to get the preliminaries of his mission over as soon as possible.

The adjutant of the battery, a Lieutenant of the reserve who was a wine and spirit merchant in civilian life, seemed to be in a great state of excitement when Vierbein went in to see him.

He kept on repeating that he had "very little time for anything".

"Sorry, Corporal, I've very little time for anything."

Vierbein stated his regiment's needs: radio transmitters and trained personnel to operate them. Requested by Colonel Luschke. Request confirmed by Divisional H.Q.

"Yes, we've got them," said the Lieutenant. "We've got them all right, But not just at this moment. Just at this moment, you see, everything here is at sixes and sevens. The C.O.'s getting married in a few days' time."

Vierbein, who couldn't quite grasp what the C.O.'s marriage had to do with supplies of men and material for the front, said: "This is a matter of particular urgency."

"And so is the other, my dear fellow, I assure you," said the adjutant, leaning the whole of his two hundred pounds against the back of his well-upholstered arm-chair.

"Colonel Luschke felt quite confident that there would be no difficulty of any sort about this matter, Lieutenant."

"And there is no difficulty! Who said anything about difficulty? No one's going to accuse us of making difficulties for anyone, least of all where the needs of the front are concerned. Oh no, my dear fellow. On the contrary. Very much on the contrary, I assure you. You won't have to wait long."

"Good, Lieutenant," said Vierbein, much relieved.

"Look, the regiment's been waiting some months for this stuff already. It won't do it any harm to have to wait another twelve hours."

"No, Lieutenant."

"Oh, and one more thing," said the Lieutenant affably; "congratulations on your Iron Cross."

"Thank you," said Vierbein and left the room.

He had hardly arrived back at the Staff Troop when he received orders to report to the orderly-room. The Sergeant-Major looked at him coldly.

"You're to report to Lieutenant Schulz right way," he said. "You haven't been getting yourself into trouble, I hope?"

"I've hardly had a chance, Sergeant-Major."

"One never knows with you front-line fellows. You haven't been home an hour before you're in trouble of some sort, most of you. We had a fellow here the other day—hadn't been back twenty minutes before he'd knocked down a man and raped a girl. Now we don't stand for anything like that here, you know."

"We don't stand for it at the front either, Sergeant-Major."

The Chief, whose only interest in life was to keep his cushy job behind the lines, swallowed this in silence. He rose to his feet and said: "Well, I'll take you into the Lieutenant then."

The door of the acting C.O.'s room was suddenly flung open so that it banged against the wall. And there stood Lieutenant Schulz—large and important, larger and more important than ever. His uniform was in a magnificent state. Everyone in the orderly-room jumped to attention. His voice was like some mighty fanfare of trumpets.

"Aha! Our old friend Vierbein!" he cried.

Vierbein confirmed this.

"Come here then! Come here, my long-lost child."

Vierbein went to him, clicked his heels and announced with faultless precision: "Corporal Vierbein, No. 3 Troop, Luschke's Artillery regiment, seconded to the reserve battery, for the purpose of obtaining men and material!"

Lieutenant Schulz let out a great laugh.

"That's the stuff, Vierbein," he cried. "A man after my own heart, eh?"

"Yes, Sergeant-Major."

Schulz looked as if he would burst, he was laughing so much. He whinnied like a brewery horse. Then he slapped Vierbein on the back and said:

"Still the same old spirit, eh? The spirit of the good old days. 'Sergeant-Major' eh? But we've gone up a bit in the world since those days, Vierbein!"

"Yes, Lieutenant," said Vierbein, still completely overwhelmed by this unexpected display of goodwill.

"Just take a look at him, Sergeant-Major," said Schulz. "This fellow was once the lousiest member of my whole troop. And now look at him: a Corporal. And not just any Corporal either, but with the Iron Cross First Class on his chest."

"You don't say," said the Sergeant-Major, putting on a show of admiration.

"What did you get it for, Vierbein?"

"Destroying tanks, Lieutenant, seven of them."

"Trained in my school," cried Schulz. "It sticks out a mile, Sergeant-Major. The lousiest member of the troop. And now —seven tanks destroyed. And a Corporal into the bargain. Come in, Vierbein."

Schulz collapsed into an enormous arm-chair and indicated another chair to Vierbein, who sat down obediently.

"Cigar?" said Schulz.

" No, thank you, Lieutenant."

Schulz laughed sarcastically.

" Same little milksop, eh? Never mind. You've shown we made a man of you. Tell me about this business with the seven tanks now."

" There's nothing to tell, Lieutenant."

" No false modesty now, my dear fellow. And when I say: tell me, I mean: tell me. Understand?" His voice sounded just as it used to be in the old days—a blast of hearty goodwill, with a slightly ominous ring to it.

" That's right," said Schulz with satisfaction. " Well, it's the same the whole world over. The best men get to the top. Look at me now. When the war started I put in for a commission. I passed top out of my training course. That goes without saying. Became a Lieutenant. Eventually ended up here in charge of the staff troop. And now, as the C.O.'s getting married, I'm his representative for the time being. For all practical purposes, Vierbein, I'm now in charge of the battery."

" I'm sure your wife's very proud of you, Lieutenant," said Vierbein naïvely.

Schulz snapped at him at once. " My wife's none of your business, man," he said.

" I only thought, Lieutenant, that . . ."

" My wife is absolutely nothing to do with you, do you understand? We're discussing service matters here. You can leave private affairs out of it. See?"

" Yes, Lieutenant."

Quite unintentionally, Vierbein had touched Schulz on his one sore point. His goodwill had burst like a balloon. His wife was the cross he had to bear—more of a cross than ever these days. He simply couldn't bear to talk about her.

Schulz stubbed out his cigar. It left an unpleasant smell in the room.

" Well, what is it you want here, Vierbein?" he asked.

Vierbein went into details. He particularly stressed the urgency of the matter and Colonel Luschke's personal wish that everything should be expedited as smoothly as possible.

" Since I am representing the C.O. at the moment," said Schulz pompously, " I shall be dealing with the matter myself."

" If I might make one request, Lieutenant . . ."

" While I'm dealing with the matter, Vierbein, you will of course automatically be attached to the staff troop, of which I shall continue to remain in command. Do you understand me?"

"Yes, Lieutenant," said Vierbein meekly.

"And I want to see plenty of the old spirit, Vierbein. Never forget that!"

Well hidden behind No. 2 gun, Captain Witterer peered keenly through his field-glasses in the direction of the enemy. Behind him stood Corporal Krause, the adjutant under training. He was peering keenly at his troop commander. The sentry who was stumping up and down in the open beside them, seemed utterly disinterested in everything.

"Most remarkable," said Witterer significantly, lowering his field-glasses.

"Yes, sir," said Krause without much idea of what it was that was so remarkable. Still he acted as if he knew; that never did any harm.

The enemy lines lay fully exposed to view on the opposite hill. Brazenly exposed, thought Witterer. A number of fox-holes and communication trenches could be seen clearly. The enemy, like themselves, had built his position round a little village. Several figures could be seen moving about quite openly.

"Unbelievable," said Witterer. "Not the slightest attempt at concealment! And there's supposed to be a war on!"

"And what's more," said Krause, playing up to him, "they haven't even got any artillery over there!"

The sentry said nothing. He thought his own thoughts. His main concern was to try and keep warm. He was also glad to remember that his relief would be due in half an hour's time. His friends would be waiting for him to join them in a game of skat. This was the fullest extent of the sentry's thoughts.

"When did you last open fire here?" Witterer asked the sentry.

"Open fire?" replied the latter, almost as if he had some difficulty in understanding what the words meant. "On who?"

"God! What an outfit!" muttered Witterer.

And Krause added keenly: "A terrible outfit, sir."

Witterer looked at the gun, noting incredulously the little white marks on the barrel which indicated the number of tanks it had destroyed. Then he looked at the little pile of shells covered with a tarpaulin, which lay beside the gun. And then he looked over towards the enemy even more keenly than before. And Krause looked with him.

Witterer said: "I want to see all N.C.O.s for a conference immediately. Let's say in half an hour's time. In Lieutenant Wedelmann's quarters."

Krause repeated the order word for word. Witterer was very impressed. He was once again convinced that Krause was a born adjutant. It gave him great satisfaction to have his judgment confirmed so unmistakably in this way.

With long powerful strides, the Captain set off at once for Lieutenant Wedelmann's billet. He found him sitting at a table with a Russian grammar open in front of him and a notebook and pencil close by.

"It seems to me," said Witterer, trying to be hearty, "as if the situation should be reversed. It's about time the people round here started learning German."

"But the people round here don't happen to be living in Germany," said Wedelmann, without any particular friendliness.

Witterer took this remark for a joke and laughed politely. He was always prepared to show himself in a good humour when circumstances permitted.

"Well," he said, "that's a matter of opinion," and he gave another short laugh.

Wedelmann was too good an officer to contradict someone senior in rank, particularly when the man in question was his own C.O. He had himself always attached a great deal of importance to discipline.

"And now, Herr Wedelmann," said Witterer, "to come to the point: activity on the front may be starting up any day now, and we shall again find ourselves involved in a war of movement."

"You're right there," said Wedelmann and he tried to keep the irony out of his voice. "Yes, there's a good chance of that."

"And do you consider that the troop is ready for such an eventuality?"

"Well, we've had some experience in action and we didn't do too badly."

"Agreed, but since then you've been hibernating here for some months and have forgotten everything."

"It won't take more than a day for us to get it all back again. Ninety per cent of our people have been in action, you know."

"Yes, but they will have forgotten everything they ever learnt. A man who has forgotten how to salute properly will also have forgotten how to deal with the enemy. Don't you see what I mean?"

"To some extent," said the Lieutenant waiting. "But you've got to be careful. The front isn't the same thing as the barrack square, you know. You won't achieve anything here by shouting at people. As for written orders, well, they have a certain amount of use in the latrines, but that's about all."

"Herr Wedelmann—war is no joke, you know!"

"You don't have to tell *me* that!"

At this moment Corporal Krause appeared and announced that the N.C.O.s were all present and correct. He barked the statement out in a manner which astonished Wedelmann.

"Right then, we'll begin," said Witterer eagerly. "Bring them in!"

Krause acknowledged the order with a salute. But he stayed where he was.

"Do you want Sergeant Asch in as well, sir?" he asked.

"Is *he* here? I thought he was organising the entertainment show."

"He's back already, Captain. He says he can't do anything more until to-morrow morning."

"What do you think, Lieutenant? Is it necessary?" asked Witterer, making it quite clear that he expected a reply in the negative.

"Sergeant Asch is the troop adjutant," said Wedelmann quietly, "at least, for the time being. It's usual for the adjutant to be present at such conferences."

"All right, if you think so . . ."

"Quite apart from which, Sergeant Asch is an experienced soldier. His opinion is always well worth listening to."

"What are you waiting for then, Corporal?" said Witterer, rather crossly, to Krause. "Let's get going, for goodness' sake."

The N.C.O.s—those, that is to say, who were in charge of the guns, of the machine-guns, of communications, of supplies and of transport, together with the Sergeant-Major, Adjutant Asch and Adjutant Krause—all piled into the little room. Lance-Corporal Kowalski pushed his way in among them at the last moment as if his presence there were the most natural thing in the world.

At a sign from Witterer they all tried to find somewhere to sit down. A few—and these of course included Soeft—managed to find chairs for themselves, and the rest had to be content with the straw which covered a considerable part of the floor. The little room was absolutely packed with men. A sour

78

clammy smell of sweat and clothing immediately became noticeable.

"Open the window, Krause," said Sergeant Asch.

Krause hesitated for a moment and looked across at Captain Witterer. The Captain, however, seemed preoccupied with his notes.

"Is there something wrong with your hearing, Krause?" asked Sergeant Asch.

Krause muttered something to himself and pushed the window open. Kowalski grinned delightedly. The little scene was by no means lost on the other N.C.O.s.

Captain Witterer looked up.

"Gentlemen," he began, "I think you'll agree we've been having a pretty easy time of it for the last few months."

"Who does he mean by 'we'?" muttered Kowalski.

"But things will be taking a more unpleasant turn before long and we must all see to it that we're properly prepared."

"May we smoke, please, sir?" asked Soeft, in a sudden access of discipline. High-sounding phrases always made him rather formal, without however producing any other practical effect on him.

"Of course you can," said Wedelmann. "Don't ask idiotic questions."

Soeft handed round his leather cigar-case which was stuffed with cigars, as usual. He offered one to Captain Witterer, who refused it curtly. Kowalski bit the end off his cigar. There was a great striking of matches. And shortly afterwards an immense cloud of smoke went pouring out of the little window into the open air.

"Yes," said Witterer, very energetically. "Well, the point is we've got to have everything shipshape here as soon as possible. I shall be having a practice alarm for the whole troop some time to-day. There'll be another to-morrow morning. And I want everything to be put into full marching order. All supplies and equipment—everything."

"Impossible," said Soeft, very emphatically. "I'd have to pack up my Kolchos!"

"What?" said Witterer, thinking he couldn't have heard properly. "Your Kolchos, did you say? And what is that, may I ask?"

Wedelmann explained. "Corporal Soeft has organised a sort of private farm for No. 3 Troop in the course of the winter," he said. "Economically speaking, it's rendered us almost entirely self-sufficient."

Soeft nodded agreement, not without a certain pride. Witterer looked straight at him: "Yes, well, we'll have to have a talk about that later."

"By all means," said Soeft amiably.

Witterer had not yet fully recovered from his surprise. He found some difficulty in picking up the thread of his argument again.

"Yes," he said. "A practice alarm with everyone in full marching order. And we'll repeat that two or three times, until we're able to pull the whole thing off inside an hour."

Sergeant Asch looked as if he had an objection he wanted to make. But Wedelmann who was sitting opposite him shook his head. Asch shrugged his shoulders and kept silent.

"Now let's just run over the amount of materials required for a normal day in action," said Witterer.

"Excuse me, Captain," said Wedelmann very correctly, anxious to set a good example to his subordinates, "but we don't think of things in those terms here."

"But surely you've worked out some sort of average figure for your requirements in action—or is this not the case?"

"But any figure of that sort which one arrived at," went on Wedelmann, still thoroughly correctly, "would be quite worthless. What you mean, perhaps, is the standard equipment figure?"

"Oh well, don't let's quibble over words," said Witterer, with unusual generosity. "What I want to know is: How long will our fuel last?"

"About two weeks."

"And ammunition?"

"About four weeks."

"And food?"

"About three to four months," said Soeft calmly.

Witterer started again and stared at Soeft. Then he pulled himself together and said: "Well, as far as I can make out, we're well stocked with supplies. Two weeks' reserves are the most we need. It follows, gentlemen, that we have too much ammunition."

There was an expectant hush among the assembled N.C.O.s. Wedelmann looked a little restless. Asch thrust his chin forward.

"You could cut the air in here with a knife," said Sergeant-Major Bock eventually. "It's much too hot." He took off his greatcoat.

Several others followed his example. Witterer himself took off his greatcoat. His tunic was beautifully pressed and quite spotless, but it was also distressingly free of decorations.

" Now where had we got to?" asked the Captain.

" The ammunition," said Krause. " The Captain had just reckoned that we had two weeks' too much ammunition."

" Better too much than too little," said Wedelmann, who could see what was coming.

" Gentlemen," said Witterer, " I have to-day seen for myself that the ammunition is simply rotting away."

" We've stored it in the manner prescribed by regulations, Captain," said Sergeant Asch with remarkable coolness.

" There are more than enough targets in our sector. I saw that for myself to-day, too. Why is it that we're not bringing them under fire? There's no shortage of ammunition."

" What's more," added Krause, " the enemy has no artillery to reply with."

Asch looked across at Wedelmann, who however avoided his glance. He seemed to be very interested in the long bony fingers which he had spread out across his knee.

" Excuse me," began Asch, " but there hasn't been a shot fired on this sector for weeks, apart, that is, from the routine firing of the machine-guns and the occasional rifle-shot at a stray dog."

" That proves nothing," said Witterer, " except that people have been fast asleep here. On both sides, too."

" A few hundred yards ahead of us," said Asch, " are the infantry, spending a good deal of their time in filthy little holes in the ground. But when they're not actually on guard they can move back to some huts they've got just behind their lines. Opposite the infantry are the enemy, living under exactly similar conditions. They have their huts too. And under these circumstances, the infantry, that is to say, our infantry, feel it's pointless to exchange fire."

" And how exactly can it be ' pointless ' to inflict casualties on the enemy, Sergeant Asch?"

" Because the enemy will immediately inflict casualties on us, Captain."

" But casualties are what one expects in war, Sergeant. Did you not know that?"

" Captain," said Sergeant Asch. " Every action must have an objective. Either one is defending one's own position, or trying to dislodge the enemy from his. But there's no question of anything like that in this case. An isolated action is bound to be pointless. The infantry have grasped that much. They

81

don't fire at the enemy's ration carriers and the enemy doesn't fire at ours."

"What on earth's going on here?" asked Witterer sarcastically, "a war or a game of grandmother's steps?"

"We're just avoiding unnecessary bloodshed—that's all."

"And don't forget, my humanitarian friend, that at the present moment we have superiority in artillery."

"That superiority could be reversed overnight," said Asch, quite undismayed. "If we start shooting at the enemy he'll bring up artillery of his own at once and start shooting at us. And the infantry will then have to spend their time in their fox-holes."

"Sergeant Asch," said Witterer sharply. "You seem to be lacking in both endurance and the necessary offensive spirit. I find that regrettable in someone of your rank. There's rather more point to this war, you know, than just being allowed to have our meals in peace. We're shooting to kill, remember."

"I do earnestly recommend," said Wedelmann quietly, "that we don't undertake anything without warning the infantry in our sector beforehand."

"Don't worry, I'll get on to them," promised Witterer. And he looked determinedly at his second in command. He was really bitterly disappointed to find him so lacking in the offensive spirit too. And once again he said to himself: what an outfit! And he swore to himself that he would soon have things looking very different.

"And as far as Sergeant Asch's observation are concerned, I do agree . . ."

"Ah yes—as far as Sergeant's Asch's observations are concerned, what I should like to know is what steps have been taken to organise the entertainment show?"

"The basic preparations are already complete," said Asch, with an air of indifference. "There are one or two practical details that have to be cleared up, that's all."

"Then clear them up, Sergeant. And as quickly as possible. I attach far more importance to the speedy and efficient carrying out of orders than to the airing of questionable suggestions about how to conduct things at the front."

"So I see," said Asch very calmly. "Very good, sir."

Lieutenant Wedelmann had a parcel tucked under his arm and

was on his way to the house in which the girl called Natalie, or Natasha, lived. One or two soldiers whom he met on the way grinned knowingly as he passed. The few remaining inhabitants of the village acted as if they hadn't seen him.

When he arrived at his destination he went in at the narrow gateway, climbed carefully up the rickety wooden steps and knocked on the little door.

"Just a moment," called Natasha. "Wait, please. I will be ready soon." It was a rich, warm, slightly guttural voice.

"All right," said Wedelmann.

The door was fairly thin and he thought he could hear the girl moving about behind it. Some heavy object, a case of some sort presumably, was dragged across the floor. There was the sound of paper being torn up.

Wedelman smiled to himself at the girl's fussiness. Typical of women, he said to himself. They're the same the whole world over.

His thoughts were suddenly interrupted by the appearance of two curious eyes, under a mop of fair hair, peering at him from the bottom of the steps. They belonged to a child, a little girl of about ten years old.

"Hello," said Wedelmann amiably.

"Dirty swine," said the little girl, no less amiably, in German.

Wedelmann was rather perplexed.

"Hey," he said. "What's that? You mean Good morning, don't you?" And he repeated the words slowly and distinctly: "Good morning."

"Good morning, dirty swine," said the child as amiably as before.

Wedelmann shook his head vigorously. He felt irritated. He wondered what was going on. Ah well, this was Russia. He shrugged his shoulders and knocked on the door again.

"Just coming," cried Natasha. "Please do not be impatient."

She wants to make a good impression, he thought. There seemed to him to be something quite definitely flirtatious about her behaviour.

She opened the door. She was a little out of breath. Her eyes were shining and her full round face was flushed. Her hair hung rather untidily over her forehead.

Wedelmann was slightly disappointed. She hadn't tidied herself up for him, after all.

She invited him into her tiny little room which was more like a closet than a room. The few objects lying about it were already familiar to him: a bed, a table, some books and notebooks, a rickety chair, a stove. There was a flat chest in one corner, covered with clean sheets of newspaper. Everything was very primitive, but at the same time very neat and clean.

"Sit down, please," she said, in her best schoolroom German. He sat down rather warily on the bed. He had been invited to sit down on it on his first visit, when he had been told that the chair wasn't strong enough to bear his weight.

"Would you like some tea?" she asked.

He accepted, and watched her busying herself with the kettle at the stove. She had broad shoulders, and a fine figure altogether. . . . But that, said Wedelmann to himself, is beside the point.

"I once had a real samovar . . ." she began.

"I know, I know," said Wedelmann quickly, and he was secretly delighted to be able to turn his thoughts to some other subject; "you once had a real samovar but the Germans requisitioned it. And then you had several cups and glasses, but the Germans requisitioned them too. Now you've only got one glass and one cup left. Yes, I know all that."

"Now, you're angry," said Natasha, looking at him thoughtfully. "Are you angry with yourself? Or just in a bad mood? Or what is it? What's wrong?"

"What's usually wrong with a dirty swine?" said Wedelmann, doing his best to laugh.

"Aha!" cried Natasha, "so you've been talking to one of our poor little children."

"She came up the steps after me."

"You mustn't be angry with her. Someone just taught her the word. She doesn't know what it means."

"Germans, I suppose."

"Of course, who else? The child doesn't know what she's saying. It's the only German word she knows. She says it to every German. You mustn't be angry with her."

"I suppose the Germans murdered her mother and father."

"Yes, exactly," said Natasha, with great emphasis.

Wedelmann took the cup she handed to him, without a word. He put it on his knees. He looked at the girl and however hard he tried, found it impossible not to think her attractive. Her thin hands betrayed a certain nervousness which she was only just keeping under control. Her dark eyes shone with a strange mixture of tenderness and hardness.

"You hate us, don't you?"

Natasha shook her head.

"No," she said, "But it's not easy for me to love you. Why did you Germans have to come here?"

"Forget it," said Wedelmann. "There's no point in talking about all that. Let's talk about something else."

"There is nothing else."

Wedelmann put his cup down carefully and pulled the little parcel which Soeft had given him out of his greatcoat pocket. He held it out to her.

She hesitated. Her hands moved about more nervously than ever. Then she said:

"I haven't done anything to earn that. What am I supposed to do for it?"

"Nothing," said Wedelmann, "nothing at all." Didn't she understand the feelings he had towards her then? They were entirely unselfish, or so he thought. "Take it. It's a present. It's only some chocolate."

She reached out for it. "Just a present?" she asked. "No obligations?"

"Of course no obligations," cried Wedelmann, and he felt genuinely indignant at her lack of trust in him.

"You are giving me something I want as it is—don't you see?"

"I am giving *you* something? How's that?"

"By just letting me be here with you. I feel I'm in another world when I'm with you. I forget everything but the inside of this hut. My whole way of thinking changes. I even breathe differently. I become another person. That's a real present!"

She reached forward for the teacup which he had put down, leaning right forward so that he could almost feel her breath on his face. She filled it and handed it back to him. "Thank you," she said.

Wedelmann spilt some of the tea when he tried to drink it. She laughed and he laughed a little too. Then she suddenly blushed deeply as if she had shocked herself.

He reached out and took her hand. He let his fingers wander slowly over her wrist and up her arm.

Suddenly she tore herself away from him. The cup fell to the floor and broke.

"No," she cried, "not that! Please, not that!" And very softly, almost inaudibly, she added: "Please!"

Wedelmann felt confused. He stood up awkwardly.

"I'm sorry," he said. "I didn't mean to annoy you. I'm afraid I've behaved like a . . ."

There was a loud knocking at the door. Wedelmann started

back. He hadn't heard any footsteps approaching, which was strange considering how badly the floor-boards on the veranda creaked.

Natalie herself was thrown into a new state of confusion. Nervously she tried to straighten out her dress with her hands, although this wasn't necessary at all. A slight flush spread over her face giving it a rather blotchy look. Before she could say a word the door slowly began to open.

Sergeant Asch poked his head cautiously round it.

"Not disturbing you, I hope?" he asked.

"Of course not," said both Natalie and Wedelmann, almost at the same moment.

Asch grinned affably.

"I'm sorry," he said. "But it simply couldn't be helped. The Colonel would like to see you, Lieutenant. As soon as possible too."

"Right," said Wedelmann, almost eagerly, springing to his feet. He was glad to be able to extricate himself from this rather painful situation.

Asch meanwhile sat down in the Lieutenant's place.

"Oh, there's not all that much of a hurry," he said. "But if you think you really must—then don't let me detain you. I've come in your car. It's waiting outside. I'll take over from you here."

"Oh, no you don't, Asch. You're leaving when I do," said the Lieutenant.

"Must I?" said Asch, looking at Natalie.

"I'm afraid it's time for us to say good-bye, Fräulein Natalie," said Wedelmann, very courteously, so that Asch stared at him in astonishment.

"Come back soon," said Natalie softly.

"Good-bye, Natasha," said Asch, grinning. "I'll be waiting for you outside," he called to the Lieutenant as he went out.

But Wedelmann followed him out and they went down the rickety steps together. The little Russian girl was waiting at the bottom. She beamed at Wedelmann.

"Good-bye, dirty swine," she said.

"Good-bye, snotty-nose," said Asch, quite unperturbed.

Wedelmann waited until Asch was out of sight and then he got into the car and told his driver to take him to the main base to see Colonel Luschke.

As the car slowly made its way in and out of the well-worn ruts in the road, Wedelmann's thoughts went back to Natalie, the girl whom Asch was able to call Natasha after being with her only a few minutes. What an uncomplicated fellow Asch was!

"Do you want to go to Regimental H.Q. or straight to the C.O.?" asked the driver. He had to repeat the question before he could get an answer.

"Straight to Colonel Luschke," said Wedelmann.

The car churned steadily along the road. The sky was heavy with snow clouds. They seemed to be sagging with the weight of the damp spring snow. Wedelmann could think of nothing but Natalie.

"Here we are," said the driver.

Wedelmann jumped out of the car.

"Go and get yourself warm at Regimental H.Q.," he said to the driver. "I'll come and fetch you when I'm ready."

He went into the little wooden house in which the regimental commander had his quarters. He found Luschke poring over his map table.

"Come over here, Wedelmann," Luschke called out to him. "Look, now. This is a map of our sector. What do you see?"

"Nothing that I haven't been seeing for the last three months, sir."

"You will have your little joke, Wedelmann. Or perhaps your brain has frozen up. But never mind, my dear fellow, the thaw's coming—there's still some hope for you."

Wedelmann smiled warily at his C.O. And his C.O. smiled grimly back.

"And what do you really see, Wedelmann?"

"The same ludicrous situation, sir. A great bulge in the front at our sector. We've driven a sort of wedge into the enemy line at this point and we are, ourselves, at the tip of it. It would have been better to shorten the line here. That would automatically have strengthened it and at the same time reduced the strain on men and material."

"You will be astonished to learn, Wedelmann, that that is what has just occurred to Divisional H.Q."

"I am indeed astonished, sir."

"They have realised that it is preferable to begin a spring offensive with as massive a concentration of forces as possible, and without inconvenient bulges."

"From a straightened front, in fact?"

"Exactly, Wedelmann," said "Lumpface", nodding at his favourite pupil with satisfaction. "Before the whole shambles begins all over again, we are to withdraw and take up a new line farther to the rear."

Wedelmann looked thoughtfully at the map.

"And as it is at this point that we have penetrated farthest," he said, "it is presumably from here that we will have to make the largest withdrawal. About forty kilometres, I reckon."

"About that. Anyway, we're taking up new positions farther to the rear—you'll be getting full details as soon as everything's ready. Then we'll be moving in the course of a single night; we'll take the Russians completely by surprise. They'll know nothing about it."

"Too easy," said Wedelmann confidently.

Luschke screwed up his eyes, "For you, Wedelmann, perhaps, but what about Captain Witterer? He has absolutely no experience."

"He makes up for that in keenness, Colonel."

"Let's hope so," said "Lumpface", thoughtfully. "But nothing can go far wrong as long as you're still with the troop. And by the way, Wedelmann: this plan is top secret, of course. You and I are the only two people in the regiment who know anything about it so far. Remember that, when you start making preparations. Go as carefully as possible. Your troop will be the last to leave—you'll move at the same time as the infantry."

"My troop? Surely you mean Captain Witterer's, Colonel?"

"My dear Wedelmann," said Luschke, grinning to himself. "Don't start playing the injured innocent with me. As soon as I feel convinced that No. 3 Troop can do without you, you'll see what I have in store for you. And then an even more idiotic expression will come over your face than I see there at present, which is saying something. Until then, however, Wedelmann, I'd be obliged if you'd get down to work. I have to rely on you entirely."

The Siamese twins, Corporals Bartsch and Ruhnau, were quite willing to take Vierbein under their wing as soon as he had paid his tribute of a bottle of schnaps. By lunch-time they were busy initiating him into the secrets of life on the home front.

"The thing is to make yourself indispensable in some way," said Ruhnau.

"And as far as possible invisible," added Bartsch.

Vierbein spooned up his stew and listened out of politeness, but without any particular interest. He didn't want to antagonise the two "night-fighters" as they were fond of calling themselves. ("Fifty-nine shot down to date!")

"I'm in charge of the gas-mask store," said Ruhnau. "It's the ideal job."

"And I'm in charge of workshops," said Bartsch. "I'll be here as long as the barracks themselves."

"And what about an air-raid?" asked Vierbein, chewing methodically. He said it more to show that he was listening than out of any real wish to know how this would affect them.

"An air-raid!" cried Bartsch in horror. "I'd lose my job!"

"It wouldn't be so bad if they dropped gas-bombs, of course," said Ruhnau thoughtfully.

Bartsch beckoned a mess orderly over to him and pressed his plate into his hand without a word. He merely gave him a quick knowing look. The man disappeared at once. It was a minute or two before Vierbein realised what was going on for there was a full plate of stew on the table in front of them already. But then the orderly reappeared and put a brimful plate down in front of Bartsch. At first sight it seemed to be exactly the same stew as all the others were eating. But the Corporal at once began to poke around in it and unearthed several large pieces of meat.

"The man in the kitchen's all right," said Ruhnau, nodding at Bartsch who nodded back at Ruhnau.

Suddenly Ruhnau said to Vierbein:

"You're not staying here, I hope?"

"No, no. Certainly not."

"He means you're not thinking of getting a job here, in charge of gas-masks or workshops or anything like that? Now or at any other time?"

"No, I am not. I promise you."

"That's all right then."

The Siamese twins who just then were thinking of themselves primarily as "mine-sweepers" continued to chew stolidly, although without any real relish. Bartsch carefully selected one or two particularly fat pieces of meat from his plate. Ruhnau threw a half-chewed bone over his shoulder.

Then one of these two stalwart "blockade-breakers" said to Vierbein:

"You see, we're men of confidence here. Do you know what that means?"

"No," said Vierbein, "I've never heard of such a thing."

"Ah, but you don't know the C.O. here?"

" No, All I know about him is that he's just about to get married."

" Yes, well he ought to be just about up to that," said Ruhnau, who happened to have his mouth open at the time.

He then ordered three glasses of beer which he graciously allowed Vierbein to pay for. Bartsch then said that cigars wouldn't be a bad idea either. The canteen contractor had managed to get hold of some that were almost up to peace-time standards. Vierbein was allowed to pay for these too.

" You see," said Bartsch puffing out a great cloud of smoke, " The point is that the C.O. simply has no idea how to run things here."

" Nor has the adjutant," added Ruhnau after a long pull at his beer.

" And so he has to have someone who will take the whole thing off his hands."

" And that someone is our good friend Lieutenant Schulz."

" I see," said Vierbein, who felt he was beginning to under-stand.

" And as even Schulz can't manage entirely by himself, he has to have a little assistance."

" And we are that assistance."

" We are absolutely indispensable."

" And quite apart from that we know too much."

Vierbein was gradually beginning to appreciate his own position. In whichever direction he looked he saw Schulz confronting him. Unpleasant as this prospect might be, there was nothing to be done about it. Schulz just had to be accepted as a natural phenomenon. Now Vierbein ordered another round of drinks and then excused himself, for he had been ordered to report at the reserve troop staff office " first thing that afternoon ". When he got there he waited patiently for a matter of an hour or so in the ante-room before Lieutenant Schulz condescended to allow him in.

Schulz, very much aware of the dignity of his position as deputy C.O., sat in the same chair in the same room as that from which Colonel Luschke had formerly exercised his uncanny vigilance over the barracks. He occupied the chair as if it were a throne. His arms were stretched out wide so that his hands reached almost from corner to corner of the enormous desk.

" Vierbein," he began, " I'm happy to announce that officially the regiment's requirements in men and material are able to be fulfilled immediately."

He paused. Then he looked searchingly at Vierbein. Then

he looked out the window. And then he looked back again at the papers spread out in front of him on the desk. Anyone who didn't know how officers were accustomed to behave would have thought that he was wrestling with some tremendous decision.

" Officially," repeated Schulz, " they can be fulfilled immediately. Theoretically that is. But I, Vierbein, am a man who believes not in theory but in practice."

The Corporal didn't dare to contradict him. Anyway there was no denying the fact. Schulz was a man who believed in practice all right. It just depended on what sort of practice one meant.

" So I'll have to tell Colonel Luschke that . . ."

" . . . that everything is proceeding according to plan," interrupted Schulz.

The Corporal was now quite unable to understand what was going on. Unfortunately he was bold enough to say so.

Schulz gave a superior sort of smile which was anything but friendly.

" As a man who believes in practice," he proclaimed solemnly, " I cannot undertake simply to deliver men and material. My conscience will only allow me to deliver trained men and tested material. Do you follow me, Vierbein?"

" I think so," said Vierbein, trying hard to conceal his astonishment.

" Corporal Vierbein," said Schulz with devastating logic. " In the course of your military career, you have learnt among other things how to wait. You will therefore wait now. The training of the men and testing of the material must be completed before I can take the reponsibility of forwarding them to the front."

" And when will that be, Lieutenant?"

" In four or five days. We've got an artillery display coming off here in four or five days' time. Within twenty-four hours of that being over the regiment will find itself in possession of everything it needs."

" I'll tell Colonel Luschke that," said Vierbein. And he stressed the words carefully so that Schulz should realise that it might be unwise to let such a message get through to the Colonel.

Now Schulz had no knowledge of the swift channels of communication at Colonel Luschke's disposal. He thought to himself : all right, go and tell him, my little man. It takes at least a week for a letter to get to Russia. And before Luschke can get wind of the little game I'm playing with Vierbein, everything here will have planned out to my entire satisfaction. And that is exactly as things should always be.

"In the meantime," said Schulz, rubbing his hands, "you will be available for duty with us. That can't do you any harm. You're seconded to the reserve battery for the duration of your mission, and the reserve battery at the present moment happens to be myself."

Vierbein stood there as stiff as a post. For the moment he found himself incapable of coherent thought. He stared at Schulz and Schulz mistook the stare for a sign of submission.

"We'll find something for you to do all right," said the Lieutenant. "You're not exactly a fool."

"Might I request a free pass for this afternoon," asked Vierbein with the last ounce of discipline left inside him.

"And why not!" cried Schulz, condescendingly. "We're not inhuman here. You've just come from the front. You've a good deal of dirty water to get off your chest. I understand perfectly. But be careful, Vierbein? Don't go and get yourself into trouble of any sort. You understand what I mean, Vierbein? I regard anything like that as equivalent to a self-inflicted wound."

Corporal Vierbein, who considered himself lucky to have got away from Schulz at all, left the barracks in a hurry. He went straight to the Café Asch, where his friends were waiting for him with some impatience. Ingrid, every inch a war bride, threw her arms round him and kissed him. Then she held him a little away from her. Her eyes shone with admiration. When she caught sight of his Iron Cross First Class she kissed him all over again.

"How proud I am of you," she said tenderly.

"And I'm delighted to see you," said old Asch, giving Vierbein his hand. "And the fact that you're a hero doesn't interfere with my pleasure at all."

The café was almost empty at that time of the afternoon and Vierbein was led through it to the rooms in which the Asch family lived on the first floor. Ingrid held his hand and old Asch had an arm round his shoulder.

"Now tell us all about it," said Ingrid as soon as they had sat down.

"Let him eat first," said old Asch. "Eat and drink. I know just how he feels."

"I'm afraid I must be off almost at once," said Vierbein,

with a keenness which he felt sure must make a good impression. "I have an important message to deliver."

"Oh, the war will still be on to-morrow," said Father Asch opening a new packet of cigarettes.

"But this message can't be delayed a moment," said Vierbein. "I just called in to say hallo."

"Nonsense," said old Asch. "Here you are for the time being and here you're staying. The Führer can wait. Wasn't he a soldier himself once? Well, there you are. He's learnt to wait."

"But you mustn't stop him from doing his duty, Father," said Ingrid feelingly. "If the message is an important one . . ."

"Duty? What do you mean? He's got a duty towards us, hasn't he?" Old Asch uncorked a bottle of wine. "He's done his duty as a soldier and a good deal more, I dare say. Well, now he can sit and have a drink in peace."

"Oh, Father!" said Ingrid reproachfully, "sometimes I think you've no enthusiasm for this war at all."

"That happens to be a fault I'm rather proud of. Let's drink to it."

They raised their glasses and smiled at each other. They were all delighted to be together again. Their eyes radiated happiness and affection.

Vierbein told them a little about Herbert Asch. He promised them a fuller report when he had more time.

"Anyhow," he said, "he's quite all right. He's well, in excellent spirits and has enough to eat. You've nothing to worry about."

"It says that much in the newspapers," said old Asch. "And there are even some people who believe it."

Vierbein squeezed the hand of the girl beside him. He was overjoyed to see her again, to hear her voice and be able to hold her hand.

"Dear children!" said Father Asch after a long pause, staring at them in admiration.

"Do you need writing-paper?" asked Ingrid. "And ink?" Vierbein nodded. Old Asch shook his head sadly.

"I'm beginning to be afraid," he said, "that if we go on like this we may really win the war."

Ingrid and Vierbein paid no attention to him. They set about preparing the message with great solemnity. The girl brought paper and ink. Vierbein sat up straight and tried out the pen. Then he began to write.

When he had finished writing out his report to Colonel

Luschke, he read it through all over again very conscientiously. He added a comma here and a full stop there. Then he signed it.

"Is it going straight to the Colonel?" asked Ingrid naïvely. She looked proudly across to her father.

"Well?" said old Asch. "And what's so wonderful about that? I've got several letters from a real General in my files. He used to be the representative of a motor firm here, before the war took him off and made him a General."

"But he is a General now, anyway, Father."

"Yes and I've written to him as such. Pretty sharp letters too. He's not only a General but has a General's debts."

Vierbein allowed a weak, almost unmilitary smile to cross his face. Asch was surprised and delighted by it. Ingrid tactfully overlooked it.

"Right," she said, after helping him fold up the message. "And now we'll both go out to the post with it."

"No, that won't do," said Vierbein. "This is a very urgent message. I must take it to the C.O. of the airfield and he'll send it straight on to Russia."

"Oh, must you?" said Ingrid, hardly able to hide her disappointment. "But that'll take the whole afternoon."

"I'm afraid I must," said Vierbein, seriously upset because he couldn't comply with Ingrid's wishes. And he repeated: "I'm afraid."

Old Asch pushed the brandy bottle away impulsively.

"What an age this is!" he growled. "Ever since we became a nation of heroes we haven't had a moment to ourselves. There's always someone or other to make us jump to a word of command. And what do we do about it? We obey! We can't help it. It's in our blood—a taste for the whip, the muzzle and ersatz coffee!"

"But Father, don't you know there's a war on!"

"Yes, I do. But you can borrow my delivery van, the two of you, to take the message to the airfield. I need some so-called flour for the so-called cakes."

"Oh, thank you, Father."

"Thank you very much, Herr Asch."

"Don't thank me. Thank the Führer," said old Asch. "We wouldn't have any of this but for him."

Corporal Vierbein was the sort of man to whom every order

was sacred, and a request from a superior officer was equivalent to an order, particularly when the superior officer's name was Wedelmann. But in his simplicity he was rash enough to ask for Frau Lore Schulz's address from his two room-mates, Bartsch and Ruhnau.

The Siamese twins looked at each other knowingly. At the mere mention of a woman's name their brains seemed automatically to synchronise.

"Good God, man!" cried Bartsch. "You're asking for one of our best addresses. You don't get that without a fee."

"And if you like," said Ruhnau with a broad grin, "we'll let you have a set of instructions at the same time."

"It's just that I have a call to pay there," said Vierbein with some reserve. "I'm not interested in anything else."

The two "thousand-pounders" looked at each other and bellowed with laughter.

"That's a good one!" roared Bartsch. "That really is a good one!"

Eventually after solemnly promising the two dashing "night-fighters" a bottle of schnaps from the Café Asch, Vierbein succeeded in obtaining Lore Schulz's address.

"Give her our love!"

"Tell her to keep the bed warm for us!"

These insinuations bewildered Vierbein. To him Lore Schulz was a respectable married woman—the wife, what was more, of a superior officer. Such thoughts in connection with her were right out of the question. Besides, Vierbein had secretly retained a special admiration for Lore Schulz, who had shown herself sorry for him at a period of his life when he had been feeling rather sorry for himself. She had been good to him then and he felt grateful to her.

While he was getting ready to go out, the two "marauders" were laying their plans for the "Ladies' Night" party which was to take place in the officers' mess that evening. Lieutenant Schulz was organising it and had given them certain special duties.

"But be more careful this time," said Bartsch to his friend. "Do you remember last time how you hung a lavatory seat round the adjutant's neck when he was tight?"

"And who was it locked the ladies up in the lavatory so that Schulz had to send an orderly in backwards down the ventilation shaft to open it up? If he'd found out it was you who did that, you'd have had your marching orders by morning. You were signing your own death-warrant, man!"

95

Vierbein hurried away to escape from this conversation. Carefully he wrapped up the bottle of brandy which Wedelmann had given him and set off from the barracks into the little town. He found the house he was looking for near the market-place. There was a plate on the door which read:

LIEUTENANT SCHULZ
First Floor

Ring once for service matters
twice for other matters

Vierbein climbed up to the first floor and after thinking the matter over for a little while, rang twice. Then he took a step back and drew himself up in a stiff, rather formal manner.

He wanted to make it quite clear that he had merely come on an errand with which he had been entrusted. He was aware that it might well be Lieutenant Schulz who would open the door to him. In which case he had decided to present the bottle of brandy immediately "with best wishes from Lieutenant Wedelmann, to Lieutenant Schulz and Frau Schulz"; to salute smartly, turn about and go away again.

He waited with a sense of gathering foreboding. Then he rang again. Again twice—still on "other matters". Then he heard footsteps approaching. And then the door on which the name "Lieutenant Schulz" was so neatly engraved, slowly began to open.

Vierbein breathed a sigh of relief when he saw that it was Lore Schulz who had opened it. He saluted and then said:

"Might I have a word with you?"

"Herr Vierbein!" cried Lore Schulz in astonishment. "So you're still alive! What a delightful surprise at this hour of the evening! Where have you come from?"

"If you will permit me," said Vierbein, breathlessly. "Allow me to——"

"But why don't you come in? Or do you still think I might bite? But you can't go on standing there in the passage."

"Oh, I don't know," said Vierbein, feeling more and more embarrassed. "I don't see why not. I only wanted to . . . I mean I didn't want to disturb you . . ."

"Come in," said Lore Schulz, smiling at him. "*You* could never disturb me. And what from, anyway?"

She opened the door wide and Vierbein stumbled over the threshold into the apartment.

Lore Schulz laughed. "You must mind your step, you know," she said jokingly.

Vierbein mumbled a few words of apology. He wouldn't leave his things in the hall. He walked into the sitting-room with his cap in his hand and his belt still buckled tightly round his waist. After Lore Schulz had twice asked him to sit down he gingerly took a seat on the very edge of a chair and looked about him nervously.

"If you're looking for my husband," said Lore, amused, "I'm afraid you're out of luck. He's not in, as usual."

"I was admiring your room," said Vierbein awkwardly.

He now looked at her properly for the first time. She had hardly changed at all. She had filled out a little, certainly, and not only in her face. Her mouth, on the other hand, seemed to have become smaller and her eyes lay a little deeper in their sockets. But on the whole she was as attractive as ever.

"We've all grown a little older, Herr Vierbein, haven't we?"

"More mature, I'd say," he answered and he took care to say it very emphatically.

"It depends which way you look at it." There was a note of resignation in her voice, but it was a resignation in which she seemed to take a certain amount of pleasure. "I'd say that you were more mature and that I was older. But we both probably go on making the same mistakes as before."

Vierbein had no answer to this. So he picked up the parcel which he had laid across his knee and presented it to Lore Schulz.

"This is for you," he said, "with very best wishes from Lieutenant Wedelmann."

Her eyes lit up for a moment.

"Good God in heavens!" she cried in amazement. "From Wedelmann! It's not possible. The dear silly fellow. So he still thinks about me. Me of all people! It's hardly credible. And how is he?"

"Fine, needless to say. That is in the circumstances."

"And he hasn't forgotten me?"

"No," said Vierbein. And he felt tempted to add: it doesn't exactly look like it, does it? But he was too tactful to say this. Besides, he had no wish to prolong his visit unnecessarily.

He half rose to his feet.

"You're not going already?"

"I must," said Vierbein, very firmly. "Besides, I don't want to . . ."

"To meet my husband here," Lore Schulz laughed a little bitterly. "My dear Herr Vierbein, you don't need to worry about that. Lieutenant Schulz is a very busy man. By comparison with him, Sergeant-Major Schulz was permanently on leave."

"Anyway, you'll be at the 'Ladies' Night' party in the mess?"

"I'll be honest with you," said Lore Schulz, going over to the door with him. "I shan't be going to the mess to-night. Neither to-night nor any other night. I don't fit in there. I've been told that pretty clearly often enough."

"Who by?"

"My husband, of course."

"I see," said Vierbein. He felt rather helpless.

"When we were living in barracks," said Lore, "I at least had a few friends of my own. Acquaintances, anyway. But not any longer. Things are changed now. In those days my behaviour was sometimes considered 'impossible'. Nowadays I'm wholly unworthy of him. You see, my husband is firmly convinced that he's been bettering himself all this time and that I have merely stayed where I was."

Vierbein didn't know what to answer. He opened his mouth and no sound came out. But his indignation was plainly visible on his face.

"I won't keep you," said Lore Schulz. "You must have friends who'll be wanting to see you. I don't grudge you them. I couldn't grudge you anything, Herr Vierbein. But I do envy you."

"Thank you very much," he said. He felt more confused than ever.

He hurried away to the Café Asch where they were already waiting for him. Anton, the head waiter, bustled over to him at once and said, "They're all upstairs."

Vierbein ran up to the Asch's private apartment. Ingrid opened the door and offered her mouth to him bravely as a true war bride should. She knew how to honour the men back from the front. Then she said: "I think you might have come a little sooner."

"I had an order to carry out," said Vierbein with a certain dignity.

"Oh well, that's all right then," said Ingrid without expressing any curiosity as to what this order was.

The walls of the long room were covered with family portraits. Waiting for him there at a table spread with a clean white cloth, were old Asch, Foreman Freitag and his daughter Elizabeth, the wife of Sergeant Asch. Mother Freitag was not there. She was excused because someone had to stay behind and look after the baby.

Vierbein sat very proud and erect in the place of honour. The others grouped themselves eagerly round him.

" There was a suggestion that we should decorate your place with laurel leaves, Herr Vierbein," Asch told him with a wink. " But we decided not to in spite of Ingrid's energetic protest. They would only have made it difficult for you to sit down. That's the trouble with honours and decorations—they do rather interfere with the rest of one's life. A distant relation of mine has got the Knight's Cross[1]—and he refuses ever to undo his collar except when going to bed. He keeps it done up even when washing. That just shows you how stiff-necked one can get about things."

They all laughed. But they had come to hear Vierbein and they now insisted that he should tell his story. Vierbein, however, was no story-teller. He was obviously embarrassed to find himself the centre of attention.

Old Freitag soon realised this and began to ply him with questions. This was more to Vierbein's taste. He gave his answers thoughtfully. By joining forces the two fathers managed to draw a certain amount of factual information out of him.

" It's supplies that will really decide the issue of the war in the end," said old Freitag. " If our equipment consists of worn-out vehicles which are not a hundred per cent reliable, then we'll be badly let down when the thaw comes and in another year they won't be fit for anything but scrap."

Vierbein didn't want to be the cause of any misunderstanding.

" I can't, of course, give you any concrete details about the way things are outside our troop. But our vehicles are in a very bad state. The demands on them are too great for proper servicing."

Asch was of the opinion that only the Führer knew what was really happening. Freitag thought that the men at the front probably knew what was coming instinctively.

While the two of them discussed the point, Ingrid and Elizabeth seized their chance and drew Vierbein to one side. But before they could satisfy their curiosity an appalling disturbance broke out on the landing.

[1] Worn round the neck.—*Translator*

A moment later Anton, the head waiter, appeared in the doorway, gesticulating wildly. And behind him loomed the grinning faces of Bartsch and Ruhnau. The Siamese twins were "heavily loaded". Their eyes were bright, their voices hoarse and you could almost see the cloud of alcohol in which they moved.

"We've come to fetch our old friend Vierbein," bellowed Ruhnau.

"We've come to appeal to his conscience," roared Bartsch.

"I thought you were on duty in the officers' mess to-night," said Vierbein. He found the intrusion extremely embarrassing.

"We were on duty. But we're finished with all that now. Schulz threw us out."

"And now we need consolation. We've come for that bottle of schnaps you owe us, Vierbein. Come on, now. Screw it out of that father-in-law of yours. You promised me, you know."

"I didn't promise anything of the sort," said Vierbein. He was worried. "I merely said I'd speak to Herr Asch about it."

"Then speak to him, man! There he is!"

"He'd be wasting his breath," said old Asch. "You're not getting another drop out of me. You've had far too much as it is."

"In that case," said Ruhnau, "let's go and see Frau Schulz."

"Yes, let's do that," agreed Bartsch. "And we'll make her bring out that bottle of schnaps Vierbein gave her."

"What's that?" asked Ingrid sharply.

"He took her a bottle of schnaps. And why shouldn't he? He's not the first person to do so by any means."

And with that the Siamese twins went staggering away again. The noise they made could be heard for some time after they had left the room.

The new day crawled exhausted over the horizon. It crawled slowly towards the sentry who stood slumped over the barrel of the gun he was guarding.

The sentry saw that this morning was exactly the same as a hundred others that had gone before it. Thick clouds had swallowed up the sun. And the frost bit greedily into the earth.

"Perhaps it will snow," thought the sentry. "But then perhaps it won't. The main thing is: it isn't raining. The moment it starts raining the winter will be washed away and the war will look different at once."

The sentry looked across to the hill on the other side of the valley. And there, a few kilometres away, he saw a man stamping his way through the snow. He, too, was a sentry.

And this sentry, thought the sentry, has an Asiatic face and speaks Russian. His skull is shaven and his uniform is brown, but he's doing exactly the same thing as I'm doing. Exactly the same.

It's funny, thought the sentry, he's doing exactly the same thing as I'm doing.

Soeft was an early riser. He had spent the night in the main base, as he often did. A man like Soeft had a number of beds at his disposal.

While he shaved he had a short conversation with a Sergeant friend of his who was one of the chief clerks in an important supply store. This man lay on his palliasse, eyeing Soeft craftily.

" Good shaving cream this," said Soeft, " I could do with five tubes of it."

" What are they worth to you?"

" A goose."

" We get goose in tins," said the Sergeant pretending not to be interested.

" In tins!" said Soeft contemptuously. " This is fresh goose I'm offering you. No one wants to eat goose out of a tin when he can get the real thing."

" Three tubes for one goose," said the Sergeant. " You can't do as much with that livestock of yours as you could once, you know."

" Why's that?"

" Because we're taking up new positions soon. Or so it seems. They're beginning to transfer stuff secretly already."

Soeft slowly put down his razor.

" We must have a little talk about this," he said.

The orderly who brought Luschke his hot water every morning found the Colonel already seated at his map table. It looked as if he was asleep there. His tired lumpy face was covered with a thin stubble.

"Don't stare at me like that, man!" said the Colonel. "Haven't you ever seen an unshaven man before?"

The orderly hurriedly put down the bowl of water and disappeared.

Luschke reached out for the morning reports and quickly ran his eye over them. Weather report—little change likely. Ammunition report—stocks as previously reported. Special Divisional report—increased activity among enemy agents. Check and tighten up security. Casualties: no casualties.

The Colonel pushed the papers away from him and stared at the map. As he did every morning. And, as every morning, he said aloud to himself: "To hell with it."

And then he went over to his bowl of water which was standing on a stool and pushed his head into it. Several times.

The same day at home began like a healthy young man waking after a refreshing sleep. The sun was suddenly there shining down on the little town out of a clear blue sky.

And the barracks were awake at once.

And the soldiers turned out of their beds to the shrill sound of the whistle and the roaring of the orderly N.C.O., just as they had been doing there for years.

The only difference was that the soldiers seemed to have grown older. Several of them had paunches and there were a good many round shoulders and bow legs.

But they were all being treated as if they were young recruits. And they didn't object. Many of them seemed to think that such treatment was just part of the order of things.

Corporal Vierbein stood with them in the wash-room. He had stripped to the waist and was letting the water run over his neck and shoulders. The others watched him with some misgiving.

"That makes you feel better," said Vierbein.

And the man who was standing next to him, a man with a lined face and long thin hands which were trembling with the cold, said: "When I was a young man I used to do that."

"But you're not old yet," cried Vierbein.

"I'm not too old to be a soldier certainly," said the man. "I've got varicose veins, flat feet, ulcers, two children who're

slowly dying and a wife who goes to bed with other men—
but I'm a soldier."

And Vierbein said nothing.

Sergeant Asch was writing a letter to his wife. And as always
he said that he was well, that he thought of her all the time,
and that she wasn't to worry. Everything, he said, would turn
out all right in the end.

Wedelmann, meanwhile, was devouring his breakfast. He ate
slowly and without much relish. Every now and again he took
a sip of the hot brown water which went by the name of coffee.

"I envy you," said Wedelmann. "You know where you
stand."

"But so do you, Lieutenant."

"You've got a wife and child."

"And you've got Germany and the Führer."

"Don't try and be funny, Asch," said Wedelmann severely.

"Excuse me, Lieutenant," said the Sergeant. "But do you
think you know what Germany really is? And do you think
you know the sort of man the Führer really is?"

"I'm not going to discuss these things with you, Asch."

"Who are you going to discuss them with, then, Lieutenant?
With Colonel Luschke? Captain Witterer? Or Corporal Vierbein perhaps? Not much choice really when you consider the
importance of the subject."

"Get on with your letter and leave me in peace," said
Wedelmann, crossly. "You're not a bad fellow, Asch, in many
ways, but you'll never be a good German."

"Oh, I don't know," said Asch. "Perhaps one day when
there's a good Germany."

When, "at the crack of dawn"—that is to say at about eight
o'clock—Corporal Krause was rash enough to try and wake
Lance-Corporal Kowalski out of a deep sleep, Lance-Corporal
Kowalski simply went on strike.

"Clear off," he said, "or I'll . . ."

Krause suddenly adopted a severe disciplinary tone. "Get
up, Kowalski." Kowalski turned his back on him.

"I'll report you to Captain Witterer," shouted Krause.

"No you won't," said Kowalski. "You wouldn't dare admit

to your new Captain that you were so hopeless. You, a Corporal, and unable to get a Lance-Corporal to obey you! Really! Such a thing is unheard of—at least in Witterer's eyes."

Krause, who now saw that Kowalski had him cornered, changed his tactics.

"You can't do this to me, man!"

"Oh, can't I?" said Kowalski, and he pulled his blankets up over his head.

"Kowalski," said Krause and, however much it hurt him to do so, he allowed a soft, wheedling note to come into his voice: "It's something big! You don't get this every day of the week!"

"What is it then?" said Kowalski, turning over with curiosity.

"It'll astonish you," Krause promised conspiratorially. "All I can say is it's something really big."

"All right then," said Kowalski, slowly getting out of bed, "I'm no spoil-sport."

Ingrid Asch sat at the breakfast table opposite her father and drank her coffee. The old man was reading the *Völkischer Beobachter* and seemed to find it amusing.

"The war's getting more and more total every day," he said. "Even the Führer is now sleeping on a camp-bed. What do you say to that?"

Ingrid said nothing. She stirred her coffee and took her time about it. She hadn't been listening to what her father was saying. She was thinking.

"He's sleeping in a camp-bed," repeated old man Asch forcefully. "Now who the hell is going to believe that? My friend the General—the one who owes me so much money— once had himself photographed beside a field kitchen. The caption said: 'The General shares the food of the ordinary soldier.' Like hell he does! I happen to know quite well that he lives largely off *pâté de foie gras*—with truffles of course. He organised himself two cases of it last time he was home on leave."

Ingrid was still wrapt in her thoughts. She paid no attention to these aspersions on her beloved Führer.

"Is there something the matter with you, child?"

"Father," she said suddenly. "Do you think Johannes is being unfaithful to me?"

"Vierbein? Of course not! And if he is, then only with that

whore the Goddess of War. You seem to approve of that, though."

"Please don't talk like that."

"My dear child," said old Asch, very seriously, "if I were in your place I'd know what to do to keep him faithful. But as your father, I can only say: Wait until this is all over. You're still very young. You won't end up an old man, don't worry."

The girl called Natasha sat by the window in her little hut. She had a board across her knee with a sheet of paper spread out on it. She was writing very seriously in big round letters, with considerable concentration. She was like a child learning to write.

And this is what she wrote:

"Wedelmann, No. 3 Troop—4 guns, 32 vehicles." And then she crossed that out and wrote instead the one word: "Wedelmann."

A deep furrow appeared across her otherwise unlined brow. She was leaning forward and her full broad shoulders were slightly hunched. She was breathing heavily.

She started writing again and under the word: "Wedelmann" she wrote:

"Height 5 feet 11 ; weight 140 pounds; Eyes, blue; Hair darkish brown; Nose straight; Mouth thin, Teeth perfect."

She gave a little laugh and rather surprised herself with it. Then she suddenly became very serious again, and hurriedly scratched out everything she had written. She turned the sheet of paper over with an air of determination.

And once again she wrote:

"No. 1 artillery regiment: C.O. Colonel Luschke: 3 infantry regiments, C.O.s Hanke, Niekisch, von Behringer; 1 tank regiment equipped with Mark IVs, C.O. Schwaiger."

She went on writing like this until the paper was covered with names and figures. Then she looked at it for a long time.

Suddenly she got up, opened the door of the stove and threw the piece of paper into the fire. And she stared for a long, long time into the flames, as if hypnotised by them.

Captain Witterer stood beside his brother officer, a Captain in the field security police, on a hill just outside the main base encampment. And just behind them, at a respectful distance, stood Krause and Kowalski.

Two men were digging a hole just in front of them. They shovelled away with slow rhythmic movements. Two field security police leant on their rifles and watched them.

"Isn't that enough?" asked the field security Captain.

One of the two field security police went over to where the men were shovelling and looked into the hole. Then he nodded and said: "Yes, that's enough."

"Well, what are you waiting for then?" asked the Captain.

One of the field security police went up to the two men and took their shovels away from them and threw them down on one side. Then he loaded his rifle. The other did the same.

Captain Witterer went a little closer to the grave. The two men knelt down and he saw the backs of their necks exposed.

"I always get my men to aim into the back of the head," said the field security Captain. "One shot is usually enough."

One shot was enough. It tore the whole of the back of the head away. Brains spurted out on to the ground and some watery-looking blood flowed from the wound. The two men collapsed and slipped into the grave.

"All right, shovel them over," said the field security Captain.

Lance-Corporal Kowalski spat and turned on his heel.

"I am to put myself at your disposal," said Soeft, blinking at Lisa Ebner.

Lisa Ebner stared in astonishment at this strange guest who had forced his way in on her and sat down uninvited, with almost incredible self-assurance. Sergeant Asch seemed to have beautiful manners compared with him.

"Well," said Soeft encouragingly, "what can I do for you?" His little eyes sparkled.

"Did Captain Witterer send you?"

"Of course. Or did you think I came of my own accord?"

"It's not impossible."

"It is if you know me," Soeft assured her. "I don't need to come to you, you know. I have quite a lot of customers in this particular stretch of territory. A wide range, in fact. Besides, you're not really my type."

"What do you want?"

"I'm here to grant you anything you wish," said Soeft, seeing himself as a sort of Caliph of Baghdad. "What do you need?

Soap, stockings, fur boots? *Foie gras?* A couple of really good bottles of something?"

"And what do you want in return?"

"Ah! Captain Witterer will present the bill," said Soeft with a knowing grin.

"Get out!" cried Lisa Ebner.

"Steady now!" said Soeft, trying to calm her down. "You're throwing away a fortune!"

"Get out!" repeated Lisa Ebner.

A new sentry relieved the sentry on the gun position and the new sentry looked exactly like the old one. He moved in exactly the same way and thought exactly the same thoughts.

Perhaps it will snow, he thought. But then perhaps it won't. The main thing is: it isn't raining. The moment it starts raining the winter will be washed away and then the war will look different at once.

And the sentry looked across the valley to the hill where the enemy had dug himself in.

And he thought to himself: the sods, the poor sods. And I'm just a poor sod like them.

The world seemed full of poor sods.

Once a week, usually on Thursdays, Corporal Soeft used to go the rounds of the gun positions. When he did so he gave himself the airs of a General and was treated with almost as much respect as if he were one. Sometimes he seemed more like a king, the King of the Commissariat, receiving the homage of his devoted subjects.

In fact his tour had no other purpose than to discover the taste and appetite of his numerous customers.

He usually took a small entourage with him, and this time had the adjutant-under-training, Corporal Krause, in his wake. Krause realised at once that this was a very special honour and did his best to seem as obliging as possible.

When, however, Soeft threw out the suggestion that in addition to the field-kitchen truck he was really in need of an auxiliary field-kitchen truck, Krause showed a certain reluctance to commit himself.

"An auxiliary field-kitchen truck would save no end of

trouble if we were to move," said Soeft. "It doesn't matter whether it's advance or a retreat—the direction is immaterial. I could then keep up our present high standard of living under all circumstances. But to do that I do need an auxiliary field-kitchen truck."

"You may be right," said Krause cautiously, with what he thought was great diplomacy.

"I am right," said Soeft curtly. "I know what I'm talking about. For instance, just suppose we're serving *schnitzel*. We can't take the field-kitchen truck itself round to everyone. For the troop to be able to have several helpings I need two trucks at least: one to do the actual frying of the *schnitzel* all the time and the other to be taking it round to the men."

"I see," said Krause, slowly nodding agreement.

"So you will do your best to impress the urgency of the matter on the C.O. Make it clear to him that some action has to be taken if he wants to get through the war without loss of weight."

"I'll do my best," said Krause. "Certainly you'll find me more co-operative than Asch," he added, putting out a feeler.

Soeft grinned to himself. And there was something about this grin that was reminiscent of Colonel Luschke. Nor was this surprising for the General Field-Marshal of the Commissariat had adopted it from the Colonel himself. The Colonel was a man whose methods even a man like Soeft had to respect. And like the Colonel, the ration king refused in any way to have a price dictated to him. He acted as if he simply hadn't heard the word Asch at all.

They went to the gun positions and visited each gun in turn, where a "smokes and grub parade" was sounded as soon as they appeared. Everyone paraded. Soeft first distributed cigarettes to the gun crews from his private stores, making a point of remembering the cigar smokers. Then he noted any deficiences in the way of supplies. There was still a shortage of matches. Soeft promised that this would be remedied within twenty-four hours. And the men knew that the matches were as good as theirs already.

Then he announced to the crews that he was once again prepared to offer them a special Sunday dinner—"as much as you can stuff inside you and nothing to pay." He pulled out his note-book and asked: "Right then—what would you like?"

"Liver!" shouted No. 1 gun crew which had crowded round him eagerly, half-way between the main dug-out and the slit trench. Their mouths began to water. They could see and taste and smell the liver already. Soeft looked worried. He raised his enormous nose and looked sadly at them through his little eyes as if he felt deeply hurt.

"What?" he said, and there was a note of reproach in his voice.

"We said we'd like liver!" shouted the men, suddenly becoming anxious about their Sunday dinners. "You said we could have anything. . . ."

"I mean, what sort of liver?" said Soeft with dignity. "Pig's liver, or calf's liver? Fried or boiled? With sweet-sour sauce or how?"

The men stared in wonder at Soeft, as if he had beeen some fabulous creature, a sort of unicorn of the commissariat, a white whale among ration kings. They nodded dumbly and pushed closer to him. The man was a genius. Almost all of them knew that Soeft was in fact a crook and a black marketeer, but nobody held this against him. Didn't he work the black market in their interest? Long live Soeft! The longer he lived the better were their own chances of survival.

No. 1 gun crew eventually decided on calf's liver, flavoured with onions, and Soeft noted this down in his little book.

No. 2 gun crew wanted fresh pork and *sauerkraut*. No. 3 gun crew, mutton and beans. The leader of No. 4 gun crew leant nonchalantly against the barrel of his gun, grinned at his crew and said: "We want caviar!"

"Caviar," noted Soeft without turning a hair. And he left the men standing there in utter amazement.

"You know," said Krause, after they had left the gun positions, "they're beginning to take it out of you. They just think of the most impossible things they can ask for."

"With me," said Soeft, "nothing is impossible. That's one of the things I pride myself on."

"You're simply spoiling them."

"My dear friend and comrade in crime," said Soeft, suddenly stopping in his tracks. "Kindly leave me to worry about that. As long as my patrols continue to go out the men are entitled to their share of the booty. Here we are at the moment sitting on our bottoms and waiting. And waiting for what? Death on an empty stomach? Not on your life!"

They went over to the field telephone and Soeft got on to the men at the observation posts, and then to the Sergeant i/c transport in his provisional workshop. He noted down the wishes of the ammunition section. And even the medical

Corporal, whom Soeft was in the habit of addressing merely as "Medical orderly Neumann", was allowed to attach himself to a section for the purposes of his Sunday dinner.

"And what are the wishes of the headquarters staff?" Soeft asked the adjutant-under-training.

"What about roast duck?" asked Krause tentatively.

"Why not?"

"If you don't mind I'll just ask Captain Witterer what he would like first."

"Yes, do that," said Soeft. "But be as quick as you can about it. I've got to have all orders in by midday to-morrow at the latest. My friend in the butchers' section won't wait any longer."

"I'll certainly let you know by then," Krause assured him. "And shall I find out what Captain Witterer would like to drink too?"

"By all means," said Soeft generously. "But while you're doing that see if you can also find out anything about a possible withdrawal."

"Withdrawal?" asked Krause in surprise. "What put that idea into your head? We're absolutely glued to the spot here—at least until the great thaw comes."

"Perhaps," said Soeft, "but perhaps not, too. In any case, I've heard a faint rumour up at Divisional H.Q. The Quartermaster appears to be packing up his things in preparation for a move."

"Well, it's the first I've heard of it," said Krause in genuine astonishment. "I imagine Captain Witterer knows nothing about it."

"It's enough for me if I know," said Soeft. "But it'll come to Witterer in time, and with luck he'll hear more of the details. So keep your ears open and if you find out anything useful, let me know in plenty of time. You see, it's not only my stores I'm worried about, I've got my whole Kolchos to move."

"All right," said Krause. "And don't worry, I think we'll get Witterer to play with us all right in the end, you know."

Soeft grinned and as he did so deep lines appeared across his forehead. Then he said:

"Ah, well! We shall see what we shall see! The two things I'm most interested in are my auxiliary field-kitchen truck and my Kolchos. Do what you can about them. If you take too long I may have to put Sergeant Asch on to the job for me."

"Oh, you don't need to do that," said Krause hurriedly.

"I'll soon see what I can do for you." And then he added: "Besides, Asch wouldn't play."

"Perhaps I'd better sound him out."

"Soeft," said Krause and there was an almost conspiratorial note in his voice. "Obviously one has to reckon with a number of conflicting cross-currents in this sort of life. But if I have your support, not only in these matters but in others as well, then I think the two of us will manage all right. But you've got to make your decision—if you don't mind me putting it like that."

"Decision? What about?"

"In favour of me or of Asch."

Soeft beamed like a contented baby. But his eyes twinkled slyly.

"My dear old fellow," he said, "I'm a business man. You must realise that. And my favour goes to the man who does the best business for me. So see what you can do for me, won't you?"

To get round Captain Witterer, Krause exploited his position of a well-disciplined subordinate to the full. The Captain was sitting by the telephone in his quarters, looking thoughtfully into the distance. He graciously bade his adjutant sit down.

"I've just been going round the sections with Corporal Soeft," said Krause, with the keenness of a schoolboy who wants to keep in his teacher's good books.

"Good," said Witterer, only half paying attention.

"Corporal Soeft is organising a special Sunday dinner for each section."

"Fine," said Witterer, playing with the telephone.

"Of course, Corporal Soeft has done some most remarkable things for the troop. But now he wants to excel himself. He's got a really first-class idea. But in order to carry it out he needs an auxiliary field-kitchen truck among other things."

"A what?"

"An auxiliary field-kitchen truck, Captain."

"Never heard of it. There's no such vehicle as that in Wehrmacht regulations. And I know what I'm talking about. As you know, I framed a number of the more important regulations myself."

"Corporal Soeft," said Krause, "wants to try out what he thinks is a very promising experiment."

"In my troop? My dear Krause, there's one thing I must make quite clear to you: in the event of any sort of trouble cropping up, the only thing that counts with me is Wehrmacht regulations. Wehrmacht regulations are the soldier's Bible. They alone make possible a concentration of strength to bring a disorganised enemy to his knees."

Krause said nothing. He boldly tried to give the impression that his silence meant agreement, and he almost succeeded. Certainly he wore a very submissive expression. It was disappointing that this first sally on Soeft's behalf should have proved a failure but he wasn't going to let himself be discouraged.

Witterer was still thinking of the telephone conversation he had had with Colonel Luschke only a few minutes before. Suddenly he asked:

" Who's this Corporal Vierbein? "

" Oh, he's Sergeant Asch's blue-eyed boy," said Krause promptly.

" Aha! " said Witterer, not exactly sure that that was the sort of answer he had wanted.

" Is this Corporal Vierbein seconded or on leave? "

" No one's quite certain," said Krause, thinking himself very cunning. " Officially, on the personnel report, he counts as being seconded."

" Who was responsible for that actually? "

" Sergeant Asch, I suppose, sir—that's to say, officially, Lieutenant Wedelmann."

" This fellow Asch," said Witterer, " is beginning to get on my nerves."

" I can quite understand that," said Krause with emphasis.

After further fruitless researches into the exact nature of Corporal Vierbein's present status, Witterer found himself obliged to apply to Sergeant Asch for information. But Asch wasn't to be got hold of. He was, so Witterer was told, back at the main base " on something to do with the job he's been given there."

" What a state of affairs! " cried Witterer, indignantly.

" That's just like Asch," Krause assured him. " He's probably calling on those dancers again. He seems to be having a splendid time there. From what I've seen . . ."

" Well, what have you seen? "

Krause was at last able to let himself go about Asch. With a wealth of imagination, but always in strictly correct and formal terms, he told the Captain a long story about having seen Sergeant Asch drinking together with Lisa Ebner in the Welfare Institute.

" Write all that down in the form of a report," ordered

Witterer. "It may come in useful later. And now go and get hold of Lieutenant Wedelmann. I want him to take over from me here for the time being. Then get hold of Kowalski. We're going in to the main base ourselves to see what this concert party is like. They're giving their first performance there to-night."

The first public performance of "The Four Penguins' Concert Party" took place in the former Soviet Hall of Culture, which was used for lectures, stage shows and films. This was packed half an hour before the performance began. There was a general buzz of excitement, and a thick cloud of smoke rose to the ceiling. Grim-faced military police, known familiarly as "blood-hounds", acted as ushers. One of them shouted: "No smoking." And someone in the audience shouted back: "I want to see that in writing!"

The audience consisted of representatives of all the various staffs, workshops and supply columns. There were also a few front-line troops. The rank and file were in the majority.

The two front rows were reserved for staff officers. There were even three full-scale Generals expected together with their entourage. A band started to play and the troops beat time with their feet, taking a delight in making as much noise as possible.

One of the military policemen called out again: "No smoking!" And another held up a board on which was printed: "No smoking. Commanding Officer."

Someone promptly called out: "The Commanding Officer is not to smoke."

Captain Witterer had himself driven up to a side entrance. Here he generously dismissed Krause and Kowalski "for the duration of the performance". He left the two men standing there and went off to find the dressing-rooms.

"Right then," said Corporal Krause. "In we go."

"I'm off duty," said Kowalski. "I've got my own plans."

Krause muttered his disapproval and left him. At the door he showed a ticket which Witterer had given him. He went into the hall and sat down in the one but last row, waiting to be entertained.

Kowalski looked at his watch and saw that there was still a little time before the show began. He therefore went in by the same side door as Witterer had used, also in search of the dressing-rooms. On one of his visits to the main base he had casually made the acquaintance of the oldest of the three girls and he now rather wished to extend it. Her name was Charlotte. When he had found out her dressing-room, he knocked on the door and went in. He had a broad grin on his face. Charlotte was sitting in front of a mirror, in an evening dress.

" I hope you have plenty of imagination," he said, " because then you can imagine that I'm bringing you a bouquet of flowers!"

" My favourite flowers are carnations!" said Charlotte staring at him coolly.

" Hey presto!" said Kowalski, stretching out an empty hand. " Three dozen of them!"

" You're too generous," said Charlotte. " A real stage-door Johnny, in fact."

" Then may I take you out when the show is over?" asked Kowalski. " What about a little supper for two?"

" Oh, so you know about supper too?"

" Of course—it's something to eat."

Egon, the conjurer and manager of the group, opened the door, without knocking, and put his head round into the room.

" Ready?" he asked briskly. " Curtain up in five minutes."

" I've been ready for hours."

" Surely that's obvious," said Kowalski, thinking himself very gallant.

" Visitors again," said Egon crossly. " I thought we were going to have no more of that, Charlotte?"

" I simply haven't the strength to throw this great ox out!"

The conjurer weighed Kowalski up for a few seconds. Then he became embarrassed for he sensed the man's prowess as a boxer. And he told himself that his own appearance was far too valuable to be worth risking in a fight.

" I don't think you've really got the strength either," said Kowalski. " But would you like to try?"

" The whole place has turned into a sort of dovecot," said Egon, furiously, but retreating at the same time towards the door. " People in and out the whole time. Half the entire officers' corps seems to have called to see Viola. And some fellow has just come flying out of Lisa's dressing-room, at top speed. It's all just what we wanted to avoid."

Charlotte shrugged her shoulders. Kowalski made as if to

roll up his sleeves. Egon shook his head and shot out of the dressing-room, slamming the door behind him.

"You won't find a seat if you don't go soon," said Charlotte to Kowalski.

"Don't worry," he answered. "I've got whole rows reserved for me."

"Well, if *you* don't go, Herr Kowalski, *I* shall have to."

"Oh, that would be too much," said Kowalski, with exaggerated courtesy. He gave her a bow of almost medieval proportions and left the room.

He wandered over to the main entrance where he organised himself an entrance ticket and walked into the hall. He looked about him for a moment, sizing up the situation. Then he made his way purposefully to the front where he sat down right in the middle of the front row.

One of the "blood-hounds" came swooping over to him at once and said that the seats were reserved.

"Fine," said Kowalski, nodding approvingly.

"They're reserved for the General, man!"

"Well, what about it?" asked Kowalski leaning back in his seat and looking up expectantly.

"Is there something wrong with your hearing?"

"Most certainly not. What's the trouble, though? I come from the General. I'm keeping his place for him."

Kowalski crossed one leg over the other and grinned up at the military policeman with a half-friendly, half-patronising air. The latter eventually managed to swallow the explanation but only after a delay of several seconds. Then he finally withdrew.

Lance-Corporal Kowalski folded his arms. He knew how to carry off this sort of thing. It was one of the oldest tricks in the world, but it always worked. No one was ever prepared to risk a possible row with a real General.

Kowalski looked expectantly first at the curtain and then at his watch and saw that it was already long past the hour when the show was due to begin. He shook his head in disapproval and then turned and looked round the hall.

There were still a number of empty seats just behind him. A little farther back there was a whole swarm of officers, including a number in the medical and administrative branches. Farther back still sat the N.C.O.s and men wedged tightly together, shoulder to shoulder. And right at the back, at the side, Kowalski saw Sergeant Asch leaning against the wooden partition.

The Lance-Corporal beckoned over the military policeman in charge of the first two rows. The military policeman was too astonished to move at first, then after a little hesitation, he came over.

"Do you see that Sergeant standing over there at the back?" said Kowalski pointing to Asch.

"Yes," said the military policeman.

"Well, bring him over here, will you?" said Kowalski. His self-assurance was completely disarming. The military policeman was about to open his mouth in a vigorous protest when the Lance-Corporal added by way of explanation: "He's the General's son, you see."

"Oh," said the policeman, and he went over to Asch at the back and brought him up to tne front row.

"Sit down, you goof," said Kowalski grinning. "Make yourself at home. Just between ourselves, we're protégés of the General's here."

"You've got a nerve," said Asch, taking a seat. "But I don't care. The worst they can do is throw us out. I've been getting in some practice at that already this evening."

"So it was you," said Kowalski. "I might have known it. Witterer threw you out of the dressing-room of that girl with the big round eyes."

"And how the hell do you know that?"

"One has one's contacts," said Kowalski very mysteriously. Then he looked at his watch again and shook his head vigorously. He beckoned the military policeman over to him, even more peremptorily than before.

"Tell the officer in charge to begin," said Kowalski. "It's high time, anyway. The General will be coming along later."

The field security man again found himself wrestling with a strong secret feeling of misgiving. But he eventually overcame this and disappeared to the back of the hall. He just couldn't believe that there was anyone in the world who would dare to try and make a fool of him like that. Such a thing was just inconceivable—at least in the Wehrmacht in which he was the terror of all saboteurs.

He therefore presented himself to the officer in charge and told him that "the General's son wished to inform him that the General would be arriving later and that in his, the General's son's opinion, the show could start immediately."

"He, the General's son, can . . ." But he gave the signal for the show to begin.

The lights slowly went out and there was a sigh of "Ah!"

from the troops and some high-pitched whistling. A wiry-looking staff officer looked round in disapproval.

"Here we go," said Kowalski, nudging Asch.

There was another "Ah!" from the troops as the curtain parted and Frau Charlotte was revealed in the soft glow of the footlights.

"I can't believe it!" shouted a soldier in sheer delight.

There was some laughter, and the same wiry-looking staff officer who had turned round before, now stood up to his full height and stared severely out over the excited audience.

"Boo!" cried someone from the safety of the back of the hall.

"Boo!" cried several others.

And even in the semi-darkness the staff officer could be seen slowly turning red in the face. He looked as if he were about to say something but before he could get anything out Charlotte had begun to speak.

"My dear friends," she said, and her warm motherly slightly mocking voice came over without the slightest difficulty. "To-day we want to try an enjoy ourselves and forget the war for a little!"

"I've forgotten it already," said Kowalski under his breath, but loud enough for Charlotte to hear him from the stage.

She peered into the hall and recognised the Lance-Corporal sitting just below her. He grinned cheerfully back.

"All of us here," she said, "bring you best wishes from home. We consider ourselves representatives of all the women who would like to be here with you. Your mothers and your sisters."

"And our girls," called out someone.

"Them too," said Charlotte. "But we only represent them symbolically."

There were several cries of "Shame!" And a deep sigh was clearly audible the entire length of the hall. The wiry-looking staff officer shuddered.

Then Charlotte announced Lisa Ebner. And as she was doing so Captain Witterer came in on tiptoe with squeaky boots and sat down at the end of the second row on a chair that had been reserved for him.

Lisa Ebner was wearing a silky black dress which fell in pleats from the hips. Her eyes seemed larger than ever. Her long slender hands wandered nervously over the guitar even before she had begun to play.

"She's got stage-fright," said Kowalski. "She should have had a stiff one before she came on."

She sang a little song about love and faithfulness and a bunch of wild flowers that—ah!—fades all too soon. And yet every spring the flowers bloom again. . . .

The applause was not particularly loud, but Captain Witterer rose to his feet and clapped continuously and this was enough to stop Asch from clapping altogether.

Charlotte then announced Viola, the dancer. The footlights were dimmed and the blonde Viola came on to the stage and took up her position. She was wearing a sort of Hungarian costume. Balkan anyway, for she had red boots on.

" Can't see much," said Kowalski rather disappointed. " Still, that'll come later. She comes on several times."

Viola tripped energetically about the stage, throwing her arms and legs about, rolling her eyes and letting her hair fly in all directions. When she had finished there was a storm of applause. The very beams of the hall seemed to shake. Viola blew kisses to the audience. Someone at the back had to be held back by force.

After Viola came Egon, the conjurer, who went on for at least half an hour. He made a great point of getting the audience to share in his tricks, let them take cards, divided rings among them, asked for hankerchiefs and produced gold coins out of a Staff Quartermaster's nose. This last trick was particularly well received. When Kowalski tried to take part in the tricks, however, Egon pointedly ignored him.

Then Charlotte recited an almost vulgar poem, Lisa sang some slightly *risqué* songs and Viola wore less and less every time she appeared. The applause even from the front rows was thunderous. " The Four Penguins " were undoubtedly a great success.

At the end Asch extricated himself from the audience and climbed straight across the stage to the dressing-rooms. He found Lisa Ebner sitting in front of a mirror, combing her hair. She looked up at him.

" Well," she asked curiously, " what did you think of me?"

" Wonderful," said Asch and it sounded as if he meant it. " Simply wonderful! But now you must get back to your billet."

" Must I? But we've been invited out to a party?"

" Just as I thought," said Asch. " Of course you won't be doing anything like that. You're too good for that sort of thing. Far too good."

" Do you really mean that?"

" Come on! I'll see you home."

"All right, I'll go if you come with me," said Lisa Ebner smiling at him. She put on her overcoat which Asch held out for her. Then she seemed to lose her balance for a moment. She stumbled and clung on to him.

"Careful now," said Asch, catching hold of her.

"How strong you are," said Lisa Ebner.

"Not particularly," said Asch. "But strong enough to stop myself from being weak with you."

"Are you sure?"

"Of course. Come on."

They had hardly left the Hall of Culture when Captain Witterer appeared in the dressing-room. He was looking for Lisa Ebner but couldn't find her anywhere. He happened to run into Lance-Corporal Kowalski, who was not in the best of tempers as a result of a rather awkward little interview he had just had with the military policeman.

"Have you seen Fräulein Ebner anywhere?" asked Witterer.

Kowalski, who was trying to get into Charlotte's dressing-room which was already packed with people, stared at him uncomprehendingly. He was still boiling with rage.

"Why do you ask me?" Why don't you ask Sergeant Asch?"

"Aha," said Witterer. "So that's how it is, is it?"

Corporal Vierbein watched the Siamese twins crawl out of bed next morning in utter disgust. They opened their mouths in gigantic yawns as they staggered about the room.

"You ought to be ashamed of yourselves," cried Vierbein.

Vierbein was already dressed. Bartsch stared at him expressionlessly out of watery eyes. He and Ruhnau were suffering severely from the after effects of the large quantities of third-rate alcohol they had drunk the night before.

"My God, man!" groaned Bartsch, clinging to the side of his bed. "What we have to go through!"

"This war's certainly no joke," moaned Ruhnau.

Vierbein was determined to show them the contempt he felt for them.

"What the hell do you mean by bursting in on the Asches like that yesterday evening? You were like a couple of bulls in a china shop. Well? What did you mean by it?"

"Don't! Don't! It hurts too much to have to think about anything."

The two spent "torpedoes" lay together face downwards

on one of the beds and felt their bursting skulls. They found themselves staring at the floor where a host of horrible worms seemed to be crawling about. Ruhnau moaned again.

"Vierbein," said Bartsch. "If only you knew what a mess we've got ourselves into, you'd have some sympathy for us."

"We've signed our own death-warrant, Vierbein," cried Ruhnau. "Pity us. You can order the wreaths now."

"Do us the last honours, Vierbein. A real hero at the grave-side—that would be some comfort to our sorrowing parents, at least."

"What happened?" asked Vierbein. Confronted by so much misery, his anger vanished completely.

"We met a dog. The dog was our downfall."

"It was the wrong dog, you see."

"What *are* you talking about?" asked Vierbein.

"A dog. We tied a lavatory seat to it at the officers' mess party yesterday evening. Unfortunately this dog didn't belong, as we thought, to the Quartermaster's wife. Schulz can't stand her. It belonged to the lady the C.O. is going to marry!"

"And Schulz traced it to us, which was why we had to take off so suddenly—like a couple of rockets, in fact!"

"Serves you right!" said Vierbein.

"Pity us, Vierbein!" cried Bartsch. "For if Schulz is still anything like as furious as he was yesterday, there's no knowing what may happen. It could mean the worst!"

"He might even post us," said Ruhnau, in a voice like the grave.

"Not to us at the front, I hope," said Vierbein.

The word "front" nearly sent the Siamese twins into paroxysms. The embarrassment they had caused Vierbein was no longer of any concern to them. They themselves were now concerned in a matter of life and death. Panic-stricken they rushed off to their duties, where they waited eagerly for any sort of word from Schulz. But no word came. Their nervousness increased hourly, gradually depriving them even of their appetites, which was clear enough proof of the seriousness of the situation.

Finally, just before the midday break, they sought out the Sergeant-Major. He treated them with complete neutrality which gave them grounds for hope again. They succeeded in eliciting from him the information that Schulz hadn't put in an appearance in the staff troop office that morning. He was at Battery H.Q. where he was dealing with a number of routine matters and personally superintending the final preparations for the C.O.'s wedding.

So the issue was left in the balance. The situation was far from clear. Almost anything might happen.

In the end they could bear it no longer and summoning up their last ounce of courage decided to ring up Schulz themselves. In a state of considerable excitement they got on to Battery H.Q. The adjutant answered.

"Would you be so good, Lieutenant, as to ask Lieutenant Schulz whether he'll be wanting us to-day?"

As always, the adjutant took care to answer with perfect military correctness.

"If Lieutenant Schulz wants you, he'll let you know himself."

"Yes, Lieutenant. You see, if we weren't wanted, we thought we'd drive out to the equipment stores about that filter."

"I see," said the adjutant. "Hold on a moment."

The next few minutes were intensely exciting. Bartsch, who was holding on to the receiver, trembled slightly without being aware of it. Ruhnau also had his ear glued to the receiver.

The thousands of gas-masks which lay on racks round the store seemed to be grinning down at them. There was a smell of rubber and chlorine. Ruhnau found it unpleasantly stuffy and opened the window.

Bartsch was breathing so heavily he had to sit down. He felt bathed in sweat. He strained every nerve down the telephone. He was on the point of praying. This was a thing which had never happened to him in his life before.

Suddenly the adjutant came back at the other end.

"No," he said, "you're not wanted this afternoon."

Bartsch put down the receiver and looked at Ruhnau. Ruhnau looked at Bartsch. As a routine precaution he made sure that the receiver had been put back properly. They both thought the matter over for a while.

"Well, and what does that mean? Does it mean that Schulz really doesn't want us, or that he doesn't want to have anything more to do with us? Has the whole thing been forgotten, or is the reckoning still to come?"

"Oh God, man. It can be a damned hard war at times!"

"If only we had a schnaps at least?"

"Or several schnapses!"

"We ought to drink up those bottles we've got in store at that little inn down by the bridge. We may not have so much longer to drink them in."

" Let's go there. We've got to go into town anyway now about the new filter. We told Schulz we were going!"

They climbed into the Opel which they had managed to wangle for their own personal transport and roared into the town.

They went straight to the inn by the bridge and demanded their supplies. But the landlord would allow them only three of the four bottles which he had been keeping for them. He held the fourth one back for himself as a fee for " cellarage ". They called him a crook, a swindler, a black marketeer and a lot of other names, but none of this worried him in the least. Such lack of sensitivity on his part made them take their bottles elsewhere to avoid having to pay him " corkage " as well.

They went and sat down in the Café National in the next street and there they ordered tea, which they poured away under the table and replaced with schnaps. The very first sip gave them a new interest in life. By the time they were on to their second cup the situation even seemed fairly rosy.

Thus refreshed they began to take in their surroundings for the first time. They discovered two girls who were obviously determined to spend their afternoon off as pleasantly as possible. The two mighty " air-screws " asked " the ladies " to join them at their table and after a token hesitation, " the ladies " did so. Tea was ordered for them, too.

By the time they had emptied the first bottle of schnaps, the two " rockets " were addressing " the ladies " as " du ". By the end of the second bottle, they were becoming even more intimate. " The ladies " giggled and the girl who was waiting on them cleared her throat indignantly. But the throat clearing stopped as soon as she found a twenty-mark note being stuck down the front of her blouse. Certainly she wouldn't tolerate an attempt on the part of the two " howitzers " to make sure that it was completely secure there. But she tolerated everything else.

By the third bottle, things were becoming lively. From time to time one of the girls would let out a little squeal. Bartsch and Ruhnau had their hands full. And the manageress of the café began to get anxious. She stood in the background raising her massive arms to heaven in horror.

" Have you got a room to let?" asked Bartsch.

" Shame on you!" cried the manageress. " Do I look that sort of woman?"

" Yes!" chorused the Siamese twins in triumph.

And the manageress immediately began to threaten them

with the police, the military police and all the rest of it. When she actually made a move towards the telephone, the two "thousand-pounders" decided on a rapid change of front. They offered their arms to the ladies, who had been readjusting their clothes in the meantime, and all four went staggering out into the street.

A few yards father down stood a solitary horse and cab. The Siamese twins immediately pronounced it "requisitioned" and installed their companions inside it. Bartsch climbed in eagerly. Ruhnau said he would take a look round for the driver. But there was no sign of him. He had obviously gone off for a drink in a nearby tavern. So the Corporal untied the reins from the lamp-post and staggered up into the driving-seat himself.

"Everyone ready?" cried Ruhnau. "Right! We're off!"

He cracked the whip and the old horse set off obediently. The wheels turned briskly over the cobbles. The cab-driver, hearing the noise, rushed out of the tavern and stared in amazement. A Corporal in his driving-seat was something he hadn't seen before. "Stop!" he cried.

Ruhnau whipped up the old horse, which trotted on ahead. The cab-driver trotted along behind, waving his arms and calling on them to stop. Inside the cab "the ladies" could be heard squealing and giggling in triumph. Bartsch hoisted a flag which consisted of a piece of underclothing.

Thus, to the laughter of the bystanders, the cries of Ruhnau, the squeals of "the ladies" and the curses of the pursuing cab-driver, this extraordinary equipage left the centre of the town for the suburbs, where it headed for the barracks.

The sentry, an inexperienced young oaf with watery eyes and sticking-out ears, opened his mouth wide in astonishment.

"Open the main gate," shouted Ruhnau from a distance. "I've got an officer in here!"

The sentry rushed to the main gate, and pulled it open. As the cab passed through it, the sentry sprinted back to his place and did his best to present arms. Whereupon Bartsch produced a different piece of clothing from the inside of the cab and waved back with it.

The swaying, creaking old cab came to a halt in front of the staff troop building. The horse snorted. Ruhnau jumped down from the box and cried: "And now, away like nobody's business!"

And the two "M.T.B.s" immediately disappeared into the barrack block.

The abandoned cab, from which two very drunk partially clad "ladies" now began to emerge, immediately became a source of considerable interest. One or two soldiers leant out of the windows of the barrack block, and among these was Vierbein.

Ruhnau and Bartsch came tearing into the room feeling simply delighted with themselves. They rushed at Vierbein, roaring with laughter.

"Come on, Vierbein!" they cried. "There are ladies to see you! You must come down."

"You're tight!" said Vierbein.

In the meantime a considerable uproar had arisen at the main gate. For the cab-driver had arrived, panting and puffing, and, overcome with fury, was demanding admittance. The sentry, however, was determined to keep this unruly and unmannerly civilian out at all costs.

"I'll go down," cried Bartsch. "You, Ruhnau and Vierbein, get the women away. Hide them in one of the N.C.O.s rooms! What are you waiting for, Vierbein? Have you no sense of comradeship?"

And Bartsch trotted down into the barrack square and across to the gate, where the sentry was on the point of taking the safety-catch off his rifle in his determination to keep this intruder out of the barracks.

"What's going on here?" asked Bartsch. "What's all the row about?"

The cab-driver, naturally, didn't recognise Bartsch, who had been sitting inside the cab when it drove off. He threw himself on this apparently friendly N.C.O. and implored him to let him have his cab back. Bartsch pretended not to understand what it was all about and asked for details, to gain time. Then, after listening for some minutes to an account of what he knew perfectly well already, he declared generously: "I'll look after the matter for you myself!"

Bartsch got the cab-driver a pass from the guard-room. The man was obviously touched by such consideration for his welfare. Then Bartsch made a show of setting out on a search with him. He took him on a detour round several of the barrack blocks and only after some time brought him to the spot where the cab now stood empty.

The cab-driver rushed up to the horse and threw his arms round his neck. "I can understand how you feel," observed Bartsch sympathetically, standing behind him. "My father's a cab-driver, too."

"You're the only decent human being in the place," said the cab-driver, again visibly touched. He was still puffing desperately.

"Oh, I don't know," said Bartsch, with admirable modesty.

Sergeant-Major Bock could tell at once that all had not gone well with Witterer the evening before. The Captain seemed to have suffered a rebuff of some sort at the entertainment show. He appeared determined to work it out of his system with an even more furious burst of activity than ever.

"Is my car ready?" he snapped, after signing a number of orders about the necessity of troops carrying gas-masks with them at all times and always going about fully armed.

"It's just outside, sir," said the Sergeant-Major.

"What? It's already there? Why hasn't the driver reported to me?"

"The Captain only ordered him to bring the car round."

"And report! That goes without saying, Sergeant-Major. Where I'm concerned, anyway. Kindly make that clear to the lazy swine in future."

Bock managed to avoid answering this. He got away with it easily enough for the Captain was fully engaged with the preparations for his departure. These were being made in full compliance with the orders which he had just signed. He strapped on his service revolver, and then loaded himself up with gas-mask, map-case and steel helmet. Then he patted the field dressing which, as prescribed by regulations, was sewn into the lining of his tunic. And then, with his usual springy stride, marched rapidly out of the room.

Corporal Krause was waiting outside with the car. He, too, was in full war-paint. Kowalski sat at the steering wheel, eyeing the two heroes. Compared with the way in which they were equipped, he looked like a peaceful civilian.

"Where's your gas-mask?" asked Witterer.

"In the back of the car," answered Kowalski promptly, knowing very well that it was nowhere of the sort.

"Why aren't you wearing it?"

"Much too cumbersome," said Kowalski. "It would get in the way. Either I sit here and drive the car, or else I tie a gas-mask round my belly and sit in the back, but I can't do both."

"If I understood your order aright, Captain," said Corporal Krause, who couldn't afford to antagonise such a useful contact as Kowalski, " it is sufficient if the gas-mask is kept within easy reach."

"Well, what are you waiting for?" cried Witterer. "Gun positions! And let's see how the C.O.'s driver can drive!"

He hadn't quite finished sitting down before Kowalski let in the clutch. Witterer was jerked backwards and for a fraction of a second had the unpleasant sensation that his neck was breaking. Then the car roared forward sending a great fountain of dust up in the street behind it. Kowalski seemed determined not to avoid a single puddle. He tore through the slush, covering Krause, who was sitting at the back, with mud.

As Kowalski approached the gun positions, driving across the open in full view of the enemy, Witterer roared at him: "Have you taken leave of your senses, man?"

"What do you mean, have *I*?" asked Kowalski.

"Take cover, man!" cried Witterer. "You're not here to give them target practice!"

Kowalski headed straight towards a large tree, jammed the brakes on hard and ended up within a couple of inches of it. "All change!" he cried. "Terminus!"

Witterer didn't know whether to laugh or swear at him. It would be better to laugh, he thought. How else could one react to a clown like Kowalski? But he wasn't in at all a good mood, which was hardly surprising after the calamity of the previous evening. So he preferred just to put on an enigmatic expression. He levered himself out of the car, taking care to keep under cover all the time. Krause imitated his every movement, rather as if he were his reflection in a mirror.

"Put the car right out of sight," ordered Witterer.

Kowalski nodded and putting the engine into reverse ground his way painfully back across the landscape. Eventually he disappeared behind a house where he switched off the engine.

Witterer, closely followed by Krause, now ran over towards No. 2 gun. To the delight of the sentries, they hopped across the landscape like a couple of hares. Just before they reached the gun itself, Witterer leapt into a slit trench. Krause leapt in after him and would have landed on top of him if at the last moment he hadn't managed to give a twist to his body which landed him instead in the middle of a large puddle. The sentry, who was standing close by, found the whole performance extremely entertaining.

Witterer, with his face now set in a grim expression, began fiddling with the field-glasses that hung round his neck. He kept his head down carefully and, leaning against the front of the trench, peered anxiously through his glasses in the direction of the enemy. He felt himself to be really in action at last. He tried to analyse his sensations and decided that he was like a surgeon who picks up his scalpel for the first time knowing perfectly well that he will always perform even the trickiest operation with outstanding success. He decided that he would write about all this at some length in a letter. In several letters probably.

So there they were—the enemy lines. A set of zigzag trenches in the distance, exactly like the German ones. A few isolated fox-holes on the little chain of hills opposite. Some well-worn paths. And the whole thing apparently fast asleep.

Suddenly Witterer said: "But it's simply not possible! Just have a look, Krause."

Krause obediently took the field-glasses from Witterer and looked through them intently. Some snow trickled into his sleeve, where it melted and ran down in a little stream to his elbow.

"Well?" said Witterer impatiently and with unmistakable sharpness. "Don't you see anything?"

"Nothing special, Captain. Or rather, nothing that strikes me as special."

"Good God man!" said Witterer, even more sharply than before. "Look straight ahead of you! Three thousand yards. Group of trees. Four bars to the left—a bushy-top tree. See it?"

"Yes, Captain."

"Well? What's moving across your field of vision, there?"

"A man," said Krause. "A ration-carrier, I suppose. He's going over to the trenches on that hill on the left."

"And the fellow's walking about bolt upright. He's openly defying us."

"That's true," said Krause, seeing what was in Witterer's mind. He couldn't decide whether to encourage him or try to restrain him. "Yes, sir. He's defying us all right. But they've been doing that every day at noon now for weeks." And, still not certain what was the right attitude to adopt, he added: "We do exactly the same."

Witterer snatched the field-glasses back from Krause and looked through them again with great concentration. He focused them as sharply as possible. The sight of the enemy ration-carrier calmly walking along in full view of him, made him grind his teeth with rage. This was the enemy! The fellow

127

was strolling about unconcernedly in the very cannon's mouth, the mouth of his—Captain Witterer's—cannon. It was too much.

And without lowering his field-glasses, Witterer said: " Gun stations!"

Krause jumped. He had a long-drawn-out moment of horror. Then he passed on the order to the sentry.

" Gun stations!"

"What?" the sentry shouted back. "What's the matter?"

" Gun stations!" shouted Krause.

The sentry shrugged his shoulders. Why not, he said to himself. I suppose the old man wants a practice alarm. It's a bore, but there's nothing one can do about it. He set the noisy little hand siren going and began uncovering the ammunition. This was the regulation procedure.

Witterer paid no attention to any of this. He took it for granted. He continued to look steadily across towards the enemy. And he smiled to himself.

No. 2 gun was ready relatively quickly. The men had heard Witterer approaching. The noise Kowalski made with the engine had woken them up from their after-lunch sleep. The leader of the gun crew, Corporal Rauch, who was always ready to carry out orders but whose personal inclinations were for a life of civilised ease, reported to Captain Witterer: " All ready, sir."

" See your target?" asked Witterer. He gave him the necessary details.

" On target!" said the Corporal.

" Right, then," said Witterer. " Give the orders to fire."

" Seriously?" asked the Corporal, not seeing the frantic signs Krause was making to him from behind Witterer's back.

" Good God, man," cried the Captain, with what he imagined to be real soldierly indignation. " You don't think war's a joke, do you?"

The lines round the Corporal's mouth hardened and he trotted back to the gun crew. The orders he gave were all right as far as they went, Witterer thought, but too slow.

" Faster," cried the Captain. " More life in it!"

" Range three thousand!" said the Corporal, calmly, looking through the range card which he had pulled out of his sleeve.

" On target," reported the gun-layer.

The Corporal gave the order to load. Then he looked across at Witterer again and the whole gun crew looked with him. Witterer was still standing in the trench watching every movement of "his" enemy. His blood was up. He could feel the excitement of battle surge through every vein in his body. His heart—his soldier's heart—was beating faster than ever. And he felt this to be a thoroughly manly trait.

"Come on!" he cried.

"Fuse to explode on impact," ordered the Corporal, with the faintest possible shrug of his shoulders. He grinned at his men in embarrassment. The loader pushed the shell into the gun and closed the breach.

"One round," cried Witterer.

"Fire!" ordered the crew leader.

A sharp crack split the peace of the morning. The barrel recoiled and ejected the empty shell-case. Then it slid slowly back into its original position. The shell whined through the air.

Witterer was still smiling calmly to himself, but his lips were now slightly parted. He felt a little cramp in the hand which had been holding the field-glasses. He had thrust his left foot out sideways and was stirring up the mud at the bottom of the trench with the toe of his boot.

A puff of blue-black smoke went up on the hill opposite about fifty yards away from the ration-carrier. Witterer watching through his field-glasses saw the enemy soldier utterly taken aback with astonishment. Then he looked about him wildly. And he began running desperately in the opposite direction to the shell-burst.

"Too short!" cried Witterer. "Another round."

The Corporal again gave the order to load and fire.

This time the shell landed behind the target. The enemy ration-carrier immediately changed direction again and began hopping about like a kangaroo. He stumbled, fell flat on his face, picked himself up again and struggled on with his load through the heavy snow.

"He's scared to death!" cried Witterer, delightedly.

"No doubt about that, sir," said Krause, close beside him.

"Another one!" cried Witterer. "Simply obliterate him."

The gun-crew leader now merely had to order a slight shortening of the range and he would have been almost bound to hit his target. But he felt sorry for the fellow leaping wildly about through the snow over there with the ration can on his back. The whole thing was too ridiculous.

So he gave the order: "Same again! Fire!" He didn't even watch to see where the shot fell. He knew it wouldn't hit. And that was all he cared about.

"Too far!" shouted Witterer, stamping with disappointment. "Damnation!"

"Another round?" asked the Corporal.

"Go on until you've wiped out the target!" cried Witterer. "Until you've smashed that little manikin over there into a thousand pieces."

But before Corporal Rauch could again give the order to fire, the field telephone rang. Rauch was clearly delighted by the interruption. He bent down and picked up the receiver. And then trying to hide a grin, he said: "It's for you, sir. The infantry commander."

"What does he want?" asked Witterer, impatiently.

Corporal Rauch obediently inquired of the infantry commander what he wanted. When he heard the answer he had considerable difficulty in keeping a straight face. Then he spoke out loud and clear: "The infantry commander wishes to know who the half-wit is who's opened fire. He strictly forbids it."

The gun crew stared eagerly at Witterer. He was overcome with rage and roared back: "Tell the man he can stuff it."

"Captain Witterer says you can stuff it," said the gun-crew leader down the telephone as loudly and clearly as before. Then he carefully put the receiver back again, with something almost like devotion.

Witterer was having a desperate struggle with himself. Then suddenly he said, very abruptly and quite unnecessarily: "Cease fire!" He jumped out of the trench, athletic as ever and called the gun crew over to him. "That wasn't very impressive," he said. "But we'll be having some more practice. We'll soon get things into shape around here."

Then he turned to Krause and said loud enough for everyone else to hear: "And now we'll go and settle up with that little Heini from the infantry."

But he didn't go straight over to the infantry. He decided first to telephone Colonel Luschke. And in order to get himself into the right mood for the conversation, he got Kowalski to drive him back to rear base.

"Well, we saw something to-day anyway!" said Witterer, as he sat jolting along beside Kowalski.

Kowalski grinned. As always, he knew all about what had happened.

"We certainly did."

The Captain seemed actually to be proud of his achievement. "We'll call that little engagement Operation Leap-Frog."

"It'll certainly be talked about for some time to come," said Kowalski emphatically. "You can be sure of that."

"And what are the girls like around here?" asked Witterer. He felt considerably set up by his first experience of action. "The Russian girls, I mean?"

"You'd better ask Lieutenant Wedelmann about that," said Kowalski. "I think he may be able to help you."

Captain Witterer's assault on the enemy lines endangered the entire system of equilibrium which had been so carefully built up over so many months on that particular sector of the front. The echo of the shell-bursts reached the ears of Colonel Luschke plainly enough. Luschke made a note of the fact in neat little letters on his writing-pad. And that was all he did for the time being.

The first person actually to get Luschke away from his Russian novel to the map-table was Captain Witterer himself. He was taking the liberty, so he said, of making his report, entirely of his own accord. A small engagement had taken place which he might perhaps make so bold as to christen Operation Leap-Frog. And Witterer made it clear that he thought he had every right to feel pleased with himself.

"Just a minute," said Luschke, putting down the receiver. He fished around in his pocket for an enormous blue-and-white handkerchief, slowly unfolded it and let out a tremendous sneeze. He followed this up with several more. And while they were going on he reached out with his left hand for his writing-pad.

After a considerable lapse of time, during which Luschke folded up his handkerchief and put it back into his pocket, opened the writing-pad and found himself a pencil, he picked the receiver up again and asked: "What time? What was the target? What were the results? How many rounds were fired?"

"Only three rounds," said Witterer, slowly, beginning to realise that the whole affair was much more complicated than he had realised in the first place. "That's all."

"Captain Witterer," said Luschke. He spoke crisply and remarkably softly. "I thought I had put one or two categorical questions to you. I should be glad of categorical answers. Without any embellishments on your part. Right then. Would you be so good as to give them to me?"

Witterer now endeavoured to satisfy Luschke with that particular form of barking long-windedness which in German military circles passes for conciseness. He was certain he would be successful. Besides, he had had considerable experience of superior officers.

And when Witterer heard Luschke answer, "Aha!" he imagined that all was well. But the next moment he had to think again for he heard the Colonel say in that soft ominous voice of his: "You'll be hearing from me later."

Luschke knew what a devastating effect it had on anyone if you left them in a state of uncertainty like this. He took no immediate steps to follow the matter up. He jotted a few words down in his note-book, underlined one of them, and then pushed the pencil away from him again. But he didn't go back to his chair. He stayed where he was, at the map-table, pulled his novel over towards him and tried to go on reading.

A little later a telephone call came through from the infantry. He had been expecting it. But it was no longer the battalion commander who was protesting but the regimental commander himself.

"That surprises me very much," said Luschke. "I thought you would shelter behind Divisional H.Q."

"We'll try and clear the matter up between ourselves," said the infantry colonel. "That is, if we possibly can."

"Are you afraid there'll be trouble, my dear colleague?"

The regimental commander was in no way surprised by this form of address, for he was used to Luschke.

"Just after your No. 3 Troop had finished their idiotic bit of nonsense, the Russians opened up with a mortar. Three of my men were wounded, one of them seriously."

Luschke let the pencil drop from his fingers.

"And what do you expect me to do about it?" he asked, and his voice sounded harsh. "Express my regrets?"

"Give that half-wit of yours a kick up the bottom. The fellow must have been tight."

"Tight? Intoxicated?" said Luschke, thoughtfully, and his left hand played with the edge of his writing-pad. "You may be right there. Intoxicated, yes, but not with alcohol!"

"I don't understand, Herr Luschke."

"If that's all you don't understand about this war, then I congratulate you!"

"I'm afraid I can't afford the luxury of trying to follow your train of thought, Herr Luschke," said the regimental commander. "All I'm interested in is in seeing that this sort of idiocy doesn't occur again. Will you kindly see that it doesn't? No individual actions can be tolerated by any unit whatsoever. It seems to me that it would be more worth while to grasp that than to spend one's time philosophising about the war."

Luschke picked up the pencil again and began drumming on his writing-pad.

"My dear colleague," he said, so fulsomely that this very goodwill had a sarcastic ring about it, "it's possible to look at a case of this sort from a number of different points of view. And one such point of view might go something like this: An officer of mine finds a target and brings it under fire. That is all. It's the sort of thing that happens in war, you know."

"So you're determined to shield the man, Herr Luschke?"

"I attach considerable importance to freedom of action. Even in a case of this sort."

Luschke's right eyelid twitched for a moment when he heard the infantry commander abruptly put down the receiver.

Then he pulled a brief-case towards him, opened it and looked through some papers. He eventually found what he was looking for; a report from Corporal Vierbein which had reached him that day via his old friend the Commandant of the airfield.

Luschke once again read through what Vierbein had written. Then he carefully underlined a couple of sentences, and picking up the telephone asked to be put through to Lieutenant Wedelmann, who had obviously been expecting his C.O. to ring up and answered at once.

"How are you, my dear fellow?" asked Luschke. He sounded suspiciously friendly.

Wedelmann thought he knew the sort of thing the C.O. wanted to hear.

"When this business occurred this morning, Colonel, I was . . ."

"What are you talking about, Wedelmann? What business? I'm not interested in anything to do with business. I merely asked you how you were?"

"Very well, thank you, Colonel," answered Wedelmann, taken aback.

"Good. That's all I wanted to know. If there's anything else I want to know I'll ask you."

"Yes, Colonel."

"I have some news from your friend Vierbein, my dear Wedelmann."

"Good news, sir?"

" Just guess."

" Has anything gone wrong, Colonel?" asked Wedelmann anxiously. " I can hardly think it has. But if it has, I simply can't believe that it was Vierbein's fault in any way."

" Yours, then, perhaps, Wedelmann?"

Wedelmann said nothing. He was trying to think of any mistake he might have made but none occurred to him immediately.

" You only gave Vierbein papers seconding him. Now he's stuck with the reserve battery. Leave papers and a separate movement order in addition would have been simpler."

" Would it be any good sending him leave papers now, Colonel?"

" That rather depends," said Luschke, slowly. " It depends on whether Vierbein has given up his papers or still has them in his pocket. If the latter's the case the damage can be repaired fairly easily. But if he's handed the papers in it would complicate things still further."

" What are the Colonel's orders then?" asked Wedelmann. It was an old trick which nearly always worked.

" Orders? My orders are that you shouldn't make mistakes like that in future."

" Very good, sir," said Wedelmann, feeling very foolish. He should have known that one couldn't put anything like that over on Luschke.

As he replaced the receiver he was aware of a mild, but rather confused feeling of resentment againt the C.O. for whom he normally had so much respect. Sergeant Asch came into the room at that moment and threw his greatcoat down carelessly on to the heap of straw in the corner.

" What did the Colonel want?" he asked. " Was he congratulating us on our gallant feat of arms this afternoon?"

" Not a word about it," said Wedelmann, lying down on the straw. " No. It's Vierbein. He's got stuck."

" Because of his papers?"

" Now, don't start crowing, Asch. It just so happens that you were right. Good. We made a mistake. But we can put it right again. We'll send leave papers after him by air—he'll have them by to-morrow morning."

" And do you imagine Captain Witterer is going to sign them?"

" The date on his leave papers will naturally be the same as that on the papers seconding him. And I was still troop commander when they were issued."

"Good," said Asch. "Then I'll make them out for you."

"Yes, do that, Asch," said the Lieutenant stretching out his legs. He looked at his boots. For a moment it seemed almost as if they were the only things of any importance in the world.

The Sergeant went and stood in front of Wedelmann.

"And what about Captain Witterer?"

"*What* about Captain Witterer, Asch? Kindly leave me in peace, will you? I've got other things to bother me."

"Lieutenant," said Asch stubbornly. "It's just that Captain Witterer fired a number of rounds off into the blue this afternoon."

"He did not fire them into the blue, Asch. He fired at a target."

"He sent a ration-carrier running for his life! And for that he had to use artillery?"

Wedelmann looked worried. He shook his head.

"My dear Asch," he said. "We must respect the decisions of our superior officers. How can we tell what really happened? He may have had perfectly good reasons for what he did. Where would we be if we all decided to wage our own independent wars over Witterer's head?"

"We'd have a better chance of survival!"

"Asch!" said Wedelmann, "you're a hopeless case. Captain Witterer seems to be like a red rag to a bull to you. What have you got against him?"

Asch leant against the edge of the table.

"Lieutenant," he said, calmly, "you know quite well that you really think just the same as I do. But you don't find it quite so easy to abandon your principles. Or at least you won't discuss the matter openly with a subordinate. But, in fact, you don't respect a man just because he's your superior officer any more than I do."

"Forget it, Asch," said Wedelmann determined to leave the subject. "It won't get us anywhere."

"Why don't you face up to facts, Lieutenant?" said Asch. "You know as well as I do what you think of Witterer. He's a candidate for a bullet in the back if ever I saw one. Look, Lieutenant: Colonel Luschke is fighting this war for his Fatherland. His trouble is he doesn't know just where to find his Fatherland at the moment. You are fighting it because you believe in your Führer and Fatherland and you want to keep it a clean war. But this man Witterer is a very different proposition. He's fighting the war for its own sake. He enjoys it. He enjoys the idea of killing men and walking about with a chestful

135

of medals. And I haven't got any use for a creature like that. Nor have ninety per cent of the troop."

"Stop it, Asch," said Wedelmann sharply. "Stop it at once, or I'll have you court-martialled."

"After Captain Witterer? Or with him?"

Wedelmann stared as Asch in fury and amazement. He had gone deathly pale. His hands were trembling. He suddenly turned round, seized his cap and belt and hurried out into the open.

He stood by the door of the hut for a moment and took a deep breath of fresh air. The cold air did him good. He automatically fastened on his belt . . . Then without any idea of where he was going, he strode away into the distance.

He had soon left the main street of the village behind him. He took no notice of the salutes of some men of his troop, who were busy changing their billets much as wild animals change their lairs. He didn't even pay any attention to where he was going, until he suddenly found himself heading for the house in which Natasha lived.

The Russian girl had seen him coming. She was standing by the door with a shawl thrown round her shoulders. When he came up to her she smiled a little shyly, but with obvious friendliness.

"How nice of you to come and see me," she said.

"Is it all right?"

"But of course." Still rather shyly she gave him her plump firm little hand and he shook it vigorously. Then she opened the door for him and with what seemed an almost mischievous gesture, showed him in first.

Once in her room she sat down opposite him, as usual. She looked at him inquiringly. She could sense his embarrassment and his restlessness and this made him sympathetic to her.

"Something wrong?"

"Does it show?"

"Woman can tell these things."

"So you are a woman," he said, trying to make a joke of it. "The last time I was here I thought you were just a citizeness of Soviet Russia."

"Do you want me to be?"

"Of course not," cried Wedelmann, almost angrily. "I'm delighted to know that you wonder about such things as whether I'm unhappy or not. And I have plenty to be unhappy about I can tell you. If I had my way I'd sit with you all the time. But I don't have my way."

"You'll be leaving here soon, won't you?"

"What do you mean?" It seemed an odd question to ask. Admittedly the big withdrawal was imminent, but she couldn't possibly know anything about that, and again he said: "Why do you ask that?"

"You won't stay here for ever," said Natasha, avoiding a direct answer. "War's like that. There's nothing one can do about it."

Wedelmann looked at her searchingly. Seconds passed. And he saw that she was agitated about something. It didn't seem necessary to ask what this something was. "Would you miss me, Natasha?" he said.

"Yes," she said simply. And it sounded as if she meant it.

He felt for her hand and she let him take it. He squeezed her hand and she didn't seem to mind.

"Why does there have to be war?" she asked.

"But for the war we would never have met."

"What a thing to say!" she answered and withdrew her hand. "That's just an easy excuse, but it's a rotten one. We might have met at some big sports gathering, or on holiday, or in a theatre, or in a picture gallery, or anywhere like that. Why does there have to be a war to bring two human beings from different countries together?"

"But I'm not responsible for the war, Natasha!"

"No, but you help to carry it on."

The day following the row over the stolen cab, a letter from the cab-driver arrived at the reserve battery. This was both a threatening letter and a thank-you letter at the same time.

The wretched man again complained bitterly about the theft of his property and demanded that those responsible should be punished. He threatened to report the matter to the local Nazi party organiser, who was a relation of his wife's and a close one at that. However . . .

However, continued the cab-driver, he felt bound to mention his indebtedness in this matter to the sympathetic intervention of a certain Corporal Bartsch. The said Corporal Bartsch had shown not only sympathy but real co-operation. His, the cab-driver's, faith in the Greater German Wehrmacht had been profoundly shaken by the incident, but if one person had been able to restore it, it had been the above-named Corporal Bartsch. Nevertheless . . .

Nevertheless, ran the cab-driver's letter, which showed clear signs of collaboration with his wife's close relation, the local Nazi party organiser—nevertheless, duly licensed hackney-carriage driver as he was, he could hardly be expected to leave the matter there. He found himself compelled to ask for the maximum punishment for the culprits. Otherwise . . . .

"Otherwise—what?" asked Lieutenant Schulz, who had just finished reading the letter through.

The adjutant, the Lieutenant who was a wine and spirit merchant in civil life, said:

"Otherwise presumably this close relation of his wife, the local party organiser, will step into the picture."

"I don't care if the Gauleiter himself steps in!" cried Schulz. "We won't budge an inch." And he didn't mean a word of it.

"Of course not," said the adjutant. "Of course not." And he too knew that Schulz had spoken completely insincerely.

"If it weren't for this bit in the letter about Bartsch," said Schulz, waving a hand towards the desk, "about Bartsch pacifying the cab-driver, I'd assume that it was Bartsch and Ruhnau who were responsible. It's just the sort of thing they would get up to!"

"Absolutely!" agreed the adjutant. "But it does seem that it's Bartsch we had to thank for preventing a scandal."

Schulz thought for a moment. Then he said: "Our relations with the local party authorities are all right as far as I know?"

"Yes," the adjutant hurriedly assured him. "They're excellent. And the C.O. whose representative you are, is anxious that they should remain so."

Schulz nodded. "Right then," he said. "In that case there are only two possibilities. Either we find the culprits and put them through it. Or we settle the matter out of court, so to speak."

"Of course."

"Go and find Corporal Bartsch for me, will you?"

The adjutant hurried away. Within a relatively short space of time Bartsch, who had been prepared for the summons, was standing in front of his temporary C.O.—of course with his inseparable companion, Ruhnau, by his side. Schulz seemed to take this for granted. It was what he had expected.

He let them both stand at attention in front of him while he looked them up and down in silence. Then he cast a quick glance at the cab-driver's letter and looked the two thugs straight in the eyes.

" I've had about enough of you two," he said.

" Yes, Lieutenant," they both called out together. And whatever Schulz said, they would have continued to agree with him. They knew how to deal with Schulz.

" No punishment would be too bad for you."

" No, Lieutenant."

" But I am again prepared to temper justice with mercy."

" Yes, Lieutenant." A note of relief was plainly audible as the Siamese twins agreed to this with one voice.

" You managed that business with the cab-driver very nicely," said Schulz.

They stared at their inquisitor in astonishment. They had completely misunderstood him. They imagined that he must now know all, and that instead of holding it against them he was taking it as a joke. His sense of humour was well known. They grinned broadly and nudged each other furtively.

" What have you got to grin about, Ruhnau?" asked Schulz, slightly bewildered. " It's got nothing to do with you. As far as I know it was Bartsch alone who pacified the cab-driver."

" Oh, I see," said Bartsch inadvertently.

" What's that?" said Schulz. He was suspicious at once.

" Nothing, Lieutenant. Just . . . just . . . I see," answered Bartsch, giving Ruhnau a nudge in the ribs.

" Now, listen you two, I hope it wasn't you who . . .?"

" But, no, Lieutenant. Certainly not."

" Of course not, Lieutenant. Not us."

Schulz's whole training made him a suspicious man and he missed nothing. His eyes narrowed and he began to think hard.

" We've got an alibi, anyway, Lieutenant," lied Bartsch quickly. " We were playing skat with Vierbein all afternoon."

" Yes, skat," added Ruhnau.

" I didn't know Vierbein played skat?" asked Schulz incredulously.

" Well, he's not much good at it, Lieutenant. We beat him easily in fact. But he's got nothing to spend his money on at the front. We had to help him get rid of it."

Schulz waited a moment or two before saying very emphatically : " Right. For the time being then I'll assume that you're telling the truth. I may even have a few hands of skat with Vierbein myself. But what I'm more interested in at the moment is this: Bartsch, do you think you can square this cab-driver altogether?"

"Easy, Lieutenant," replied Bartsch, very confidently. "I'll fix everything so that the cab-driver feels the whole thing's really been a stroke of luck for him."

"All right, then," said Schulz, trying to conceal the relief he felt. "Within three hours I want to have a report on my desk saying that the matter has been dealt with. Off you go then!"

The Siamese twins shot out feeling greatly relieved.

Schulz nodded to the adjutant and said: "They're a couple of crooks, of course, but quite invaluable. What else is there?"

The adjutant said:

"There's this matter of the C.O.'s father-in-law."

"Right!" said Schulz. And then, as if he had just had a brilliant idea, he cried: "Vierbein!"

"Corporal Vierbein?" queried the adjutant with a certain scepticism. "But do you really think we can, Lieutenant?"

"I can," said Schulz, confidently. "Send for Vierbein, and I'll show you how it's done."

While supposedly searching for Vierbein, the two Siamese twins were doing all they could, by appeals to his honour and a sense of comradeship, to get him to swear that he had been playing skat with them on the previous afternoon. To this Vierbein replied: "But I don't even know how to play!" Lieutenant Schulz meanwhile was giving the adjutant a glimpse of his flair for improvisation.

"Believe me!" cried Schulz, with supreme self-confidence, "there's no situation I can't deal with. You'll see that this fellow Vierbein is just the man we need."

Vierbein, accompanied up to the very door of the troop office by the Siamese twins' appeals for loyalty, reported to the adjutant, who took him in at once to Schulz in the C.O.'s office.

"Now then, you old skat fiend," cried Schulz, overflowing with geniality. "Come over here. Sit down. Go on, Vierbein; that's an order. Sit down. That's it. Well, now, how are things?"

"Herr Lieutenant, this mission of mine . . ."

"Oh, before I forget it, Vierbein," interrupted Schulz affably. "Don't let those two swindlers, Bartsch and Ruhnau, take all your money off you at skat, will you?"

"No, Lieutenant," said Vierbein, relieved that he didn't have to tell a lie. As he didn't play skat it was impossible for anyone to take all this money off him at it.

"But to get down to the point," said Schulz, leaning comfortably back in his chair. He stared amiably at Vierbein. This rather unsettled him. "As you know, my dear fellow, our C.O. is getting married in a few days' time."

"Yes, Lieutenant."

"Good. I shall be needing you for that, Vierbein."

"For the marriage, Lieutenant?"

Schulz thought Vierbein was being funny. He laughed heartily. He loved this sort of joke.

Vierbein blushed scarlet and Schulz laughed all the more at his embarrassment.

"To be serious for a moment, Vierbein! The C.O.'s father-in-law is coming to the wedding. He'll be arriving this evening and staying until the day after the ceremony. Now then, listen to this, my dear fellow. The father-in-law of the C.O. is an Admiral of some sort. I don't know exactly what sort, but he is an Admiral all right. One from the First World War. Do you follow me, Vierbein?"

"Not quite, Lieutenant."

"You, Vierbein, will look after the Admiral. That's it in a nutshell."

"But, Lieutenant, you mean I'm to be his batman?"

"Vierbein," said Schulz, not without a note of severity in his voice, "you seem to have forgotten some of the things I once taught you. The higher ranking the officer, the higher ranking the orderly. Normally you would need to be a sergeant to become the orderly of a full-blown Admiral. Is that clear? I hope you realise the honour I am bestowing on you?"

"Yes, Lieutenant," said Vierbein helplessly. And again he wondered at Schulz's ability always to present his own private views on any situation as if they were incontrovertible facts. "But what about the business I'm here for?"

"We're going ahead with that," said Schulz. "Or did you think it had been forgotten? While you fritter away your afternoons playing skat we're working as hard as we can, you know, supplying the front with men and material. And in order that you should not have to waste your time playing skat, at which, my dear man, you will do nothing but lose your money, I am taking steps to see that the days pass as pleasantly as possible for you."

Vierbein sat humbly on the edge of his chair. It seemed to him quite logical that he should be kept busy. It was just that he didn't quite see why he should be kept busy in the role of batman to an Admiral.

"Or did you expect, Vierbein," added Schulz sinisterly, "that just because you were wearing an Iron Cross First Class, I would kill the fatted calf for you?"

"Of course not, Lieutenant."

Schulz seemed satisfied with this answer. He beckoned to the adjutant who had been hanging about tactfully in the background. The former wine and spirit merchant came over to him at once.

"Herr Admiral Jacoby . . ." he read from a sheet of paper which he had prepared.

"What's his name?" interrupted Schulz, and he put on a very superior tone. "Jacoby? His Christian name's not Nathan by any chance? The man should have had himself re-christened." And he laughed, feeling very pleased with himself. The adjutant laughed, too, but less enthusiastically.

"Well, anyway," he went on, "Herr Admiral Jacoby will be arriving at 17.38. The C.O. and his future bride will meet him at the station. So will Herr Admiral's orderly. Herr Admiral will be staying in the German House. A car will be in attendance."

"And so on and so on!" cried Schulz. "Give Vierbein the sheet, man! The whole thing's his responsibility."

Vierbein obediently took the sheet of paper and put it away in his pocket. He prepared to leave. But Schulz held him back.

"One more point, Vierbein. Do you know how to address an Admiral?"

"As Herr Admiral, Lieutenant."

"Wrong," cried Schulz, enjoying Vierbein's discomfiture. "Absolutely wrong." And the Sergeant-Major in him broke out again. "Officers of the old Imperial Forces are to be addressed as 'Your Excellency.' How are they to be addressed, Vierbein?"

"As 'Your Excellency,' Lieutenant."

"Good," said Schulz, enjoying himself more and more. "You'll need to know that. And now we'll just have a little practice at it, to see that you don't make any mistakes."

Schulz drew himself up to his full height. He stood there like a statue.

"Now then, Vierbein. Just imagine that I am His Excellency, Admiral Jacoby. Can you imagine that?"

"Yes, Lieutenant," said Vierbein, who was beginning to feel rather bewildered.

"Good!" cried Schulz. He looked about him. "Here," he

said, pointing at the strip of carpet by the door, " is the station platform. Go and stand on it, Vierbein."

Vierbein obediently went and took up his position on the carpet.

"Here," said Schulz, who felt himself to be back again training recruits in the happiest days of his life, " here is the train, the express, that is, on which His Excellency, Herr Admiral, is arriving." He pointed at the desk behind which he was standing. "And now, are you ready, Vierbein? Here comes the train, there's Herr Admiral looking out of the window, you've recognised him . . ."

"If I might make a suggestion," broke in the adjutant, "it's more than likely that Herr Admiral will not be wearing uniform but civilian clothes. . . ."

"Well, what about it?" yelled Schulz, very much put out by the interruption. "Uniform or no uniform, he's still an Admiral isn't he? And is to be addressed as such. That's perfectly clear, isn't it? Or do you imagine that people dare to address me as Herr Schulz when I'm in my bathing shorts?"

The adjutant said no more. He wanted to say that it wasn't the form of address with which he was concerned, but the problem of recognition, but he saw that it would not be wise to interrupt Schulz a second time.

Schulz now returned to his theme.

"Right, Vierbein: now there you are on the platform; here's the train; there's the Admiral at the window. . . . What do you do?"

"I go up to the Admiral and . . ."

"My God, Vierbein! Look here—here!—is the platform and here am I, the Admiral, leaning out of the window. Now then . . ."

"I report to him . . ."

"Report then, man!"

Vierbein stood to attention in the middle of the carpet, looked meekly up at Schulz and bellowed: "Corporal Vierbein detailed to His Excellency as orderly."

"Go on, Vierbein."

"Corporal Vierbein begs to request His Excellency's suitcase."

"That's it, man," cried Schulz with satisfaction. "That's the way. 'His Excellency' all the time. Plenty of volume. That'll impress the old boy. We'll show the Navy that the Army knows its stuff all right."

Then he took pity on Vierbein and dismissed him, not without once again reminding the astonished adjutant:

"Trained in my school, you see, my dear fellow! A man like Vierbein doesn't forget it so easily. When I remember what he used to be like . . ."

Corporal Vierbein was still feeling rather dazed when he walked out of the battery office. The Siamese twins were waiting for him.

"Well, how did you get on?" asked Bartsch, simply bursting with anxiety.

"Everything all right?" asked Ruhnau tensely.

Vierbein was still deep in thought about His Excellency the Admiral and ignored the two creatures altogether. They followed him a little way along the passage still trying to get information from him. Then they were brought up short by the thought that perhaps things weren't as bright as they had imagined.

"If this fellow has gone and double-crossed us," said Bartsch, menacingly, "we'll give him something to think about. We'll make his experiences at the front seem like a holiday treat."

"The best way to do it," said Ruhnau, "would be to tell Schulz that Vierbein had been tampering with his honour."

"Lore, you mean? But what if it goes wrong?"

"It mustn't go wrong."

"But if it does?"

"Then all three of us will be off to the front together. But at least we'll have had a bit of fun first."

"Be careful, man, for God's sake! Or the laugh may be on us."

The barn which Asch had selected for the Four Penguins' performance in No. 3 Troop's sector contained plenty of space. Its one drawback was that it also contained the greater part of Soeft's supplies, and was where he parked his lorries. However, in return for a concession by which he was to be responsible for the building and general supervision of the ladies' lavatories and dressing-rooms, he eventually agreed to give permission for it to be used.

"We're all ready," Asch was able to report to Witterer that afternoon. "The performance can take place to-morrow evening at eight o'clock."

Witterer nodded. "Quite good, Asch," he said. "There's

nothing more we can do now. The final decision as to whether the barn is suitable or not must, of course, rest with the performers themselves."

"I've taken the trouble to ascertain their requirements, Captain. I think I can say I know what would suit them."

"That may be, Asch. That may well be. But I would nevertheless prefer it if a member of the troupe, Fräulein Ebner, for instance, were to come and look over our arrangements first. I suggest therefore that you go and invite the lady to come out here this afternoon. I'd go myself only I'm waiting for an important telephone call."

"I don't really think it's necessary, Captain."

Witterer ignored the remark.

"You can take my car, Asch, for this once, and get Kowalski to drive you to the main base. It's just after three now—I'll expect you back here at five with Fräulein Ebner."

Asch found Kowalski hanging round the field kitchen, as usual. He refused to move at first, but when he heard what their destination was, he changed his attitude at once. Five minutes later the two of them were hurtling along through the dirty snow at a great pace.

Lisa Ebner was lying on her camp-bed reading when Sergeant Asch came into the room. She sat up, pushed the book to one side and smiled up at him.

"What an honour!" she said playfully.

Asch shook hands with her without waiting to be asked, sat down beside her on the camp-bed. She stared at him in amazement but didn't move to one side. Her lips parted a little in curiosity.

"And what do you want with me, Sergeant, may I ask?"

As he didn't reply, she said softly:

"Well, I'm waiting, Sergeant."

"What for?"

"For something. For a kiss perhaps?"

"And what would you do if I gave you one?"

"I don't know. Better try and see."

"I'm not a guinea-pig," said Asch, brusquely. "Not for *you* to experiment on anyway."

"But I like guinea-pigs. I'm very fond of animals, you know."

Asch sat up. He was determined to put an end to this little romance.

"Now just listen," he said slowly.

"Yes?"

Asch shook his head crossly, like a horse whose nose-bag is slung too low.

"Look here, Lisa," he said. "I've come on business. I'm to take you out to Captain Witterer. Officially, so that you can approve the preparations we've made for the concert."

"And unofficially?"

"You know perfectly well! Anyway, I've been to see you and I've carried out my order. Now I can go again."

"Without me?"

"Of course. You refused to come. You refused to accept the invitation. For obvious reasons."

"And what are these reasons, may I ask?" asked Lisa.

Asch stood up abruptly.

"Are you really pretending you don't know? You don't want to play with fire, my girl, do you?"

"Well, sometimes I do feel rather cold," said Lisa Ebner flirtatiously.

Asch went over to the window and stood there with his back to it. He didn't want Lisa Ebner to be able to see his face too well and he wanted to see her with the light full on her. He looked round the primitive little room. There was a smell of scent. "You're too young," he said. "You're only a child still."

"And you—you're not exactly an old man!"

"You're much too good for this sort of thing."

Lisa Ebner sat up. She shifted the weight of the upper part of her body on to her two arms which she pushed out behind her. Her mouth was slightly open and her teeth were just visible. She smiled.

"Are you in love with me?" she asked tenderly.

"What *are* you talking about, child," said Asch abruptly. "I'm merely looking after your interests. I don't want to see you go to the dogs here."

"And what if I'm in love with you?" asked Lisa. She was at the end of her tether.

"Then try and prove it to me."

"How?"

"How? By staying here, locking the door of your room and writing to your mother."

"And what do I get for doing that?"

"No premature lines on your face. A virgin body and a clear conscience."

Lisa Ebner slowly sank back on to the pillows until she was lying full length again. She relaxed and took a deep breath. Her firm little breasts rose and sank regularly. Asch stared at her as if hypnotised. When she noticed this her smile grew wider.

There was a loud knocking at the door and Kowalski came gaily into the room. Charlotte, thé girl who acted as compère to the little troupe, was standing just behind him. Lisa didn't alter her position at all. Asch looked rather confused.

"We're off!" cried Kowalski. "I've taken the liberty of engaging a chaperon." And he winked roguishly at Charlotte.

"I don't think it would be a very good thing if you went alone," said Charlotte to Lisa.

"It's never a good thing for a human being to be alone," cried Kowalski, who was in the best of moods.

"Fräulein Ebner isn't going at all," explained Asch.

"What's that?" cried Kowalski. "Is she not only a singer of respectable songs but a spoil-sport as well?"

"Aren't you really coming?" Charlotte asked her colleague curiously.

"She doesn't want to," said Asch. "And I can well understand it."

Lisa Ebner didn't move. She kept on looking straight at Asch and her pretty, rather hungry eyes seemed to grow larger and larger. And still she said nothing.

"To hell with it!" cried Kowalski. "What's going on here? Has the lady lost the power of speech?"

"I've said what she's got to say, for her, Kowalski."

"That's just like you, Asch! So you want to spoil an old soldier's fun, eh?"

"Herr Kowalski," said Charlotte, smiling. "What do you mean by fun exactly? I hope it hasn't got anything to do with me by any chance?"

"What an idea!" cried Kowalski innocently.

Then he went over to Asch, who was still standing by the window, and began to try and persuade him: "You can't leave me in the lurch like this, old man. You've no idea how long it took to talk her round. Angels' tongues weren't in it. And I've made a pretty powerful impression, man! I've become quite a cavalier. And now you want to mess the whole thing up? Asch, if you really were a friend of mine . . ."

"How much longer is this little business going on, I'd like to know," said Charlotte grimly. "Aren't you really coming then, Lisa?"

147

Lisa still kept on looking at Asch but this time she said quite clearly: "No."

"Right," said Charlotte. "Then neither am I."

"Damnation!" cried Kowalski, in a fury, pulling his cap off and throwing it to the ground. "It's pure sabotage! You're sabotaging Captain Witterer's orders, Asch. I hope you realise that. Normally I wouldn't care a damn but this time I must say it's a bit too much. For the last time I'm asking you. . . ."

"Is he always like this?" asked Charlotte ironically.

"Only when he's in love," said Asch.

Lieutenant Wedelmann turned his back on the uneasy atmosphere that was developing in his sector and went to see Natasha. He couldn't bear the hours of useless waiting, just sitting about in his hut with nothing to do while the storm gathered force around him.

Natasha was as pleased to see him as ever. Perhaps even more so than ever. He accepted the inevitable cup of tea, said how good it was, although it was almost undrinkable—very low-grade tea, over which, however, a great deal of trouble had been taken. Then they looked at each other for a long time, rather sadly, rather tenderly, rather dreamily.

"I suppose everything'll be starting up again soon," said Natasha, looking thoughtfully at the tea steaming gently in her cup.

"War never dies down really: it just stops for breath now and again."

"It's a pity," said Natasha, and it was as if she were speaking of the weather, "that it doesn't give us longer to get *our* breath back."

"You shouldn't bother your head with such things, Natalie."

"You can call me Natasha if you like."

"Thank you, Natasha."

"You're trying to reassure me, I know. Men like doing that. They think reassurance is what women want. But it isn't. We just want to know the truth. We're not really the weaker sex, you know."

"Truth? What is truth? How do you expect me to know? I can't see any further ahead than from one day to the next. I feel more and more like a sort of football—a feather blown here and there—a grain of sand."

Natasha slowly shook her head. "Now I think you're underestimating yourself. One determined individual can do more than a whole crowd who don't care what happens to them."

"Are you trying to give me courage, Natasha? To convince me of something? But what? And why?"

"I'm just thinking, that's all. Putting two and two together. For some days now there've been rumours that the front is on the move. It's not just machine-guns that are firing now but mortars and artillery. I don't like it."

"How is it you know the difference between mortars and artillery?" asked Wedelmann, surprised. "You might be a soldier the way you talk."

Natasha flushed slightly and Wedelmann found this charming.

"One learns these things in war-time," she said. "I was a student before the war. I wanted to be a teacher. But the war was my university. And I learnt how to steal potatoes, make tea from herbs, milk cows and tell the difference between mortars and artillery."

"Anyway," said Wedelmann, who felt a little confused by Natasha's ready answers, not least because they seemed to conflict with her essentially feminine character, "anyway, you mustn't be alarmed. That disturbance yesterday seems to have been caused by a misunderstanding. The real reason seems to have been that someone got a little above himself."

"Do you know that, or is it just what you think?"

"It so happens that I know it. But why are we talking about these things? There are other things to talk about, aren't there?"

"Such as?"

"Love, for instance."

"Love in war-time! What do you mean? Have you got someone you love—back in Germany?"

"No."

"You don't expect me to believe that?"

"You must believe it. I haven't got anyone. With us, you know, to become an officer is to cut oneself off from whole sections of society. And the rest are just there to be married into. But what is to happen if one can't find anyone one wants to marry?"

"Do you really want to marry then?"

"But, yes! You know, Natasha, to have a woman who belongs to one, and a child who looks up to one, and a little house of one's own—that's really living."

"And have you never found anyone you wanted to marry?" asked Natasha, softly. Her eyes flashed darkly.

Wedelmann stretched his legs out comfortably. He felt snug and secure in the warm little room. The trouble that was brewing up between the lines seemed a thousand miles away. He felt the whole of his body slowly relaxing, from the soles of his feet to the muscles in his neck.

"Yes," he said. "There was a woman I would have liked to marry. In fact, there were two. One was a girl who served in our N.C.O.'s canteen in the barracks—she had a warm heart and a cool head. She married a man who's now one of my Sergeants. They've got a child and are as happy as one possibly can be in the circumstances. And they deserve their happiness."

"And the other one?"

"The other one? That was a strange business—her name was Lore. A sort of dead-end kid—if you know what that is, Natasha. At first I just felt sorry for her—she was unhappily married you see. But then I grew to like her more and more. She had an almost childish appetite for life. And, in addition, she had a happy disposition. Of course she could be like a wild animal too: a wild cat, you might say."

"She sounds charming, I must say," said Natasha, with some force.

Wedelmann ignored the touch of jealousy. "But let's not talk about all that," he said. "It doesn't get us anywhere. And I won't ask you about the men in your life either."

"I don't mind what you ask," said Natasha and her voice sounded hard. "I was engaged. The man I loved was killed. Right at the beginning of the war. Perhaps it was you who killed him."

"It's possible," said Wedelmann, staring at her as if she were a complete stranger. "Anything is possible."

"Not anything," said Natasha, no less stiffly than before. "For instance, I could never love the man who killed my lover."

Wedelmann said nothing. He put his cup down abruptly so that it rattled in the saucer. Natasha also fell silent. She looked down to the end of the bed where the Lieutenant was sitting rather awkwardly. And it was as if she could see right through the bed to the box with the transmitter in it which lay beneath. And the knowledge that it was there gave her confidence. She had to force herself to look away.

That was really the end of their conversation. Wedelmann made several attempts to say good-bye but at the last moment always put it off. Natasha, too, was quite determined to let him go if he wanted to but, at the same time, seemed unwilling to admit that their rather painful conversation was at an end. They were both relieved when Asch came to take Wedelmann away.

"Sorry, Lieutenant. But Colonel Luschke's just rung up. . . ."

"Oh, all right. . . . Please excuse me."

"Of course," said Natasha.

She shook hands with him politely but wouldn't look at him. They said no more to each other. Natasha went in front and opened the door for them without a word.

"A bit cool, eh?" said Asch as they went down the steps.

"If you mean the weather," said Wedelmann, "then I agree with you."

"Yes, the weather's cool, too," said Asch. "There's still a lot of snow to come."

"And did you say the Colonel had rung up?" asked Wedelmann as soon as they were in the street. "What business is that of mine? Captain Witterer is the C.O. now."

"Colonel Luschke expressly asked for you, Lieutenant. He's coming straight up to the gun positions."

"Such sudden interest makes me suspicious," said Wedelmann, jumping over a puddle of slush.

"I can't say I'm surprised after what's happened," replied Asch.

When they arrived at forward base they saw the regimental commander's car already parked there. Colonel Luschke himself was standing by a pile of wood relieving himself. Captain Witterer, with Corporal Krause in attendance, remained at a respectful distance. Luschke stumped over towards them, adjusting his dress as he did so. Witterer and Krause sprang to attention and saluted. The Colonel nodded grimly. "If you were as good at fighting a war as you are at clicking your heels," he said, "I wouldn't have to leave my stove."

"Quite, Colonel," said Captain Witterer, who felt, not without justification, that the remark had been directed primarily at him.

Luschke had pulled his dirty, crumpled cap well forward over his eyes. Suddenly he turned his great potato nose menacingly at the new-comers.

"You're pretty late, Lieutenant," said Luschke. "Did they have to search for you? But if you were with a girl, Wedelmann, then I'll forgive you."

"In that case I'm forgiven, Colonel."

"With pleasure," said Luschke with a grin.

Then the Colonel turned to Witterer.

"Captain," he said. "You must know that I have considerable understanding for human weakness. It's the would-be saints who get on my nerves—almost as much as the swine."

"Very understandable, Colonel," said Witterer.

"I mean, if someone doesn't drink, it makes me suspicious. Of course, a real soak won't last long in my regiment. But I see nothing wrong in a glass or two now and again. Same with girls."

"I entirely agree with you, Colonel," said Witterer.

The Colonel raised his eyebrows.

"I dare say we agree where little girls are concerned. But when it comes to warfare, my good sir, our attitudes seem to be very different. Very different, indeed."

Witterer swallowed this reproach with a good grace, a feat which was made easier for him by Luschke turning abruptly away and marching off with short, determined steps towards the guns. The others started after him at once.

"The map," said Luschke, curtly.

Captain Witterer hurried forward proffering his map to the regimental commander. Luschke quickly found his position on it without slacking pace. He was heading for No. 2 gun.

"Oh, please take cover, sir," cried Witterer.

The Colonel ignored the remark. He took up his position on a little hill just beyond the gun, about ten yards nearer the enemy lines. His entourage had no alternative but to follow him.

Luschke stared out towards the enemy. Then he looked at the map. Then he said: "Captain Witterer, have you any idea of the effects of your little game yesterday afternoon?"

"No, Colonel," said the Captain, truthfully enough. He noted the Colonel's use of the word "effects" with a certain cautious optimism. Effectiveness counted for a good deal in Witterer's vocabulary.

"I have had a report," said Luschke, without taking his eyes off the enemy lines, "that the enemy brought up artillery during the night."

"That was to be expected," said Asch. "Is it known how much?"

"No," said Luschke. "The enemy was not so obliging as to tell us."

"We could try and find out, Colonel," suggested Captain Witterer with praiseworthy keenness.

"And how, may I ask, Captain?" asked Luschke with some interest, though he still did not turn round.

"We could send a patrol over, Colonel."

Luschke stood motionless on his little hill. He seemed to pull his head down into his narrow shoulders for a moment and listen. There was the sudden sound of something rushing through the air over their heads, followed by a dull thump in the earth behind them. Then some metal splinters came whistling shrilly past them.

Witterer had ducked and was on the point of throwing himself flat on his face. His knees were slightly bent and his shoulders were hunched. He looked rather as if he were just about to sit down on a lavatory seat.

"Are you leaving us, Captain?" asked Wedelmann, barely audibly.

Luschke stood there quite motionless. He might have been a tree.

"Mortar—medium calibre," said Asch, calmly. Then he turned round, walked slowly back ten yards or so and disappeared into a slit trench.

A second shell followed immediately afterwards and was again too short. Luschke turned round and stared at his entourage in silence. Witterer was now standing stiffly to attention; Krause's attitude was equally exemplary beside him. Wedelmann looked utterly disinterested.

Luschke looked past them to the slit trench out of which Asch was now poking his head. A broad grin spread over the Colonel's face. Then without any change in his expression, he looked at Witterer.

Witterer seemed to regard this as some sort of challenge to his qualities of leadership.

"Sergeant Asch," he cried. "I gave no order to take cover."

"It wasn't necessary," answered Asch. "We don't need orders for that sort of thing."

"Kindly follow our example in future, Asch."

"But why?" Asch called back genially. "It seems to me that you're setting anything but a good example."

"But, you dare to . . ." Witterer looked at Luschke who still had a broad grin on his face, and then across to Wedelmann who stood there motionless. "What do you say to that, Lieutenant?"

"I quite agree with Asch," Wedelmann answered, leaving the group and getting into the slit trench just as the third shell burst close by.

Luschke laughed shrilly and Witterer had the uncomfortable feeling that "Lumpface" was laughing at him.

"God, what a crew!" cried the Colonel, in the best of humour. Then he strode quickly over to the slit trench and disappeared into it.

For a second or two Witterer and Krause stood there forlorn and helpless. Then they, too, hurried to follow their superior officer's example. The fourth shell burst dangerously close. It accelerated their progress. They dived practically head first into the slit trench, which was now full to capacity.

"Athletic as ever," cried Luschke, quietly.

Witterer's steel helmet had slipped sideways and he now straightened it under the critical eye of the Colonel.

"Your belt, too, Captain," said Asch, helpfully.

Witterer pulled his belt straight. The buckle had slipped round over the left-hand pocket of his tunic.

"What were you saying just now, Captain," asked Luschke, with sinister affability. "Something about sending out a patrol?"

"Always provided the Colonel agrees."

"Naturally," said Luschke. "And who would you suggest to lead this patrol? Not yourself, surely?"

"Perhaps an experienced N.C.O., Colonel?"

"For example?"

"Sergeant Asch for example."

"I'm not volunteering," said Sergeant Asch, firmly.

"And why not?" asked Luschke, curiously.

"I'm no celluloid hero," said the Sergeant.

Luschke grinned more broadly than ever.

"And neither am I," he said.

Admiral Jacoby—addressable as Your Excellency, father-in-law of the Commanding Officer of the Reserve Artillery Battery, the man to whom Vierbein had been detailed to act as orderly—turned out to be a most sympathetic man. For Admiral Jacoby in the course of more than two decades had lost the habits of service life and relaxed all sense of discipline, and now fully appreciated the pleasures of being human.

When after saying good-bye to his daughter—who was by no means as young as she might have been—and his future son-in-law, he arrived back at his hotel, he found himself alone with Vierbein. He at once showed himself to be thoroughly reasonable.

"Don't bother about that, my dear fellow," he called out jovially, as Vierbein began unpacking his trunk. This was one of the duties expressly laid down for orderlies in Wehrmacht regulations. "Or do you think I'm too old to do it myself?"

"Oh, no, Your Excellency," cried Vierbein gallantly.

"And you can drop the 'Your Excellency' when we're alone together."

"Very good, Your Excellency."

"It isn't usual among war-time comrades."

Vierbein snapped open the catch of the trunk as a proof of his comradely feelings and at once proceeded to unpack. Admiral Jacoby insisted on lending him a hand. A quarter of an hour later they were polishing up the Admiral's medals together. There could be absolutely no doubt about their being comrades."

"Quite a collection, eh?" said His Excellency, running his finger along the row of medals as if they were the keys of a xylophone. "When you become an Admiral you get this sort of stuff by every post. Of course, some of them are different. This one for instance now—I got that from His Majesty himself."

"Did Your Excellency know His Majesty?"

The Admiral, who had arrived wearing a civilian suit—a navy blue one naturally enough—but had brought full-dress uniform with him in a special trunk, had now slipped on a comfortable smoking-jacket. He looked around for his slippers, and Vierbein, attentive as ever, brought them over to him.

"His Majesty and I," said His Excellency, putting on the slippers, "used to get on very well together, if I may use such a bold expression. His Majesty was gracious enough to consult me from time to time about various naval problems that arose and I think I may say His Majesty came to value my advice almost as much as that of the Admiral of the Fleet himself."

Corporal Vierbein was amazed. The grey-haired old man with the lined, weather-beaten face, a really tough-looking old salt, was a man straight out of German legend and thus a man after Vierbein's boyish heart. And it was a matter of astonishment to him that such a great commander could be so friendly.

His Imperial Majesty's Admiral asked about Vierbein's own

decorations and then suggested that they should take a little glass of something together.

Vierbein knew that Ingrid Asch was waiting for him and he tried to think of some excuse.

"It's very good of Your Excellency, but we have to be back in barracks by . . ."

"Don't worry about that, my dear fellow. So long as I'm here you're under my personal protection. If you're late, or want to get off early or anything like that, you've only got to say: 'Admiral's orders' and I'll cover up for you! We're comrades, remember, we've got to stick together!"

The Admiral rang for the waiter.

"Three carafes and two glasses!" he ordered. "We'll be drinking 'church windows'."

"Church windows, sir?" asked the astonished waiter.

"You haven't been to sea, apparently! Not served with the Navy, eh? Not even as a steward? Never been hunting in East Prussia either?"

The waiter shook his head.

"You surprise me," said the Admiral, staring fixedly at the pale, gaunt figure of the waiter—a typical civilian.

"Well, then: 'Church windows' are made of equal quantities of rum, arrack and red wine. The three colours suggest stained-glass; hence the expression 'Church windows'."

"Very good, Your Excellency," said the waiter obediently and immediately disappeared. He returned a short while later with three full carafes, ready to carry out the Admiral's slightest—his very slightest—wish.

Corporal Vierbein managed to avoid looking at his watch. He felt very flattered by the Admiral's goodwill towards him and didn't want to disappoint the old gentleman. Ingrid would have to wait. He was sacrificing himself in the course of his duty and he had no doubt that his decision was the right one. Besides, he was grateful. He had expected his new master to be aloof and almost inhuman. Instead, he found him genial and fatherly.

Admiral Jacoby, in his turn, enjoyed the unqualified respect with which Vierbein treated him. He had always got on well with the lower deck and this sort of jovial good-fellowship was just what he had missed so badly in all the long years which had followed his pensioning-off after World War I.

"I have written my memoirs, you know," he said, "*War and Peace*. But, of course, there could be no question of them appearing while His Majesty was still alive."

During the shameful episode of the Weimar Republic he had spent his time planting cabbages—in Pomerania, never very far from the sea, and because he wanted to keep himself in good shape, he had taken an interest in a firm which transported sugar-beet, a firm, needless to say, which operated a fleet of steamers. The coming of the Third Reich—the head of which held a distressingly low military rank—brought a return of the good old days when he could put on his full-dress uniform with all its trappings.

"The present Supreme Commander," said Admiral Jacoby, "cannot unfortunately be compared with His Imperial Majesty—though I'm not, of course, saying anything against him. All I will say is this: that His Majesty always wore naval uniform for preference."

Vierbein maintained a respectful silence and drank up his drink bravely, in a series of little sips. The Admiral mixed a fourth " church window " and held it up to the light where it glowed richly. He then swallowed it down with considerable relish. A bold flush spread over his weather-beaten face. It was easy to imagine him on the bridge of his ship leading a fleet into action.

" I've nothing against this war," said His Excellency, " even though I'm not entirely happy about it."

Vierbein waited breathless for some astonishing revelation. His Majesty's personal adviser was about to give to a mere Corporal of the German Armed Forces—of the Army too— the benefit of his wisdom on world affairs.

" They're not concentrating enough on sea power," he said. " It could have unfortunate results. On the whole, though, this war has had the effect of bringing all the national elements together. And I must say that up to now our achievements have been thoroughly respectable."

And he looked into his glass with a slow, far-away smile. Yes, apart from the unaccountable neglect of the Navy, he had nothing to complain of. Even the feeblest specimens of the race were beginning to bestir themselves. His daughter, for example. She had been sitting at home vainly hoping for something to happen to her for years now: then along came the war; she joined up and before she knew where she was she found herself marrying a Commanding Officer. Not perhaps the very finest type of Commanding Officer—he was only a reservist after all—but a Commanding Officer all the same. " There's no knowing what a war like this may not lead to," he said.

After the fifth " church window " the Admiral's comrade,

Vierbein, was allowed to take his leave. He was to come back at about ten o'clock the next morning. Without cleaning materials. He might try and find a tailor who would press the Admiral's uniform, though.

Corporal Vierbein, rather the worse for the Admiral's hospitality, was swaying slightly as he executed his farewell salute. He wanted to go and see Ingrid Asch, but the hellish mixture of rum, arrack and red wine had such a powerful effect on him that he had to lean against a wall for support.

He felt weak at the knees and his head seemed the size of a pumpkin. He went straight to the barracks, threw himself down on his bed, and fell at once into a heavy sleep. For several hours Vierbein was oblivious of everything: of the vicissitudes of war, of the uneasiness of the home front, of the need for a girl, the goodness of Admirals and the unexpectedly potent qualities of "church windows".

When he woke up it was already broad daylight. The orderly Corporal was standing over him with a conspiratorial grin. He bent down and whispered: "Don't be a spoil-sport. Schulz would never forgive you."

Vierbein sat up at once and immediately felt an excruciating pain in the back of his head. He had a hang-over. His mouth was dry and his eyes didn't seem to be functioning properly. It took some time for him to realise what was going on in the room.

"I've taken the looking-glass down," said the orderly Corporal.

And with an effort Vierbein saw that Corporal Ruhnau was lying in bed with his face painted pitch black. The same was true of Corporal Bartsch. Both their faces had been thickly coated with boot polish.

"It's a splendid joke," whispered the orderly Corporal, nudging Vierbein in the ribs. "We painted them up last night when they were dead drunk. They'd been trying to break in on Lore Schulz. And the best part of it is that each will think that it's only the other whose face has been blacked."

Vierbein shook himself. He still could hardly grasp what was going on. His skull felt as if it were about to burst. Then he looked at the blackened faces of the two "blockade breakers" and found that the situation had certain elements of comedy.

"Schulz is waiting outside in the corridor with some friends of his," said the orderly Corporal. "And the curtain's just about to go up. And in case you should think of putting them wise, remember that Schulz wouldn't think that at all funny."

Vierbein just managed to get out of bed and drag himself over to the wash-basin. There he put his head under water. Several times. And gingerly he began to feel his skull.

In the meantime the orderly Corporal went over to the door and flung it open. Lieutenant Schulz was standing outside with his entourage. He nodded eagerly.

The orderly Corporal put his whistle to his mouth and blew it with all his might.

"Alarm!" he shouted. "Alarm!"

The "marauders'" beds lay side by side. Both men leapt into the air simultaneously, jerked their eyes open and stared at each other in astonishment. Their mouths also opened. And suddenly they took in what had happened during the night. And they both burst into a roar of laughter.

"Alarm!" yelled the orderly Corporal.

The "night fighters" continued to bellow with laughter. And each of them was convinced that he alone had cause for laughter. Each thought that it was only the other whose face had been painted black.

"Didn't you hear? Alarm, you oafs!" shouted Schulz by way of encouragement. "Come on now, look lively!" And his little pig's eyes sparkled with delight.

The two Corporals, swaying slightly, pushed themselves somehow into their clothes, snatched down their steel helmets and staggered out of the room. Schulz and his companions were practically choking with laughter. The battery adjutant, purple in the face, took the liberty of nudging Schulz in the ribs, an action which Schulz affected to ignore. Vierbein, standing in the background, slowly shook his head.

There was a sudden roar of laughter in the corridor outside. Several dozen other ranks were standing round the two black-faced Corporals, on whom the truth was slowly beginning to dawn. They rushed over to the looking-glass which hung near the hall-door and stared into it in utter amazement. Then, swearing furiously, they rushed back into their room again followed by a storm of laughter.

There, wild with rage at being made such fools of, they found themselves suddenly confronted by Schulz. Their jet-black faces were positively distorted with fury. And each felt an overpowering urge to spring straight at Schulz's throat. But mad as they were, they weren't quite as mad as all that.

Schulz was gasping for breath. He wiped a tear from his

left eye. He hadn't laughed so much for years. This was really what he called a joke, a real man's joke—soldier's humour at its very best.

Then, with lightning transition, he was suddenly deadly serious. He made a sign to his entourage and they withdrew at once. He fixed the two "thousand pounders" straight in the eye.

"That's what comes," he said, in an ominously quiet voice, "of trying to put your dirty paws on women who don't belong to you."

"But it was a mistake," said Bartsch, grovelling. "We went to the wrong door."

"We promise it won't happen again," said Ruhnau.

"And what about the bottle of schnaps you were trying to get from my wife?"

"But that was for you, Lieutenant."

"We were only thinking of you, Lieutenant."

"What bottle of schnaps was it, you miserable worms?"

They stood there dumbfounded, black in the face, looking suddenly utterly wretched.

"Come on, out with it!"

And as Schulz still got no reply from them, he added: "All right, if you don't feel like talking to me, I'll find you another troop commander to talk to—quite some distance away from here."

The Siamese twins seemed to turn pale beneath their coating of boot polish. They stood there wild-eyed, rooted to the spot. Then one of them gave the other a violent nudge.

And Bartsch said: "It's the bottle Vierbein brought your wife."

For a few seconds Schulz stood there absolutely motionless. He had thrust his chin forward and his hands hung down loosely at his sides. Then he turned smartly about with almost faultless precision, and stormed out of the room.

"You dirty swine," said Vierbein, in disgust.

Bartsch slowly shrugged his shoulders. "You can't blame us, man. Our lives were at stake."

"Yes," said Ruhnau, nodding portentously. "There is a war on, you know."

"You've got nothing to lose, man. You're going back to the front anyway. It's quite different for us."

"Do you see that, or don't you? You don't see it? Where's all this front-line comradeship they talk so much about?"

"Oh, to hell with both of you," said Vierbein with un-accustomed sharpness.

"What manners!" said Bartsch.

"And that's the sort of creature whom we've got defending the Fatherland!"

The two "mine-sweepers" began scrubbing the boot polish off each other's faces. For this they used turpentine and soap, scrubbing-brushes and saucepan scourers. When that was no use they tried petrol.

After an hour of this the orderly Corporal reappeared, grinned at the two "washerwomen" as he called them, and said to Vierbein:

"You're to come to Lieutenant Schulz at once."

Vierbein nodded. It was what he had been expecting. He was ready for it. And he was determined to stand up to what-ever was in store for him like a man, and not to let himself be bullied. After all, he had a job to do.

Schulz was waiting for him, enthroned behind the desk which had once been Luschke's.

"Vierbein," he said, in a surprisingly matter-of-fact tone, "you will be taking part in to-day's preparations for to-morrow's artillery display."

"I'm very sorry, Lieutenant," said Vierbein, correctly, "but His Excellency the Admiral has ordered me to attend him."

"But we need you here, Vierbein."

"I don't know whether His Excellency the Admiral . . ."

"I'll allot someone else to him. Either Bartsch or Ruhnau. Both perhaps."

"But His Excellency the Admiral expressly ordered me to be there at ten sharp to-day."

"All right then, Vierbein. I suppose you'd better go. But I want to see you at the preparations for the artillery display this afternoon. It'll do you nothing but good. And, besides, it's what you're here for, in a way. We'll be testing the radio equip-ment which Colonel Luschke has asked for."

"Very good, Lieutenant."

"And perhaps to-morrow you can take over a gun yourself at the display. We'll be firing at dummy tanks. The General will be there. And you can show him how it's done."

Vierbein understood what had happened. Within the last half-hour or so the General must have suddenly announced his intention of attending the display. Schulz, as deputy C.O., saw this as his great chance. And Vierbein, whose skill as an artilleryman most fortunately happened to be at his disposal, should lend him a hand. Yes, Vierbein saw what was going on all right. His long association with Asch was beginning to put even him wise to this sort of thing.

" As far as the other matter's concerned," said Schulz slowly, turning a paper-weight round and round in his fingers, " I find it impossible to believe that such a distinguished soldier as yourself, Vierbein, would be so foolish as to play with fire in that way."

Schulz fell silent. And Vierbein astonishingly also said nothing. Each waited for the other to speak, and each waited in vain.

The silence in the room was complete. Then the sounds of the barrack began to penetrate it: the singing of marching songs and the shouting of orders. They were almost indistinguishable. The Lieutenant got up and shut the window himself, with a powerful heave.

Then he spoke:

" Vierbein," he said, " you now have a chance to show me that you're a real soldier at last. I shall be delighted if you succeed in doing so."

The Colonel was standing in the church with his legs planted rather wide apart, his body bent slightly forward. It was as if he were leaning against some invisible railing. He was standing where the altar had once been. A hissing acetylene lamp had now taken its place.

Luschke stared at the white heat biting its way into a sheet of iron. The soldier with the thick goggles over his eyes worked away with great concentration. The presence of his Commanding Officer had speeded his work up considerably.

The main body of the building was packed with vehicles and every sort of mobile piece of machinery. Captain Witterer made his way towards his Colonel with his usual springy stride. He came to attention a little to one side of the Colonel—the man with the acetylene lamp was directly in front of him—and brought his hand up smartly to the peak of his cap.

" Captain Witterer reporting."

Luschke touched the side of his forehead with the tips of two fingers and continued to stare at the shower of sparks. Secretly he regretted that his men were using this place as a repair shop. He knew that they cursed him for coming here so often. His presence automatically meant that they had to work harder. But this was one of the places he enjoyed visiting most.

"Captain Witterer reporting!" repeated the new C.O. of No. 3 Troop.

"You don't suppose I'm deaf, do you?" said Luschke, without looking up.

Witterer hastened to deny this. He stood there at attention for a little longer, then surreptitiously transferred to the at-ease position and waited.

An almost imperceptible smile crossed Luschke's face as he stood there contemplating the spurting flame. His men couldn't possibly know what brought him here so often. And it was a good thing that they didn't. For, in fact, he didn't come on their account at all. He came here drawn by the magic of the old ruined church. There was about it something of the vastness and stillness of the landscape in which it stood, this landscape that now lay scarred and furrowed and trampled by death.

The Colonel slowly raised his head. It was as if he were beginning to be aware of the men around him. None of them dared look at him. All bent industriously over their work. Witterer felt it necessary to come to attention again.

But Luschke's eyes went up to the walls and along them to where the great windowless gaps reached up towards the sad open sky. It seemed to him that the hands of some giant corpse were reaching up to God for mercy—all in vain.

Then he turned sharply round, took two short paces towards Witterer and said:

"How long do you need to get your troop ready to move?"

"Forty-two minutes," answered Witterer promptly.

"How do you know that so exactly?"

"We've practised it, Colonel. Only three days ago it took the troop nearly an hour. Yesterday we did it in forty-two minutes dead. But I want to get it down to thirty minutes."

"And are you quite certain, Captain Witterer, that your men aren't making a fool of you?"

"Quite certain, Colonel. The reports which have come in . . ."

"Have been checked by you?"

"Partly, yes, Colonel."

"Partly, eh?" Luschke gave a short, satisfied laugh. "It'll take you a long time before you're wise to all their little tricks, Witterer. That fellow of yours, Soeft, for example. Why, he needs an entire convoy to get his stuff away!"

"But Corporal Soeft reported that his section was ready to move in twenty-five minutes. Both to me and the Sergeant-Major."

"All right, then," said Luschke sourly. "And I suppose you'll have it down to ten minutes before long. However that may be, you try and get your outfit ready for the road within two or three hours and you'll be doing all right. It's always a difficult business getting going again after a long lull like this. Of course, once the wheels of war start turning, then the difficulty is to try and get them to stop."

"Yes, Colonel," said Witterer, hoping to convey that he had understood all the implications of his Commanding Officer's remarks.

The Colonel turned round and went over to a pillar in a corner at the back of the church. Witterer trotted after him obediently.

"Captain," said Luschke when they got there, "you and your troop will get yourselves ready for a change of position in three days' time. Our destination lies thirty-eight kilometres to the rear."

"To the rear, Colonel?"

"Does that upset you, Captain? You don't seriously imagine that we do nothing but advance, do you? Why, last December a whole army moved back here from Tula, a distance of several hundred kilometres, and only a short time afterwards the Führer announced that the campaign in the East was at an end. Shall we say he made a little mistake?"

"Yes, Colonel."

"And now we're re-grouping for the spring offensive. We want to have a jumping-off point. Or, looked at another way, you could say that we're correcting the mistakes of the last three months. Call it a straightening of the line, Captain."

"Yes, Colonel," said Witterer. There was a note of disappointment in his voice, such as was only natural in a soldier whose desire to get at the enemy was being so cruelly thwarted.

"In three days' time, then. To-morrow you can reconnoitre the new position with Wedelmann. My adjutant will give you the details. But I don't want any fuss made about it. The whole affair's secret. When the moment comes, we'll march off at night, disengaging under cover of darkness. A complete surprise. The Russians must wake up next morning and find us gone."

"Very good, Colonel," said Captain Witterer, and he added a short sharp laugh, for he couldn't help thinking of the idiotic faces of the enemy when they discovered what had happened.

Luschke looked at Witterer with interest. He took a secret pleasure in the man's ridiculous reactions. And he felt more convinced than ever that there was a lot more fun to be had out of Witterer yet. He hoped it would only be fun.

"I suppose I may take it that the Colonel is still in favour of the front-line entertainment show taking place regardless of the change in the situation? For purposes of deception as much as anything else?"

"I don't grudge the men any diversion of that sort. But it does seem to me that you, Captain, are less in need of it than most people."

"What do you mean, exactly, Colonel?" asked Witterer, beginning to feel slightly nervous.

"What I say."

"Since I've been here, Colonel . . ."

"Don't think I'm not delighted by your concern for the spiritual and moral welfare of your officers and men, Captain. I can see you have quite a bent for organising entertainment. But I shouldn't like you to concentrate on it at the expense of everything else."

"No, Colonel."

And with a sudden sharp hiss, Luschke said:

"When were you last at the hospital?"

Witterer stood there at a loss for several seconds. He found the way Luschke stared at him, like a snake confronting him in the middle of his path, very disconcerting. And he managed to stammer out the words: "I haven't been there at all, Colonel. There's nothing the matter with me."

"Some men of your battery," said Luschke, with tantalising softness, "are at present lying in the field hospital—three of them to be precise—according to to-day's report. One man is wounded, another is a case of frost-bite and another has inflammation of the lungs. Has it never occurred to you that their welfare needs consideration too?"

"But, of course, Colonel," stammered Witterer, "I was going to . . ."

"Then don't let me stop you," said the Colonel, turning away abruptly and looking very intently at the faded remains of a fresco down which the water was pouring in little black rivulets, which would soon have ruined it completely.

Witterer felt that he had been dismissed. He saluted the Colonel's back smartly and hurried away at top speed.

Corporal Krause, who was waiting for him outside the

church, wrenched open the door of the car. Lance-Corporal Kowalski sat slumped over the wheel. Witterer got in without a word. Krause shot into the back. Kowalski started up the engine.

"To the hospital!" snapped Witterer.

Kowalski let in the clutch so fiercely that the car shot forward in a series of wild jerks. He brought it under control again and added: "The hospital? Incredible!"

"Kindly keep your idiotic remarks to yourself. Lance-Corporal," shouted Witterer furiously.

"They're not idiotic at all," said Kowalski, calmly.

"Hold your tongue, man," shouted the Captain.

Kowalski shrugged his shoulders and trod on the accelerator. He had merely been confirmed in one of his basic beliefs, namely that it was unwise ever to let yourself get into a discussion with an officer.

The car swung across to a halt beside a long, low, wooden building. A Red Cross flag hung limp over the main entrance. Witterer climbed out, smoothed out the creases in his great-coat and said to Krause: "You drive over to Fräulein Ebner. Say that I'll be over to see her in about an hour's time."

Corporal Krause repeated the order, word for word. Kowalski listened to his performance with interest. He marvelled at the Corporal's sense of discipline. The moment he'd finished, Kowalski let in the clutch and roared away to enjoy a little mild flirtation with Charlotte.

Witterer, in the meantime, entered the hospital, stalked into the ante-room and found himself confronted by a nurse who seemed quite unimpressed by his Captain's rank. She was busy making up lists from a large quantity of information she had written down in front of her.

"If you don't mind," said Witterer, in a markedly unfriendly tone, after he had been waiting there for several seconds without having had the slightest notice taken of him, "I would like to visit my men."

"What are their names? What part of the hospital are they in?"

Witterer was now really annoyed. He immediately expressed his displeasure at this "quite uncalled for manner of interrogation." The nurse gave him back as good as she got. The two of them roared at each other for a time.

"Kindly remember where you are!" shouted the nurse.

"Good God!" shouted the Captain, "are we people here to

166

serve you, or you here to serve us? What sort of a shambles is this?"

On the word shambles, one of the doctors came into the room. He looked for a moment as if he were about to take an energetic part in the discussion, but he became friendly as soon as he saw Witterer's rank. Each officer was very conscious of his own importance, and they were soon getting on excellently together. Within ten minutes Witterer was in possession of fairly full particulars about his men.

" I'm very anxious to have them fit again," he said. " And as soon as possible, too. We need every man we've got at the front—particularly at the present moment."

" I see," said the doctor.

Witterer nodded. Now he thought he understood what the Colonel had meant by sending him here. It was obvious! Luschke was not motivated by any sentiment. He merely wanted his commanders to get their units up to strength. The time had come when not a man could be spared. The days of leave passes, secondings, sick-lists and all the rest of it were over. Witterer realised why he had been sent.

Witterer, turning these thoughts over in his mind with some satisfaction, paid little attention to his surroundings. He was taken into a large ward full of patients, most of them lying on well-filled straw mattresses. They even seemed to have sheets.

One very pale man, wrapped up in a lot of blankets, stared weakly up at him. This was someone from his own troop. Witterer introduced himself and asked a few questions. He found nothing to take exception to in the man's answers, though they were not exactly optimistic.

" How are you feeling?" he asked.

It was the man with inflammation of the lungs.

" Much better, Captain."

" That's it! We'll have you back with us in a few days' time—you'll be pleased about that, won't you?"

" Yes, Captain," said the man very weakly.

Witterer looked at his watch, added a few more words of encouragement and took his leave. The man with inflammation of the lungs stared blankly after him. He saw a broad back, a fine pair of trousers and a fat revolver-holster resting on the Captain's right buttock.

Witterer's visit to the man with frost-bite went much the same way. In this case, too, though he found what seemed tolerable keenness, positive optimism was missing. The man's left hand was thickly swathed in cotton wool. A greyish-green ointment, with a very strong smell, oozed through the bandages like pus.

"The main thing," said Witterer, "is that your right hand is all right. Or are you left-handed?"

"No, Captain."

"Well, there you are!" said Witterer, not forgetting to take another glance at his watch. Then he said good-bye to him, too.

Outside in the corridor, he stopped and took a deep breath. The stench of the anti-frost-bite ointment made him feel sick. There was something repellent about ill people, and the room had been full of them. They had stunk and they had stared at him. If you had to go, that wasn't the way to do it, he thought with disgust. That was the way old women died. Heroes died in the glory of their youth or not at all. And above all, they didn't stink.

He successfully fought off the desire for a cigarette. He looked down at the worn floor-boards in the corridor and listened to them creaking as he walked across them. He saw a dark spot and stopped in front of it. Blood, he thought. And it filled him with a strange pleasure to be standing there where blood had been shed. The war had come one step nearer still. He shuddered with delight.

He drew himself up and walked into the room where those with wounds below the waist were lying. The great wave of stench which met his nostrils sent him staggering back again. It completely took his breath away. And on top of that there came the continual whimpering of a man racked by fever. The fellow might at least try and pull himself together, thought Witterer, with manly disgust.

He strode past several mattresses without paying any attention to the men lying on them and made straight for the member of his troop whose name, bed number, and nature of wound were written up on a card at his feet. "Perforation of the lower bowel," read Captain Witterer.

"I'm your new C.O.," he said. "Captain Witterer."

The wounded soldier smiled feebly. His face was a greyish-yellow. His eyes were sunk deep in his head and shone feverishly. His mouth was no more than a straight line in his face.

"And how are you, my dear fellow?"

The man threw back his blankets. Witterer saw the bandages swathed thickly round his hips. They were stained a watery red. He bent over them with something like a professional interest.

"Well," he said. "It could be worse."

"Yes, sir," said the wounded man.

"Just a moment," said the Captain turning round, for the door had opened behind him. Corporal Krause was standing there. He made his way over to Witterer. "Well?" asked the latter.

"Fräulein Ebner regrets . . ." began Krause.

"What does she regret?"

"That she's unable to wait for the Captain. She has some rehearsing to do."

"Really!" said Witterer with evident displeasure. "So she has some rehearsing to do, eh?"

And he looked at his watch and said to Corporal Krause: "So it's taken you a whole hour to find that out?"

"I'm sorry, Captain," said Krause, "but I couldn't be any quicker. I lost Kowalski."

"Did he go off on his own again?"

"He was with a woman called Charlotte."

"What the hell does he think he's doing?" cried Witterer, suddenly losing control of himself. "I've had enough of this."

He left Krause without another word. And the look he gave his adjutant made his displeasure abundantly clear. Lance-Corporals without any sense of discipline; women without any sense of co-operation. What a state of affairs! And yet these persistent rebuffs from Lisa were a sure sign that she felt she couldn't trust herself with him. The funny little thing! She was actually afraid of him. Well—perhaps it wasn't altogether incomprehensible.

Witterer went back to the wounded man from his troop. He bent over the bandages again and shook his head. He'd have to write this man off for the time being. He wasn't likely to be ready for the spring offensive. After a few more words of encouragement, he left him lying there and hurried out of the room to get away from the stench.

Before getting into his car, he said to Krause:

"We need every man we've got, Krause. Every single man. We must call in every man we can."

"Even Corporal Vierbein?" asked Krause keenly.

"I said every man, Krause."

"Very good, Captain."

"See that it's done then! And as for you, Kowalski, you're dismissed. You're not my driver any longer."

"Very good," said Kowalski, preparing to get out of the car.

"What do you think you're doing now?"

"Carrying out your orders, Captain," said Kowalski, offering Witterer the key of the car. "And delighted to do so."

"Get in again at once!" shouted Witterer, almost choking with rage. "And as soon as we get to rear base you will report to me—on a charge."

"With pleasure, Captain."

The news that Kowalski was up on a charge again spread rapidly round the troop and was received everywhere with suppressed delight. Kowalski himself was more amused than anyone. He explained at some length, to anyone who cared to listen, on the remarkable personal qualities of the new troop commander. "Ox-brain" was his name for him.

When the Sergeant-Major heard the news he hurried off to Captain Witterer at once and was bold enough to ask outright whether it was really true what he had heard, though he could hardly believe it, namely that the Captain was considering punishing Lance-Corporal Kowalski.

"Yes, it's quite true," said Witterer, unpleasantly. "He's going to be punished."

"I beg to advise against such a course of action, Captain."

"You're wasting your time, Sergeant-Major. My decision stands."

"But I beg to suggest, Captain," went on Bock with a hint of truculence, "that you are wasting your time trying to punish Kowalski! It's quite impossible. He simply doesn't care. With respect, Captain—I may say he doesn't care a damn."

"I'll soon change all that," cried Witterer, thirsting for revenge. "He doesn't know me yet. I'm not going to let myself be treated by the fellow as if . . . as if I were just a wet rag. Bring him in to me at once."

The Sergeant-Major shrugged his shoulders. Then he gave the Captain a salute which was by no means the smartest he could muster, and left the room. He shook his head disapprovingly. He knew of old that this was no way to run the troop.

He took his time about finding Kowalski. First of all he tried to get hold of Lieutenant Wedelmann, but was unsuccessful. Asch couldn't be got hold of either. The Sergeant-Major even considered whether he should ring up Luschke but his hand fell back from the receiver at the last moment. After an hour during which he had done absolutely nothing, a furious telephone call came through from Witterer demanding Kowalski dead or alive. The Sergeant-Major sighed dismally as he put the receiver down. Then he went out to fetch Kowalski.

"Now then, Kowalski," said the Sergeant-Major, in a truly comradely tone. "You won't make trouble, will you?"

"What an idea, Sergeant-Major," the other reassured him. "I wouldn't dream of spoiling the fun."

"Treat him correctly."

"But I aways do."

Bock pushed Kowalski ahead of him into Witterer's room. Kowalski gave his name, rank and number in the approved manner. The Captain buckled on his belt, put on his cap—all this was also in accordance with regulations: both the man on the charge and the officer dealing with it had to be properly dressed. He took up a formal stance in front of the culprit.

He held up a sheet of paper and read out from it:

"I hereby sentence Lance-Corporal Kowalski to three days' close arrest for repeated insolence towards his troop commander and other senior ranks of his troop, and for an attitude prejudicial to good order and discipline."

"Damnation," said the Sergeant-Major, under his breath. "That's no way to sentence anyone. That's mere wishy-washy nonsense. A man can only be sentenced on a specifically framed charge. A lot of generalities like that won't do."

"You're no longer my driver," yelled Witterer at Kowalski. "From now on you're to drive nothing but ammunition. Well? What have you to say to that?"

"Very many thanks, Captain."

"Out of here!" roared Witterer. "Out of my sight!"

"With pleasure, Captain," said Kowalski. He came smartly to attention and left the room.

Sergeant-Major Bock stamped out after him without waiting to be dismissed. Things were looking blacker than ever—for Witterer as well this time. When Luschke received the official report of the charge and sentence—and according to regimental orders sentences had to be reported within forty-eight hours of being promulgated—there would be hell to pay. He had no sympathy for Witterer, but the trouble was that he would be in the line of fire himself.

"Excuse me, Sergeant-Major," said Kowalski, with some curiosity. "But when can I begin my sentence."

"Steady now," said the Sergeant-Major, "there's no need to rush things."

"But according to regulations," explained Kowalski with a certain relish, "the sentence must be put into effect as soon as possible. And I'm waiting for mine to begin."

"Now don't be difficult, Kowalski," said Bock. "Perhaps the Captain only meant it as a joke."

"I don't see it as a joke at all," cried the Lance-Corporal, with some dignity.

The Sergeant-Major waved him away and went to his quarters. Kowalski followed him like a shadow. He was having a fine time.

"What do you want now?" asked the Sergeant-Major crossly.

"My punishment, that's all."

"God, Kowalski, you're a stubborn devil!"

"I insist on having my punishment," explained Kowalski, thoroughly enjoying the trouble he was making for everybody.

Sergeant-Major Bock walked away from Kowalski without a word. He took a heavy mackintosh down from a hook and put it on. Then he went outside to the barn and got out his motor-cycle and side-car.

Kowalski followed him there too. He came to attention and said: "If I were you I'd take a look at the valves . . . they don't sound too good to me."

"Get out of my way, you!"

Bock trod on the starter and the engine sprang into life for a moment and then died out.

"Too much throttle," said Kowalski, with the air of an expert.

Bock pulled back the throttle and trod on the starter again. Once more the engine sprang into life. He let it warm up for a bit. While he was doing this, he looked across at the Lance-Corporal with some hostility.

The Lance-Corporal came nearer and said: "Do you hear those valves? They're making a terrible noise." And he added with a broad grin: "Ox-brain made a hell of a mess of that sentence, didn't he? Come on now, admit it. Oh, I know the regulations all right. And if there's as much as a comma altered on the charge sheet, I'll complain to Luschke."

"Out of my way!" shouted the Sergeant-Major, letting in the clutch and roaring off at a tremendous speed.

Bock went sailing up to the forward base in search of Lieutenant Wedelmann. But he wasn't to be found either in his quarters or up with the guns. The Sergeant-Major swore and continued his search. Sergeant Asch wasn't to be found, either. Lance-Corporal Kowalski finally took pity on him and gave him the tip-off: Natasha.

Wedelmann and Asch were sitting in the Russian girl's hut drinking tea, this time out of some cut-glass which the Lieutenant had found for her. They were talking about the war—it was the only subject anyone ever talked about with Natasha.

"We didn't begin this war," she said seriously. "For us it's a patriotic duty."

"For us, too," said Wedelmann, no less seriously. "It's a national necessity. We attacked you first but only in self-defence."

"Excuse me," said Asch, "but some years ago there was a sexual murderer near where I live, Schlapprosch was the creature's name, and before committing one of his crimes, he always knelt down and said a prayer. He was absolutely convinced that he was carrying out God's will."

Neither Natasha nor Wedelmann said anything in reply. It was quite clear what their silence meant. Asch, they thought, simply didn't understand them. They were sitting side by side, quite close to each other on Natasha's narrow bed. His right hand and her left hand were just touching and they made no effort to move.

Asch was sitting on the only chair. It creaked with every movement he made. He seemed very much amused by something. His eyes shone with a mixture of sarcasm and pity. He leant back and crossed his legs.

"You know," he said, "when I have the two of you in front of me like this, it's easy enough to see which way the wind's blowing."

"Don't let us keep you, Asch, if you're anxious to be off."

"You're both marching towards the millennium," went on Asch, unperturbed, "but each in the opposite direction. Each is convinced that he has discovered the perfect philosophy. And what's even worse: each thinks that his philosophy is the only one there is."

"I really think it's time you were going, Asch. You don't seem to feel at home here."

"I'm listening to him," said Natasha. "What he says interests me very much. He can't shake my convictions."

"Nor mine," said Wedelmann, passionately. "And that's just why it's quite unnecessary for us to have to listen to him."

"I'm not trying to persuade you," said Asch, in a calm and

friendly tone. "I'm not even trying to enlighten you. You're both too far gone for that. This is the age of mass-produced minds. And there you are, the two of you, both expert performers for your parties, one red, and the other brown—you're in love with each other, I take it, but for you love between two human beings has to come second to other things. The Soviet Union, or the Reich must come first, for both are striving to make the world a better place. The happiness which two human beings are capable of giving each other simply doesn't count. One can't help wondering what is the point of human beings producing children. To supply soldiers for the defence of their country? Or to continue to live through such children?"

"You have no sense of patriotism," said Natasha proudly. "I am defending my country so that I can live in it in peace."

Wedelmann said, no less proudly: "And presumably you'll never grasp the fact that the race is all that matters. The individual human being is nothing apart from the race to which he belongs."

"You're hopeless," said Asch. He stood up. "God is above all of us. We can be brought together by our love for each other. All men can be brothers. Nothing—absolutely nothing —can justify war."

And Asch left without looking at either of them again. He slammed the door behind him. They could hear him going noisily down the steps. There was an oppressive silence in the room. From somewhere out at the front came the distant rattle of a machine-gun.

"He doesn't understand us," said Wedelmann. He seemed worried.

"Perhaps even he will understand us one day."

Wedelmann slowly shook his head.

"No," he said, "Asch is a hopeless case."

Natasha took his hand affectionately. He turned towards her and looked at her. There was both excitement and fear in her eyes. They were soft and dark and glowing. He put his mouth to each of them in turn.

He felt her eyes closing. He held her hands. They began to tremble. But her head didn't move.

They stayed like that for a long time, neither daring to move. He could feel the coolness of her breath on his face. His mouth slid downwards, and he could feel her lifting her face towards him. He kissed her on the mouth. And then she drew back a little.

Each let their eyes wander over the other's face. They were hardly breathing at all. Then they kissed again.

"I love you," each said to the other.

They separated and looked at each other in wonder. It was a long time before they moved again. They shuddered as the rattle of the machine-guns again came towards them from the front.

"Come on," said Wedelmann. "Come with us."

"Where to?"

"We must stay together," he said. "For as long as we can."

"But, we're together now."

Wedelmann shook his head.

"We won't be much longer. We're moving. Any day now."

She fell back, as if she had fainted. She took her hands from his and said: "Don't talk about it. Please don't talk about it."

"But we must talk it over."

"No."

"Do you want me to leave you, then?"

"No."

"Then you must come with me."

"No."

"But you must," he said. "We've got such a short time to ourselves—such a horribly short time. We must make it last as long as possible. You must come with us. We'll be gone in a couple of days."

A tragic look came into Natasha's eyes. He thought that she must be afraid, afraid for him, for both of them, for their love for each other. And, strangely enough, this made him happy. I've never been so happy in my life before, he said to himself. I didn't know there could be such happiness.

"I love you," he said.

Natasha closed her eyes. Her face was pale and her lips were thin and drawn. She held her breath. Her eyelids trembled for a moment, as if she were in pain. Then she let her breath out again, almost violently. She opened her eyes and stared at him. Then she asked:

"When will you be going?"

"The night after to-morrow."

"Just your troop?"

"No, everyone. We're moving. We're straightening the front."

"How far back are you going?"

"About forty kilometres. Why don't you come too? I'll see that you're all right. It'll be weeks before the front really gets on the move again. And these weeks will belong to us. Natasha, you must listen to me. Look—you're all alone here. It was only the tide of war that brought you here. It doesn't matter to you where you are—the only thing that matters is that we should be together."

"The night after to-morrow," said Natasha. It was as if he were hardly there any more. She wouldn't look at him.

"Well, are you coming?"

"I really do love you," she cried loudly. "You must believe me."

"Yes," he said. "I believe you."

She threw herself into his arms, as if she wanted to bury her head in his chest. "Whatever happens," she gasped, pressing close to him. "Whatever happens, remember I love you."

"Is everything ready for this evening?" Schulz asked the adjutant.

The adjutant took a list of the guests out of his brief-case. He also took a carefully prepared plan of the seating. A party was to be given in the mess at eight o'clock that evening in honour of the Commanding Officer and his bride. Schulz was organising it.

"Oh, and by the way," said Schulz, as if the idea had only just entered his head. "Don't forget that we've got to pay special attention to His Excellency the Admiral. We'll detail Vierbein to wait on him throughout the evening. That'll create a good impression."

The adjutant turned his fat, well-nourished face towards Schulz. He looked worried, though not excessively so. He enjoyed his present position as adjutant far too much not to accept Schulz for what he was. It was only in such a position that he could be what he was pleased to call a soldier and at the same time keep an eye on his wine and spirit business. No, he was not the sort of man to make trouble, or, indeed, do anything which might disrupt the elaborate structure of mutual confidence that he had built up between himself and his superior officers.

"Vierbein will stand behind His Excellency throughout the meal," said Schulz, reconstructing in his mind's eye a scene from some super-film which he had seen just recently and which appealed strongly to his ever-increasing sense of the theatrical. "He will come forward whenever His Excellency sits down or stands up, but will otherwise remain at a distance of three paces behind him. He will wait on no one else but His Excellency."

"Very good," said the adjutant, looking as if he had a bad pain in the stomach.

He left the room as soon as he could. It was all very well for Schulz. He just did the planning. It was he who had to carry the plans out. He went over to the telephone. Just before he lifted the receiver he told himself that war was a damned hard thing. There was no doubt about that.

His first call, of course, was to his own firm from which he thoughtfully ordered fifty bottles of champagne. Then he rang up the Sergeant-Major and told him that Vierbein, Bartsch and Ruhnau, together with five other orderlies and three extra men to help in the kitchen, were to be detailed for duty at the party that night.

Then he went over to the mess itself to supervise the final preparations like an experienced head waiter.

Schulz was the first to appear, half an hour before the party officially began. He was wearing his best uniform. It fitted him exceptionally well. He also wore a spotless white collar. Naturally he came alone. He had decided that his wife wasn't fit to go out in society. Everyone knew of and accepted this decision. Some even respected him for it. He himself accepted the necessity for it with regret but with commendable fortitude. Only that morning he had had yet another, and as he thought, final quarrel with his wife on this point. She simply would never understand him.

A few minutes later, the orderlies and the other auxiliary staff for the party met together in the kitchen.

Schulz wanted to see if the drinks were the right temperature. He poured himself out a brandy—a large one, of course. Then, with his half-empty glass still in his hand, he went to inspect what he called the "supply columns" under the command of his trusted lieutenants Bartsch and Ruhnau.

These two "eight-tonners" looked up at him with guarded respect. The remainder of their staff made vain attempts to swell out their chests beneath their white mess jackets. Schulz, still holding on to his glass of brandy, looked them up and down with a critical eye. No spot or stain was too small to escape his notice.

He then tasted the food to see that it was up to standard, and checked the temperature of some of the other drinks. He found one or two things to criticise but his criticism was tempered with praise, and this was a clear enough indication of his mood.

But his good mood wasn't to last long. It collapsed immediately on the arrival of His Excellency the Admiral, for His Excellency the Admiral arrived without Vierbein.

Schulz circled twice round His Excellency, being allowed on the first occasion to shake the Imperial adviser's hand and being asked, on the second, where his wife was. Schulz was overwhelmed with confusion by this. So much so that he didn't dare ask His Excellency—he, Schulz was afraid to ask the question which was tantalising him, namely: where was Vierbein? On second thoughts, however, such a question, perhaps, would have been going a little far. It might even have proved a tactical error, for if His Excellency had been a Luschke—which most fortunately was not the case—His Excellency would have been able to answer back; "Don't you even know where your own men are?"

Schulz rushed straight off to the kitchen where Bartsch and Ruhnau were just testing the quality of the cold table. "Listen to me, you two oafs! Go and find Vierbein for me at once!"

"Very good, Lieutenant," shouted both of them at once, though without much enthusiasm.

"And look sharp about it. If you don't have him here double-quick, it'll be the last you see of the Fatherland for some time to come."

The two "bull-dozers" quickly gobbled up a few more delicacies and washed them down with a couple of glasses of champagne. Then they raced away.

They found Vierbein surprisingly quickly. As they had hoped, he was sitting upstairs in the best room in the Café Asch, hand in hand on the sofa with his bride, Fräulein Ingrid. Old Asch, not wishing to disturb the two lovers, had tactfully withdrawn with the excuse that he had to go and see his old friend Freitag. He knew he was quite safe to do this. There was no danger of either of them overstepping the mark.

Bartsch and Ruhnau grinned broadly at the romantic scene which met their eyes. They nudged each other and winked. Then they sighed exaggeratedly. They seemed to find it all a huge joke.

And one of them said to Vierbein: "Vierbein, Schulz wants you. It's nearly nine o'clock now. What's it worth to you if we don't find you before ten?"

"Three bottles of wine," said Ingrid, who was slowly

adapting herself to the customs of the time. "Three bottles—for eleven o'clock."

"Sorry," said Bartsch. "Two hours' search would be going too far."

"One hour's all right," said Ruhnau. "We can explain that away easily enough."

"Of course I'll come at once if I'm wanted," said Vierbein. "Even though I don't much like being called away in the middle of my leave."

"What do you mean your 'leave'? You're seconded here, aren't you?"

Vierbein put his hand to the leave papers in his tunic. They had come to him straight from the front that evening. The C.O. of the airfield had sent them by special courier. Vierbein had wondered for a time what he was meant to do with them but there was now no doubt in his mind.

"I'm on leave here," said Corporal Vierbein. "And as soon as my leave is up I'm to take back certain trained radio personnel and their equipment."

The two "flame-throwers," Bartsch and Ruhnau, were at a loss what to do with this information. It was too categorical to give them much opportunity of getting round it. So they merely acted as if they hadn't heard it and started all over again. They were on the point of settling with Ingrid for three bottles of wine for a ninety-minute search when Vierbein said:

"I'd rather come straight away. Then the matter will be settled once and for all."

"But what's the hurry when you're on leave, man?"

"Schulz doesn't know that. And besides: orders are orders!"

"Oh!" said Ingrid, crossly. "How maddening it all is! They don't seem to leave you alone for a moment!"

Vierbein laid a restraining hand on her arm.

"I'll be back soon," he promised.

"This isn't a hotel," said Ingrid, angrily. "You can't just come and go as you like."

"I'll be as quick as I can."

"Well, I'm going to bed."

"I'll be back in half an hour," promised Vierbein. "It won't take longer than that to get it all cleared up."

And he left with Bartsch and Ruhnau, who were complaining furiously. They had a number of very unflattering things to say about him. They had been deprived—cheated they would have said—of a profitable piece of business. The only compensation was that they would at least be able to reinstate themselves with Schulz. They had proved themselves reliable watchdogs. He could hardly help complimenting them on their efficiency.

But Schulz found neither the time nor the opportunity to do any such thing. The Vierbein problem absorbed all his attention. He rushed straight at the Corporal shouting: " Why didn't you carry out my order, Vierbein?"

" I beg to inform the Lieutenant that I did carry out his order."

" You were to wait on His Excellency. Have you been waiting on him?"

" I reported to His Excellency but His Excellency said he didn't want me."

" And who gives the orders around here, Vierbein?" asked Schulz. His voice was ominously quiet. " Me or this Admiral?"

Vierbein couldn't think of the answer to this. Schulz noted the fact with pleasure. He jerked his thumb several times in the direction of the mess ante-rooms. Vierbein hesitated for a moment but then obeyed. Lieutenant Schulz noted this with even greater pleasure. And he allowed himself another brandy— again a large one.

When he went back to the mess ten minutes later, dancing had already begun in the dining-room, which had been cleared of furniture for the occasion. He looked into one of the bar-rooms for a moment and there—actually sitting in the special corner which was usually reserved for the C.O.—there sat Vierbein—Vierbein of all people—a champagne glass in each hand, bowing stiffly from the waist. And next to Vierbein sat His Excellency, this ludicrous Admiral!

It took Schulz some seconds to master his rage. This drinking session of Corporal and Admiral went very much against the grain. He sidled up closer and surreptitiously beckoned Vierbein over to him. Vierbein excused himself from the Admiral for a moment, got up obediently and followed Schulz out into the little corridor where the lavatories were.

" Do you imagine you're a guest here, Vierbein?" asked Schulz, glowering at him.

" His Excellency, the Admiral, asked me to sit down, Lieutenant."

" And you actually dared plant your bottom on the chair specially reserved for the C.O.?"

" After I had twice been told to do so by the Admiral—yes, Lieutenant."

"And who's in charge here?" asked Schulz. It was his favourite gambit. "Some old salt from the Kaiser's navy or a Lieutenant of the Greater German Wehrmacht?"

Vierbein maintained a stubborn silence.

"Return to barracks at once, Vierbein!" cried Schulz.

Vierbein took a gulp of air, shut his eyes for a moment, opened his mouth and said:

"Might I beg to inform the Lieutenant that I shan't be sleeping in barracks to-night."

Schulz couldn't believe his ears. Was this really Vierbein he was talking to? It couldn't be. "Let me smell your breath," orderd Schulz. "I want to see if you're drunk."

Vierbein breathed at him. Schulz sniffed and then shook his head in utter amazement. "You haven't been drinking," he said slowly. "But what's the matter with you? Do you feel ill?"

"I'm on leave," said Vierbein, with his last ounce of courage.

"Don't be an idiot," said Schulz roughly. "You're seconded for duty here. Or have you left your brains behind at the front?"

"If the Lieutenant will permit," said Vierbein, unbuttoning the top left-hand pocket of his tunic. He took out the papers which he had received only a few hours before. He held them out to the Lieutenant.

Schulz, who was still gasping with astonishment, took them from him almost in a dream and started looking through them. At last he said: "Well, then, I must be drunk."

He threw the papers back at Vierbein and left him without a word. Vierbein, who didn't like the look of things at all, sighed deeply. Then he hurried out of the mess, much worried by the thought that Schulz would probably be after him as soon as he had recovered from the shock.

Nor was his supposition incorrect. Hardly had he left the building when Schulz came rushing back through the ante-rooms, bellowing for Vierbein. But he bellowed in vain. He sent for Bartsch and Ruhnau and said: "Go and fetch that Vierbein for me, you miserable couple of idiots—or you're off to the front to-morrow."

The two "mine-sweepers" went off, cursing, to look for Vierbein again at just about the same moment as Vierbein arrived at the Café Asch. But Ingrid had been as good as her word and gone to sleep. Vierbein was on the point of forcing his way into her room in desperation when old Asch laid a kind but restraining hand on him. The old man gave him a friendly piece of advice: he should go off where he would be welcome at that time of night and could find what was denied him here.

And so it came about that after wandering about the town for some time, Corporal Vierbein finally paid a friendly visit to Frau Lore Schulz. And was made very welcome.

War Correspondent B. M. Eberwein arrived at Luschke's regiment with instructions to cover the withdrawal according to plan—"another page of glory for our troops." The Colonel didn't see him but sent him straight up to No. 3 Troop. Eberwein arrived there early in the afternoon.

Eberwein considered himself an "ace" among correspondents, and there were even quite a lot of other people who thought the same. He possessed plenty of imagination and absolutely no sense of responsibility. He got his "piece" back twice as fast as anyone else. And the methods by which he did so were his own professional secret.

Captain Witterer gave the great Eberwein the heartiest of welcomes. He felt deeply honoured by his presence. It made him very proud and pleased that it should have been to him, Witterer, that Luschke chose to send the great man. And he imagined that he now had better grounds than ever for supposing that Luschke was well disposed towards him. But appearances can be very deceptive.

Eberwein gave an elegant salute and asked dryly: "Well, when does the balloon go up?"

"To-morrow night," said Witterer.

Eberwein began to think. He had a well-fed appearance. He knew how to look after himself all right.

"To-morrow night, eh? If I'm to have the pictures and my piece back in Berlin by the day after to-morrow, I'll have to hurry. I'd better start at once."

Witterer put the newspaper man right.

"To-morrow night, I said. Not before."

Eberwein saw that he was dealing with a beginner. He calmly folded his pink, plump little hands and said: "Improvisation is the secret of success! Even in our job. Together with inspiration, of course. We have to look ahead. We work out what's going to happen and set it all up beforehand."

"Aha," said Witterer, beginning to understand. "You mean you pose your pictures?"

" That's the expression laymen use," said Eberwein, putting him in his place. " We professionals call it pre-actuality."

" I see," said Witterer, not without a certain respect. " Well, naturally, I'm at your disposal."

" Excellent, Captain," said Eberwein. " But I won't trouble you personally for the time being. What I'd like is a few competent N.C.O.s who can help me to get everything set up —the actual pictures will only take me a quarter of an hour or so."

" I'll be glad to do anything I can to help," Witterer reassured him in friendly tones. " And, in any case, I'd be delighted if you'd be my guest at a little entertainment we're giving this evening."

Eberwein accepted the invitation gladly. He then started to use his imagination. He worked fast and headlines soon began to form themselves in his mind. " Heavy Artillery Covers Retreat "—" No. 3's Tank Busters At It Again "—" From Auditorium Into Battle."

Witterer's first step was to allot Soeft to Eberwein so that the newspaper man should be properly looked after. He then added the N.C.O. in charge of transport and Corporal Krause to the party. Witterer, himself deeply interested in all that was going on, also stayed at Eberwein's side, apparently with the intention of dealing with any difficulties which might arise.

The distinguished war correspondent and his enthusiastic assistants then took the C.O.'s car up to the gun positions. Kowalski's job had been taken over by a certain Lance-Corporal Dammhirsch. After they had gone three kilometres this man Dammhirsch drove them into a six-foot slit trench with such force that Eberwein felt for a moment that he had broken every bone in his body. Witterer had a two-inch cut on his forehead. He cursed and swore. And these three kilometres were the limit of Dammhirsch's experience as driver to his C.O.

His successor was a certain Lance-Corporal Trinkler. Trinkler had a habit of spitting. He was always trying to spit right over the bonnet of the car, though when in motion he naturally had no success. The spit merely splashed back, partly against the windscreen and partly into the face of the occupant of the front seat, who, in the present case, was Captain Witterer. After the first disaster of this sort, Trinkler confined his spitting within more modest limits. But late that afternoon he ran out of petrol and Witterer and Eberwein had to go two kilometres on foot. By the evening Kowalski was once more reinstated as the C.O.'s driver.

In the meantime, War Correspondent Eberwein had developed into a little tyrant. Like many men who wear uniform but are not proper soldiers at all, he insisted on being taken very seriously. With Witterer looking keenly on, the men of No. 3 Battery had to make the best of it while he systematically put them through their paces.

First picture: "The decisive moment! Captain Witterer, C.O. of the renowned No. 3 Troop stands beside the gun scanning the enemy lines through his field-glasses." He had made a point of choosing No. 4 gun for this purpose, for it stood behind a hill and therefore could not be seen by the enemy. The N.C.O. i/c ammunition had placed a small charge of explosive at a safe distance from the photographer and the heroes who were being photographed. And Eberwein took his picture just as the charge was detonated. Three detonations were necessary before the photographer was satisfied.

Second picture: "A perilous incident! A caterpillar nearly topples into a trench. But the men just jump off in time and with a superhuman effort "—clicked the shutter—" the machine is righted." Strained faces, steel helmets slipping sideways, boots digging desperately into the frozen ground. The picture was taken from a low angle while the caterpillar was tilted over from the opposite side with levers.

Third picture: "Enemy tank knocked out at close range! A giant Russian tank in flames; only a few yards away a soldier in a shallow fox-hole on the point of hurling yet another grenade." This tank had been lying near the forward base for something like four months now. It was no more than a huge dismantled steel coffin that had been stripped even of its tracks. A can of petrol had been poured over it and then set alight. The flames roared magnificently. The Corporal hurling a hand grenade was none other than Soeft himself. He played his part to perfection.

"You've got a fine body of men in this troop, Captain," said Eberwein, with genuine admiration when he had taken about two dozen pictures.

"There's nothing wrong with the material," said Witterer. Eberwein nodded.

"But of course it's leadership that counts," he said, laying the flattery on heavily.

Witterer took this as his due. He knew just how good he was. He had never had any doubts about himself. He wondered what his friends would say when they saw him on the front page of the *Völkischer Beobachter*. At the head of his men. Shells bursting all round him. Face to face with the enemy.

Lance-Corporal Kowalski reported to him as he had been told to. Witterer looked him up and down sourly. He found it extremely galling to have to take this creature back as his driver, though even he had to admit that he was superb at his job.

"Kowalski," he said, "you will go and fetch the ladies for this evening's show. Sergeant Asch is expecting you. He's transporting their gear."

"And when can I serve my sentence?" asked Kowalski, in a friendly enough tone.

"We'll postpone that till later," said Witterer, "when we've got more time. And you can rest assured, Kowalski, no one's going to forget about those three days of yours."

"I shouldn't like them to, Captain."

Witterer wondered for a moment whether this ought not to be classed as yet another insolent remark on the Lance-Corporal's part. But, after taking into consideration the exact phraseology and tone of voice in which he said it, he decided that for once this was not the case. Nevertheless, he found his dislike for this awkward customer greater than ever. It had almost reached a pitch of loathing. He couldn't stand the fellow or his suspiciously genial grin. He resolved to get himself another driver at the first possible opportunity.

Shortly after that Witterer found himself engaged on the telephone in a small, but, to his way of thinking, by no means insignificant controversy with Lieutenant Wedelmann. Wedelmann had spent the morning reconnoitring the new position. He informed him that he didn't feel like attending the entertainment show that evening.

"We officers," said Witterer, with ill-disguised hostility, "have to set an example to our men."

"I quite agree," said Wedelmann. "But not in a matter of this sort."

"Do you want to make nonsense of my arrangements then?" asked Witterer. "I've expressly released you from duty up with the guns for this evening."

"That's very good of you," said Wedelmann. "But I have my own plans."

"I shall expect you," said Witterer and it was clear that he meant this to be taken as an order. "I shall expect you to be present this evening. And when the show is over, I shall expect you to attend a little supper-party I'm giving in my quarters for the performers."

"Yes, sir," said Wedelmann, dejectedly, putting down the receiver.

Witterer had a perfectly good reason for wanting Wedelmann to be present. He smiled a long, self-satisfied smile. Then he sent for the Sergeant-Major and heard his final report on the arrangements.

"Eight o'clock sharp, then," said Witterer. "When everything's ready, report to Lieutenant Wedelmann and he can then report the parade to me."

"Yes, sir," said Sergeant-Major Bock. He saw what Witterer was up to now. He wanted his moment of drama: the former troop commander reporting the parade to the present one, and thus demonstrating his inferior status to the entire assembled troop. Bock didn't like that.

"And what about the members of the other units?"

"They'll be considered as part of the parade."

"But what if there are senior officers among them?"

"They will be requested to exclude themselves from the parade."

Bock went out sullenly. He felt very dissatisfied. Not only with Witterer, but with himself. He wasn't doing enough to keep this upstart in his place. He saw this as something to reproach himself with. First of all he had thought that, as a new broom, the man might do a certain amount of good. But he hadn't reckoned on the new broom sweeping on and on like this. Witterer was stirring up a little too much dust in the process.

Meanwhile, Witterer began making his own elaborate preparations for the evening. First of all he got Krause to fetch him some hot water from the field kitchen. He shaved thoroughly, washed his feet and cut his finger-nails. Finally, he went to his spare trunk and took out a clean pair of socks and a clean set of underwear, and put these all on. Then he sprinkled himself with eau-de-Cologne, took a long look in the looking-glass and found his appearance thoroughly satisfactory. He was certain that Lisa would fall for him now.

Then he got his billet smartened up a little. The soldier who had been specially detailed for this job by Krause brought in a lot of new blankets and spread them over the table, the chairs and the camp-bed. A sort of bar was erected on a long chest in the corner, and on it were placed numerous bottles provided by Soeft, together with glasses, some sweets and a plate of cakes. Witterer sampled some of these, nodded contentedly and determined to give Soeft the highest praise for his work.

He considered where Lisa Ebner was to sit. And he came to the conclusion that she should obviously sit next to him on the camp-bed. This had been arranged to look like a sofa. And in his mind's eye he saw her already sitting there: neat and charming, soft and cat-like, and, as always, just a little helpless. What a delightful person she was! And then two or three hours later, about midnight, the other guests would withdraw. The trusty Soeft would arrange to evacuate them. And he would be left alone—with Lisa.

And Witterer smiled at himself in the looking-glass, even more pleased with himself than a few minutes before.

And then the visitors started arriving in the barn where the show was being given. Infantry and artillery sat peacefully side by side, and even medical personnel were tolerated. A Corporal was thumping away on some sort of piano which Soeft had got hold of and every now and again the audience would join in the chorus, when it managed to recognise the tune.

Outside the barn, Sergeant-Major Bock had assumed the role of traffic policemen. Fortunately he found that people obeyed him. The thought of the pleasures in store for them made everyone well-behaved.

"No pushing, now," he shouted, although there was no sign of anyone pushing at all. "Everyone with a ticket will be able to find a place."

Soeft, who was waiting the arrival of the ladies with some impatience, watched the Sergeant-Major with amusement. He turned to Krause and said:

"The Chief's getting in some practice for peace-time."

"How do you mean?" asked Krause.

"He'd make a perfect barker for a fair-ground!"

"Now then, no pushing!" shouted Bock busily.

An infantry Major arrived, followed by a small entourage. Noticing that the Major was wearing the Knight's Cross, the Sergeant-Major saluted smartly, spoke a few conventional words of welcome, and led him to a seat in the front row.

Shortly afterwards four more senior officers arrived, including a tank Captain with a dog. Bock refused to allow the dog in. The Captain remonstrated vigorously. Bock remained adamant. Then Captain Witterer himself appeared on the scene, smelling strongly of eau-de-Cologne. The two officers came to an understanding at once. And the dog was allowed in.

The performers arrived punctually. Sergeant Asch brought the baggage and the conjurer together in a small truck. The conjurer sat muffled up in the back, tortured as usual by the fear that he might catch cold and lose work and salary as a result. He thought he should have been provided with proper transport, not just a cattle truck like this. He was in a great state of misery and looked extremely cross.

Kowalski brought the ladies in the C.O.'s car. He sat splayed out like a peacock behind the wheel, steering almost gracefully with two fingers of his left hand, while his right arm encircled the seat beside him which was normally occupied by Captain Witterer.

But it was Charlotte, the little concert-party's announcer, who occupied it now. Lisa Ebner and Viola, the dancer, were in the back. Lisa's large, round, inquisitive eyes stared out from under an enormous driving-rug. Viola beside her seemed to be asleep. She appeared utterly indifferent to all that was going on.

Kowalski and his passengers were surrounded by an interested crowd immediately on their arrival. And it seemed to Kowalski that the curious and admiring glances which the troops directed at the girls were in some way really a tribute to him. Bock, Soeft, Krause, the N.C.O.s i/c transport and ammunition, the cook, the medical Corporal and the orderly-room clerk all hurried forward to help the ladies out. Even Kowalski himself looked for a moment as if he were prepared to help Charlotte with her case, and this caused general surprise. However, he allowed Krause the pleasure of carrying it in the end.

Witterer cleared a path for himself through the crowd. A broad smile was set on his face, as he cried out: " Welcome, ladies! Welcome!" And he shook hands with all three of them, holding Lisa Ebner's hand particularly tight. " Now, then," he said, " what about a little schnaps just to warm you up?"

Charlotte had taken over command of the troupe now that the only man in the company, the conjurer, appeared to have succumbed to a combination of his inferiority complex, the cold and the disgraceful treatment that had been handed out to him. She shook her head.

" No," she said. " Work first. And then perhaps play afterwards."

" I expect the ladies will want to tidy up," said Witterer courteously. " My own quarters are at their disposal."

"We're quite tidy enough as it is, thank you," answered Charlotte. "We don't need to make any preparations."

"Besides," said Sergeant Asch, "we've rigged up a ladies' room just next to the stage. It would probably be more convenient."

"If the ladies would just like to go to the toilet," put in Soeft, helpfully.

Charlotte burst out laughing. Viola, the dancer, screwed up her eyes and looked at Soeft like a little girl looking at a dwarf in a fairy story. Lisa went rather red and looked across at Witterer, who seemed annoyed.

"I'll gladly show the ladies the way," went on Soeft.

"You seem to have thought of everything," said Charlotte, with gentle irony.

"Well, then, shall we begin?" said Sergeant Asch, breaking a painful silence. "Or are we going to go on talking here all evening?"

He led the way and the ladies followed him. And Witterer followed them. Soeft ran round in front of them all, opened the side door into the barn, pushed aside the curtain and ushered them in.

"When the war's over," said Asch, "you ought to try for a job in one of those hotels where they let rooms by the hour."

"My day-dream," said Soeft, smiling blissfully. "In Paris for preference!"

Witterer said good-bye to the ladies—"Until after the show, then!"—and gave one last lingering look into Lisa Ebner's beautiful big round eyes. Then he hurried round to the main entrance and marched into the barn. No one came up to report to him. Wedelmann hadn't arrived yet and Bock was keeping in the background. Witterer's military pride was cut to the quick.

But the look which the Major with the Knight's Cross gave him hurt him still more. Witterer felt that he was suddenly standing there without any clothes on. And the infantry Major said loudly, so that everyone round him could hear:

"So you're the prize shot of yesterday afternoon!"

And Witterer wasn't at all sure that the word he used was "shot".

He was glad when the curtain went up. The mood of the audience grew more and more animated, as was only to be expected. The infantry Major's Knight's Cross shone more and more alarmingly. War Correspondent Eberwein took some of his celebrated " action " photographs. And all the time Sergeant Asch kept a watchful eye on Lisa Ebner.

Asch was fully aware of the preparations that Witterer had made for later on. Equally suggestive were the glances with which Witterer followed Lisa Ebner's appearance on the stage. It was Sergeant Asch's view that Captain Witterer wasn't nearly good enough for Lisa Ebner, alternatively that she was far too good for him. And he was determined to take action accordingly.

But he had to waste a lot of valuable time dealing with the conjurer, whose demands were becoming more and more insistent. First of all the barn was too cold for him; then the atmosphere was too stuffy; then he began criticising the placing of the spotlights; and then he insisted that the distance between the stage and the front row of the audience was too small. Later he complained about the unfairness of the audience which, for purely erotic reasons, preferred the girls' acts to his own for which they had absolutely no understanding.

" Well, and why not? " cried Kowalski, leaping angrily to the defence of womanhood. " You don't think we're going to have a special performance just for your sake do you? Pansies only? "

" Really, you disgust me! " cried the conjurer.

" I'm delighted to hear it, " said Kowalski, winking at Charlotte.

The performance came to an end amid a howl of applause. Viola, sultry and pretty, was called back over and over again for her curtain call. Witterer decided that it would be a good idea to invite the infantry Major with the Knight's Cross in for a drink by way of reconciliation.

" You might as well make it several, you old prize shot, " cried the Major. " For all we know, some of us may be out of reach of a drink for ever by this time to-morrow evening. "

Witterer ordered Krause to look after the ladies and to bring them round to his billet when they were ready. He then took the infantry Major by the left arm and smiled at him warmly. The infantry Major bore this stoically.

" Well, " said Witterer. " We'll all soon have a chance of proving what we're really worth, eh? "

" To hell with that, " said the infantry Major openly enough. " If I had things my own way I'd spend the rest of the war in bed. "

" And why not? " said Witterer, thinking himself very much

the old soldier. "After all, you've already won your Knight's Cross."

"What, this piece of tin?" said the Major cynically. "Do you know what that cost me? The lives of twenty-two soldiers, a bullet in the groin, and a bad conscience for the rest of my life—that's to say it'd take me more than a lifetime to get my conscience clean again!"

"Ah, yes, war's a damned hard business," said Witterer, trying not to show his embarrassment.

"It's not only hard. It's dirty and rotten as well. Just a dirty rotten business from beginning to end."

By this time Witterer and his strange guest had arrived at his billet. He again looked round it and found everything in perfect order. He let his eyes rest lecherously for a moment on the corner of the bed where Lisa was to sit.

He invited the infantry Major to sit down. The Major did so, groaning heavily. He looked about him with a slightly pained expression. "This place looks like a brothel!" he said.

Witterer gave an embarrassed laugh and tried to think how he could get rid of his unsatisfactory guest as quickly as possible without giving offence. The man was simply too coarse for him. He had no manners at all. He can't ever have had much enthusiasm for the war.

Corporal Krause, the adjutant, appeared on the scene. He looked distinctly nervous. He stumbled over the carpet as he made his salute.

"Well?" asked Witterer. "Are the ladies coming?"

"I beg to inform the Captain that the ladies have already left. With Sergeant Asch."

"Hell and damnation," cried Captain Witterer. "What do they think they're playing at?"

"So it's not a brothel after all," mused the Major.

"Send my car round at once!" shouted Witterer.

"I beg to inform the Captain that Kowalski has gone with them."

"Don't get excited, Prize Shot," said the Major. "Just write the ladies off until next year. You'll have to get used to the fact that there are more men killed than conceived in war—however hard you try to adjust the balance."

Sergeant Asch signalled to the driver cf the little truck to go slower. They had now arrived at the main base. The conjurer, who was sitting on his case at the back, tired and irritable and still tortured by the fear of catching cold, sighed loudly with relief.

Kowalski, following on behind, swayed comfortably about the road with his car-load of ladies. He didn't miss a single pothole. The springs creaked and groaned. Kowalski was convinced that his passengers were having a fine time.

"Here we are!" Asch shouted back to him.

"Right! Now the fun begins," said Kowalski.

Asch had jumped out of the truck and was already unloading the baggage. Somewhat reluctantly, the conjurer helped him. Kowalski looked eagerly on.

"Well, we'll just say good-bye then," said Asch.

"Good God, man, what's the matter with you?" cried Kowalski, honestly indignant. "I don't feel nearly entertained enough yet. Besides, I managed to screw three bottles of champagne out of Soeft. That's an event in itself. It needs to be celebrated!"

Asch avoided catching Lisa Ebner's eye. She was staring straight at him. He shook his head and said:

"We won't bother the ladies any longer."

"I've got a date anyway," said Viola, who never liked to begin her real day's work until after midnight. "Take my case up for me, children. I'm in a hurry. Till to-morrow, then."

"She doesn't do too badly," said Kowalski, looking after her in astonishment. He seemed particularly interested in her hips. "What swagger!" he said, in admiration. "She must have been a camel in some previous incarnation!"

"Not only in a previous incarnation!" said Charlotte dryly. "But now what about you two heroes? Are you going to stay here and freeze to death or come up for a drink?"

"I'm right with you," said Kowalski, hurriedly collecting the various pieces of baggage.

"And what about you, Herr Asch?" asked Charlotte, mockingly. "Are you going to stay down here and wait for your friend?"

Asch was undecided. "I don't quite see the point," he said.

"It's so that you can keep your promise," said Lisa Ebner, and her voice, which was usually so soft, sounded almost angry.

"What promise?"

"We were told that if we would come straight back here immediately after the performance, a certain Sergeant Asch would be very pleased. Moreover, we were told that we'd be able to have a little chat and drink a bottle of champagne together."

"Who said that?" asked Asch in astonishment.

"I did," said Kowalski. "Who else do you think? And didn't I say what was in your mind?"

"Apart from the fact," said Charlotte, "that I don't think either of you have any idea what a mind is, I must admit that it was only because of that we left when we did."

"Exactly," said Lisa Ebner, decisively. "Otherwise we would have stayed with Captain Witterer. And I'm already sorry that we didn't. I don't like being lied to—especially in this sort of way."

"I don't take that as being directed at me," said Kowalski, now heavily laden with baggage. "I merely give expression to the thoughts of other people."

And with that Kowalski set off, followed by a laughing Charlotte. Lisa Ebner left Asch without another word. Snatching up her guitar so suddenly that it twanged against her breast, she went up after the other two. The conjurer had vanished long ago, as if the victim of one of his own tricks.

Asch stood all alone in the cold for some time, thinking things over. Then he brought the flat of his hand down sharply on the little truck's mud-guard. He bent down, loaded himself up with the rest of the baggage, and followed them into the building.

There was no one in the corridors. He could hear the sound of snoring behind closed doors.

Asch pushed open the door of Viola's and Charlotte's room. Kowalski was kneeling on the floor beside the stove blowing some life into the still glowing coals. The Sergeant let Charlotte take the cases which belonged to her.

"And the last one," she said with a significant smile, "belongs next door."

Asch nodded to Kowalski, who grinned at him. He went out of the room and shut the door behind him. Then, without knocking, he went straight into Lisa Ebner's room and put down the case.

"Anything else you want?" he asked.

Lisa Ebner looked at him out of her big round eyes. Then, as if he simply wasn't there, she unbuttoned her coat with slow deliberate movements, took it off and threw it on to the bed.

"Why do you think I didn't stay with Captain Witterer?"

"Because you're a sensible girl. Much more sensible than I realised."

Lisa Ebner didn't answer at once. She looked at him again

for a moment, searchingly. Then she sat down on the camp-bed, picked up first one leg and then the other, and pushed her shoes off without untying the laces. Then she leant over and found a pair of slippers from a corner, again picked up one leg after the other, and put the slippers on.

Then she said, with some feeling: " I'm fed up with being sensible."

" Well, sleep well," said Asch. " And be thankful you're sleeping alone. To-morrow morning you'll wake up just as sensible as ever."

Lisa Ebner stood up quickly, as if a sudden idea had just struck her. She stared at him intently for a long time. And as she stared at him, she took hold of her sweater and pulled it over her head. And she let it fall on the floor beside her. Her hair was all untidy and her eyes were shining.

" What are you doing, Lisa?" asked Asch, quietly.

" I can do what I like."

" You'll catch cold."

She continued to look straight at him. She drew her small, sinewy frame up to its full height. He saw the beginnings of her breasts, her white shoulders and her slight little arms.

Asch went up to her, put his hands on her shoulders and made her sit down on the camp-bed. She obeyed without a murmur. She sat there looking up at him.

Asch sat down beside her.

" Lisa," he said very seriously, " you're one of those rare girls whom men love, rather than just want to go to bed with. There are a lot of people who'll want to spend their whole lives with you. So far, I've only met two women I've been able to say that to, and have said it to."

" Who's the other one?"

Asch smiled. Then he went on: " Don't just throw yourself away, Lisa. You're much too good for that."

" But I'm in love," she said, with conviction.

" If you really think you're in love with Witterer, then you don't know what love is."

" Not with Witterer," she said, indignantly, " with you!"

" Lisa!"

She threw herself desperately into his arms. It was as if she wanted to bury her head in his breast. Her small, nervous hands felt for his shoulders. Her hair had a soft, sweet smell and her breath was hot on his cheek. Her whole body seemed to be on fire.

" I love you," she said, almost inaudibly.

Asch's hands were still on her naked shoulders. He held her

firmly. Slowly he bent his head down until his lips touched her hair.

Then he pushed her away from him and said:

"This won't do, Lisa."

She stared at him helplessly.

"Why not?"

"You don't know what you want."

"But I do," she said, indignantly, and her eyes quickly filled with tears. And the tears overflowed and poured down her narrow, eager little face. "I do know what I want. And I can't help it. I'm made that way. And I'm going to stay that way. And you must take me as I am."

"Don't forget that I'm a married man."

Asch felt that he had to defend himself with all his might. He would have to be hard and brutal, if necessary.

He stood up and moved away from her altogether, so that the little table stood between them. And he pretended that he was looking straight at her but, in fact, he was looking at a point on the wall just beside her head.

"What do you think you're doing, Lisa?" he said, brutally. "You're no better than an animal. An animal on heat. You ought to be ashamed of yourself."

Anger showed on her pale face. She stopped crying. Her lips trembled and he saw that she was clenching her teeth.

"How dare you talk to me like that!" she said, with a last desperate sob.

"You don't deserve any better. Listen, this war may last another two or three years. When it's over you'll be twenty-three. Only twenty-three. Do you want to be an old whore at twenty-three?"

"Get out of here! Get out at once!"

"You'll be gone to-morrow," said Asch. "And I shall be several kilometres and a whole night nearer the end of this bloody war."

"I never want to see you again! Never!"

"I don't expect you will either," said Asch. He walked slowly out of the door, and there was a hunched look about him as he went.

He turned round once more before he shut the door behind him.

"See that you keep out of trouble," he said. "You're too good to be wasted."

He stumbled a short way down the corridor and then stood

there motionless for a moment. He raised his hand and ran it gently along the wooden partition of Lisa's room.

"It had to be like that," he said. He tried to smile.

He moved along the corridor. He went to the door with a notice on it saying: "Requisitioned. By order of the Commanding Officer. Occupied by two Ladies."

He knocked and waited. There was a short pause and then he knocked again. The door opened and Kowalski appeared in his shirt-sleeves.

"Coming?" asked Asch. And he knew it was a pointless question.

But the Lance-Corporal answered:

"Yes, of course. Right away."

Then he vanished and reappeared five minutes later in the corridor. He seemed tongue-tied. They wandered past rooms full of sleepers, down the steps and out into the open air.

They stopped in front of the entrance. Asch looked up at the sky which was grey and heavy. The clouds hung very low.

"There's dirty weather brewing up," he said. "To-morrow night'll be hell."

Kowalski also seemed lost in contemplation of the threatening clouds. He took a series of deep breaths, as if testing the quality of the cold damp air. Then he said, absent-mindedly:

"You know, that woman's a menace, Asch."

Asch realised at once that he was talking about Charlotte.

"She doesn't seem one," he said.

"But she is, all the same," said Kowalski, adding with some hesitation: "You know, a few more days with her and I'd become quite respectable. Astounding, isn't it?"

"You—respectable, Kowalski? You know you don't mean it!"

"I wouldn't have believed it myself this evening," the other assured him. "But I was in serious danger, I can tell you."

"Aren't you getting confused with the lady herself?"

"Not at all, Asch." Kowalski seized his friend by the arm and looked at him with genuine anxiety. "Listen, man—I had every intention of . . . well, you know how it is."

"And you didn't bring it off? Kowalski, you're not getting too old for the job, are you?"

"Ah, man," sighed Kowalski. "I hardly know what's happening to me. This war's got me on its conscience, all right. Yes, well, as for this woman, I meant to . . . And she herself wasn't disinclined. But just as I was getting down to things, she asked

196

me what I thought of marriage. A great deal, I said, it's something I respect—particularly in others."

"And did she clock you?"

"Worse, man. She laughed. She simply roared with laughter. And now I'm wondering whether she was laughing at me."

"Was there someone else in the room then?"

"You're not taking me seriously, Asch," complained Kowalski. "And she wouldn't take me seriously either. No one takes me seriously. I'm slowly turning into a professional clown."

"You've had too much to drink, Kowalski."

"That must be it," said the other, considerably relieved. "Yes, that must be it. I must be tight. This would never have happened to me if I'd been sober. Never!"

"Well, come on, you old dog. Witterer probably wants a word with you. And with me, too."

"As for Witterer," said Kowalski, "I'll flay the man alive. And that goes for all the other Witterers in this world too."

"You'll be kept pretty busy then."

"Every Witterer in the world," repeated Kowalski, angrily. "They're to blame for my failure this evening. And I'm not going to stand for it. I'll show you how to deal with that nonentity."

It was a damp, heavy night all along the front. Earth and sky seemed to have melted together on the horizon. The snow through which the sentry stamped his rounds stuck to his boots like dough.

The sentry made his way slowly round the gun. He kept on the move in order to keep warm. His hands were thrust deep into the pockets of his greatcoat. His collar was turned up. His face stuck up out of it, a grey, indeterminate lump.

Suddenly he stopped and listened. And the night also seemed to stop and listen to his breathing. And he thought he caught the drone of distant engines.

"Impossible," he thought. For the sound, muffled as if by a heavy layer of blankets, was coming from the Russian lines. And the Russians, as he knew quite well, were fast asleep.

Let them go on sleeping!

Soeft lay with his little eyes closed, his mouth wide open and an expression of blissful happiness on his face. His enormous nose was pointed towards the ceiling. He was bellowing the song about the obliging young girl who was so hot that she wore no underclothes:

> " And just as God had made her
> She did what all men bade her
> And the General roared with might and main
> ' Now, come on, do it once again.' "

And his bosom friends, the Sergeant-Major and the N.C.O. i/c transport joined in the chorus with him.

A thick haze of smoke lay over the room. The top of the table was wet with spilt schnaps.

" Ah, well," said Soeft, thickly, " if you've got no women, drink's better than nothing."

" And if you must have dead men, then let them be this sort," said the Sergeant-Major pointing at the row of empty bottles and thinking himself very clever.

Soeft nodded.

" The war will be starting up again to-morrow. And I tell you: food is more important than ammunition. And more important even than food is Soeft."

" You tell Witterer that!"

" Ah, to hell with Witterer. The war will look after him, all right. It's put paid to better men than him before now."

At home the night seemed still and peaceful. The first hint of spring stole softly through the bluish darkness. War had put out the lights in the streets of the little town.

Corporal Vierbein sat beside Lore Schulz. He was determined now to show his courage on the home front as well as in battle. And Lore Schulz seemed willing not to put his heroism to too severe a test.

" Herr Vierbein," she said, and the standard lamp threw a soft light on to her eager upturned face, " would you say I was just a sort of ' reserve ' where you're concerned?"

" No, Frau Schulz," said Vierbein, and he was astonished at his own bravado. " You're an integral part of the front!"

" Ah," she said slowly, " but who knows how easily I might be overrun?"

And then she added, even more slowly than before: "Would you like to test my defences?"

Colonel Luschke lay on his bed, fully clothed. He was unable to sleep. His lumpy face was wet with sweat. His hands were folded on top of the blankets, but he wasn't praying.

After a time he threw off the blankets and got up off the bed. He felt his way over to the map table and put his hand up to the electric lamp which hung from the ceiling. He switched it on. It burnt dimly. The battery was low.

The Colonel's bow-legs were stuck into woollen stockings. His riding-breeches had slipped down, for he had undone his braces when trying to get off to sleep. The Iron Cross First Class shone dully on his tunic, which lay in heavy folds across his chest.

Luschke looked rather like a tired, overworked dwarf; and he knew that he did. He supported the top part of his narrow frame on his hands, as he bent over the map. He looked at the thin lines which marked the roads along which his regiment was to withdraw the following night.

His face showed signs of strain.

He put out a hand for the reports which had come in the evening before: Movement of enemy troops anticipated in the sector; weather report: unchanged; enemy agent's transmitter detected in divisional area; absolute ban on any movement of troops before nightfall to-morrow.

He switched out the light, went over to the window, pulled the curtain back and stared out into the darkness. A few isolated snow-flakes came tumbling out of the sky. They melted as they struck the window-pane.

"There's something really filthy brewing up," said Luschke sourly to himself.

Old Asch came tiptoeing out of Ingrid's bedroom and went across the corridor to the living-room. His old friend Freitag, who was sitting over a bottle of wine, looked up at him as he came in.

"She's asleep," said old Asch. "And she's sleeping alone."

"Aren't you a little sorry?"

"I would have understood," said old Asch, after a moment's thought. "I'd have done the same myself."

Foreman Freitag took a sip of wine. Then he said:

"According to Vierbein, things are dead quiet on much of the front. Nearly as quiet as here."

"Well, why not? Or do you imagine they're all mad to have a go at the Russians?"

"What the ordinary soldier thinks doesn't come into it."

"But the war couldn't be carried on without them, all the same."

"Did we want the First World War?" asked Freitag.

"Of course not."

"Then it didn't take place, I suppose?"

The old café proprietor cut the end of another cigar. He took his time about lighting it. Then he asked:

"Why do we obey this Führer of ours?"

"We can't help it. It's a national characteristic, man! There's something sacred about orders to us Germans. And about all orders too. It doesn't matter who gives them—men of honour, half-wits or criminals!"

Natasha clung to Lieutenant Wedelmann. Their hearts were full and they lay as close to each other as they could. He thought he could feel her trembling.

"Don't go," she said.

Wedelmann gently broke away from her.

"I must go. To-morrow's going to be a strenuous day for us. And then there'll be a night when we don't see each other. But after that we'll be together again."

"Don't go," she repeated. And she said it so that it sounded both like a plea and an order at the same time.

Wedelmann bent over her and his lips searched for her mouth. She kissed shyly and tenderly, as if it were the first kiss of all.

"It has to be like this," he said.

She shook her head vigorously.

"You should never leave me," she said. "Never. You ought to stay with me for ever." And she added, almost inaudibly: "I don't want to be alone any more."

"I love you more than anyone else in the world."

"How I loathe this war!" she cried out suddenly.

"And I loathe it, too," said Wedelmann. He hardly knew

what he was saying any more. He stroked her trembling hands tenderly for a moment and then went out.

She stared after him. She stared at the closed door for a long time after he had left. She listened desperately to the silence of the night.

She buried her face in her hands. After a while she pushed them up through her hair. She knelt down suddenly and it seemed almost as if she had fallen.

She bent right down and felt for the chest under her bed. Quickly she opened it and pulled out a few pieces of clothing —a scarf, some stockings and a crumpled dress. Then she pulled out a little box and put it on the table.

It was a short-wave transmitter.

Lore Schulz was stroking Vierbein's hand. She loved his hands. She loved all hands that were, as she put it, " nice " hands.

" My life's terribly lonely, believe me," she said.

" I do believe you," Vierbein assured her. He was prepared to believe anything she said.

" That is, if you call it a life," she said. " I'm practically in prison here. I'm not allowed into the mess. I'm not good enough for the officers apparently. And too good for the N.C.O.s. Civilians, of course, are out of the question. So what is there left for me?"

" I have a friend," said Vierbein, struck by a sudden thought, " who is an Admiral."

Lore Schulz sat up in astonishment. " Really?" she said.

" And my friend the Admiral is the most decent man in uniform I've ever met. And if I asked him to do something for me, he'd do it. I'm certain of it."

" And what could you ask him to do?"

" He's the C.O.'s father-in-law. He's come here specially for the wedding. And I'll tell him about you. I'll tell him how pretty you are and how good you are and how gay. And I'll ask him to escort you to the wedding."

" You'll really do that for me?" asked Lore Schulz, excitedly.

" Gladly," said Vierbein. " You deserve it."

And almost inaudibly, he added:

" So does he."

An urgent telegram arrived at the little town's post office in the course of the night. It ran: "Corporal Vierbein—Leave Cancelled—Return to Unit immediately—Witterer, Captain, C.O., No. 3 Troop."

Captain Witterer, who was by now on his last legs, was still sitting up with the infantry Major. The Major's capacity for drink seemed unending. He drank and drank and showed no signs of it. "I don't sleep much," said the holder of the Knight's Cross.

"Soldiers don't need much sleep," said Witterer, who was nearly dead with exhaustion. Krause, who sat beside him, was already beginning to drop off.

"To hell with that," said the Major. "I only don't sleep because I can't sleep. Who could sleep in a filthy hole like this? But I'll break out one day—go completely off my head. And I must say I'm looking forward to the moment already."

"To-morrow night's the night," said Witterer, still doing his best to get rid of his guest. It looked as if he would never leave. "We'll need all our strength for that."

"So long as the Russians don't try and follow up the withdrawal it'll be a walk-over," said the Major.

"Is the Major afraid there may be trouble," asked Witterer, suddenly showing interest. And Krause also pricked up his ears.

"What else is the whole war but trouble?" said the holder of the Knight's Cross, unconcernedly.

"But the people at the top know what they're doing. . . ."

"Do they hell?" said the Major, very emphatically, pouring the contents of an entire tumbler down his throat. "Waging war on a map is a very different thing from lying around in the mud yourself. There's a difference, too, between blood and the mark you make on a map with a red pencil. Some men are killed—right, rub them out with an india-rubber! One man vomits his lungs up into the snow. But the other's only vomiting because he's drunk too much red wine!"

"But what if the Russians really do try and follow up the withdrawal?"

" Then you'll have another chance to show what a prize shot you are, my friend!"

" You ought to be glad you didn't," Charlotte said to Lisa Ebner, as she sat beside her on the bed the next morning.

" *He* was the one who didn't."

" Then write him a post-card and thank him."

" I would have shown him how much I loved him. He would never have forgotten."

" Child," said Charlotte, smiling, " what do you mean by ' never '? Three days? A year? For as long as the war lasts? Times like these affect the memory. We all suffer from amnesia these days. My husband was killed in Poland—did I remain faithful to his memory?"

" But that was two years ago."

" It was a little under ten months before I was sleeping with someone else."

" But if you loved him . . ."

" Two months after that I slept with another man. And with three or four others in the two months after that."

" Why did you do it?"

" I'd got into the habit and couldn't stop myself," said Charlotte honestly. And she looked thoughtfully at her clothes which lay scattered on a chair and over the floor. " But now, I don't want that any more."

" What do you want?"

" I want to get married," she said simply. " I want to know where I am. These men who undress me with their eyes all the time, repel me. If the war had a face I'd spit in it."

Schulz was flirting with his Commanding Officer's bride-to-be. The lady was still in high spirits, though her future husband had dropped off and was snoring peacefully in his arm-chair.

Schulz turned on what he thought of as his charm.

" Dear lady," he said, and he sat his massive form down beside her. This in no way appeared to displease her. " Dear lady, your future husband for whom I have the greatest respect, knows that he can rely on me in every eventuality. In every eventuality."

"We both think very highly of you, Herr Schulz."

"I'm most honoured to hear it," he replied, promptly. It was as much as he could do not to wink at himself.

The C.O.'s bride was a thin, almost scraggy-looking creature, with a pale complexion and mousy hair. She had a pale mousy personality too. But her eyes shone with a sort of joyful eagerness. As far as Schulz was concerned, she was a woman. Was she not to marry his own C.O.? And Schulz had a weakness for women.

"He's asleep," she said, nodding sideways at the snoring C.O. and smiling at Schulz. She liked his broad manly appearance. This man was part of her future now, her future with her soldier husband. A by no means unimportant part of that future.

"Allow me," said Schulz. He rang the bell. An orderly appeared and Schulz said curtly: "Send Bartsch and Ruhnau to me at once."

The man disappeared. And soon after Bartsch and Ruhnau themselves arrived and came smartly to attention, waiting for orders. They swayed slightly as they stood there, but otherwise, seemed fit for duty.

"You will take the Commanding Officer home," said Schulz. "And see you go carefully. None of your monkey tricks. I want you both on parade to-morrow for the artillery display."

The Siamese twins grinned obediently.

"And if you will permit, dear lady," said Schulz, turning on all his charm, "I shall be delighted to escort you home myself."

Slowly night began to creep away from the front. And earth and sky seemed to have blended completely. It was snowing. The snow-flakes fell like drops of water. They were thin and scattered. And they melted as soon as they had fallen.

The sentry on the gun had crept under a sheet of canvas for shelter. He stared in the direction of the enemy. And he listened as hard as he could, with his eyes almost closed.

The distant drone of engines was coming nearer and nearer. They were big, powerful engines and their noise was muffled by the snow. The sentry could almost see the enemy vehicles churning their way along the slushy roads.

But what sort of vehicles were they? Heavy trucks? Or tanks?

"It's ridiculous," thought the sentry. "What the hell's going on?" And he reminded himself that sound was four times as loud during the night as during the day. And this knowledge reassured him. He felt tired, dog-tired, dead tired in fact— why shouldn't the Russians be feeling just like him?

And the snow continued to fall. Noiselessly. And it changed into drops of water as it fell.

Thin, scattered snow-flakes, hardly noticeable at all.

When the war began to show signs of life again, the first to depart was the ace war-correspondent. Eberwein needed no experience of the real thing to be able to write a vivid description of it. He left first-hand experience to those of his colleagues with too much ambition and too little imagination.

The second person to get on the move was Soeft. He, admittedly, had every intention of coming back. He was merely indulging in the luxury of anticipating this carefully camouflaged top-secret withdrawal by twelve hours or so. There was a ban on all movement before nightfall. But Soeft began to get his men on the move during the early part of the afternoon.

Of course he didn't ask anyone's permission to do this.

First of all he loaded all food, wines and spirits, and tobacco, on to his new Henschel eight-tonner. And while he was about it he took the opportunity of sending three cases out to a cover address in Germany by the one but last goods train to leave the main base—to supplement his own private stocks.

" If you want to send three cases," said the Sergeant-Major who was the right-hand man of the officer in charge of the goods station, " you must deliver five altogether—forty per cent for us, that's the new tariff."

" Anyone would think the Jews were running this place," said Soeft, reproachfully.

" Well, if you don't want to accept those terms, then don't," said the Sergeant-Major, adamantly, " but clear your stuff off the loading ramp so that other people can get on to it."

Soeft looked with growing irritation at the pile of boxes, sacks and cases that were waiting on the goods platform. The troops who were to do the loading sat around, idly smoking or dozing, waiting for the arrival of the one but last train. The officer in charge stalked proudly up and down like a cock on a dunghill.

" One case for three," said Soeft, finally, " and a special food parcel all to yourself."

"With caviar?" asked the Sergeant-Major bluntly.

"With two pounds of caviar," said Soeft.

"All right, then," said the Sergeant-Major, as if he were making a great sacrifice. "For you, I'll do it. One does what one can for people after all. And seeing how long we've known each other. . . ."

"Cut it out, you old crook," said Soeft genially. "You know very well that for sharpness there's nothing to choose between us."

After concluding this little transaction, Soeft started off with the Ford and the Henschel on his first official round of evacuation. The protests of the Sergeant-Major who was afraid that this might lead to trouble of the worst sort, made no impression on the Ration King at all.

"You simply can't do that, Soeft," said the Sergeant-Major, imploringly.

"Oh yes, I can," said Soeft, putting a padlock and chain through the iron grill which had been fixed up to the back of the Henschel. He had already done the same thing to the Ford. He gave his specal key an extra turn and put it away in his pocket. Then he grinned happily. He was the sort of man who never trusted in anyone. He always preferred to take three times too many precautions rather than one too few. There was always the possibility that there might be another Soeft around in the neighbourhood somewhere.

"You know perfectly well," said the Sergeant-Major, supplicating and reprimanding at the same time, "that according to our marching orders, this troop is not to get on the move until 22.00 hours. And the guns are not to move before midnight. You know that perfectly well, Soeft."

"All I know," said Soeft calmly, "is that you seem very windy already."

"All unnecessary troop movements are to be avoided."

"But my movements are entirely necessary," said the other, "and therefore unavoidable."

"We've got to reckon," said the Sergeant-Major, stubbornly, quoting from divisional orders, "that the enemy has our movements under continual observation."

Soeft nodded and climbed up on to the Henschel.

"And that's why I'm moving now," he said. "If he has—which I very much doubt—it's just one of those little ideas the people on the staff like to get into their heads—and certainly they have plenty of time to give their imaginations a free rein—but anyway, if he has, then he'll know that the hard-working

Soeft spends his days driving all over the area trying to find something to put in that great belly of yours, Sergeant-Major. If I don't drive around to-day, man, he'll get suspicious and begin to think that something is up. Understand?"

"Oh, all right then," said the Sergeant-Major. "Do what you like. But on your own head be it. I don't know anything about it, see?"

"No one'll doubt that," said Soeft, giving the signal to drive away.

It was just about an hour later that Colonel Luschke came through on the telephone to complain of Soeft's activities. He quickly dealt with the Sergeant-Major and demanded to speak to Witterer. But Witterer was nowhere to be found, though Bock searched everywhere for him.

"Well, tell him to ring me up immediately," said Luschke, "and don't forget, Sergeant-Major, I said *immediately*."

Bock assured him that he had understood perfectly. He was trembling slighlty as he put down the receiver. He cursed Soeft with a terrifying wealth of vocabulary. Then he put everyone he could possibly find on to the task of locating Witterer, and himself continued to telephone for him until the wires grew red hot.

Captain Witterer, followed everywhere by his shadow Corporal Krause, was firmly convinced that the greatest moment of his life was approaching. Ever since he had first put on uniform, and indeed for some time before, he had looked forward eagerly to his first experience of action and now it seemed the moment was at last upon him! In something like a real state of elation, he supervised the final preparations for the withdrawal, and needless to say, left nothing to chance.

First of all he made the ammunition section practise loading up until the men's tongues were hanging out with exhaustion. Then he made the cook prepare a meal with the field kitchen all packed up and ready to move. He even made his way into the men's billets and inspected their kit; that's to say he made them unpack it and drew a sharp distinction between necessary and unnecessary articles and gave Krause orders—which Krause immediately wrote down—that no article designated by him as unnecessary should be allowed to be taken in a man's kit.

The men stood there with their eyes popping out of their heads.

Then he went and put the machine-gun crews through their paces. He was at this for nearly an hour. It brought him to the verge of desperation for the more he put them through it, the slower all their movements became. His voice grew hoarser and hoarser.

"Take their names, Krause," he shouted finally. "Take all their names! And we'll practise it all over again when we get into the new position."

Krause took their names. The Captain flexed his knees athletically. The machine-gun crews stood there at attention, goggling at their troop commander in astonishment. Only the Corporal in charge of them was looking up at the sky.

"I'm here, man, not up there," cried Witterer.

"It's snowing," said the Corporal, calmly.

It was snowing. The snow-flakes which were tumbling out of the sky were large and heavy and soggy with moisture. They fell noiselessly, fairly widely scattered at first.

"Yes, it's snowing," said Krause.

"I can see that," cried Witterer. "I don't need anyone to tell me that. And what if it is snowing? I don't care if the snow-flakes weigh a hundredweight each—it doesn't alter anything. If we have to wade up to our necks in mud, we'll pull off a respectable withdrawal whatever happens, understand?"

"Yes, sir," chimed in Krause immediately, although he didn't feel too happy about it.

"If any one of you fellows let me down," shouted Witterer, "I'll tear him to pieces with my own hands when we get into our new positions."

A runner came panting up. He was breathing very heavily, although he hadn't really been over-exerting himself. But it was a convincing performance.

"The Captain is to ring up Colonel Luschke—immediately."

"You mean," said Witterer correcting him sternly, "that the Commanding Officer, Colonel Luschke, is looking for me and wishes me to get in touch with him by telephone with the least possible delay."

"That's right," said the runner.

Captain Witterer flung one last devastating look at the goggling machine-gun crews, another—a more satisfied one this time—at the large stack of ammunition they would have to move, and strode away, always followed by his faithful Krause, to the nearest field telephone.

This was installed in one of the troop's observation posts, in a little Dutch barn which the men had converted by means of boards and mud and blankets, into a primitive shelter. It was a windowless little hovel, packed with men and equipment.

Witterer was rather put out to find the inhabitants paid little attention to him.

" Come on, out of here the lot of you," he shouted. " I want to telephone."

" Come on, out of here," shouted Krause. " Hurry up. The fresh air will do you good."

" You go out, too, Krause," ordered Witterer.

The soldiers pushed their way, grumbling, out of the hovel. Krause followed them out like a sheep-dog. His bark was more like a poodle's, for none of the troops paid the slightest attention to him.

After the Captain had carefully switched off every extension, he grabbed the telephone and put a call through to the Colonel. Two minutes later the Colonel came on to the line. And, as always, his voice was soft and purring.

" Captain Witterer here, sir. I was to ring you up."

Luschke cleared his throat. Then he said:

" Captain, what do you imagine is the point of giving orders?"

" To have them obeyed, sir," answered Witterer promptly.

" I'm very glad to hear you say that, Captain," purred the Colonel softly. " And I'd be glad if you'd tell your men that—and as soon as possible."

" Very good, sir."

" For unfortunately your own wholly invaluable appraisal of the situation does not appear to be shared by the men under your command. Do you know what the excellent Soeft is up to at this moment?"

" I imagine he's up at rear base, Colonel."

" You imagine, my dear Captain? I'd prefer it if you said you knew. For if you did know what Soeft was up to, my dear Captain, you'd also know that your troop simply doesn't give a damn for your orders. Soeft is at this moment transporting supplies to the rear with a fleet of vehicles fit to transport the baggage train of three generals."

" I'll look into that, sir. . . . If that's really true, Colonel, I'll have the fellow put under close arrest."

" If that's really true, did you say? Do you doubt my word, Captain? No? That's extremely good of you, I must say. And ' close arrest ' did you say? Listen to me, you poor fish—I'd be grateful if you put your house in order, but kindly go about it in a reasonable manner. Have you ever heard of such a thing as establishing confidence and co-operation? You have? Well, now. But perhaps you are not quite clear what these words mean? Or are you?"

" Yes, Colonel."

" Good. But it would be even better if you not only knew the meaning of these words, but adjusted your behaviour in accordance with it. Mutual confidence and co-operation. You ask Lieutenant Wedelmann about those things. Or make some inquiries of Sergeant Asch. Let your own men put you wise. They could all have told you that something was seriously wrong. And, by the way, I might add that this is the first time Soeft has ever taken off on his own like this without informing his troop commander beforehand. That ought to make you think."

" Yes, Colonel."

" Captain Witterer," said Luschke, and there was once again a soft, sinister note in his voice. " May the Lord have mercy on you if you succeed in upsetting my No. 3 Troop. Always provided, that is, that the Lord is still interested in Germany. You've got a first-class bunch of men under you there, and you're to conduct your share of this war *with* them and not *against* them. If there's any trouble, Witterer, and it should become clear to me that you're responsible for it—my God, man, you'll then learn what ' Lumpface ' is really like and in such a way that you won't forget him in a hurry."

And with that the telephone conversation came to an end. Witterer stood there for several seconds, holding the receiver in his hand and staring into the gloom. He was shaken. Severely shaken, one might say. But he wasn't beaten yet.

Captain Witterer broke off the little round of last-minute preliminary training which he had been so keen to give his men and withdrew to his quarters. Here he took a reckoning of the situation. Corporal Krause lent him assistance, with considerable circumspection, on the whole, but with sycophantic alacrity whenever he felt his active participation was called for. The telephone conversation was still having its repercussions.

" I'm the C.O. here," said Witterer. " And what I demand is confidence."

" Very naturally," said Krause, positively oozing confidence.

" And above everything else, co-operation," said Witterer.

" Yes, sir," said Krause, co-operatively.

" I hope I can rely on you in this respect," said Witterer.

Krause looked loyally up at his C.O. and his loyalty seemed

unmistakably genuine. There was no need for him to say anything. Witterer nodded approvingly.

Then he said:

"Besides, I hope you realise that you hold a position of special confidence here?"

"Naturally, Captain," Krause assured him with some solemnity.

"Good," said Witterer. "Well, we'll see."

Then he paced up and down the room for a while, with his hands behind his back, trying to set at rest the gnawing sense of unease which his telephone conversation with Luschke had left him with. His chin was thrust forward and his eyes half closed.

Suddenly he stopped, looked challengingly at Krause and said: "How well do you know Colonel Luschke? What sort of a man is he?"

Krause saw that this was an important moment. By asking him this question, Witterer had really shown his confidence in him. A Captain was asking him, a Corporal, to give his opinion of a Colonel. He knew that, for the first time, he had now really become Witterer's right-hand man, his most intimate adviser.

"I don't think there's anyone who knows the Colonel really well," Krause said warily.

"Not even Lieutenant Wedelmann?"

"I hardly think so, sir, though it must be admitted that the Colonel has a high opinion of the Lieutenant."

"As a man?"

"More as a troop commander—for his achievements, I should say. The troop's success has been quite remarkable."

"Aha," said Witterer, who felt no embarrassment about discussing these things with Krause. He seemed to be getting near the heart of the matter now.

And his pacing up and down the room became just a little more agitated. Then it stopped altogether. He saw that he was on the point of discovering what this was all about. And he said to himself: Witterer, you're a man who's weathered many a storm in your time. You've had full Generals as your immediate superiors before now. You've coped with the most complex moves in the game of red-tape. And you'll cope with Luschke too—not perhaps right away, but in time.

"Right," said Witterer, more to himself than to Krause. "So the Colonel favours confidence and co-operation. That's all a lot of nonsense, of course, but he shall have it."

"And he's impressed by courage," said Krause, quite calmly and almost inaudibly.

"And he shall have that too! And plenty of it!"

And then, still apparently perfectly calmly, but sensing that what he was about to say was the most powerful bait he could possibly throw out to Witterer, Krause said: "Of course what the Colonel hasn't yet got is a Knight's Cross."

"My God!" was all Witterer said for a moment. He seemed astonished and yet, at the same time, greatly relieved. Then he added with conviction: "You've hit it! That's it all right!"

"The Colonel," said Krause, keeping himself cleverly in the background, as if out of modesty, "was about due for the award last autumn. But the Divisional Commander came ahead of him on the list."

Witterer nodded. He wasn't nodding to Krause so much as to himself. And he said to himself: So that's the way the wind blows! The old boy seems to have persuaded himself that his only chance of getting the Knight's Cross is if the success of No. 3 Troop continues. And so long as Wedelmann was troop commander here this success, and his Knight's Cross, seemed assured. And he doesn't think that he stands as much chance with me in command as with Wedelmann. But that is just where the Colonel is wrong. I must make this clear to him. He shall have his Knight's Cross. With oak leaves, too, for all I care. I shall be quite content if I manage an Iron Cross First Class, or a German Cross in gold for myself.

Right then: Co-operation! Right: Mutual confidence! He shall have them. He shall have everything he wants. Witterer laughed a short, care-free laugh. His usually boundless self-confidence slowly began to return.

"Ask Lieutenant Wedelmann to come and see me at once," he said to Krause. "Sergeant Asch can come too."

"Very good, Captain," said Krause.

"But first of all," continued Witterer, "ring through to main base and try and get Fräulein Ebner to come to the telephone."

"Very good, Captain."

And while Krause set about putting these orders into effect, with commendable briskness and skill, Witterer spread his maps out in front of him and looked at the pencillings on them: present position—new position—line of withdrawal. And the excitement of battle, distinctly damped by Luschke's uncalled-for remarks down the telephone, once more began to stir in his veins.

The telephone rang loudly. Lisa Ebner on the line. Witterer

quickly adjusted himself from his role of battle-scarred hero to that of romantic cavalier.

"I'm sorry you weren't able to stay yesterday evening," he said.

"I'm sorry, too," said Lisa Ebner.

"I hope Sergeant Asch looked after you all right."

"I threw him out."

"Really?"

"On his ear."

"I'm very pleased to hear it," said Witterer, delighted.

"I'm not so pleased, Captain."

"No, naturally not," agreed Witterer, sympathetically. "Certainly you would have had a much nicer evening with us."

"I have no doubt of that. I'm only sorry we can't make up for it this evening. We're packing up to go."

"Perhaps I could drop in on you for a moment this afternoon? You won't be moving before nightfall."

"I'd be delighted," said Lisa Ebner, rather awkwardly.

"Excellent," said Witterer, and he smiled as charmingly as if she had been in the room with him. This conversation made him feel very much better. To know that he was respected again and not just by anyone but by a most attractive young woman who knew a real man when she saw one—all this was a great solace to his pride.

He got up when Wedelmann and Asch came into the room, and even took a couple of steps towards them. This surprised the Lieutenant agreeably but made the Sergeant thoroughly suspicious. Krause withdrew to the stove and listened carefully. No one seemed to take any notice of him.

"Gentlemen," said Witterer, bustling round them, "I've asked you here so that we can just quickly run over one or two points together. Sit down, won't you?"

Wedelmann and Asch sat down. Witterer remained standing in front of them. He smiled down at them. "Right then, gentlemen—the preparations for the withdrawal are as good as complete. But as neither of you are still on general duties with the troop, I've taken the liberty of allotting you special jobs."

"What were you thinking of exactly, Captain?" asked Wedelmann.

"It's quite simple—as neither of you are in command any more, you shall have certain supervising duties."

"Are we to be traffic policemen?" said Sergeant Asch. And he directed the question at Lieutenant Wedelmann, who shrugged his shoulders.

Witterer was determined to ignore the remark, but at the same time he told himself that it was the last remark of Sergeant Asch's which he was going to ignore in this way. He said:

"Your task will be primarily to support me in my role as troop commander. You, Lieutenant Wedelmann, will proceed to the new position at nightfall and superintend the arrival of the troop there. You, Sergeant Asch, will provide yourself with a motor-bicycle, and escort the men while actually on the move."

"A sort of watch-dog, you mean?"

"Something like that, Sergeant. If there are any breakdowns, you're to see that they're put right and all that sort of thing. Or don't you feel strong enough for the job?"

"Oh, I feel strong enough for it, all right, Captain," said Asch, quite unperturbed. "But not really stupid enough. What you're detailing me for is something that is properly speaking the job of each individual section commander, and under the over-all supervision of the N.C.O. i/c transport."

"But what," said Witterer, with a superior smile, "if unforeseen circumstances should occur, Sergeant Asch?"

"Since when," said Asch, stubbornly, once more turning to Lieutenant Wedelmann, "has it become necessary to have a Sergeant i/c unforeseen circumstances?"

"It's clear what you're expected to do, Asch," said Lieutenant Wedelmann, without making any attempt to conceal his indignation.

"I'm sometimes rather slow at grasping things," said Asch. "And I always make the mistake of thinking that other people are as stupid as I am."

"Gentlemen," said Witterer, with a certain forcefulness, and he once again managed to ignore Sergeant Asch's little aside, "There are two things to which I attach particular importance: mutual confidence and co-operation."

"I seem to have heard that before somewhere," muttered Asch.

"And it is to these two qualities that I appeal now. Confidence and co-operation. In addition to these, of course, come courage and good discipline. And then, gentlemen," and Witterer now spoke as if this was very much just between themselves, "what I want above all is a troop that will function smoothly. All our soldierly qualities must come to the fore. And I expect you two to set a good example."

"Anything else?" asked Wedelmann, getting to his feet.

"Officially, nothing," said Witterer. "Unofficially, just one more thing, and that's something for your ears, Sergeant."

Asch who had remained seated, looked up at Witterer in curiosity. "And what would that be?" he asked.

"Your personal qualities do not particularly concern me," began Witterer, and there was a trace of contempt in his voice. "You organised the entertainment show very well indeed and I have nothing but praise for you there. That your personal behaviour was not up to the same standard, as Fräulein Ebner has just informed me over the telephone, is a matter for regret, though I don't hold it against you. But what I am entitled to demand is that in the forthcoming test you should show to the full those soldierly qualities for which you have a reputation. Do you follow me?"

"Perfectly," said Sergeant Asch.

"As for discipline," concluded Witterer, with sudden sharpnesss, "we'll have a little talk about that later."

"By all means," muttered Asch grimly. And he and Wedelmann left the room.

"And now we two," said Witterer to Krause, feeling that he had come off very much best in this little encounter, "we two will just go and pay our farewell respects to Ivan. And we'll make it a farewell he won't forget in a hurry."

The Captain got Kowalski to drive him and Krause up to the gun positions, where two gun crews were immediately sent to the guns, and three minutes later given their targets.

"Fire!" cried Witterer.

The barrels recoiled with the force of the explosions. The shells went whining towards the enemy and exploded among a row of houses on the hillside opposite. A tongue of flame shot upwards, followed by a thick cloud of black smoke.

"And again!" shouted Witterer from his slit trench. The light of battle burned in his eyes.

And he turned to Krause, who was beside him in the slit trench and said:

"Now we can give it to them! Nothing matters now, Ivan can bring up as much artillery as he likes. We'll be away from here before he can do anything with it."

But at that moment there was a sudden gurgling sound through the air. It came nearer and nearer—turning slowly into an ominous muffled howl. Witterer dived down to the bottom of the trench. It was as if the earth were being torn up all round him. Shell splinters went whining through the air.

"But they've got artillery already," said Krause, in utter amazement.

A man on No. 2 gun suddenly screamed. Another only a few

yards away from Witterer, stood there rigid, with a fountain of blood spurting out of his neck, presumably hit in the jugular vein.

"Take cover!" roared Witterer.

Again there came the sound of an approaching shell, the ground heaved and mud and shell splinters went flying in all directions.

"Stretcher!" yelled a man, on a high long-drawn-out note like a siren.

"Hell and damnation," cried Witterer, after he had recovered from the shock, "what's happening? Order to observation post: locate battery immediately! We'll soon put paid to those swine."

A wounded man was carried off on a stretcher. Another went crawling wildly out into the open, screaming like a wounded animal. The gun-crew leader sprang out to try and bring him back.

"That fellow should pull himself together," said Witterer, brutally. And his remark was plainly audible for the enemy guns had stopped firing and it was suddenly as if they had never fired at all.

"Head wound presumably," said the crew leader, holding on to the wounded man who was struggling desperately.

Witterer climbed out of the trench and strode off to the rear. Krause trotted after him.

"What I'd like to know," said Witterer, when he was once more inside the car, "is where Ivan has suddenly got his artillery from? There's something wrong somewhere."

"Why on earth shouldn't he have artillery?" said Kowalski, as he started up the engine. "You'll soon get a chance of seeing how he uses it too. That was just the beginning."

The artillery display, "and simultaneous testing of new radio equipment" which had been ordered by Schulz, in his capacity as deputy C.O., for nine o'clock, had still not begun by half-past ten.

The guns had been in position since seven. The crews had reported ready for action by eight; the radio personnel by eight-fifteen. And shortly before nine Lieutenant Schulz arrived with the battery adjutant and Corporal Vierbein.

At ten o'clock the officer in charge of range safety announced that the safety measures were complete. At about the same time, the target officer announced that the towing targets, four in number, were ready in their sheds. And at half past ten a telephone message came through to say that the General could be expected to arrive at eleven o'clock.

Schulz, every inch the deputy C.O., decided to make good use of the interval. He once more put the gun crews through their paces, standing there with his watch in his hand, critically watching their every movement.

Corporal Vierbein sat a little apart on a hill. He forgot for a few minutes that Schulz had him here on parade with the battery as a sort of show piece. The mild spring sunshine fell on his young, rather sad-looking face, warming him pleasantly.

"Now once again, you clumsy oafs," cried Schulz. "And pull yourselves together or I'll give you something to remember me by for the rest of your lives. Ready? Right—into positions!"

The four gun crews were sweating their guts out. They cranked handles, raised levers, slammed bolts across, struggled up with the gun carriages. There was a clanking of metal. Sweat poured down their faces. Schulz laughed brutally.

"Five seconds over the average!" he yelled. "And you call yourself gunners! And to think that I've had a hand in your training! You're not fit to shovel cow-pats! What are you?"

"Not fit to shovel cow-pats!" chorused the gun crews.

"Now then once again!" cried Schulz. "Change position—move!"

Vierbein, sitting on his hill, seemed not to hear any of this. He stretched his arms out behind him and leant back. He looked out across the open country, and saw rolling hills, a beech tree or two and the rich green of the fields. He felt as if he were lying stretched out on a carpet.

And suddenly he seemed to see Lore Schulz kneeling on this carpet in front of him. And he looked at her eyes which were half closed and at her mouth which was beginning to open. Her eyes were a mysterious green and her mouth was blood-red. Then the red alone seemed to remain and it spread and spread until it was nothing but a shiny wet pool of blood. The green of the grass grew paler and paler and whiter and whiter until it suddenly turned into snow. The white snow-fields of Russia.

Vierbein shuddered. And he felt for the top pocket of his tunic, as if to make sure that it was properly buttoned. A rustle of paper came from the pocket. It was the telegram from Witterer calling him back to the front.

"The General's coming!" shouted a sentry, specially put there for the purpose.

"Now pull yourselves together, you swine," bellowed Schulz. "I want you to show the General that there's something else you can do besides put food into your bellies. And just remember one thing: if everything doesn't go perfectly smoothly, I'll see to it that you're trained for the front in such a fashion that death will seem a treat in comparison!"

The General appeared with a small entourage packed tightly into two large motor-cars. He was a small, thick-set, rather fat little man, with the face of a store general-manager, and the gait of a goods-yard inspector. A brown dachshund followed at his heels, but made off towards Schulz as soon as it saw him and prepared to raise its leg over his boots.

Schulz brought the parade to attention with the necessary words of command. The visiting officer saluted. The men stood stiffly to attention. A church clock could be heard striking twelve in the distance.

"Good morning, men," roared the General.

"Good morning, Herr General," the men roared back.

The General nodded in approval, shook hands with Schulz, said jovially: "Well now, and let's see what you can do!" and surrounded by his little cluster of officers, went and stood expectantly on the little hill which was to be his observation post.

And with that, at approximately a quarter past twelve, the display "together with demonstration of radio equipment", which had been scheduled to start at nine, was ready to begin.

But it did not begin.

First of all the men couldn't be found to tow the targets. Then when they had been found, there was no one to signal the all-clear. Then when someone had signalled the all-clear, the sights of one of the guns were damaged by clumsy handling of ammunition and had to be changed. Then there was no all-clear again. Finally when the all-clear had been given for the second time the rope on one of the target-towing machines broke.

The General who had begun by talking genially with his entourage, gradually grew silent. He did his best to glare sternly ahead of him, but only succeeded in staring idiotically at the horizon. He snorted angrily. He began flicking his gloves rhythmically up and down the outside of his riding-breeches.

Lieutenant Schulz was bursting with rage.

Then after they had all been standing there for an extremely painful three-quarters of an hour, the first round was fired closer and the next one closer still. None of the first eight rounds hit the target and the first target vehicle rolled out of sight undamaged.

"Rotten!" shouted the General and began punishing his riding-breeches with his gloves more furiously than ever.

Schulz went bright red and bit his lip. But when the second target vehicle also rolled out of sight untouched, he clenched his fists with suppressed fury.

"Worse still!" said the General.

And then Schulz played his only, and as he thought, unbeatable trump.

"The next attack will be carried out by Corporal Vierbein!" he bellowed.

Corporal Vierbein went over to the gun which was due to fire, and looked the crew up and down. The crew looked him up and down. It was obvious that they couldn't care less what happened.

Vierbein knew from the very first moment what the result would be. He could do nothing with the crew and they could do nothing with him. Contact or understanding between them was impossible—they were worlds apart.

Corporal Vierbein gave his orders calmly and deliberately. Round after round was fired. None hit. The third target vehicle rolled out of sight undamaged.

"The worst shooting I ever saw in my life!" said the General.

"The little runt!" choked Schulz.

"I've never seen anything like it," said the General. "Utterly rotten. Beneath all contempt!"

And he looked daggers at Schulz, who was trembling at the knees. The dachshund wagged his tail with joy and the General said: "You don't seem to be in the right job here, Lieutenant."

And then the General left. And behind him trotted the dachshund. And behind the dachshund, with long faces and much shaking of heads, trotted the entourage.

Schulz stayed where he was. And the officers of the reserve battery who remained with him looked as if they were standing round a freshly-dug grave. An oppressive silence fell over the scene.

Suddenly Schulz roared out: "Vierbein!"

And as the Corporal came to attention in front of him,

Schulz roared again: "I'll never forgive you for this, Vierbein! Never, do you hear? You did it on purpose. You were shooting like a . . . like a . . . you did it to spite me, Vierbein. But I won't let you get away with it, you little runt. You're done for now. Done for, do you understand? Finished. You haven't a hope."

"But Lieutenant . . ."

"Return to barracks immediately, Vierbein. On foot, too. And I want to see you do the nine kilometres in less than ninety minutes, do you hear? You will report to me at three o'clock this afternoon. And you'd better make your will beforehand, you rotten little swine!"

Corporal Vierbein turned about so smartly that he kicked up sand all over Schulz's trousers. Then he set off at once on his long walk home. He trotted off down the main road heading for the town, a solitary, inoffensive little figure. The officers' cars overtook him, covering him with dust as they passed. Schulz stared menacingly out of the back of one of them. Then the guns overtook him, and the trucks carrying personnel who had been taking part in the shoot. The thick clouds of dust completely enveloped him.

And Vierbein kept on walking. And the farther he walked the more determined became the expression on his face. The spring sun brought the sweat out on him. The sweat collected under the rim of his forage cap and ran over his face, leaving little rivulets in the layer of dust which had formed there. He looked as if he were crying. But he was determined not to cry.

He reached the barracks at twenty-five minutes to three. He washed off the dust and the sweat, and punctually at three o'clock was standing before Lieutenant Schulz in his service dress.

"Right," said Schulz—and he was trembling with suppressed rage—"Right then, we'll begin!"

"I beg to inform the Lieutenant," said Vierbein calmly, "that His Excellency the Admiral is expecting me."

Schulz started. That was true. He'd quite forgotten about the Admiral. This rather spoilt his plan. He wanted his pound of flesh. His pound of Vierbein's flesh. Did the fellow really have to go to the Admiral?

"Bartsch and Ruhnau can go to him instead," said Schulz. But the Siamese twins weren't to be found for the moment, and Schulz eventually had to agree that His Excellency the Admiral couldn't be kept waiting any longer. Because of this guest's special status there could be no question of trying to find even less suitable substitutes. Besides, time was getting on. The wedding was due in an hour.

"All right," snarled Schulz. "For God's sake go to His Excellency then. The ceremony in the church is at four. You'll form part of the guard of honour, Vierbein. But at five o'clock the party comes to an end. And twenty minutes after that I want you back here again. See, runt? Not a minute later."

"I beg to be allowed to ask the Lieutenant if the radio equipment and personnel are ready yet?"

"Out of here," roared Schulz.

Schulz, who was now determined to stop at nothing, looked after Vierbein with murder in his eyes. It made him very angry to think that he had actually been responsible for giving this swine his soft job with the Admiral. He could have kicked himself for it now.

He looked at his watch. There wasn't much time. It was a good thing that he had his best uniform with him in the barracks—his full-dress uniform, that was, with all his decorations, service trousers, patent leather shoes and ceremonial sword. He signed one or two papers, inquired tentatively if the General had . . . But no, the General had taken no action yet.

Feeling rather relieved, Schulz quickly changed his clothes, got into the car which had already been waiting for him for half an hour and had himself driven over to the Hotel Excelsior, where the guests, in accordance with the plan he had drawn up, were assembled before the wedding.

And as he walked into the hotel it was as if someone had suddenly hit him over the head.

He simply couldn't believe what he saw. By all that was holy (but then what was holy to Schulz?) he just couldn't believe his eyes. For there in front of him he saw Lore, his wife. In her best dress. And standing beside her was His Excellency the Admiral.

Schulz thought he would have to sink through a hole in the floor. His wife Lore, one of the laziest and most ignorant creatures who ever lived, a completely undisciplined, utterly worthless hussy—actually standing there with His Excellency the Admiral!

Schulz, who was now hardly in control of himself, dragged her to one side. "What the hell do you think you're doing here?"

"Take your filthy hands off me! You're not at home now!"

"How did you get here?"

Lore couldn't resist the oldest joke in the world,

" Through the door, of course."

Needless to say he didn't think it funny. He had his barrack square face on. And he opened his mouth wide, very wide, as if determined to bawl her out there and then, just as if she were indeed one of his recruits on the barrack square.

" Ah, my dear Lieutenant Schulz," said His Excellency the Admiral. " I envy you your charming wife."

" Oh?" said Schulz, utterly bewildered.

" Why have you been keeping her from us all this time? If it hadn't been for my young comrade in arms, Vierbein . . ."

" Vierbein!" said Schulz, in an absolute paroxysm of rage, " Vierbein again!"

And completely forgetting himself, Schulz left His Excellency the Admiral without another word and went hurrying off in search of His Excellency the Admiral's orderly, who he found hiding in a corner. He advanced on him as if he intended to kill him.

" Vierbein," he said, and his voice was choking so much with rage that what he said was barely audible. " Vierbein, I have you at last. You are delivered into my hands. You will come with me to the barracks at once."

Corporal Vierbein drew a deep breath and then said bravely: " I beg to be allowed to inform the Lieutenant that I am home on leave, and that I have to return to the front by air this evening. I beg to be given charge of the radio equipment and radio operators."

" I'll teach you to talk to me like that, you swine!" bellowed Schulz at the top of his voice, so that the wedding guests all turned round and stared in astonishment.

With the fall of darkness, the German troops began to disengage. Their intention was to proceed some forty kilometres to the rear by a night march, and there re-group. Everything went according to plan at first. The whole organisation seemed to be functioning with the utmost smoothness.

Only the weather refused to function exactly according to plan. But the snow was still not thick or wet enough to cause real trouble.

Witterer was heard to remark with typical smugness:

" A thin veil of camouflage—just what we wanted!"

In any case the front slowly began to get on the move.

The various staffs went first, that's to say all the higher and more important staffs, in so far as they were not a long way to the rear already. They were followed by the various dependencies of the higher and more important staffs: ordinance and meteorological units, special wireless cars, the archives and files, and of course vehicles packed high with personal baggage.

Captain Witterer stood on a little hill and cocked an ear into the darkness. The sounds of motor engines could be heard on all sides. Vehicles formed themselves into long convoys and went swaying off into the night. The roads slowly filled up. All the roads in that particular sector of the front.

Witterer felt himself to be nearer to the heart of the war than ever before. It was as if in these few minutes he was able to see the whole situation at a glance. Standing there listening on his little hill, he almost mistook himself for the Commander-in-Chief himself.

"Listen," he said to Krause. And once again he listened in rapture to the sounds of the night. "The war is on the move again."

The war was indeed on the move. The lanes and side roads along which the columns of vehicles were moving were the brooks and ditches, as it were, from which were fed the streams flowing along the secondary roads. These in their turn fed the rivers along which the main flood of war poured down the main roads.

The more important staffs were followed by the staffs of medium importance. And with them went the baking and butchering companies, the field hospitals, the signals people, the military police and the ammunition columns.

This left behind only the thin line of actual fighting men: the infantry with the artillery behind them and the anti-tank guns in between.

"We're responsible for the safety of hundreds of thousands of men," said Witterer, not without a certain pride.

"Yes," said Krause. "It's a splendid feeling."

The night seemed filled with the roar of engines. And the roar seemed to be coming from all directions at once. It seemed to stretch far beyond the horizon.

Captain Witterer looked at the dial of his watch, as he had already done many times that evening. It was now just before eleven o'clock. He nodded, climbed down from his little hill, and went over to the troop's rear base, closely followed, of course, by Corporal Krause.

All the vehicles were drawn up silent and motionless in the

main square. The drivers and their mates were lounging against the bonnets, or squatting in the drivers' seats. Most of them were smoking. Hardly anyone spoke.

Sergeant-Major Bock stood in the middle of the square with Sergeant Asch. They also were smoking and not speaking. They stared at the gently falling snow-flakes.

"All ready?" asked Witterer, in ringing tones.

"All ready," answered the Sergeant-Major.

"Is Soeft back yet?"

"Yes, sir. He came back an hour or so ago. But he's gone off again now."

"I want to have a word with him sometime," said the Captain. "He's got a surprise coming to him." He looked at his watch again. "Three more minutes," he said. "And then we're off."

"It would be better," said Asch, speaking out calmly and clearly in the darkness, "if we were to wait another three hours."

Witterer started and then went straight across to Asch. The Sergeant-Major quickly made way for him. The men pricked up their ears with interest.

"Are you giving the orders round here, then, Asch—or who is?"

"It's the people who understand the situation who ought to give the orders. Plans made in offices are just about worth the paper they're written on."

"Sergeant Asch," said Captain Witterer, with infinite complacency, "you can't run a war without planning, you know."

"Or without improvisation," said Asch.

"The orders for to-night, Sergeant Asch, have been very carefully worked out by the ablest brains in the Wehrmacht. This is a masterpiece of strategy."

"I should say that what these able brains have worked out is a prize piece of dilettantism. They forgot to make any calculations for the weather, among other things."

"It's not for you to criticise, Asch."

"But one's allowed to have one's own thoughts still, isn't one?"

Sergeant-Major Bock, anxious as always to smooth out any trouble that looked like arising, now called out:

"Exactly half past eleven, Captain."

"Order to march!" rapped out Witterer.

But before Sergeant-Major Bock could pass on the order, Sergeant Asch's voice was heard saying: "Captain, all the roads are jammed. It's been snowing since this morning. The going's heavy everywhere. It'll be quite impossible to keep up normal progress under these conditions."

"What are you waiting for, Sergeant-Major?" said Witterer.

"There's something in what Sergeant Asch says," said Bock, warily.

Asch followed this up at once.

"If we set off now," he said, "we'll be stuck before we've gone more than a few kilometres. All we'll be able to do is sit there on the road with our engines overheating. On the other hand, if we simply wait until the traffic clears . . ."

"Enough of this!" roared Witterer. "Kindly keep your mouth shut, Asch! And you too, Sergeant-Major. Orders are orders as far as I'm concerned. And if my orders are to move off at eleven o'clock, then I move off at eleven o'clock. Hail, rain, snow or sunshine!"

"Very good, sir," said the Sergeant-Major dourly.

"All right," said Sergeant Asch, "then off we go, but if we haven't got stuck fast by the time we've gone three kilometres, then my name's not Asch, but something rather like it."

"Everyone in his place!" shouted the Sergeant-Major. "Engines started! Forward!"

The convoy moved slowly out of the square and down the village street. The heavily-laden trucks drove without lights. Only when one of the drivers put on the brakes, was the glow of the red lamp visible from the back. Engines whined and roared. Sergeant Asch brought up the rear on his motor-cycle.

"I must say, I admire the Captain's patience," said Krause.

"It is now exhausted," replied Witterer.

He looked after the departing convoy. Then he got into his own car, in which Kowalski was sitting, fast asleep.

"Just look at that," said Witterer. "A war in progress and the fellow's asleep. Wake up, man!"

"What's the matter?" asked Kowalski, who was awake in an instant. "Extra rations?"

"Is all the baggage in?" asked Witterer.

"Have you put all the baggage in, Krause?" asked Kowalski.

"Yes, sir," replied the other, slightly confused. "The Captain's battle kit is stowed in the back. His personal baggage has gone with Soeft."

"Battle kit?" asked Kowalski, with interest. "What the hell's that? Never heard of it."

"Well, then I'll have to put you wise, Kowalski," said

Witterer, grimly, feeling his kit in the back. "It seem to me you've still got a lot to learn."

"And I'm not the only one," mumbled Kowalski to himself. Witterer had no time to try and catch what he said. For at that moment a motor-cycle came roaring up. The valves made an infernal clattering noise.

It was Sergeant Asch. He steered his way over to Witterer, stopped in front of him and switched off the engine.

"The column's stuck already," he said. "About two kilometres down the road."

"I suppose you're delighted," said Witterer, bitterly.

"There's little enough reason to be," Asch spoke in a matter-of-fact voice. "The roads are completely jammed. It was inevitable. The new snow is lying about four inches deep. The trucks have to follow in the ruts if they want to move at all. But they can't move. Because there isn't an inch to move anywhere. All the columns are stuck."

"And you sit there making speeches, Asch!"

"I'm just telling you."

"Well, clear off, man! Your job is up with the column. Ride up to the main road and see what's blocking the traffic."

"I've been up there already," said Asch.

"Well?"

"The columns which were supposed to have started at nine are still stuck. They've been waiting for more than two hours."

"Well, you go and wait too, then! Two hours as well, if needs be. Twenty hours if needs be. And if you're as useless as I think you are, then you'll wait there till you rot or the war's over. But every order I give gets carried out, understand?"

"Really?" said Kowalski slowly, "*every* order."

"Shut up, man," yelled Witterer.

Asch started up his engine and roared away. Krause seemed ready to leap after him, if he were to get the order to do so.

Witterer kicked savagely at the tyre on the rear wheel of the car.

"Yes, there's plenty of air," said Kowalski.

"Take his name, Krause," said Witterer furiously. "Write it all down, word for word."

Krause sat down in the back of the car, switched on his torch, dimmed the light by shining it through a blanket and began to write. Witterer paced up and down the empty square. Kowalski slowly lit himself a cigarette.

"It's impossible to rely on anyone any more," said Captain Witterer. "The whole place is an utter shambles! Let's hope

226

at least that Wedelmann has arrived at the new position by now."

"I think we can assume that," said Krause keenly. "Lieutenant Wedelmann set off at three o'clock as planned. With motor-cycle and side-car, one truck and a girl interpreter."

"A what, Krause?"

"A girl interpreter, sir. Or rather that is how Lieutenant Wedelmann describes the lady he has taken with him."

"He has what he calls a girl interpreter?"

"Well," said Kowalski, and it was as if he were conducting the conversation exclusively with Krause. "And why not? You'd do the same. Every unit has its interpreter. Soeft even has two. He calls them his kitchen assistants. Do you mean to say you've never heard of that?"

Witterer didn't say anything. He thought for a moment. The matter seemed worth looking into.

"Is she attractive?" he asked. "This—er—interpreter?"

"She certainly is!" said Kowalski. "Though whether she's equally obliging to everyone . . ."

"I should think she'd find a troop commander good enough," said Witterer, with a curt, manly laugh. And he took his place beside Kowalski and put on his steel helmet.

"Where to?" asked Kowalski. "The new positions?"

"You won't be able to get through just yet, Kowalski."

"I can always get through if I want to."

"But I want you to go up to the guns," said Witterer. "We've still a good deal of surplus ammunition left up there."

And as he spoke the heavens seemed to split open all along the front. A giant sheet of flame leapt across the horizon. Other sheets of flame followed at short intervals. Then the air was rent by the whine of shells winging their way through the night.

"They seem to have some surplus ammunition too," said Kowalski, dryly.

Witterer leant forward and listened, intently. And he too realised that it was the enemy, Ivan himself, who had unleashed the barrage. His shells were shrieking their way into the German lines.

"But where have they got the artillery from all of a sudden?" asked Krause.

"I suppose Father Christmas gave it to them," replied Kowalski.

"Ah, to hell with it," said Witterer, pretending to rise above it. "What sort of people do they think we are? Idiots? They're just making a lot of noise to try and frighten us. They've noticed something going on and they're sending over everything they've got. They'll have shot their bolt in ten minutes or so. And in an hour we'll be off! According to plan."

Once more a sheet of flame ran along the horizon. The shells howled and shrieked and whined their way through the air. Only a few kilometres ahead of them the whole earth seemed to burst into flame, as if a volcano were erupting there.

"Up to the guns then," said Kowalski.

"Steady," said Witterer. "Don't lose your head. I think the best thing would be to drive over to Regimental Headquarters first."

Colonel Luschke was crouching over his map—and this was before the din broke out at the front. He seemed to have grown smaller. He looked rather like a collapsed drunk who hasn't the strength to move any more. But his sharp cunning little eyes wandered tirelessly backwards and forwards over the map.

For the last three hours now the main base had been busy evacuating itself to the rear. Luschke and his staff did not evacuate with it, for they were not part of the main base proper. It was getting on towards midnight. He waited, although he couldn't exactly say what he was waiting for. But of one thing he was certain, and that was that he wasn't going to move away from the enemy until the front-line troops themselves got on the move.

He rang for his adjutant, who appeared immediately. He was in full marching order, but didn't come to attention. Luschke didn't like his Regimental Headquarters to be turned into a parade ground. The adjutant therefore behaved rather like a uniformed civilian. He had nothing to do now but wait for fresh orders from his Commanding Officer. Everything else was in a state of flux.

"What's the weather like?" asked Luschke.

"The snow's getting thicker. The barometer's almost down to zero."

"What's the situation on the roads?"

"All jammed."

The Colonel nodded curtly. That was to be expected. Bad weather, and all the roads would be blocked. This night evacuation was sheer lunacy—sprung from the bird-brain of some fanciful strategist well behind the lines. The surprise element indeed! A war like this was, in the long run, just one huge piece of calculation. Unfortunately people who fancied their powers of imagination, were usually hopeless at mathematics.

"Any reports in from any of the troops?"

"Nothing special. Everything's going according to plan so far."

"Nothing else to report?"

"There's a Corporal from Intelligence waiting outside who wants to have a word with you."

"A Corporal from Intelligence wants to have a word with me? Isn't that lot moving, too, then?"

"Most of them have already gone, Colonel—but this particular fellow seems to be hanging on."

"Right. Anything else?"

"The Commandant of the airfield rang up. He's got news of Corporal Vierbein. The reserve battery have been making trouble for him."

"Making trouble? Making trouble for a Corporal sent back by me?"

"Apparently, Colonel."

Luschke's eyes narrowed, a sure sign that he was thinking hard. He stretched a long finger out over the map and began to tap out a little march. Then he said:

"Is there much congestion on the line?"

"As a matter of fact it's surprisingly clear at the moment. All the staffs are on the move. Hardly anyone's using the telephone at all."

"Then try and get me through to the C.O. of the reserve battery at once. Say it's a top priority call. Make it urgent top priority. Well, what are you waiting for?"

"But Colonel if . . ."

"When the war starts up again here, my dear man, I'm going to need those transmitters. And the war is already beginning to show signs of life. I can feel it in my bones. Let's use the telephone to worry those dead-beats back home while we can. Or are you getting finicky in your old age?"

The adjutant hurriedly denied this and withdrew. The Corporal from Intelligence then came in. He stood shyly in the doorway for a moment. The adjutant could be heard yelling from the next room as if trying to make himself heard in Germany even without the telephone.

"Shut the door, will you?" said the Colonel to the Corporal

from Intelligence. "And then come a little closer. I won't bite, you know."

The Corporal came closer. He looked like a short-sighted schoolteacher. Every one of his movements gave him away as the eternal civilian. He seemed to be wearing uniform solely by accident. He looked at Luschke in embarrassment, as if wanting to apologise to him for his very existence.

"How did you come to get into Intelligence?"

"I'm an electrical engineer by profession," said the Corporal, smiling modestly. "From Königsberg. And I speak fluent Russian. I went to Russia for my firm before the war. I was installing radio equipment there."

"And why haven't you been evacuated with the rest of your lot?"

"There's some peace to be had round here just now," said the Corporal, and his smile broadened a little. "Most of the staffs are on the move and there's no red-tape to have to deal with. And I'm particularly lucky to find you here."

"We'll see how lucky that is in a minute," said Luschke. "Do you work for the *Sichereitsdienst,* for the Gestapo, or counter-espionage?"

"I don't have anything to do with the political police," said the Corporal, looking straight at Luschke. "Nor do I wish to have."

"Well, that makes you more sympathetic to me at once."

"I gather that, Colonel," said the Corporal calmly. And he added: "We have our ears to the ground, you know."

"Have you been tapping my telephone conversations?" said Luschke, in a quiet menacing voice.

"There's a lot of telephone tapping going on," said the Corporal. "And it's on the increase. There'll obviously be more and more from now on."

"Thanks for the hint," said Luschke, curtly.

"Glad to give it," said the Corporal.

Luschke seemed to crouch lower than ever behind his map. But his eyes were bright. An excited flush had come over his lumpy face.

"So we're of the same way of thinking, eh?"

The Corporal nodded. "They haven't started thought-tapping, yet."

Luschke shook with silent laughter. He looked more than ever a tough nut to crack at that moment. It was clear that there were more people of his way of thinking that he had dared to hope. It was good to know that.

"And is that all you wanted to say to me, Corporal?"

"Not quite all," said the other, "though it's the most important thing."

The telephone rang shrilly. Luschke took off the receiver and listened. Then he turned to his visitor with a grin and said: "I've got an urgent top priority call coming through from Germany. If you'd like to listen you can take the extension."

"Not necessary," laughed the Corporal, waving his hand almost affectedly.

"Who's that?" shouted Luschke down the telephone. "Schulz! I can't believe it! Are you the C.O. there then?"

The Colonel listened with obvious relish. Schulz's voice, which was usually so full of self-confidence sounded agitated. It was a great source of worry to him that he never seemed able to get away from Luschke in the end.

"Unbelievable!" cried Luschke, sarcastically. "The C.O.'s getting married, so you're standing in for him? The born stand-in, eh, Schulz?"

Schulz was sweating blood at the other end of the line. When first told that Colonel Luschke wanted him on the telephone he had thought someone was playing a practical joke on him. But now, as the all too familiar voice cut at him like a razor across hundred of kilometres, he knew at once that it was no joke. No joke at all.

"Lieutenant Schulz," said the Colonel, "you seem to have forgotten about me. I feel very offended. But I'd be delighted to refresh your memory."

"Colonel," said Schulz very keenly, thinking that he would manage to avert disaster at the last moment, "those demands of yours are all being seen to and . . ."

"Lieutenant Schulz," said the Colonel, "if you're making trouble there . . ."

"But, of course I'm not, Colonel," Schulz reassured him.

"But just supposing you were, Schulz, even the tiniest bit of trouble, I'd put in a demand to have you posted to me at once. Do you understand?"

"Yes, sir," said Schulz, in a strangled voice.

"And if I asked for you, I'd get you, see?"

"I'll have your wishes seen to this very night, Colonel," said Schulz. "This very night."

"We're not in all that of a hurry now," said the Colonel.

And with that he brought his urgent top priority conversation to an end. He grinned with pleasure. He found it very satisfactory that his voice alone should be enough to ginger a sluggish old war-horse like Schulz into a gallop over so many hundreds of kilometres.

Luschke turned to his visitor who looked up at him with that modesty which he had shown from the beginning. He had pulled a note-book out of his pocket and was waiting for the Colonel to take notice of him again.

"Right, fire away," said Luschke, leaning back in his chair expectantly. "You look as if you've brought some ammunition with you."

"Colonel," said the Corporal, and he seemed to regret what he had to say, "there are three enemy transmitters working behind our lines in this sector. We've listened to almost all their transmissions. We've managed to decipher most of their messages and have actually located and eliminated two out of the three of them."

"So what we're concerned with is the third transmitter," said Luschke, paying close attention.

"So far we haven't been able to locate this transmitter. But this morning we were able to get a fairly close fix."

"What do you call fairly close, Corporal?"

"Within two kilometres or so."

"And where do you deduce is, or was, this transmitter operating from?"

"Somewhere in the area of No. 3 Troop's forward base," said the Corporal, quietly.

Luschke winced. Then he rubbed his left hand rhythmically up and down his chin. Finally he said:

"You'll find quite a number of different units up in No. 3 Troop's area: infantry, anti-tank guns, signals, mortars, tanks."

"Oh, yes," said the Corporal, "yes, I know that."

"Only . . ."

"Colonel, it wasn't until late this afternoon that my colleagues and I succeeded in deciphering this third transmitter's signals. And it then appeared that this trasmitter was much better informed than the other two. As long as four days ago it had already signalled that a withdrawal of some forty kilometres or so was planned for this sector."

"I'm beginning to understand," said Luschke, more to himself than to his visitor.

"Now it was only five days ago, Colonel, that this information was given out to a small group of officers down to and including the rank of regimental commander. It wasn't until three days later that the order was passed on as top secret to company and troop commanders."

Luschke stared straight at the Corporal.

"So that the question you wish to put is: Did I, four days ago, discuss the question of the withdrawal with any of my officers, presumably one of my officers in No. 3 Troop?"

"That is the question, or rather a similar one, to that which I have already put to two other regimental commanders to-night."

"And their answers, naturally, were in the negative?"

"Naturally," said the Corporal. "But whether their answers will bear up to more detailed scrutiny, is of course, something I can't say."

"And what if my answer also is in the negative?"

"Please don't misunderstand me, Colonel. I'm not putting any questions to you. Not to a man with whom I have so much in common. I just thought perhaps you yourself might care to look into the matter. For your own safety's sake—or to see whether I'm right—or for whatever other reason."

"You're almost too intelligent to be as decent as you seem," said the Colonel, after a longish pause.

"At the moment," said the Corporal, "I'm wondering if I'm not half-witted. Either I am or the Russians are."

"What makes you say that?"

"Nothing is happening, Colonel. The staffs are on the move now and have jammed all the roads. And yet nothing at all is happening at the front. And I'm asking myself if I haven't gone mad. The Russians have known for days that we were going to withdraw to-night. There's been a considerable increase in radio activity from the other side. Our agents report troop concentrations. We also know that the enemy has brought up artillery. And yet absolutely nothing happens at all!"

The Colonel got up and beckoned to the Corporal.

"Come on," he said, "we'll go outside and take a look at the war."

They both went out. The Colonel made a slightly hunched figure as he strode on ahead. Every now and again he flashed a torch. A sentry challenged them, but sprang to attention as soon as he recognised the Colonel.

Luschke was making for the church which he secretly referred to as "his" church. The snow was falling thickly and melting as it touched his uniform. But the night was a bright one, for the moon lit up the clouds and the snow shone like wet white silk.

The Colonel flashed his torch on the broken steps which

led up the tower. They stood together on a little platform, looking out through the great gaps in the ruined church.

"Listen," said the Colonel. "Out there. That's where the front is. And what do you hear? Nothing."

"Absolutely nothing," said the Corporal. He sounded almost desperate about it.

"And now listen out that way. What do you hear there? Motor engines. That's where the roads leading to the rear are. And they're jammed. Vehicles have been piling up there for the last three or four hours. And the situation is getting more and more dangerous every minute."

"And you mean the Russians know that?"

"Anyone who has any front-line experience knows that. But to wait for the right moment in which to exploit such a situation requires strong nerves. Yes, you need nerves to wait until the enemy has got into the most advantageous position for you to attack him, believe me. Nerves! And you don't learn them in school. And if what you deduce is true, Corporal, namely that the enemy has massed together forces with which to attack us now—then, all I can say is, God help us!"

The Corporal said nothing. He stared out into the night which, though light, was impenetrable. He seemed to be having difficulty in breathing.

"If I were on the other side," said Luschke, "I'd wait a bit yet."

"How long?"

"Until midnight, perhaps. That's to say another fifteen minutes."

They climbed down again and went back into the Colonel's billet. Luschke looked thoughtfully at his map and then tore it from the table. He folded it up quickly and carelessly. He called in the adjutant.

"I want Lieutenant Wedelmann to report to me at once," he ordered.

Then he turned to the Intelligence Corporal and said:

"I've been delighted to meet you. I hope we'll remain in touch."

"It's my job to keep in touch," said the Corporal, smiling shyly.

"And in an hour at the latest," went on the Colonel, "we shall know whether you're half-witted or not. But I'm very much afraid you're not!"

"If you really insist," said the Commandant of the home airfield to Corporal Vierbein. "Then you shall have your own way."

"I beg to be allowed to fly, sir," said Vierbein, thoroughly correct, as always.

The Commandant of the home airfield, a close friend of the Commandant of the airfield at the front, who, in his turn, was a close friend of regimental commander Luschke, looked at Vierbein with fatherly concern.

The Commandant listened to the sounds of the night. His bald pate shone pink in the light of the table-lamp. Outside on the runway he could hear the sound of aircraft engines. The sound of repairs came from the hangars. It was just after midnight.

"Corporal Vierbein," said the Commandant in a friendly tone, "you don't have to fly, you know. If you want to, you can stay here a few more days without any trouble at all. I'm perfectly prepared to write you out a chit saying that there's been no transport available."

"Thank you," said Vierbein. "But I've been called back by telegram."

"A telegram from Colonel Luschke?"

"No."

"If it hasn't come from Colonel Luschke personally, I shouldn't take any notice of it. Naturally you can have a seat in any of my planes any time you want—you can even have a special plane as far as I'm concerned. I'd gladly arrange that for Colonel Luschke. But absolutely between ourselves, this is a very bad moment to choose. There's a withdrawal going on to-night. They're straightening out the line. You'll land yourself right in the middle of it."

"But I might be needed," said Vierbein naïvely.

The Commandant looked up slowly from his desk. And he stared at Vierbein in utter amazement.

"Needed?" he said slowly. "What for? The war can surely get on without you for a few hours."

And the Commandant thought: Needed! He really believes he might be needed. He doesn't know that Generals think in terms of divisions. He doesn't realise that some nights several thousand Vierbeins go into the attack without a single commander sleeping any the worse for it. He's really managed to persuade himself that he's making history. But it takes a million litres of blood to write a single tiny chapter of world history. What does one Vierbein count?

"Look here," said the Commandant slowly, "you'll probably arrive in the middle of the utmost confusion. All you'll have to do is to stand around and wait until things have sorted themselves out again."

"I'll be able to find my unit, all right," said Vierbein, confidently. He had had his orders and he was a man who obeyed orders, at once to the letter, as he had been trained to do.

"All right then, if you insist," said the Commandant, eventually, and he rang the bell for his adjutant, who came in at once. The adjutant looked as if he had just seen a ghost. But no one paid much attention to him.

"Corporal Vierbein will be flying on one of the next machines to take off for the front," said the Commandant. "Preferably in some old crate that won't get there till to-morrow morning."

"Very good, sir," said the adjutant, but he went on standing there as if he were dying to be asked something.

"Well—what is it?"

"Outside," said the adjutant, and it was as if he had some wonderful secret to impart. "Outside in front of the hangar, there's an Admiral, a real live Admiral. An Admiral of the First World War presumably. And he's got a lady with him."

"Well, well!" said the Commandant in astonishment. "Are you sure you're not seeing things? If I didn't know you were a teetotaller, I'd think you were tight. An Admiral! What can he be doing here?"

"I beg to state," said Vierbein, still thoroughly correct, "that it was His Excellency the Admiral who brought me here."

"I beg your pardon," said the Commandant. "Is he your uncle, or something?"

Vierbein shook his head.

"His Excellency the Admiral is the father-in-law of the Commanding Officer of the reserve battery, who got married to-day. I was detailed to His Excellency as orderly."

"You don't say!" said the Commandant, very much astonished. "Then I must certainly see him."

And the Commandant went down to the hangar with Vierbein. The adjutant who had started to follow them down, out of curiosity, was ordered to attend to the departure of the various aircraft.

The night that lay over the airfield was cold and clear.

The stars seemed to be hanging very low. The sky was like a dark velvet canopy.

His Excellency the Admiral was promenading up and down in front of No. 1 hangar with Lore Schulz on his arm—for he was a genuine cavalier of the old school. He was conversing animatedly and Lore Schulz listened to him with respectful attention.

The Commandant of the airfield strode straight up to His Excellency and begged to be allowed to introduce himself. The Admiral gave him his hand. The Commandant took it, explaining that it was a great honour for him to be able to welcome the Admiral to the area under his command. He was entirely at the Admiral's disposal. Lore Schulz and Vierbein watched the progress of this little ceremony in astonishment.

"But I beg you, my good sir," said the Admiral with the utmost heartiness, "don't let me disturb you. You're on duty and you won't have much time. I've only come to say good-bye to my young friend Vierbein, of the artillery, you know. He was urgently in need of transport and I prevailed upon my son-in-law, the Commanding Officer, you know, to put a motor vehicle at our disposal. Our young friend had deserved that at least."

"Most certainly, Your Excellency," said the Commandant, and he too found this elderly, slightly cranky, but nevertheless extremely friendly old sea-dog very sympathetic. "I think it most commendable of Your Excellency to have accompanied Vierbein."

"Oh, I've seen thousands of men off in my time," said His Excellency. "Whenever my personal duties with His Majesty permitted, I always went to inspect the crews before they set sail, and have a word with officers, non-commissioned officers and men."

"I'd be most honoured if Your Excellency would care to inspect my airfield and its installations, while you're here," said the Commandant.

The old sea-dog beamed with pleasure. He drew himself up to his full height. It was quite like the old days again. "You were an officer of His Majesty the Kaiser's forces yourself?" he asked.

The Commandant acknowledged this with a certain pride.

"A bomber pilot in Immelmann's squadron."

That wasn't strictly true, though it sounded good. In fact, he'd merely been an air traffic control officer, nicknamed "the

237

broom" by his comrades in the mess on account of his efficiency in keeping the runways clear.

"Bomber pilot, eh?" repeated His Excellency. "In Immelmann's squadron, eh? In the days of His Majesty the Kaiser? I thought as much. Ah, those were the days, my dear sir. In those days, now, the Supreme Commander . . . whereas to-day —but we won't talk about that."

"I agree with Your Excellency whole-heartedly. Particularly on the latter point."

"I'm delighted to hear it," said His Excellency. "Really delighted."

Then His Excellency, the Admiral, turned to Lore Schulz and said gallantly:

"If you would permit me, I'd very much like to have half an hour's conversation with my comrade of the Luftwaffe. . . ."

"But of course," said Lore Schulz, obligingly. It was a great happiness to her to find herself treated with respect in this way. The eventful evening had been the happiest she had spent for a very long time.

"And perhaps you will keep our young friend Vierbein company for a while, my dear lady?"

His dear lady blushed to the tips of her neat little ears. "But by all means," she said. And she counted herself lucky that the lighting was dim enough to hide her embarrassment.

His Excellency, the Admiral, and His Majesty's former Flying Officer, now Commandant of the airfield, strode off happily into the hangar together.

Lore Schulz watched them with joy. Vierbein stared into the darkness, down the broad runways which seemed to grow narrower and narrower until they vanished altogether into the blackness of the night.

A loud-speaker suddenly droned out:

"Corporal Vierbein to the adjutant at once, please."

Vierbein nodded, as if it were in some way necessary to acknowledge the announcement.

"I'll be as quick as I can," he said to Lore Schulz.

"Don't hurry," she said, looking into his eyes. "I won't be running away from you, my dear."

Vierbein smiled at her, tenderly, a little sadly.

"How nice that you were able to come," he said.

"But nicer still if I had been someone else?"

"You're a good person," he said, a little awkwardly. "A good, decent person. I know that. And I'll never forget it. I'll never forget you."

238

"Oh, my dear," said Lore, "I'm just a little bitch—and I hardly spent any time with you at all!"

And the loud-speaker near them suddenly drowned their conversation mercilessly. It roared for Vierbein. Vierbein hurried off to the adjutant.

"Your departure's been postponed for an hour," said the adjutant. "You won't be on the third plane after all, but the ninth."

"Might I ask . . ."

"The reserve battery has just rung up. There was a Lieutenant Schulz on the line. You won't be the only one flying out. Two N.C.O.s and ten men are coming as well. A truck with men and equipment is on its way out now."

"The transmitters!" said Vierbein, and there was an unmistakable note of joy in his voice.

The adjutant shook his head in further astonishment. What an extraordinary night this was being!

"Good God, man!" he said. "Does it make you happy just to receive an order?"

"My mission is accomplished," said Vierbein.

"Well, I don't know, I'm sure," said the adjutant, shrugging his shoulders.

"So you're still alive," said the Colonel grimly, looking Witterer up and down with interest. "I'm glad to see it."

The Captain, who was wearing full war-paint, did his best to produce a regulation salute. But it wasn't a great success. He got entangled in the strap of his gas-mask carrier, and was only just able to get his hand up to his steel helmet.

"The true-born warrior," said Luschke. "If the Russians see you like that in broad daylight, you'll scare them out of their wits."

"I beg to report to the Colonel . . ."

"Just a minute," said the Colonel and he put up his hand to halt the Captain's volubility, like a policeman controlling the traffic. He picked up the telephone. He asked for a call to Divisional Headquarters, but there was difficulty in getting through. His left hand played with the map that lay in front of him on the table, and his quick, fidgety movements looked very much like nervousness. Yet his voice sounded as calm as ever.

" I want the General," said Luschke. " I'm not dealing with underlings at this stage."

Outside the front was in an uproar. Long tongues of flame leapt from the mouths of the guns so fast that it was impossible for the eye to distinguish between them. A flickering light lay over the whole horizon. And the Colonel's hut was beginning to shake under the impact of bursting shells, which seemed to be coming nearer and nearer.

The Colonel threw the receiver away. He pulled up the collar of his tunic, leant forward over the map and snorted contemptuously.

" You've just come from the front," he said to Witterer. " What does it look like there?"

" I beg to inform the Colonel, that I thought it wiser to come straight to the Colonel. . . ."

" You mean, you haven't been up to the front?"

" I was busy seeing that my men got off on time for the withdrawal, and just superintending their actual departure when the enemy . . ."

" All right," said the Colonel, curtly.

" If the Colonel thinks . . ."

" I'm not reproaching you, Captain. It's possible you've done the right thing. I know something of the background to all this. There's nothing you could have done to stop it—not at this stage at any rate."

" I wanted to ask the Colonel if there would be any change of plan."

The Colonel buttoned up his tunic. He strode past Witterer to the door, opened it a fraction and shouted : " Coffee and a cigar!" Then he went back to his map table.

" Where's Lieutenant Wedelmann?" he asked.

" He's already in the new position."

" What's he got with him?"

" A car, a truck and five men."

" Anyone else?" And as Witterer hesitated over the answer, and hesitated for a noticeable period of time, the Colonel repeated, sharply : " Anyone else, Herr Witterer?"

" A girl interpreter," said Witterer slowly.

Luschke sat down and sipped the coffee which had been brought him. Then he bit the end off his cigar, spat it out and ignored the match which the Captain held out to him. He put the cigar in his mouth unlighted.

Then he said :

" The position is still very confused and difficult to make

out. From midnight on, the enemy has been employing strong concentrations of artillery and mortars. God knows what the next stage will be. Any views?"

"It's probably bluff, Colonel. Ivan . . ."

"Say 'the enemy', please."

"The enemy, Colonel, has spotted our movements, and is now firing off all his available ammunition to try and hamper them. He'll soon have used it all up."

"I seem to remember, Captain, that you made some artillery experiments yourself a few days ago which you jokingly named 'Operation leap-frog.' At that time the enemy didn't have any artillery to speak of in this sector. One of your Sergeants described your little venture, and I must say I see his point, as an 'Invitation to the Waltz.' It seems as if your invitation has been accepted."

"But Colonel," said the Captain, secretly congratulating himself on his cunning, "the artillery which the enemy has sent into action on this sector must have been withdrawn from another one. So that on a wide view it cancels itself out."

"My dear Captain," said Luschke, sipping his coffee, while the table trembled under the weight of his elbows, "that wide view of yours is little more than an optical illusion. The point is that it's here, in our sector that the hell is going on, and everywhere else—that is to say, all that you include in your wide view, is perfectly quiet."

"But when the enemy barrage lifts, when he's used up all his ammunition . . ."

The Colonel raised his hand. He was listening for something. Witterer also leant forward. He hardly dared to breathe.

They heard nothing.

The Colonel switched out the light and went over to the window. He tore the curtain to one side and pushed the window open. There was the distant drone of engines, but otherwise nothing.

The front had gone completely quiet.

"There you are, you see, Colonel," said Witterer, much relieved.

"So far," said the Colonel, breathing the fresh air in deeply, "the enemy has merely been bombarding our front-line positions. The losses of the infantry have been kept within what's called bounds—in other words, our infantry losses can be reckoned as considerable. The withdrawal itself proceeds, if not exactly according to plan, at least without any disastrous hitches. Morale is tolerably good and not as yet endangered."

" And the withdrawal of the front-line troops will also proceed according to plan?"

" Provided that . . ."

Luschke stopped. Artillery fire had broken out again. Tongues of flame once again leapt along the horizon.

" Weak," said Witterer. " Not impressive. They've exhausted themselves already."

" That," said Luschke, barely audibly, " is our own artillery. And behind it—do you hear?—rifle fire."

" My God, you're right," said Witterer.

Luschke shut the window, drew the curtain again, went back to his map table and switched on the light. A thin layer of sweat had broken out all over his lumpy face.

" That means the enemy is attacking," he said.

" What will happen now?" asked Witterer, now utterly at a loss and making no attempt to hide the fact.

" If the enemy really is attacking," said Luschke, " then there can be only two possibilities; either the line will hold or we will be overrun."

" And what about the withdrawal?"

" That presumably will have to be delayed. Or simply stopped altogether. Or else we will have to fight a rear-guard action. A system of overlapping defence. Also a sort of operation leap-frog, my dear Captain."

" I see, Colonel."

" I'm glad you do," said the other brutally. " And I'll be even more glad when you've got back to your gun positions and rung me to inform me of the situation there."

" Very good, Colonel," said Witterer and withdrew immediately. His gait was springier than ever. Once again he felt that his great moment was approaching.

Now that he was left alone in the room, the Colonel lit his cigar for the first time. It didn't burn evenly. He didn't like the taste of it. He put it on one side and let it go out.

The adjutant appeared with the latest radio reports. Luschke looked quickly through them. The enemy was attacking on Hill 234, along the railway embankment, by the little pond, that is to say, what might be called on a broad front. Infantry attacks of medium strength. No ground gained so far. No tanks reported so far. Our own losses so far not excessive.

Always the same story, thought Luschke. At first the padded cell technique: the madman runs his head against the wall, which being made of rubber gives a little and then returns to the same position. The madman rushes at it again and the wall is a little weaker. If his skill is made of iron and his attack vigorous enough and the thing against which he is running ultimately destructible, he will destroy it in the end.

"I still can't get hold of the divisional commander," reported the adjutant. "And his intelligence officer. . . ."

"The divisional intelligence officer is a decent enough fellow in private life, but in his office he's just a stooge of the General's —don't bother about him!"

"Lieutenant Wedelmann is here."

"Ah, show him in, the wonder-child. In the meantime try and contact my colleague from the infantry."

The adjutant nodded. He was behaving more and more like a civilian these days. He came and went without saluting and never stood to attention, or spoke in military fashion. And that was how Luschke liked it. "I want a man who'll do some work, not a jack-in-the-box," he had once said.

Wedelmann came into the room, tall, thin, and serious-look-ing as ever. As he was bare-headed, he gave the Nazi salute.

"Steady now!" said Luschke. "This isn't a party meeting. Sit down. And see that you make yourself comfortable."

The Lieutenant took a seat obediently. Colonel Luschke seemed to be rather nervous. Wedelmann could understand this—the outlook, he gathered, wasn't exactly promising.

"Why do you think I've sent for you, Wedelmann?"

"Do you want me to take over command of No. 3, sir?"

"No, I want to court-martial you, man!"

Wedelmann politely kept silent. He presumed that this was just one of Luschke's grim little jokes. Not a particularly good one—but then that was forgivable in the circumstances.

"Have you come from the new position, Wedelmann?"

"Yes, Colonel, on a motor-bike. It's almost impossible to get through on anything else. Thirty-five kilometres in just on ninety minutes."

"Not bad going. If you'd had any idea of what I wanted you for, you'd have taken longer. What's morale like on the roads?"

"All right, so far. The men are a little nervous. If the enemy were to use aircraft . . ."

"Wedelmann," said Luschke, leaning back. "I've sent for you to tell you a little story. Your motor-cycle ride will have been quite an ordeal for you, and one presumably which you will have to repeat again to-night—however, the story makes it worth while."

Wedelmann sat there in expectant silence. He was genuinely

perplexed; he hadn't the slightest idea what Luschke wanted to tell him.

"This is the story," began Luschke, "of a radio transmitter, which was not a German one but which nevertheless was situated in a certain forward base where one of the Führer's most trusted henchmen was serving. And this transmitter leaked the Führer's most trusted secrets."

Wedelmann had gone deathly pale.

"That's impossible, Colonel."

"I can prove it, Lieutenant."

"No!"

"The person who was operating this transmitter knew something which, in addition to this golden-headed boy of the Führer's, was known only to an old lump-faced idiot."

"No!" said Wedelmann again.

Colonel Luschke compressed his lips. It was as if he were trying to grin, but failing. Otherwise his face remained immobile. His little eyes were both sad and cold at the same time.

"If what you say is true," said Wedelmann, "I shall know what conclusion to draw."

"Only one, Wedelmann," said the Colonel. "Leave everything else to me."

Wedelmann got stiffly to his feet. "The bit about leaving everything else to me," said the Colonel. "That's an order. Do you understand. An order from me, Wedelmann!"

Sergeant Asch knew exactly what was going to happen. He had been through it all once before, on a much larger scale, a few months ago, in December, 1941.

Then a whole army had overreached itself. Theoretically the intention had been to encircle Moscow. The forward units had got as far as Tula. And then the entire army had gone over to the retreat. And the German High Command communiqué reported a "withdrawal according to plan".

Five hundred kilometres of road had been turned into a graveyard for men and machines. Staff officers' morale collapsed. Their faith in the Führer was permanently damaged. The news seeped through that Hitler had had at least one General "dealt with" for the debacle—a procedure to which in itself the troops took no particular exception, although the cowardly way in which all the other Generals took it lying down made a very bad impression.

Ever since those days the front-line troops had had a saying: even Generals had arses, and sometimes get kicked.

For the fifth time that night, Asch rode the length of Sergeant-Major Bock's convoy. It had moved barely three kilometres in the last two hours. The heavily-laden vehicles tottered slowly along the appalling roads. Wheels churned deeper and deeper into the slush. Radiators boiled; and the snow-flakes hissed almost inaudibly as they landed on them.

The column was stuck again. A few drivers had switched off their engines. Sergeant-Major Bock was taking a nap in his car. The distant sounds of the front did not disturb him.

Sergeant Asch weaved his way through without much difficulty to the Chief's car.

He knocked on the closed windows. Bock jumped.

Then the Sergeant-Major asked through a little gap:

" Do you want to get warm, Asch?"

" What's your rum like, Bock?"

" It says it's ' pure Jamaica '," answered the other. " Tastes almost as if it were too. It cost me a box of cigars."

Sergeant Asch took the bottle and drank from it.

" Not bad," he said.

" It looks as if we're going to spend the night on this road," said Bock.

" Better than in the ditch."

" Once we get on to the main road, we'll cover the last thirty kilometres in a couple of hours," said Bock confidently.

" You ought to have been a racing-driver," said Asch. " But remember the speed of a convoy is the speed of its slowest truck. Provided, that is, we're allowed to move at all. There's the weather for instance, which doesn't seem to be obeying the Führer, and the Russians who don't seem to be giving us much consideration; and then there are our Generals who unfortunately haven't all been crippled by frost-bite yet."

" Well, I'm going to have a nap," said Bock. " It's going to be a long night."

" No, you're not," said Asch. " You're going to keep an eye on your trucks. And I'm going up ahead to see what the delay is."

" You and your joy-rides," said the Sergeant-Major crossly. " But you'll smash your skull in on one of them some day and all I'll say will be: serve him damn' well right."

Whereupon Bock got out of the car and started walking back down the line of vehicles. The men were dejected. They weren't particularly tired. The noise from the front unsettled them. They wanted to get on into the new positions as quickly as possible. They knew it was dangerous to be all jammed together along the main road like this, unable to move.

Sergeant Asch passed the end of No. 3 Troop's convoy and rode along beside an endless chain of heavy trucks belonging to other units. There were few cars. There was hardly a man to be seen off the trucks. The vehicles were stationary over an entire stretch of three kilometres. It was as if they had all driven down a dead end.

At the point where this secondary road joined the main road, however, things were extremely lively. Field security police, armed to the teeth, the famous bloodhounds, were standing there playing at point duty. They had a Major in charge of them.

Asch drove straight up, and immediately saw what the trouble was. The Major and his men were keeping all subsidiary roads blocked, except one, and along that one road rolled the vehicles of the Major's own division. As soon as vehicles from some other unit tried to make their way on to the main road, the Major nearly threw a fit.

He was a medium-sized angular-looking man. A brutal face stuck out from the huge fur collar. Whenever he felt himself challenged he rapped out a string of orders.

Asch knew that this sort of man wouldn't stop at murder. He knew his type. Such a man would get his own way at all costs. If he were to meet with any serious resistance, he wouldn't hesitate to draw his revolver and make use of it.

Asch was convinced that so long as this man dominated the crossing, the convoys on the subsidiary roads would rot before they were allowed to pass. So, said Asch to himself, the Major must be got out of the way. But how was this to be done?

Asch drove up to the crossing, tried to turn into the main road and was immediately brought up short by a military policeman who blocked his way with outstretched arms. " Halt!" he cried.

And the Major came rushing over at once as if drawn by a magnet.

" Dispatch rider!" said Asch who knew how to deal with this sort of situation.

" Let him pass!" said the Major.

Asch gave his machine full throttle and raced down the main

road. The trucks he was overtaking now were moving slowly forward. It wasn't until he had gone three kilometres that he came across another block.

A number of men were bustling about a stationary truck, cursing and swearing. An officer intervened—he swore too.

" What's the matter?" asked Asch.

" Back axle gone," said one of the men. " Overloaded. Full of food for one of the staffs of course."

" Tip it into the ditch," ordered the officer.

The driver of the broken-down truck refused to obey. The drivers of the other trucks started yelling at him. One of them tried to overtake, skidded off to the left and crashed into a tree.

" Tip them both into the ditch," ordered the officer.

A huge Henschel came slowly up and started shoving with its bumper against the truck with the broken axle. Slowly it pushed it forward off the road until it overbalanced and tipped over down a small embankment.

" All clear!" shouted the officer. " Off you go."

Asch drove on, swerving to avoid oncoming motor-cycles. He saw that it was now only motor-cycles which were able to pass freely in either direction. Two military police, riding very close together, came roaring down from the opposite direction.

" Everyone over to the right," they shouted. " Clear the road! The General's going up to the front."

The heavy trucks at once swung over to the right-hand side of the road. Asch wormed his way in behind a small bus. There was the screaming of sirens. A small troop-carrier with tracks went roaring by.

A soldier leant out of his truck and watched the General go past. Then he said to Asch: " It looks as if things must be getting nasty up there."

" It can't be too bad, if a full-blooded General's still prepared to go up," said Asch.

" Maybe you're right," said the soldier. And he looked anxiously ahead again. His own concern was to get on as quickly as possible. But the road still seemed to be blocked.

Asch put his machine into first gear and tried to get past the little bus in front of him. It was particularly difficult to see on the road here, and he switched on his headlamp. In the narrow strip of light which was thrown ahead of him he saw some luggage which he thought he recognised piled up on the back of the bus. He braked, and switched off first his headlamp and then his engine.

He opened the inside door of the driver's cabin and called into the darkness of the interior:

"Well, you heroines, how's it going?"

"That's not Herr Asch?" asked a low, now rather tired voice, which undoubtedly belonged to Charlotte.

"No, it's my ghost," said the Sergeant, and climbed into the bus.

"You!" said Viola, peevishly, wrapping herself up tighter in her fur coat, and drawing away into a corner. "This really is the last straw."

"It astonishes me to find you're not being escorted by staff officers," said Asch.

"I wonder if you could help us, Asch?" asked the conjurer. He seemed quite to have forgotten their little disagreement and to bear no resentment. In fact he was just scared. "We're stuck here and simply can't get on. Isn't it terrible?"

"But what did you expect," cried Asch gaily. "You didn't think war was going to be fun, did you?"

"Herr Asch," said the conjurer, throwing his dignity to the winds, "if only you could help us to get on a bit."

"If I were you," cried Lisa Ebner to the one official male representative of the troupe, "I'd ask help of anyone but him."

"I'm delighted to hear you're in such good form, Lisa," said Asch.

"We're cold," said Charlotte. "And hungry."

"Not thirsty?" inquired Asch, "I've got some brandy in my water-bottle."

"Let's have some!" said Charlotte.

"Get out of here," cried Lisa Ebner.

"If only you'd help us in some way ..." the conjurer implored him.

"Quiet!" shouted Asch. There was immediate quiet.

"Don't you hear something?" he asked. At first they heard nothing.

"Everyone out!" yelled Asch. And he yelled it with such conviction that the inmates of the little bus all climbed out immediately, the driver first of all.

They stood out in the open and listened. And all around them men were standing beside the stationary vehicles looking upwards. High above them, heading straight for them apparently, came a humming sound. It was coming nearer and nearer.

"It's an aeroplane," cried the conjurer in terror.

"It's what's called a 'sewing-machine'," explained Asch. "One of the oldest crates the Russians have. You just ladle the bombs out of those things with a coal shovel."

Lisa Ebner stood close beside Asch. She tried to tell what he was thinking from his face. But under the steel helmet his face was grey and shapeless and inscrutable.

The drone of the "sewing-machine" was now directly above them. And suddenly there was a high-pitched whistling through the air. The conjurer flew straight into the ditch. Lisa Ebner clutched Asch's arms. Her little hands fastened round them.

"We're not in danger," he said.

The bomb came howling down and exploded about three hundred yards away, close to the road. It was like a searchlight that flares up too bright and then goes out for ever. There came a muffled crash. Somebody screamed.

"Oh, my God!" said Lisa Ebner.

Asch tore himself away from her.

The shouts coming from where the bomb had exploded grew louder. They seemed to multiply and then distinguish themselves from other sounds which were merely cries of pain. Orders came bellowing through the darkness. And the sky seemed filled with the droning of engines coming from all directions.

Then the motors of several hundred vehicles started up too. The long convoys had only one wish; to get on, to get out of the thick wet slush on the road, to get away from the aircraft above them.

A little more of this, said Asch to himself, and then a break in the front, and there'll be almost perfect panic.

"I may be coming back," said Asch, going over to his motor-cycle.

"Aren't you staying with us?" cried Lisa Ebner, following him.

"I can't," said Asch, "I'm needed with my troop."

He climbed on to his motor-cycle, jerked it into gear, pushed forward the throttle and roared away. He drove straight up to the Major who was still in command at the crossing holding back all but his own troops.

"Herr Major," said Asch, "there's a General stuck on the road two kilometres back."

"Damnation!" said the Major. "Which General?"

"I don't know," said Asch. "All I know is the General ordered me to tell you to report to him. With three military policemen."

" Me?"

" The Major at the crossing, the General said."

" Damnation!" cried the Major. Then he ordered three of his six military police to come with him, gave a final stentorian warning to his remaining forces to stand firm and rushed away.

Sergeant Asch turned off into the side road in which Sergeant-Major Bock's convoy was still stuck. He went in search of the first officer he could find, and soon came upon a Lieutenant who was swearing freely.

" Lieutenant," said Asch. " The coast is clear. Just at the moment the crossing is free of senior officers."

The Lieutenant understood at once, rushed up to the crossing and took control himself. He stopped the Major's convoy and allowed his own men to proceed.

When half an hour later the Major came back fuming with rage, the vehicles of No. 3 Troop were just turning on to the main road. Those at the back found themselves looking down the barrel of the Major's revolver.

Sergeant Asch was on his way up to No. 3 Troop's gun positions. As he approached the front, he noticed that the traffic was getting less and less. Just behind the lines it ceased almost altogether. Here only ambulances and ammunition carriers were churning their way through the mud.

From the front itself came the sound of a war just beginning to get back into its stride. Big guns roared in the distance like sleepy watch-dogs. Machine-guns spat monotonously into the darkness. The mortars firing in series sounded like coals being tipped down a shaft.

His eyes had got used to the darkness. And the sleet which was falling more and more heavily, seemed now hardly more than a veil before his eyes. Soon this sleet would turn to rain altogether.

Asch drove into the village behind the front which had been the site of No. 3 Troop's forward base. The sound of a cater-pillar tractor's engine could be heard grinding away up near the guns. Whenever the engine threatened to die out, voices could be heard swearing furiously. Otherwise the newly awakened war hardly seemed to have reached this sector at all.

The Sergeant saw the C.O.'s car standing in front of the hut which he had formerly occupied with Lieutenant Wedelmann.

Asch leant his motor-cycle against the wall and went in. Lance-Corporal Kowalski was sitting by the stove drying his socks.

"What are you doing back here?" asked Kowalski. "Did you feel homesick?"

"I just wanted to see if you were still alive."

"So far," said Kowalski, "they seem to be leaving us alone. Witterer's quite cheered up again."

It was just as Asch had expected; first of all a barrage over the whole front, then concentration on a number of strategic points which up to the present did not appear to include No. 3 Troop's position.

"Our friend Witterer," said Kowalski, "is beginning to think that the Russians must be afraid of him."

"Has he been using a lot of ammunition?"

"So-so," said the Lance-Corporal, bending right over the stove with his sock. "Just lately our hero has been going a little more sparingly. He discovered that when the Russians retaliate they do so with deadly accuracy. It began to get on his nerves."

Asch sat down on the floor beside Kowalski and stretched out his hands to the stove. "The Russians will try and break through of course," he said.

"Not here," said the Lance-Corporal. "They wouldn't want to annoy Witterer."

"Somewhere to the right or the left of us. And then before we know where we are we'll find them on our flank or even in our rear."

"And you've come to see just how it all develops, eh? Or to watch Witterer running for his life? Or what have you come back for?"

Asch grinned at Kowalski. "I've seen half the troop on their way. Now I've come back for the second half."

Asch went on warming himself for a while and then left Kowalski sitting there and went out into the night. The situation was still quite unchanged. There was a great deal of noise going on on both sides of them, but in the sector immediately ahead there was relative quiet. The rattle of a machine-gun came from two or three kilometres away. It was followed by a few scattered rifle-shots.

Up in the gun positions the whine of the tractor's engine could still be heard as it strained to move one of the guns. But its wheels were now completely stuck and even the tracks were slipping. Men were pushing at it but without any real

251

effort, as Asch soon saw. Witterer stood there shouting orders.

Asch went and stood beside Witterer and watched.

"Don't stand around here," the Captain shouted at him. "Lend a hand, man."

"It's pointless," said Asch. "The ground is far too badly churned up. It's like soap."

"Kindly allow me to be the best judge of that," shouted Witterer.

"It's a question of experience," said Asch. "Let me try."

And without waiting for the Captain's permission Asch took command of the little group with absolute assurance.

"Cut the motor. Three men go and collect brushwood."

"Ah, that's more like it," said the driver of the tractor. "That's what I was saying half an hour ago."

"How did you get here, anyway, Asch?" asked Witterer angrily.

"On my motor-bike."

"Aren't you supposed to be with Bock's convoy?"

"Yes, I have been," said Asch.

"Well? Has it reached the new position?"

"No, it's stuck on the main road. There's nothing to be done at present. And since I was detailed to escort the guns as well . . ."

"As you see it'll be some time before we're off."

"I guessed plans had been upset. Theoretically at any rate they're due away now."

"Is it as late as that?" asked Witterer in astonishment.

Krause shone his torch for him and he looked at his watch.

"So it is," he cried. "You carry on here, Asch. I must go and put a call through to the regimental commander."

While Witterer ran across towards the field telephone which was situated in a slit trench about thirty yards away, Asch got the gun clear. He made the men put brushwood under the tracks and then lay an empty ammunition basket on top of that on each side.

"Right, now," said Asch, "Slowly forward."

The driver accelerated, the tracks slipped for a moment, and then gradually got a grip. Slowly the tractor rolled forward, pulling the gun after it, until both were once again on firm ground.

"Right," said Asch and went over to the slit trench where Witterer was telephoning.

"Very good, Colonel," said Witterer. And he repeated it three times. Then he shouted to Krause: "The map."

Krause unfolded the Captain's map, found a torch and held a pencil ready for him. Witterer seized map and pencil and marked a position which, as Asch saw, was about half-way between the new position and the old.

Then he once again said "Very good, Colonel," and climbed out of the trench with the air of a Commander-in-Chief. His greatcoat sat immaculate on his upright form. Spots of mud which stuck to his sleeves and shoulders merely gave him a tough experienced look.

"Section commanders to me!" he ordered.

His telephone conversation seemed to have left him extraordinarily pleased with himself. He looked defiantly out across the hills where the enemy were. And at this moment he really regretted that the enemy obviously didn't have sufficient strength to risk an assault.

"Of course the plums always fall to the regiments on either side of us," he said to Krause.

"They may make them ill," said Asch quietly.

"Ah, rubbish!" said Witterer smugly. "Ivan's trying to break through everywhere, but he's having no success at all."

"No one ever broke through a front at the first attack," said Asch.

"If everything goes as smoothly everywhere else as it's done here, there won't be another squeak out of the Russians on this sector in an hour or so."

Sergeant Asch joined the group of section leaders summoned by Witterer. Krause read out their names and each answered in turn: "Here!" It was as if they were all recruits again. Only Lance-Corporal Kowalski answered "Sound in wind and limb" and one or two of them laughed quietly.

Then after the "parade" had been officially reported all present and correct, Witterer began to give out the orders. First of all he let the section commanders have a look at his map. "I hope you at least know how to read a map," he said.

The section commanders took this insult tolerably well. None of them spoke. Only Kowalski said "A map? What's that?"

Witterer cast a sharp glance into the semi-darkness from which the remark had come. Kowalski alone seemed not to notice.

"Kindly find our present positions on your maps," said Witterer. "Right, got them? Let's see now."

The section leaders obediently showed up their maps, though it was obvious that they resented the procedure. They placed

253

their forefingers on the point which denoted their present position. They felt like recruits called out to a clothing parade.

"And where's your map, Asch?"

"I haven't got one, Captain. I don't need one. I know the country round here by heart."

"Report to me with a map within twelve hours at the latest," ordered Witterer. "I don't care where you get it from. Even if you pinch it from under some General's arse."

Kowalski laughed out loud and Witterer felt a certain satisfaction that his joke had been appreciated, by Kowalski of all people. But then Kowalski himself added: "Of course remember that what the General's got only looks like an arse—Generals don't have anything so vulgar!"

"If anyone makes a joke around here, Kowalski," said Witterer, "it'll be me, understand?"

"Very good," said Kowalski. "I'll remember that."

"Right then, gentlemen," said Witterer proceeding with the orders. "You now know where our present position is on the map. Now then, move your fingers eighteen kilometres westwards, that's to say to the left. You'll find a village there —Nikolski or something like that. Found it?"

"Found it," muttered one or two of the section leaders.

"Well then, there's a hill there, Hill 157—everyone got that? Right, that is our new temporary position. We'll get ourselves dug in there, and then see what happens. Everyone understood?"

Everyone had understood. Even Kowalski had nothing to add.

Then Asch said thoughtfully:

"Eighteen kilometres—that'll take us between four and five hours—if we get a clear run."

"We'll have priority over all other traffic," said Witterer.

"I assumed that, and I've taken it into my calculations," said the Sergeant.

"Right then; on the move," ordered Witterer. "And I want to see perfect discipline. Woe to anyone who falls behind or loses his nerve! And anyone I catch slacking or not looking after his vehicle properly will be court-martialled."

"My God, doesn't that man like the sound of his own voice?" said Kowalski to Asch.

"Let's only hope he doesn't mean half of what he says."

"You, Sergeant," ordered Captain Witterer, "will stay behind with the troop. I'm going up ahead."

"He's got his directions mixed up," said Kowalski. "When he says ahead he means to the rear."

"Still, I expect it suits you, Lance-Corporal!"

"Don't worry, I'll soon teach him the difference between front and rear!"

"I want to have a talk with you," said Lieutenant Wedelmann, pushing Natasha away from him as she came forward to kiss him.

"I'm so glad you're back," she said.

"I'm not staying."

It was still the early hours of the morning. It had taken him two hours to do the thirty-five kilometres. He had gone tearing through the convoy. The road grew more and more congested as he went on, but he always managed to get through, winding his way in and out of the vehicles with great skill, sometimes getting stuck in the snow, sometimes pushing his machine and sometimes carrying it, but always getting through so that now here he was face to face at last with Natasha.

He said:

"There's nothing I haven't seen: vehicles reduced to scrap, men shouting, wounded screaming—in the middle of the road there was a corpse that no one was taking any notice of. The heavy trucks just drove over him and squashed him to pulp."

"War's a horrible thing!" she said.

Without taking off any of his equipment, Wedelmann collapsed into a chair. They were in the room which he had found for himself and Natasha. He had wanted to have her with him.

He was exhausted. He made no attempt to hide the fact.

"Tea?" she said shyly.

"No."

She stood close to the wall in front of him. She didn't move. But there was an anxious look in her eyes.

The Lieutenant said: "I can guess what it's looking like up at the front. Heavy artillery barrage at several points. Infantry attacking. Losses on both sides. Pressure increasing from hour to hour. If they succeed in effecting a big break-through tonight there'll be no stopping them."

"You must try not to think about it," she said.

"I'll never be able to stop thinking about it," said Wedelmann.

"Never—as long as I live." And he added almost inaudibly: "And just at this moment I wish I hadn't got much longer to live."

"You mustn't say that. You mustn't even think it."

"Hundreds of people killed," said Wedelmann. "Thousands wounded. No conscience could stand it."

"What are you talking about?"

"I've seen quite a lot of men die in my time," said Wedelmann. "They died, and I was standing by them and was ready to die too—and my conscience was clean. But those days are over now. I know now I'm just a rotten swine."

"Nonsense," she said.

"I'm a filthy rotten swine."

"What happened?"

Wedelmann looked straight at her for the first time since he had come in. She saw desperation in his eyes, and fear, and at the same time great determination. It was as if he were suffering from a high fever.

But there was something ominously calm about his movements. They were slow and long-drawn-out as if he were in pain. He reached behind him for his holster, opened it, pulled out his revolver and laid it on the table in front of him.

"Strip your bed!" he said.

She looked at him in complete bewilderment. She didn't move, but fear was in her eyes, naked fear.

"I said: strip your bed!"

She moved suddenly as if she had just been pushed. She tore the blankets back, threw the pillows on to the floor, wrenched the straw mattress out of its frame.

"Undo the mattress!"

She opened up the mattress and spilled the straw out on to the floor.

"Clear out the cupboard!" said Wedelmann.

She threw her clothes down on top of the straw.

"Pull out your case!"

She stopped where she was. She stood there slightly hunched, a scarf in her hand, her head bent forward.

"No," she said.

"Yes," said Wedelmann, and it was as if in this one word he pronounced judgment on her.

Then he shouted: "Open the case!"

"All right," she said. "All right." And she was now just as desperate and determined as he was.

She opened the lid of her case, bent over it, and burrowed

around among pieces of material and clothing. Then from the bottom of it she dragged out something about the size of a shoe-box.

She put it down on the table in front of Wedelmann, next to his revolver.

The Lieutenant was breathing heavily. His face was as white as a sheet. One of his hands reached out towards the box and he opened the lid.

He saw that it was a transmitter.

Wedelmann seemed unable to move. His cheek-bones stuck right out of his face. His hands began to tremble.

Slowly, as if it were some invisible force that was hauling him up, he got to his feet. He put his hands on the box containing the transmitter. With a convulsive movement he seized hold of it and lifted it up level with his chest. Then he lifted it higher still, up to the level of his face, and higher still, high up above his head. And then he brought it crashing down with all his might on to the floor.

It smashed to pieces. Broken glass and pieces of metal flew across the floor. Natasha didn't move. Her eyes were closed. Blood trickled from a cut on her leg.

Wedelmann collapsed into the chair again.

"So," he said, "it's true."

And after a long pause, she said:

"Yes, it's true. And it's true that I love you too."

Wedelmann closed his eyes as if he didn't want to have to look at her. "You lied to me. You deceived me. You used me. You stopped at nothing."

Slowly she shook her head. "How little you know me," she said.

"Did know you," he said brutally.

"I never lied to you," she said. "Never. Especially when I told you I loved you. I do love you. I've never loved anyone in my life as much as I do you. And I never will again."

"And yet, this man whom you say you loved—you turned him into somebody utterly contemptible."

"I always told you that I loved my country, that I loved it at least as much as you love yours."

"I'm a soldier. I'm fighting for my country."

"And yet you won't let me fight for mine in the best way I can. I don't want to handle a rifle, I can't join the Partisans. I must do what I can do best. If I hadn't done that you wouldn't have respected me."

"I wanted to love you, that's all."

"As if love were all there is!" cried Natasha. She had grown excited and her voice was deep and strong. It now seemed as if she were the one who was doing the accusing.

"I only wanted to love you."

"You've killed Russians, haven't you? Yes or No?"

"I've fought openly and honourably with my enemy. Men were killed—yes, certainly. On both sides. You don't reproach me for still being alive, do you? I'm the only person who can do that. I'm the only person who has a right to."

"All right," said Natasha. "You've always done what you considered to be your duty. And that's exactly what I've done."

"Even war has its laws," said Wedelmann. "Its own code, its rules laid down for hundreds of years."

"Not this one!"

"This is a war like all the others."

"Not this one! We were attacked. You looted our country, shot our people, carried them into slavery."

"I've never looted or carried anyone into slavery. I've simply done my duty as a soldier."

"And if we had attacked Germany—what do you think your women would have done? Stood by and watched? Or supported you in your struggle?"

"War's nothing to do with women."

"But it's forced itself on them. And it forces women to take part in it. Some make munitions, some look after the wounded, some do administrative jobs. Right, well I collected information."

"From me!"

"Wherever I could get it from. Yes—from you too. I love you more than anyone else in the world. But you're still a German, one of Hitler's soldiers. All Hitler's soldiers are our enemies."

Wedelmann brought both his hands down suddenly on the table so that the revolver jumped.

"That's enough!" he said.

"Yes," she said softly. "That's enough."

Wedelmann put out his right hand and laid it over his revolver. It felt cold, ice-cold. He pulled it towards him.

Natasha stared round the room. It was in chaos. She was drooping forward as if in need of support. A lock of hair fell over her face.

She said: "Do what you like. I had to do it. You can shoot me right away—perhaps that would be best. You can hand me over to your people and they'll shoot me. Perhaps they'll torture me and ask me questions before they kill me. It's all the same to me. Whatever happens I shall know that I'm dying for my country. And I'll always be able to say: I loved you."

"One's country," said Wedelmann, barely audibly, "is sometimes like a halter round one's neck."

"A halter that one's proud to wear."

Wedelmann stood up. He picked up his revolver and felt the weight of it. Once more he looked searchingly at Natasha. She looked straight back at him. And each read the thoughts in the other's eyes.

"I never want to see you again," said Wedelmann, "I have never known you. You have ceased to exist for me."

"I love you too—above everything." Her eyes were soft and tragic. The tears ran down her face.

And Wedelmann went out into the night. He wanted to hide the fact that he was weeping too.

The aircraft droned on through the darkness towards the front. The pilot sat sullenly in front of his instruments. He'd had enough of the job. He might as well be driving a bus, he thought.

The two N.C.O.s, who only a few hours before had been proud to be known as "the Siamese twins," now sat grey and speechless in the belly of the aircraft, staring into space.

Beside them sat Vierbein, with his head tilted back a little as if he were looking up at the sky. But all his eyes could see were the curved metal walls of the aircraft, although the sky apparently was all around him, and even beneath his feet.

"It all really began," said Bartsch gloomily, "with that wretched dog—the one that belonged to the C.O.'s bride."

"We should never have put that plaque up at the main gate," said Ruhnau.

"What plaque was that?" asked Vierbein.

"An absolutely harmless affair, in red, white and black too. And on it was written: 'Dogs of an inferior race, mongrels or other non-Aryan breeds, are strictly forbidden within the precincts of these barracks.'"

"And it was immediately taken personally."

"Never mind," said Vierbein trying to comfort them. "You won't get treated like that with us. I can tell you that in comparison with Schulz and his barracks, life at the front is like being in a convalescent home."

And it was just as Corporal Vierbein said that, that several hundred kilometres away the front suddenly collapsed as easily as if it had been made of matchwood.

Russian infantry forced their way through the gap and lay bleeding and exhausted all over the German lines. Other infantry immediately pushed through from behind, stumbling over the first wave as they lay about the landscape like scattered twigs.

Then came the tanks and they ploughed their way relentlessly into the German artillery reducing the guns to scrap. Other tanks tore holes in the now open flanks. All along the kilometre's breadth of front a gap now yawned. It was only about as wide as a large river, but this was a river which flowed with blood.

The aircraft seemed to be heading straight for the gap. The pilot knew his course by heart. He had put in the automatic pilot and was smoking a cigarette. This bus-driver's existence bored him stiff.

"And then again," said Bartsch thoughtfully, "we should never have had anything to do with Lore Schulz."

"That creature was our ruin."

"She was an optical illusion."

"She was an utter fraud."

"Frau Lore Schulz," said Vierbein very firmly, "is a highly respectable woman."

"That's just what we're complaining of, man!"

"That's just what got us into trouble."

"I don't understand," said Vierbein.

"It's always the respectable ones who cause the trouble," Bartsch assured him.

"We gave her every chance," said Ruhnau. "We even offered her a guide to her husband's movement's—showing exactly what he would be doing twenty-four hours in advance. And if a wife doesn't take advantage of an offer like that, especially a wife with her assets, then there's something very wrong somewhere."

"She had no taste, that was the trouble. She simply didn't find us sympathetic. Vierbein, man, these women will be the ruin of the Wehrmacht. They should be given orders to consider themselves permanently ready for action, otherwise it's hopeless."

"By the way did we ever tell you the story of Sergeant Reitter? No? Well: Reitter had his eye on the Quartermaster's daughter, and as the Quartermaster is a particularly skilful provider for the battery, and thus a man who carries some weight there, Reitter was sent off to the front at once. But then it turned out that this pure little girl of the Quartermaster's was in the family way, and so Sergeant Reitter was hurriedly transferred home so that he could be forced to marry her. Then, however, came the miscarriage, so Reitter was sent promptly back to the front again. But now comes the best bit: on his next leave Sergeant Reitter succeeded in putting her in the family way again. . . ."

"Nothing like that goes on at the front, thank God," said Vierbein.

And even as he spoke, in a little village just behind the lines, Corporal Soeft was trading the three girl members of the concert party against the loan of a caterpillar tractor for twenty-four hours.

Soeft, honest business man that he was, guaranteed that the goods would be unsoiled, and of the best quality, but couldn't guarantee their performance. That was up to the recipient, or alternatively, the recipients, he said. At any rate it was a first-rate opportunity, and his price was really very moderate.

The man with whom he was doing business, a member of the "Controlling Agency for the Appropriation of Russian Home Produce," a vaguely uniformed creature who was half-soldier, half-Party man, knew Soeft of old. He knew from experience that his offers were always worth taking seriously —seriously in a commercial sense, that is. So they sealed the contract with a handshake.

For the next twenty-four hours Soeft was in possession of an almost new, completely serviceable caterpillar tractor. He knew what he wanted it for all right. In a situation like this a man with a vehicle capable of travelling over open country was as good as independent of the roads.

Now he would be able to cash in on the withdrawal in a big way! He would be able to tow away any heavily-laden trucks which had broken down and been abandoned. His profits would increase in proportion to the size of the panic. If everything went according to plan—according to plan, that is, in his sense of the phrase—before twenty-four hours were up No. 3 Troop would be able to count a millionaire among their number.

And every minute the aircraft flew nearer and nearer to the seething cauldron which this part of the front had now become.

The pilot took a bearing on his position. But he knew long before he had begun to calculate exactly where he was.

" War's a man's business," said Bartsch. " Women shouldn't be allowed anything to do with it."

" Still thinking of our friend Senkpiehl?" asked Ruhnau.

" Poor Senkpiehl! His trouble was that he *wasn't* interested in sex. That was his undoing."

" It was his own fault really. Captain Wolf's wife made plain enough overtures to him. He was a fool to say no. Off to the front with him!"

" Fate can be cruel at times, man."

" And then after Senkpiehl came Kempka. And he didn't say no. But the Captain caught him with his wife. So off to the front with him too."

" Well, there's nothing left for you two," said Vierbein, with a surprising turn of sarcasm, " but to become heroes."

" Is there much of a demand for them?"

" Everyone who fights at the front is a hero," said Ruhnau. " It says so in the papers. Heroes are two a penny. Right then, we're heroes!"

And as Corporal Vierbein sat there listening to this conversation, the dangerous breach in the front yawned wider and wider.

More and more enemy tanks rolled into it. They had been rushed up from other sectors. They ploughed all before them —the earth and the men who lay in their way. Fire, blood, water, snow and mud were all ploughed up together in the terrible sludge of war.

It was as if a dam had broken. Death came pouring through the gap like a flood. It came lapping up to the jammed roads. It washed over them. Smashed, burnt-out, looted vehicles lay about the roads like so much unwanted scrap.

Many tried to escape as long as they thought there was any chance of escape. Panic seized the columns. The long lines of vehicles shook with panic as if in the grip of a terrible fever.

Trucks ran into each other. Revolvers were drawn. Men shouted and swore and yelled and laughed and prayed and howled and cursed and wept. Engines screamed as trucks went hurtling with their loads into the mud on either side of the road. And all the time the " sewing-machines " swooped overhead and the front became closer, receded, came closer again and then swung sideways. The front was everywhere at once.

And between the front and the retreating columns stood a few officers whose eyes were still cool and whose brains were clear, some non-commissioned officers, cold-blooded as fishes and possessed of the calm that comes from years of heavy beer-drinking, and the men, who had no hope, no illusions and therefore no fear.

In the middle of all this Soeft bustled about with his tractor, having a hard time to keep out of trouble. A lot of officers seemed to take exception to his activities, but he answered all criticism with the explanation that he was acting on orders from the General himself. And his first action had been to tow the little bus which contained the concert party out of the danger zone. He had ascertained its exact whereabouts from Asch, for he had wanted to keep his side of the bargain.

Captain Witterer was taking "a short respite" in a farmhouse. This " short respite " had already lasted two hours and Kowalski seemed to think that this was quite long enough. The Lance-Corporal's hints that it was time they went up to the gun positions became more and more pointed and difficult to ignore. Finally he decided, as he put it, to take a hand himself.

The aircraft droned on over the last few hundred kilometres. It seemed to be growing light on the horizon already. The pilot found this rather surprising. He looked at his watch. It was still too early for dawn. So he told himself that it must be some petrol store or ammunition dump on fire. And he gave a huge yawn. Oh, but this was a bus-driver's war. It was enough to send any man to sleep.

" But at the front," said Bartsch, " surely there are some nice little nurses? What are they like?"

" You'll have to wait until you're badly wounded to find out," said Vierbein.

" And then what about the girls who help with the staff work?"

" Where we are there aren't any girls helping with the staff work."

" And then there are the concert parties. I suppose those are practically organised brothels?"

" I don't know. I never saw one," said Vierbein.

" Well, and what about the Russian girls?"

" Never seen any of them either."

" Good God, man," said Bartsch visibly shaken. " You're not serious!"

" If this is really true," said Ruhnau, " then I see why you're all such heroes! There's nothing else for you to do."

Slowly the pilot got ready to land. They had reached the airfield. He gave one more great yawn, then clapped his hand over his mouth and thrust his chin forward. The actual flying of an aircraft was child's play; take-off was a routine affair; but landing—landing was a man's job.

The aircraft came to a halt. The engines shuddered as they were switched off. Corporal Vierbein was the first to jump down on to the runway. He planted his feet firmly on the ground again, and felt happy after his fashion.

"Welcome home!" cried a cheerful voice.

"Soeft, man! Soeft!" cried Vierbein, running towards the Corporal and throwing his arms round him.

"Now then," said Soeft, "you'll make me think I've turned into a woman overnight!"

"Soeft, man!" cried Vierbein happily. "It's splendid to see you. Have you come to fetch me?"

"Do I look quite so stupid?" asked Soeft in reply. "I just wanted to see what the situation was up here, to pick up anything that was going."

"Well, you can pick us up, Soeft!"

"Then I really would be stupid," said Soeft. "You're early as it is. Take your little schoolboys off somewhere and have a drink. Then have a good sleep. Then and only then, report with the little darlings to the nearest control point. By that time the worst should be over."

"What's going on then, Soeft?"

"Almost everything you could think of."

"Take us up to the troop."

"Good God, man, I'm not an undertaker," said Soeft. "Be thankful you're where you are, man, and stay there. You must be off your head. You're not all that keen to appear in the casualty list, are you?"

"Section leaders to me!" cried the Captain, springing out of the car as athletically as ever. As he did so Kowalski let the brake off for a moment. The car moved on a little and Witterer nearly fell over.

"Be more careful, will you, man!" yelled Witterer.

"I was very careful, Captain," answered Kowalski.

After several telephone calls and another "short respite" the Captain had eventually arrived at No. 3 Troop's new gun positions in the early hours of the morning.

This time Witterer was without Krause, who had gone on ahead to find new billets. The Captain looked critically about him. The guns were bunched too close together. Admittedly that increased the troop's fire power, but it also made it more vulnerable. What he liked to see was a perfect balance between effective fire power and safety. But subordinates couldn't be expected to know about such subtleties.

The ground ahead of them was fairly open. There was no sign of infantry anywhere. The guns had been placed just behind a little hill over which their barrels poked inquisitively. They were ready for immediate action.

Sergeant Asch reported all section commanders present and correct. He had tacitly assumed command of the guns and Witterer acted as if he hadn't noticed the fact. The situation, the Captain told himself, was damn' serious, and this fellow Asch was said to be a good enough soldier. And it was far better that he should spend his time like this than continue to run around criticising. And he tugged at his belt.

"Anything special to report?" asked Witterer.

"No contact with the enemy so far," said Asch.

"Damn it!" said the Captain. He meant this. He would have felt much happier if he could have given a few curt fire orders over open sights.

"But it will probably come," said Asch.

"Let's hope so," said Witterer.

"I've got an observation post three kilometres ahead," said Asch calmly. "They've reported enemy infantry attacking in battalion strength."

"When? Where?"

"Just now. Heading this way. I should think you'll get the contact you're looking forward to in about half an hour's time."

Witterer stood quite still, thinking. Enemy infantry were all right—but in battalion strength? That was too much. Far too much. Who could say what might not follow them. Besides he had fresh orders from Colonel Luschke and they had to be carried out.

So he said:

"I'm sorry to say we'll have to forfeit that pleasure. We're changing position again."

"After contact, though," said Asch.

"At once!" ordered the Captain. "Out with your maps! The new position is nine kilometres west. You'll find a Kolchos there. There are three houses marked. Well, right in front of the third house is where our new position is. Got that."

"I see," said Asch.

"Any questions?"

"I see perfectly," said Asch, looking across at Kowalski.

"Right then!" cried Witterer. "Just one or two rounds to pull Ivan up short and then away like the wind."

"How many rounds?"

"Don't ask idiotic questions, Asch. Three or four—four or five. All the guns."

And the prospect of a few resounding explosions made him feel much better.

He made a quick calculation: Enemy infantry about four kilometres away, that's to say about thirty minutes in time. Series of salvoes from the guns: ten minutes. Change of position: fifteen minutes. Oh yes, there was plenty of time. "Right, let's get on with it," said the Captain."

He gave the preliminary orders, just as if he were on an artillery range. He had learnt the drill well. He carried it out perfectly, all in the correct sequence. And his voice sounded crisp and decisive.

Sergeant Asch telephoned to his observation post. He received the position of the advancing enemy and transferred it to his map. Then he held his map out in front of Witterer.

Witterer took in the position, and asked, a little less crisply than before, what Asch thought the sights should be set at. Asch wrote some figures down on the edge of the map.

"I'd begin with that," he said.

Witterer nodded. He roared out the orders, standing almost to attention as he did so. Kowalski watched him through half-closed eyes. The Captain's mouth flew open. "Fire!" came the order.

And before Asch could hear from the observation post where the shell had landed and thus make the necessary corrections to the sights, the Captain roared again: "Fire!" And yet again: "Fire!" And again: "Fire!" And again and again "Fire!" "Fire!"

His eyes were blazing. "That'll give them something to think about!" he said.

Then he gave the order; "Change of position!"

He stood there, richly satisfied with his stupendous achievement. He watched his troop going about its work and could find nothing to take exception to.

He was still standing there when the first vehicles moved off. Sergeant Asch collected the whole troop into a convoy five hundred yards up the road. Then he gave the order to move.

And soon the war-like Captain was standing alone in the landscape.

"Right then, let's go," said Witterer to Kowalski who was standing calmly by the car looking towards the enemy.

"Yes, it's about time," said the Lance-Corporal.

"You can leave that to me to worry about, man!"

"Just as you like," replied the other. "But if the Captain would care to look that way, the Captain might see what I meant." And Kowalski jerked a thumb down the valley.

Enemy infantry could be seen making their way forward, well spread out across the side of a hill. They wore brownish grey uniforms. One or two threw themselves down and began to fire.

"Away like the wind!" shouted Witterer, jumping into the car at a single leap.

Kowalski sat down in the driver's seat and looked quickly across at Witterer who had turned anxiously round to look out of the back. And the Lance-Corporal quickly turned off the petrol.

"Get a move on, man!"

Kowalski pressed the self-starter. The engine leapt into life, spluttered and died. Again Kowalski pressed furiously on the starter.

"What's the matter?" shouted Witterer desperately.

"Nothing," said the Lance-Corporal. "It just won't start."

The enemy infantry had now all thrown themselves down in the mud. There were a few rifle shots but the range was still too great for them to be accurate. Bullets whistled round the car.

"Well, do something, you swine!" shouted Witterer.

Kowalski said "Very good," and with painfully slow movements heaved himself out of the car. He opened the catches of the bonnet, lifted the bonnet up, fixed it in position and looked intently at the engine.

"Hurry up, will you," roared Witterer.

"Patience, patience!" said Kowalski, touching the distributor.

The enemy infantry, imagining themselves confronted by strong enemy forces, deployed and began to work their way forward in small bounds. There were some more shots but the distance was still too great for rifle fire to be accurate.

"If you don't hurry up, you bastard," roared Witterer, "I'll have you court-martialled."

"You might not be in a position to," said Kowalski playing with the valves.

"You're overdue for one already," bellowed Witterer. "You rotten low-down swine."

"And shall I tell you what you are?" asked Kowalski drawing himself up to his full height.

"Don't stand there blathering, man! Get the engine going! Or you'll be done for."

"We'll both be done for, you mean, Captain. Both of us."

More bullets flew past. This time they sounded different. They came with a sharp hiss, dangerously close. One struck the rear mudguard, making a hard metallic sound. Witterer threw himself flat on his face.

"What's the ground temperature like?" asked Kowalski, opening the other side of the bonnet.

He had now skilfully manœuvred the body of the car between himself and the enemy fire. He looked cautiously out in the direction of the advancing infantry. They were closer, but still not close enough to be really dangerous. Kowalski had some experience of this sort of thing.

"Oh God, man," moaned Witterer, whose morale had suddenly collapsed. "Get the thing going again for God's sake!"

Kowalski pretended to be fascinated by the sight of the cylinder heads. He drew his bayonet and banged it against them. Witterer mistook the sound. He was terrified.

"Oh, Kowalski, for God's sake," said Witterer. "You're a splendid driver, easily the best that . . ."

"I thought I was a rotten low-down swine."

"Kowalski!" cried Witterer imploringly.

A burst of machine-gun fire ripped across the ground barely twenty yards from where the car was standing. The mud spurted up and seemed to make a dead set at Witterer. He was lying close to the car. His face was pressed awkwardly into the ground, and his hands scrabbled around desperately searching for something to catch hold of.

"Kowalski! Comrade!" groaned Witterer.

"They're coming closer and closer, Comrade Witterer," said the Lance-Corporal. "They can just about see that great backside of yours now. Though it's all they can see of you."

Again a burst of machine-gun fire ripped across the ground. A few scattered shots struck the back of the car. Witterer got ready to run for it. He staggered to his feet, then rushed away absolutely beside himself with panic. His athletic stride was less graceful than usual.

Kowalski jumped into the car, turned on the petrol and pressed the starter. The engine leapt into life at once. He drove off in pursuit of the galloping Captain and took him on to the running-board. Witterer was panting furiously as he clung desperately to the side of the car.

"Yes," said Kowalski contentedly. "War can really be quite an experience."

Colonel Luschke stood at the side of the road. His hands were behind his back and his chin was thrust forward grimly. He looked as if he were on a parade ground, instead of in the middle of an extremely dangerous pocket. He looked up wearily at the early morning sun.

No one seemed to pay any attention to him. But he noticed everything. He looked at the abandoned trucks, the shouting men, and the vehicles careering about in all directions.

Lieutenant Wedelmann drove over to his Commanding Officer, braked hard just in front of him, and still sitting on his motor-cycle, produced a smart salute. The Colonel responded with something like solemnity.

Then he said: "Good morning, Lieutenant. I hope you had a good night."

"Good morning, Colonel," said Wedelmann, looking straight at Luschke.

"Put that machine of yours on one side for a moment, Lieutenant, and come and keep me company."

Wedelmann leant his motor-cycle against the wall of a nearby house. Then he went over to Luschke and stood beside him in silence.

"We've still got one or two things to discuss together, Herr Wedelmann," said the Colonel. "But we'll leave them for the moment. Tell me, what do you make of the situation?"

"I haven't had much chance so far, Colonel . . ."

"I know that, but I'm asking you all the same."

Wedelmann forced himself to concentrate and stared at the traffic on the road. "Panic symptoms," he said. "If the enemy succeeds in reaching our new line within the next two or three hours, there'll be chaos."

Luschke nodded curtly.

"Our guns are withdrawing," he said. "They're going back in bounds of ten kilometres or so at a time. So far things have gone fairly smoothly. No losses to speak of. No particular success."

"Presumably we haven't reached the critical moment yet, Colonel. The night attacks were intended more to cause confusion than anything else. It's my experience that attacks can really only be built up effectively by day."

Luschke looked up at the pale sky which seemed heavy with snow. "As a soldier," he said, "you have your points."

Wedelmann understood. He stayed where he was and didn't answer.

"And by the way I've just had a message from your No. 3 Troop. They say they've been in touch with the enemy. Infantry in battalion strength, apparently. No losses, but some success! Inflicted a dozen casualties or so. Now, just between ourselves, Wedelmann, do you think this fellow Witterer is boasting?"

"Colonel, I am a Lieutenant and Captain Witterer is my Commanding Officer."

Luschke turned his lumpy face towards Wedelmann, half-closed his eyes and said coldly: "Herr Wedelmann, I don't need any tuition from you, thank you. I asked you a question."

"My answer, Colonel, is: Yes."

"Thank you," said Luschke.

"But I'd just like to add to that . . ."

"Thank you, thank you, Wedelmann, I know all that."

The Colonel raised his left hand and beckoned curtly. His adjutant who had been waiting in the entrance to the house came hurrying over.

Luschke said: "Find out where No. 3 Troop is. Insist on them keeping in touch with me all the time. Have my car brought round. Order to all ranks: Dig in immediately on reaching new positions; combine with local infantry for defence. And I want that radio message that came through during the night."

The adjutant nodded and left, making a few hurried notes on the way.

"But you and I have still got something else to discuss, Herr Wedelmann."

Luschke went on ahead into the wooden house that stood by the side of the road. Wedelmann followed him. The regimental sign had been chalked up over the door.

The Colonel led the way through a largish room in which the adjutant and his staff were at work. Everyone took care not to look up when Luschke came in, for he hated work to be interrupted by unnecessary saluting. The Colonel went on into a smaller room. It was a sort of cell with bars over the windows. He threw his crumpled cap on to the rickety table. No one had ever seen him wear a steel helmet.

"Don't mind if I don't ask you to sit down," he said. "The

bed is full of lice; the chair will collapse when the next person sits on it; and as for the table I shall use that myself if I want to sit down."

"Very good, Colonel."

"Not because I'm a Colonel, but because my bones are slowly calcifying, my arteries hardening and my muscles growing soft and flabby. I'm not quite sure what's wrong with my brain."

The Lieutenant said nothing. Luschke watched him carefully. It was as if he were trying to size him up.

"You see, Wedelmann," he said. "That's what I like about you. Anyone else would have said: Oh, but the Colonel is in the prime of life—or some such nonsense! But you're not a toady, or if you are one, which I refuse to believe, then at least you have the intelligence to realise that you're not exactly in a position where toadying will do you much good at the moment."

"That's true, Colonel."

Luschke came closer to him. He leant against the rickety table, looked at him keenly and said: "Dealt with the situation?"

Wedelmann grew tense.

"It's true. There was a transmitter."

"Go on, Wedelmann."

"I take all the blame, Colonel."

"Prepared to face a court martial?"

"Yes, Colonel."

Luschke raised both his arms up to the level of his shoulders. Then he brought them crashing down on top of the table. The wood creaked at every point. He drew himself up again.

"A girl?" he asked quietly.

"Yes."

"I see," said the Colonel. He looked helplessly about him as if in search of some support. He walked restlessly about the room. Finally he took a few steps over to the window. He stayed there a few seconds, then turned sharply about and came back to Wedelmann.

"Do you realise what this may lead to, man?" he said.

"I'm prepared to face all the necessary consequences, Colonel."

"So you are prepared to . . . Very good of you I'm sure. The Lieutenant is prepared to face the consequences. Do you hear that, everyone? Prepared to let himself be arrested, court-martialled and put up against a wall or detailed to some punishment battalion to bury corpses and dig up mines. He is prepared to accept anything. What nobility! What nauseous nobility! But you're not alone in the world, man!"

"Colonel, I do most sincerely regret . . ."

"To hell with your regret, man," cried the Colonel. "I don't want it. I can do without that."

"I can't," said Wedelmann humbly. "It'll be with me for the rest of my life."

"What do you mean by that?" asked Luschke, going and standing right in front of Wedelmann. "Do you mean you'll never be able to look your beloved Führer in the eye again?"

"More or less," said Wedelmann weakly.

"I must say, Wedelmann, that personally I have never had the slightest wish to stare into those great sheep's eyes of his. The war I'm fighting has nothing to do with him. And if the loss of his goodwill is all that's troubling you, Wedelmann, then you haven't got much to worry about."

"I don't understand you, Colonel."

"Well, it's about time you did," said Luschke significantly. "And as you seem to be slow at grasping things, particularly on this point, I'll make myself clear to you. Listen carefully, Wedelmann: this war we're fighting is a dirty war!"

"No, Colonel. That can't be."

"It shouldn't be, Wedelmann, but it is. And the more convinced of it I become, the more I despise myself for taking part in it."

"Colonel!"

"I tell you I despise myself."

The Colonel raised his hands and let them fall to his side again, and the Lieutenant found this gesture of despair profoundly disturbing.

"I respect you for it," said Wedelmann almost inaudibly.

"I am a Luschke. But what are the Luschkes? There are only a few dozen of them in the world. Little people, priests, officials, army officers. Respectable people. They've always lived decently, brought up their children well, and died in peace. I am the last of them. And I'm not living decently, I've brought up no children and I shan't die in peace."

Wedelmann felt utterly confused. His thoughts and emotions were running wildly together. He was no longer sure of anything. He was deeply fond of this man, but he didn't understand him. He felt himself drawn towards him but he was afraid of him.

"The last of the Luschkes has helped to bring shame on his

country! I do my duty, but who do I do it for, Wedelmann? The man who unleashed this war is a dishonourable man. And that's why it's a dishonourable war."

" No, Colonel."

" Yes, Lieutenant—a dishonourable war. Deliberately unleashed. Conducted with the methods of a pimp. With utter contempt for all human life—our own or the enemy's. Inspired by a crude intoxicating hysteria. Embellished with cheap glorification. The heroism of the lunatic! A Fatherland for megalomaniacs! And this is the stuff that's poisoning all humanity. And nothing can save it."

" I don't understand all that," said Wedelmann helplessly.

" It's time you did understand, Wedelmann. Don't you realise yet what's going on? This filth that we're spreading all over the world begets more filth. One lot slaughters a thousand, the next lot two thousand, then the first lot five thousand and the next lot ten thousand. Looting here, rape there. First: houses set on fire, then trains machine-gunned, then whole cities blazing. Men killed at first then the women, then the children. This isn't a soldier's war any more, Wedelmann. You'd have to be a wild beast to find it inspiring!"

" I hate war, too," said Wedelmann.

" I know that. You hate war, but you love your Fatherland. And this Fatherland's Father is called Hitler. And the man likes to think of himself as a soldier! He's forgotten what it is to be a soldier. Soldiers fight—they don't attack people without warning, cheat, hate, murder Jews, loot whole tracts of land, take civilians off into slavery, or shoot hostages by the thousand."

" I would never have a hand in any of these things, Colonel."

" I believe you, Wedelmann. I believe you all right. But you aren't consulted or required. There are plenty of people who are only too willing to help. Criminals by instinct, murderers with their own brand of philosophy. And in these conditions, Wedelmann, men begin as soldiers and end as criminals. Last December for instance, when the first panic of the war overtook the troops, you saw the criminal element in us gain the upper hand at once: mutinies, looting, black marketeering, theft, even murder, dressed up as self-defence. Just think about that. Look at it calmly and coolly and realistically. Just see to what an extent our society has been messed up already. It's deafened by loud-speakers, by shouting and yelling, blinded by propaganda. You have a conversation with someone, you think you're talking to a human being but you're really talking to a

273

spy. Even now, Wedelmann, I think I'm talking to one of my comrades but for all I know I'm talking to an informer."

"Colonel!"

"It's true, my boy."

"And what happens next, Colonel?" asked Wedelmann after a long pause.

Colonel Luschke breathed a deep sigh. He seemed exhausted. But his eyes were still sparkling.

"Lieutenant Wedelmann," he said, and he was once again "Lumpface," the regimental commander, "Lumpface" the cunning, the unapproachable, the man with the upper hand, "Lieutenant Wedelmann, I've always had a high opinion of you as a soldier; I have never been indifferent to your qualities as a man. I therefore gather from your report that you have discovered an enemy agent's transmitter, but that the agent herself unfortunately slipped through your fingers."

"Colonel!"

"We'll fix the report up together when all this business is over. Come on now, man, take that spaniel look off your face for God's sake!"

Wedelmann was utterly taken aback. He still couldn't grasp what was happening. He knew only one thing: that he felt deeply grateful. And on top of that: that he felt great affection. More than affection: love.

"And besides," said Luschke, "I must inform you of the contents of a radio message I have received. The adjutant has the full thing, you can see it afterwards." And Colonel Luschke smiled slyly. "Herr Wedelmann," he said. "I congratulate you on your appointment to the rank of Captain. From to-day on you assume command of No. 1 Battery in my regiment."

Wedelmann stared at his Commanding Officer in astonishment. Only very graduallly did he gather what had happened. He was now so dazed that he was almost on the point of collapse.

But Luschke gave him no chance to collapse. He said:

"I'd advise you to look to the command of your battery as soon as possible, Captain Wedelmann—and in particular to its No. 3 Troop."

Captain Witterer seemed to recover with remarkable speed from the humiliation which Lance-Corporal Kowalski had inflicted on him in the early hours of the morning. The one thing he was grateful for was that there had been no witnesses. Once again he threw himself into the war full of keenness and optimism. Yet his very briskness was in itself a sign of nervousness.

From now on as far as he was concerned Kowalski was a man to be utterly ignored, although this naturally was of little consequence to Kowalski. He got Kowalski to drive him up to the new position. On their way there they came across a Corporal who, as soon as he saw the C.O.'s car, leapt down from a truck that was making its way laboriously through the mud, and called out: "Kowalski! Stop! Kowalski!"

"You're the last straw," muttered Kowalski driving slowly on.

"Stop, man!" ordered Witterer.

The Corporal came stumbling up and gave Kowalski a broad grin which seemed to bring the latter to the verge of despair. He jumped to attention in front of Witterer and rapped out:

"Corporal Vierbein reporting back from his mission to the reserve battery, sir."

"So you're Corporal Vierbein," said Witterer with interest, and he knew that the man who was now standing in front of him was the most successful gun-crew leader in the whole of Luschke's regiment. He didn't exactly look like the born tank-buster—though there could be no doubt at all from his personal papers that he was one. If anyone could win laurels for the troop then it was this unlikely-looking youngster.

"You know who I am presumably?"

"Yes, Captain," said Vierbein. He knew. The car which Kowalski was driving was the C.O.'s car, therefore the man in it must be the new C.O. who had sent him the telegram signed Captain Witterer.

"Were you able to accomplish your mission, Corporal?"

"Yes, Captain," announced Vierbein proudly. "Two N.C.O.s and ten men, together with six transmitters, are at this moment waiting at the airfield."

"I'm very glad—for your sake," said Witterer. "Besides you've come just at the right time. We badly need crew leaders with battle experience. Get in, Corporal."

"Oughtn't you to go to Luschke first?" asked Kowalski.

"I said: get in, Corporal."

"But if he's got to report to Luschke first?" said Kowalski stubbornly.

"Get in!"

Corporal Vierbein hastened to obey. It never occurred to him to object. He was merely astonished at the way in which Kowalski talked to the new C.O. Certainly he was used to

Kowalski's ways by now, but with Wedelmann he had never been more than slick and on the spot—whereas this was downright impertinence, even insolence.

The Lance-Corporal drove Witterer and Vierbein at a leisurely pace up to the new position. The roads were now free of traffic. The greater part of those convoys which had been stuck fast here for hours had temporarily succeeded in escaping from the Russian pressure. The fighting troops held possession of the field.

The guns had been placed close to the Kolchos buildings. There were five of these, not three as marked on the map. Sergeant Asch had requisitioned them all for No. 3 Troop, explaining to anyone else who showed an interest in them that he was preparing quarters for a whole regiment.

The scene was a comparatively peaceful one. The fighting was going on some kilometres away. Only a couple of lookouts had been posted in the immediate vicinity of the guns. The rest of the men had made themselves comfortable in their new billets. Some were playing cards. Most were dozing. Two were shaving. One was carefully cutting his finger-nails. Witterer disapproved strongly of all this.

" Where's Sergeant Asch?" he asked. And as no one seemed in a hurry to reply he yelled at the man nearest him:

" Do you think you're having a rest-cure here?"

" Good God, it's Vierbein!" cried Sergeant Asch appearing from nowhere. " How did you get here, my boy?" And he added at once: " You should have stayed where you were. We could have got on without you!"

" Yes," cried Witterer. " You don't need expert crew-leaders if all you're going to do is lie around and enjoy yourselves!"

Asch quickly showed the Captain round the position.

" A thoroughly healthy area, Captain. The war seems to be going all round us."

" No contact with the enemy? No success to report?"

" No success, because no contact," said Asch. " The war's going on about five kilometres away from us. It's the luck of the draw."

Witterer seemed put out. He found the situation most unsatisfactory. Here was the war in full progress and yet his troop were far from the scene of action. How was he to show what his men were capable of?

" What's happening up ahead?" he asked.

" The usual chaos," said Asch. " According to the observation post. Infantry mopping up. A few tanks knocking around."

"Tanks?" asked Witterer, with some interest.

"May I take command of my old gun, Captain?" asked Vierbein.

"You may," said Witterer patronisingly.

"Well, in heaven's name!" cried Kowalski and he looked at Asch. "There's simply no holding back these heroes."

"Corporal Vierbein!" called out Witterer. He had just had what he considered an excellent idea. "You will have a chance of showing us what you're capable of immediately. You've had plenty of rest—right then: into action!"

"What do you mean by that, Captain?" asked Asch.

"If the tanks aren't coming to us, Sergeant, then we will go to the tanks. Three to five kilometres isn't far. Get your gun ready, Vierbein! We'll give Ivan something to think about."

"Very good, Captain," cried the Corporal at once. He ran over to his gun, gave the order "Change of position," and while the men set to work went round saying hallo to them. The men nodded to him; one of them slapped him on the back; all showed how pleased they were to see him again.

This made Vierbein very happy. He smiled at these men who were his comrades. His boyish eyes sparkled with pleasure. Now at last, or so it seemed to him, he really felt "at home".

"I'll be coming with you," said Asch, going over to Vierbein's gun. He said it as if it were a matter of course.

"The Captain, of course, will not be going," said Kowalski provocatively.

"I shall be leading this action in person," declared Witterer.

Kowalski nodded. This man Witterer, he said to himself, may be a swine, but he's not a fool. He knows well enough what's good for him. A little joy-ride up to the front with Corporal Vierbein and Sergeant Asch is relatively safe and possibly a rewarding proposition.

"Sergeant Asch," said Witterer. "Your task and Corporal Vierbein's, which I will supervise myself, is as follows: To proceed up to the area where fighting is in progress, bring the gun into position there and take part in the fighting. Your main target will be tanks."

"I understand perfectly, Captain," said Asch. This ready agreement from a man whose attitude was normally so unsatisfactory struck Witterer as almost uncanny.

"Sergeant Asch," he said. "Have you any objections or suggestions to make?"

"None at all, Captain," said Asch. "This all seems to me quite in order. We used to undertake similar operations with Lieutenant Wedelmann. We may really be needed up there."

"Well then, what are you waiting for?" cried Witterer. Sergeant Asch signalled to the tractor. Corporal Vierbein supervised the coupling on of the gun. Then the two of them jumped up beside the driver. The crew climbed up over the side.

The tractor rolled slowly forward. The tracks soon got a grip. The gun swayed about behind them. Witterer followed behind the gun. He was being driven by Kowalski who was grinning from ear to ear.

Asch orientated himself by the map and gave directions to the driver. Then he looked across at Vierbein and smiled at him. "Did you have a good time?"

"I'll tell you about it later," said Vierbein.

"Good, Johannes."

Then Asch concentrated his attention exclusively on the country. There were only a few scattered vehicles about, concealed under trees or behind bushes. The sound of battle was coming nearer.

The heavy tractor ground its way across the landscape. Vierbein climbed back to count up the ammunition. Kowalski driving behind, waved to him. Witterer didn't approve of this but said nothing on account of his resolution never to speak to Kowalski personally again.

After three kilometres travelling across country Asch brought them to a halt near a small copse. He jumped down and ran up to the top of a little hill. He stood there for a moment trying to get his bearings. Then he turned round and signalled to the driver, describing a wide semicircle with his arms.

The driver understood at once. He accelerated and went churning up the hill in a wide arc. He stopped when only a few yards from the summit.

"That's it," said Asch.

"Into position!" cried Vierbein.

The gun crew jumped down, the hooks were uncoupled and the gun brought into position. Two of the gunners threw the ammunition baskets down into the snow. On Asch's instructions the tractor trundled back behind the copse, where Kowalski also parked his machine.

Captain Witterer came up the hill and looked through his field-glasses. What he saw left him gasping. The stretch of country which lay at his feet seemed to be literally spitting fire and mud. There were hardly any human beings to be seen, but they could be heard all right. Their weapons were tearing the horizon to shreds.

"Half-right: three thousand!" said Asch. "Between bushy-top tree and barn."

"Good heavens," said Witterer in a very unnatural-sounding voice.

"On target!" cried Corporal Vierbein. He pushed the gun-layer away and took over the handling of the sights himself.

"Five tanks!" said Witterer in astonishment.

"Eight," corrected Asch. He half-closed his eyes.

"Get on with it, men. Get on with it!" cried Witterer in an excited high-pitched voice. "What are you waiting for?"

"Ready to begin, Vierbein?" asked Asch.

"Anti-tank shells!" ordered Witterer.

"That's the only ammunition we've brought, Captain," said Asch. "And anyway, Corporal Vierbein's in command now."

Vierbein handed the sights back to the gun-layer. Then he gave the preliminary orders. "Fire!" he cried.

"Too short, much too short," yelled Witterer.

"Over, a long way over," he yelled after the second round.

"The third round," said Asch without letting the target out of his sight for a second, "will be a direct hit. I know Vierbein!"

The third round was a direct hit. Over by the bushy-top tree a tank burst into flames. Bluish black clouds of smoke poured out of it.

"Yes, yes!" bellowed Witterer. "That's it! That's the way! Carry on like that!"

Vierbein looked at his crew. And Asch looked at Vierbein. He loved this pale unlikely-looking hero!; he loved him like a brother.

"Tank on the extreme left," said the Corporal.

"On target!" said the gun-layer.

"Fire!"

The tank on the extreme left seemed suddenly to receive a tremendous jolt. It was as if it had run into an invisible wall. Its turret sailed several yards through the air. Then it was as if a gas-jet had been ignited inside it and immediately put out again with a wet cloth.

"Yes, yes," yelled Witterer. "That's it!"

"Now then quick, Vierbein," said Asch, for he knew what was coming. No group of tanks would allow itself to be picked off one by one like that with impunity. Lives on both sides now depended on speed. He who reacted slowest would be the first to go.

Smoke was pouring from the third tank. The other five came rumbling towards them. A mortar started firing from somewhere. Mushrooms of smoke suddenly went up all round the hill as the shells burst.

Corporal Vierbein and his crew knocked out a fourth tank. Then a heavy shell burst only twenty yards or so in front of the gun. A great wave of snow, mud and shell-splinters came flying over the crew.

" Use up what you've got left and then away like nobody's business!" said Asch, realising grimly that he was usurping Witterer's role. But he had no time to look round for the Captain now. It was a matter of seconds.

Shell after shell went racing down the barrel towards the enemy. After each round it slipped back shaking and the empty cases were ejected. The ammunition crew tore the baskets open and threw the anti-tank shells to the loader, who slammed them into the breech as if he were putting loaves into an oven.

A fifth tank was already on fire. The other three were coming closer and closer and firing as they came. Enemy shells rained down on them from all sides.

" Only twelve shells left!" said Corporal Vierbein.

" Get rid of the lot, then away like the wind," said Asch. " I'll fetch the tractor."

Asch looked round. Witterer wasn't there. He had simply vanished off the face of the earth. The Sergeant grinned contemptuously. Then he leapt down the little hill towards the copse to fetch the tractor.

But the tractor wasn't there either. Only Kowalski's car stood forlornly on the edge of the copse. That was all!

Asch shouted and Kowalski came running out of the copse pulling up his trousers. He had a thoroughly contented look on his face.

" Where's the tractor?"

" Gone. Witterer took it. He was yelling for me like a cow for its calf. But I was otherwise engaged. So he took the tractor instead of the car."

" Quick!" yelled Asch. " After him!"

Kowalski understood at once. He jumped into the car, started it up and roared away.

" Vierbein hasn't got any ammunition left," said Asch, while they rushed, swaying wildly, across the landscape. " He'll be overrun there. If he doesn't get away at once, he and his entire crew will be done for."

"That filthy swine!" said Kowalski and he pushed the accelerator right down to the floor-boards.

After a kilometre of nightmare journey the tractor came in sight. Kowalski quickly overtook it. He drove round and brought the car to a halt in front of it.

Asch jumped down and ran across.

"Turn round at once!" he yelled.

"Out of my way!" Witterer yelled back. "I'm going to fetch reinforcements." And he turned to the driver: "Drive on!" he said.

Without another moment's thought Asch drew his revolver. He pointed it straight at Witterer. He undid the safety catch and still pointing the revolver at Witterer jumped up on to the tractor.

"Get off!" he shouted at Witterer. "Off with you!"

Witterer had gone pale and was beginning to tremble. With his free hand Asch picked him up by his tunic, pulled him up and pushed him off the caterpillar. Witterer crashed to the ground and lay where he fell.

"Now," said Asch to the driver, "straight back!"

But by the time he had arrived at the gun position, Corporal Vierbein was already dead.

The sun tried to shine through, but the sky stayed dull. It had stopped snowing and it had stopped raining.

The roads were like scrap-heaps, and between the wrecks of vehicles lay the bodies of men. No one bothered about them. Everything which met the light of day seemed doomed.

The front had held. The enemy had exhausted himself. The losses which he had inflicted and which he had suffered himself were by no means insignificant. But then, since when has anything about war been insignificant?

The sentries went out on their rounds again, and again they saw the sentries going their rounds on the other side. The goal had been achieved, as the high-sounding phrase put it. And though a good deal else had been achieved besides, it was the objective which counted. The sentries knew that, though they didn't bother their heads about it much.

Everything was as it had been the day before: here were the guns, there was the enemy. One hut looked much like another and the lice bit just as fiercely here as forty kilometres farther east. But what changes were there.

A few thousand vehicles had been reduced to scrap. A few thousand men had breathed their last. And among them a man who had been a Corporal and whose name was Johannes Vierbein.

With the tractor which he had organised for himself, Corporal Soeft had managed to salvage three strange trucks and their loads. Now he was going over them in the new rear base.

Soeft didn't just salvage everything indiscriminately. He had been determined to make the best possible use of the capital which he had invested in the borrowed tractor. So that each load was carefully inspected before the tow rope was affixed to it.

He was quite content with his booty. One truck conveyed provisions, another clothing and a third a complete dental station.

"What do you want with that?" asked Sergeant-Major Bock who as a special privilege was being allowed to watch the evaluation of the material.

"Oh, you never know. I might get toothache," said Soeft.

"I don't see that it's much use for bartering purposes," said the Sergeant-Major.

"It depends entirely who you're dealing with," answered Soeft.

"Now a friend of mine, a business friend of course, has got a complete submarine stowed somewhere in the Balkans. Another's got a villa on the Atlantic. Besides, the price of gold-fillings is fairly high at the moment. And will be going higher still, I assure you."

"Can the transport section have the trucks themselves when you're finished with them?"

"Two of them, if they'll put the third in order for me. I need an extra truck now to cope with the extra stuff!" And he waved a hand, not without pride, in the direction of the piled-up cases.

"Man!" said Bock, worried. "Your baggage train gets bigger and bigger and the number of men in the battery smaller and smaller."

"The few losses hardly make any difference," said Soeft. "Not where the rations are concerned anyway. And supplies of human material are always the most forthcoming."

He was carrying a list on which the names of Vierbein and seven other soldiers had already been crossed out.

Sergeant Asch and Lance-Corporal Kowalski were digging together in the large grave. The bodies of the dead soldiers lay sewn up in canvas nearby.

"The whole troop ought to parade," said Kowalski. "And I'll tell them everything I know."

"No," said Asch. "The funeral is for the dead."

"And what about the man responsible for their deaths?"

"He'll be brought to account in another place."

Kowalski shook his head disapprovingly. They worked grimly on. Other soldiers came up and helped them without a word.

"I'm going to fetch him," said Kowalski. "He ought to be made to see what he's done."

"You talk too much," said Asch, taking the measurement of the grave. "You can't go and fetch him anyway. Because he's gone off somewhere. He's making the most of his victory."

They dug on with slow deliberate movements. There were fifteen of them altogether now. And more and more kept coming.

"I'll dig *his* grave for him one day," said Kowalski. "I'll do it all myself. And it'll be the pleasantest job I've had in the entire war."

"That's enough," said Sergeant Asch, looking round him. "The burial will take place in an hour's time. Anyone can come who wants to."

Captain Witterer stood proudly in front of Colonel Luschke, who himself sat hunched in his wooden chair. It looked as if he had stomach cramp. But his eyes were clear and cold.

"Just say that again, please, Captain."

"Numerous enemy infantry units attacked. Exact figures of losses inflicted impossible to estimate—but approximately thirty to forty men put out of action, together with two or three machine-guns."

"Yes, Captain. And?"

"Six enemy tanks destroyed."

"And these under your . . . How did you put it?"

"Under my own leadership, Colonel."

283

"And our own losses, Captain?" said Luschke, watching him carefully.

"Only one Corporal and seven men."

"Dead?"

"Yes—it was unavoidable, Colonel."

"Only one Corporal and seven men. Only." And Luschke suddenly roared at the top of his voice: "Only—one Corporal and seven men killed!"

Witterer was terrified. He clicked his heels together and stared at his Commanding Officer. Then he said: "It might have been more. The situation was extremely critical. But I think our successes justify . . ."

"Have the men who were killed been buried?"

"Yes, sir. I've given the order."

"Next-of-kin informed?"

"Yes, sir. The Sergeant-Major is doing the letters. The Corporal's next-of-kin will have a telegram as well."

"Fallen for the Führer and Greater Germany?"

"Yes, sir—that's the usual wording."

Luschke looked at Witterer and his eyes were hard. Then he said: "Get out of here! Go and report to your battery commander—Captain Wedelmann."

"To whom, sir?" asked Witterer in astonishment.

"To Captain Wedelmann. And now get out of my sight. I'll throw the Iron Cross after you when I get the chance."

The men stood round the open grave. There were thirty-eight of them—thirty-eight out of a hundred and twenty. They had all volunteered to come. They were wearing steel helmets and belts.

"Put them in," said Sergeant Asch.

Without a word the men picked up the bodies and carried them in their canvas shrouds to the open grave. Kowalski was standing in it. He took the bodies from them and laid them out carefully.

When the Lance-Corporal had finished he climbed out of the grave again. He stood beside Asch and stared down into it. The men came closer.

Sergeant Asch said: "We're burying here the bodies of Corporal Vierbein and his gun crew. No one knows how they died. They were all dead when we found them. And there's only one thing we can say for certain: they died unwillingly."

And then Sergeant Asch went on: "It can of course also be said that they died bravely. But no one really knows what bravery is. It could be the calm before death, submission to the will of Fate as it's called. I didn't hear any of those eight cry out, the war was making too much noise."

And then again he said: "Who can say whether they sacrificed their lives or their lives were sacrificed? I shan't call them our comrades. Johannes Vierbein was my friend—some of them crossed my path several times in the course of the last two and a half years of war, others I hardly knew at all. But our death my be like theirs—and that brings them all close to us."

Asch finished speaking. None of the others said anything. Their faces were inscrutable. No one wept. And the sky looked down grey and indifferent upon all of them.

"This Vierbein," said Corporal Soeft, opening another packing-case. "He was always a wretched chap."

"He was a fine fellow," said Bock coldly.

"That's what I mean—he had to end this way! He was destined for it. And I've often asked myself: now how exactly will that fellow catch it?"

The Sergeant-Major reached down into the packing-case, pulled out a slab of chocolate and bit into it. "I've written to his next-of-kin, as from Witterer. I've said he was a hero—he was too, if there is such a thing."

"And if there's such a thing as a swine—then Witterer's one."

"Vierbein's dead," said Bock, chewing methodically, "but Witterer's alive and is our C.O. Do you mark the subtle difference?"

"You're right. We can't bring anyone back to life again. It's the living who count."

"And yet, you know," said Bock. "I'm not sure that this death really did suit Vierbein. I think he should have died another way."

"How?"

"Perhaps frozen to death," said Bock. "Taken up a position somewhere, not been relieved—and what happens? He freezes to death. A man like Vierbein would rather freeze to death than desert his post."

"Quite right in theory," said Soeft. "But I've just got one little touch to add and that is: let's say that he couldn't desert his post even if he wanted to because his own Captain had taken away his only means of conveyance. Did you say something?"

"Splendid chocolate."

"I've got six cases of it."

Captain Wedelmann and Witterer stood together in front of the freshly dug grave and looked at the cross on which hung a bullet-pierced steel helmet.

A notice said: "Here lies Corporal Vierbein with seven of his gun crew." And there followed the names of the individual soldiers, seven in number. And underneath was written:

"They fell as soldiers."

"They fell," said Captain Witterer, "for the Führer and Greater Germany. You in particular, Captain, will be able to appreciate that."

"I was very fond of Corporal Vierbein," said Captain Wedelmann.

"As of every man in your old troop."

"But fondest of all of him."

"Ah, well—sacrifices have to be made."

"With Vierbein died the most decent man I ever knew. I feel now as if this war will hardly be a decent one without him."

"But come, come, comrade!"

"I am not your comrade," said Wedelmann, turning on his heel.

Colonel Luschke looked at Sergeant Asch for a long time. Then he looked at Wedelmann who was standing beside him. He had listened to their reports. Now he was silent.

"We are living," he said finally, "through great times. And strange things happen in great times. Just how great these times are you can gather daily from these." And he reached out for a pile of orders of the day which lay on his table. He pulled them towards him and picked them up one by one.

From the first of these orders of the day he read:

"The Führer and Commander-in-Chief: I have therefore flown to you so that everything possible may be done to ease the strain of this great defensive battle you are fighting and to turn it in the end to victory. If each one of you helps me to do this, then with the help of the Almighty we will win through."

He quoted from another order of the day.

" The General Officer Commanding: We have come through days of the greatest historical importance. When the Führer said to me in his Headquarters that our valiant defence had exceeded all his expectations and took my hand in both of his, I regarded this handshake as being for you, my soldiers."

And from a third he read:

" The Divisional Commander: The Division has been through a great deal of hard fighting and won a great deal of success. That has only been possible because everyone has done his utmost in his own particular job. Let it continue like that."[1]

The Colonel pushed the papers away again and looked up at Asch. Then he said:

" Well, those are one or two samples of the greatness of the times in which we're privileged to live. What do you think of them, Asch?"

" Do I have to say, Colonel?"

" And you, Captain Wedelmann?"

" The same, Colonel."

" Just one or two samples," said Luschke. "And now I'm going to quote a General Field-Marshal: I categorically demand from all of you, soldiers and members of units under my command, a clear fanatical, boundless and unconditional will to find victory. And as an outward symbol of our common determination in the fight I order you to take as your slogan: Second to none!"

Wedelmann looked away embarrassed into a corner and automatically straightened his uniform. Asch grew furious and made it quite clear that he thought this excerpt utterly idiotic. Colonel " Lumpface " Luschke grinned to himself.

" And my own order of the day," he said grimly, "runs: Give this man Witterer what he deserves and don't stand any nonsense from swine like that in future!"

The telegram which brought the news that Corporal Vierbein had been killed in action, " had fallen " that is " For Führer and Greater Germany, brave, unselfish and setting the highest

[1] The above excerpts from German war-time orders of the day are, with slight alterations, authentic.

example to the last," was delivered into the hands of old Asch, the café proprietor.

He read it and let it fall on to the table where Ingrid was sitting. He didn't say anything for a long time. Then, still without a word he pushed the telegram towards his daughter.

She opened it. She turned pale, and her breathing came heavily. Then she said:

" He was a brave soldier."

" He's a dead one now," said Asch. " One of many hundred thousand."

" . . . ' brave, unselfish, and setting the highest example to the last ' . . ." read Ingrid Asch.

" And before he died he cried: Long live the Führer and Greater Germany!"

" Many die like that," said Ingrid, in a proud, tragic voice.

" So they say," said old Asch brutally. " One's always reading it in telegrams, letters, newspaper reports and so on. If one were to believe it the whole front must be echoing with the cry. But I don't believe it!"

" Father!"

" There must be some who actually curse both him and Greater Germany before they die. There must be some. If not we're all done for."

There was only one person who wept for Vierbein. That was Lore Schulz. She had nobody else to weep for.

Sergeant Asch said:

" I'm not going to die for this sort of Germany."

" But who's asking you to?" said Kowalski.

" There must be another Germany, which is worth dying for."

" Man!" said Kowalski. " Perhaps one day there'll even be a Germany which is worth living for!"